RHYANNON BYRD's
PRIMAL INSTINCT series from HQN Books

Edge of Hunger
"Byrd successfully combines a haunting love story
with complex world-building."
—*Publishers Weekly*

Edge of Danger
"Ms. Byrd had me first intrigued and then
spellbound from the first page to the last."
—*Joyfully Reviewed*

Edge of Desire
"[Byrd] serves up plenty of action and passion
that won't be denied... Great stuff!"
—*RT Book Reviews*

Touch of Seduction
"This is another winner from Rhyannon Byrd."
—*Genre Go Round Reviews*

Touch of Surrender
"The sexual tension between Kierland and Morgan
will melt the ink off the pages!"
—*BookingIt*

RHYANNON BYRD

TOUCH OF TEMPTATION

HQN™

Recycling programs
for this product may
not exist in your area.

ISBN-13: 978-0-373-77479-1

TOUCH OF TEMPTATION

Copyright © 2010 by Tabitha Bird

Dear Reader,

I can't believe that I'm already on book six of the Primal Instinct series! Where has the time gone? It seems like only yesterday that I was writing about Ian and Molly in *Edge of Hunger*, when Kellan Scott's character was first introduced. Kellan was such a bad boy back then, and while he's still wicked where it counts, it's been a wonderful journey as an author to watch the gorgeous shape-shifter take control of his life in *Touch of Temptation*, becoming the hero we've always known he could be. A breathtaking hero who is willing to do anything for the passionate little witch who steals his heart...and awakens the possessive hungers of his beast.

It's been a remarkable experience writing the Primal Instinct series, and I hope you'll enjoy the series' scorching conclusion in 2011, as well as the beginning of a provocative spin-off series for the sexy Deschanel vampires who have been working alongside the Watchmen! But first, there's a certain green-eyed soldier named Seth who's insisting on a story of his own... ;-)

Wishing you all much happiness and a wonderful holiday season!

Rhy

For the one and only Shayla Black.
You are amazing in all things you do, Shay, and
I'm so lucky to have met you!

TOUCH OF
TEMPTATION

CHAPTER ONE

Dark temptations lead to darker pleasures...

Sunday morning

THE PROBLEM WITH TRYING to act like a good guy was that good guys played by the rules. They didn't lust after those in need of their help. They didn't act on their baser instincts. Didn't think about what was between a woman's legs when they were meant to be saving her life.

Since the moment Kellan Scott had set eyes on the youngest Harcourt witch, he'd been struggling to be good. But *Christ*, he wanted to be bad.

Bad. Dominating. Dirty. If it was explicit and it was sexual, he wanted it with her. Didn't matter how hard he tried to fight it, or how determined he was to keep himself in line. He still wanted her. And the news wouldn't have shocked anyone who knew him. In fact, it was exactly what they would have expected from a guy whose existence could be defined by four words.

Watchman. Werewolf. And world-class fuckup.

The first was easy enough to explain, if one had an open mind. Though most humans were clueless about such things, the truth was that many paranormal species lived hidden among them. They were called the "ancient clans" and for the most part the various species lived in peace with humanity. But…not always. And that was where the Watchmen came in. A highly skilled organization of shape-shifters, it was the job of the Watchmen to keep "watch" over the clansmen and -women. Though the majority of their work consisted of surveillance assignments, ensuring the secrecy and security of the clans, there were times when they were called on by their superiors to kill something that needed to be killed—which was why Kellan was one hell of a soldier, trained both in weapons and hand-to-hand combat.

And the werewolf part—well, that pretty much explained itself. Perhaps the only clarification that could be made was that he could control the changes in his body, rather than having them dictated by the cycles of the moon. And contrary to modern beliefs, he couldn't be killed by a silver bullet, though it hurt like a bitch whenever he managed to get himself shot. Still, despite the fact that the werewolves' healing abilities were some of the strongest among the shifter clans, he *could* die before he reached the natural end of his life if he bled out. For that reason, the simplest way to kill a Lycan—a werewolf—was to slash its gut open, spilling its insides. A fate Kellan had been lucky enough to avoid.

But while the first two distinctions were things he could be proud of, it was unfortunately that last one—*fuckup*—that best defined the true essence of his character. That, Kellan was most widely known for…and that was the *one* thing he truly excelled at.

As far as truths went, it was a bitter one to swallow, which was why it'd jammed in Kellan's throat a few months before…and he still hadn't managed to swallow it down.

In fact, it was that choking sense of guilt that had landed Kellan in his current set of circumstances. Those circumstances being his incarceration in the secret hideout of a raging psychopath who was out to turn the world into a living hell for humans and clansmen, alike.

When the idea for this harebrained rescue had first come to him earlier in the month, after he'd finally tracked down a lead on where Chloe Harcourt was being kept prisoner, it'd seemed so straightforward. *Find the witch. Protect the witch. Save the witch.* Suicidal, no doubt, but a beautiful plan in its simplicity—until lust had jumped in to complicate the hell out of it. Still, Kellan had seen the situation as the perfect answer to the burning question of what he was meant to do with his embarrassing waste of a life. It was hard to live up to expectations when your older brother was one of the most righteous badasses around, but that was Kierland for you. Kellan loved the guy like crazy, but he'd have been lying if he said he wasn't tired of feeling like the proverbial village idiot when measured against his paragon of a sibling.

Then again, he didn't need to be compared to Kierland to look like a tool. No, he'd managed that embarrassing distinction all on his own.

In the midst of a war, he'd made the ultimate blunder: he'd listened to his dick instead of his brain and unknowingly screwed one of their enemies. To make it worse, Kellan hadn't even figured it out until it was too late. Until he'd almost cost an innocent woman her life—a woman who was now engaged to one of his closest friends.

Talk about a mistake that you'll never live down....

Choking back a harsh growl, he used the back of his

forearm to wipe the sheen of sweat from his brow, narrowed his eyes and kept on with his task, his muscles burning as he fought to force open the door of his jail cell. Though he'd already picked the lock, the door, which was made of iron bars, was fitted with a counterweight that would have taken at least three human males to lift, and Kellan was doing it on his own. Cold air prickled against his skin, the flickering flames of the fire in a nearby hearth doing little to take the chill from the air, and yet, he continued to sweat from exertion. Continued to push himself to the point of agony, a grimace curling his mouth as his mind churned over that fateful night last fall when things had gone so wrong.

Yeah, nothing like endangering the lives of innocent people to give a guy a head-cracking eye-opener. Months later, he was still reeling from the blow. Still coated with the slimy film of shame that'd been slinking over him like some kind of toxic shroud.

It made him feel like a jackass to say it, but until that moment when the shit had hit the fan in Purity, Washington, Kellan had lived his life for one specific purpose—that purpose being pleasure. Known as the carefree "playboy" of his Watchmen unit, he'd earned a reputation early on for allowing his sexual appetites to get him into trouble. For too damn long, sliding between a hot pair of legs had been his way of releasing his pent-up frustration with life. His coping mechanism for a less-than-stellar childhood and deep-rooted emotional hang-ups. Or so he'd been told. Things had been shaken up lately in his Watchmen unit, several of his friends taking the plunge into romantic bliss, and the sudden female influence was showing its mark. Now phrases like *self-awareness* and *emotional baggage* were thrown

around like handfuls of therapy confetti. And Kellan's
new gal pals had made their opinions concerning his
dissolute lifestyle painfully clear.

You're selling yourself short.

You're using meaningless sex as a diversion.

You're acting like a thickheaded man-slut.

"Bitchy little harpies," he murmured affectionately,
knowing damn well that they were right about him. They
weren't saying anything that he hadn't already figured
out on his own.

After his colossal pooch-screw with that seriously heinous dark-haired, green-eyed female who'd been playing
him, Kellan had been forced to take a long hard look in
the mirror. Wouldn't have been so bad, except that he
hadn't cared for the man staring back at him. True, it
could have been worse. He could have been a murderer
or a rapist or some other pestilent sleaze who deserved
to rot in eternal damnation. Instead, he was just…hell.
He was a kid who'd never taken the time to notice that
his ass had grown up. That his actions had consequences.
Ones that had serious implications when his friends and
colleagues were in a fight for their lives.

It'd been a sharp blow to his pride, but one Kellan
figured he should have seen coming. The signs had been
prickling at the edges of his consciousness for a while,
making him increasingly restless. Uneasy. Little twinges
of awareness that had whispered insults in his ear. Most
of the time, it was just name-calling, but sometimes…
sometimes those whispered insults got personal, lecturing him about his choices. Warning him that no matter
how many built, stunning women he took beneath his
body, he still wasn't going to find that one thing he
needed.

Warning him that it was time to stop acting like a useless waster and actually do something with his life.

Since he agreed, Kellan had finally decided to take action. And without a doubt, he'd definitely started the new year off with a bang.

In the ballsiest move he'd ever made, he'd traded his freedom for a cell. Had purposefully allowed himself to be captured by the enemy, which had resulted in his subsequent beating, torture and imprisonment.

And all for the little witch sleeping in the cell next to his. The one delicate female who had completely turned his world on its head. Who was a complete stranger. A woman he'd never even met.

And one who he was determined to talk to, which was why he was currently doing his best to get that bloody door open.

Though Kellan had already been at the compound for two full days, he'd only had a few brief glimpses of Chloe as the guards had taken her from her cell, to the upper floors, and then back down again. But he'd gleaned as much data as he could. Flashes of perfectly smooth, pale skin. Sleek, dark hair. Fey face. He'd thought about the details until their memory was burned into his brain like a brand, scarring his sanity.

She'd been taken upstairs again in the early hours of that morning, but had finally been brought back to the underground level two hours ago. Two hours that had felt like a living hell while Kellan had struggled to get his rioting emotions under control and focus on the task at hand.

"All that matters is getting her out of this place," he muttered under his breath, same as he'd been doing since he'd first set foot within the Wasteland, where the enemy compound was hidden. A mystical region created by powerful magic, the Wasteland was a cold, dangerous, desolate realm where "nests" or family units of vampires were exiled after judgment had been passed against them. Most vampires, otherwise known as the Deschanel clan, resided in "nesting grounds" located throughout Scandinavia and Eastern Europe. The grounds were ancient, sprawling castlelike communities where extended families lived for security, the lands protected by spells that kept them hidden from the outside world. But the exiled Deschanel families were forced into the Wasteland, where it was every man, or vampire, for himself.

After traveling through the region, Kellan could vouch that it pretty much sucked for Lycans, too. And yet, he'd have done it again in a heartbeat.

He didn't know how to explain it, and so he'd given up trying. He only knew that it felt *right*. That he was where he was meant to be.

From the first moment he'd seen Chloe Harcourt's photograph, she'd been in his every thought, impossible to forget. One moment he was staring at the picture of the cute brunette, and the next thing he knew, he was doing everything he could to find her. If it was the last thing he did, Kellan intended to get this woman back to her family and have at least one selfless, worthwhile deed listed among a lifetime of mistakes.

But while the need to prove himself might have sounded like a reasonable explanation for his suicidal actions, it still didn't explain his obsession.

And there's no arguing that I'm obsessed.

During the past two months that Kellan had known Chloe's human stepsister, Olivia—ever since she'd ended up with Aiden, his fellow Watchman—he'd constantly asked questions about the little witch, desperate to learn everything that he could. And while he knew many of the basic stats—she was half Merrick, half Mallory witch, single, a bit of a loner, self-employed, had a degree in design and enjoyed art and cooking—it wasn't enough. He wanted to know every intimate detail. What made her laugh? Made her smile? What made her cry or drove her crazy? What were her favorite smells and did she prefer the sunshine or the rain? The dazzling rays of dawn… or the evocative, moonlit shadows of the night?

And he wanted to touch her. But that was the one thing he couldn't do. Not after the mistakes that he'd made…or the danger he could pose to her in his current condition.

Earlier that week, as he'd been fighting to make his way to this godforsaken place, Kellan had been infected by a poisonous vampire named Asa Reyker, whose family was among the many Deschanel nests who'd been exiled to the Wasteland.

As a Lycan with extraordinary healing abilities, Kellan's body was currently managing to cope with the poison polluting his system, so long as he stayed calm. But his ability to cope wouldn't last…and staying calm wasn't easy. The witch's scent called to those most dangerous, visceral parts of him. Parts he could barely control after traveling for so many days in his primal wolf form. He'd known what he was risking by going completely beastie for so long, but he'd had little choice. The Wasteland was a treacherous place—even more so when you were traveling alone. If he hadn't given himself over to the wolf, he never would have made it.

But that doesn't mean that I can't control you, he snarled at the predatory animal prowling the confines of his body, the beast desperate to get its hands on the witch and slake its lust.

Wanna bet? it taunted, the sneaky bastard searching for any signs of weakness it could exploit. *I'm not gonna hurt her. I just want to…play.*

Yeah, right.

Kellan's hands shook as he curled his fingers around the door's thick iron bars and pulled, his nostrils flaring as he helplessly sucked in more of Chloe's lush, intoxicating scent. He could taste it on his tongue in the way that only an animal could, the provocative flavor making his mouth water. Hunger rode him hard, battering against his reason, but he locked his jaw, struggling to tighten the reins on the wolf….

"You're losing it, Lycan. You need to take a deep breath and calm down."

The soft, huskily spoken words belonged to Raine Spenser. She was another prisoner—and one who'd suffered far more than Kellan had. Part-vampire, part-psychic, Raine had been captured several weeks ago by Ross Westmore, the raging psychopath who was holding them…and who had forced Raine to use her powers against Kellan's fellow Watchmen by killing her sister and kidnapping her little brother.

From what Kellan and his friends had learned, Westmore was behind the recent return of the immortal Casus, one of the most violent of the ancient clans. For the past thousand years, the entire Casus race had been rotting away within Meridian, the metaphysical holding ground where they'd been imprisoned for their crimes against humanity…and a rival clan named the Merrick. Though the Merrick had eventually bred with others, and the clan's bloodline became dormant, the recent return of more than a few Casus had set off a chain reaction, awakening the primal blood within many of the Merrick descendants, most of whom were now allied with the Watchmen. It'd become one of those classic good versus evil kind of conflicts, and now all hell was breaking loose, with the safety of the world hanging in the balance.

The Casus were out to destroy the Merrick and unleash their sadistic hungers on the world, the Watchmen were determined to stop them, and they were all after some nifty little crosses called the Dark Markers. As the only known weapons that could kill a Casus's soul and send it to hell, the Dark Markers were the hot ticket that everyone wanted a piece of. The Watchmen also suspected that the Markers could somehow be used to bring about "the flood"—a scenario in which the gates of Meridian would break open, allowing the monsters to escape. If they were right, it would explain why Westmore and the Casus were seeking the weapons as seriously as Kellan and his friends. But they didn't know for sure…and although Raine's powers were strong, she claimed that Westmore was one of her blind spots, which made it impossible for her to tell Kellan why the bastard wanted them. It also meant that she couldn't tell him what Westmore had planned for their future.

Kellan had already been at the compound since last Thursday. If he hadn't figured a way out by the upcoming Friday, he was confident his brother would launch an attack on the compound to get him out. Kierland knew where he was, and according to Raine, his brother had made unlikely allies in the Wasteland who were ready to help them. But Friday was a long five days away, and Kellan wanted both Chloe and Raine out before then. Though Raine had managed to negotiate her little brother's release, as well as a reprieve from her torture by threatening to withhold information that Westmore wanted, and Chloe had been deemed off-limits to Westmore's men, he still worried about them being surrounded by such monsters.

And when it came to Chloe, Kellan couldn't discount the risk that he personally posed to her safety. The wolf might be a part of him, but when it came to the little witch, he didn't trust it any more than he'd have trusted a wounded animal. It was in pain from the poison, seething with hunger for her, and like any wild animal, it cared for naught but its own wants and needs. Which was why he'd be staying the hell away from her once they'd escaped, leaving her under the protection of Kierland and the others.

But first, he had to get her out, and if they ended up having to fight in order to escape, then he was going to need the little witch's cooperation. They needed to talk, and one way or another, he was going to get her to acknowledge him.

"Kellan, did you hear me?" Raine's soft words were edged with a touch of impatience.

"Yeah, I heard you," he rasped, careful to keep his voice as quiet as possible. Although Kellan's cell was situated between the two women, and the walls between each cell were made of solid sheets of metal—which meant that Raine couldn't see into Chloe's cell—he knew the psychic was monitoring Chloe for him with her powers. "Is she still out of it?"

"The drugs they gave her to calm down were pretty potent. She's still sleeping off the effects, but should be fairly clearheaded when she finally wakes up."

The thought of those drugs being injected into her system by Westmore and his quack physician made Kellan curse under his breath, his fingers digging into the iron bars with enough force that they could have snapped.

Although Chloe's mother had been a Mallory witch, her father, who'd died when she was young, had been a direct descendant of the Merrick clan. When Kellan had been taken captive three days ago, he'd learned that the primal Merrick blood within the witch was already awakening, desperate for its first feeding, its hunger weakening her more each day. Since keeping her healthy was part of Westmore's plan—at least for the moment—he'd had his doctor try to improve her condition by "feeding" blood into her system through an IV. To keep her calm, they sedated her beforehand, which meant she'd been fairly out of it since Kellan's arrival.

And the thought of what they might be doing to her while she was so defenseless made him see red. Literally.

"Are you sure they haven't touched her?" he forced out through his gritted teeth. "Haven't harmed her in any way?"

"I'm sure. I've heard Westmore warn the others that she's to be left alone. He gets furious if they even look at her the wrong way, because she's meant to be Calder's *gift* when he escapes Meridian."

Thanks to their prior confrontations with the Casus, Kellan and the other Watchmen knew that Calder was the name of the monster who'd taken charge of things in Meridian and was now working with Westmore to bring about the Casus's escape.

Raine added, "Calder was adamant that she's not to

be touched—or awakened with a real feeding—until he's here to claim her."

In other words, until he was there to carry out her rape and murder.

Wanna tear the bastard's throat out, his wolf snarled, and Kellan nodded, this time in complete agreement with that feral part of him. The only godsend to this entire nightmare was that Calder apparently didn't plan to escape from Meridian anytime soon, which meant that he didn't pose any immediate danger to Chloe.

Unfortunately, the same couldn't be said about Kellan.

"She's scared of me," he said to Raine, and even with his anger and exhaustion riding him hard, the regret in his tone was clear.

"Why do you think that?"

Kellan snorted. "You've heard what happens when I try to talk to her through the wall that separates our cells. I know she can hear me, but she won't even respond."

"It's nothing personal. She's just…wary of *all* men, but not scared. She simply doesn't trust her effect on them."

He paused in surprise, thinking over what Raine had said. He'd assumed that Chloe's reticence had been simple fear because of what he was. A stranger. Not to mention a werewolf. And one who was looking every bit the predator after what he'd been through to get to her.

But apparently he'd been wrong.

Shaking his head, he asked, "Are you saying that she won't talk to me because she's afraid the Mallory curse is going to affect me?"

"That's exactly what she doesn't want to happen. She

already feels guilty enough that you risked your life to come here for her. The last thing she wants to do is start tampering with your emotions."

As a Mallory witch, Chloe possessed an unusual power that heightened the emotions of those around her to extreme levels. Though Kellan had heard of it before, Olivia had explained the Mallory curse to him in greater detail, describing how it had locked into the varying powers of the once-powerful Mallory witch clan and channeled them into the mother of all spells.

"I didn't come after her because of some bloody curse," he muttered.

"I know that and you know that. But Chloe…well, she doesn't know what to believe."

He grunted in response, wrenching the door open another inch, the gap almost wide enough that he could squeeze through. But he had to be careful. In order for his plan to work, Kellan had to break out of his cell without actually damaging the door, leaving Westmore and his goons none the wiser.

"How's that door coming?"

"They weren't fooling around when they built these cells, but I've almost got it."

As far as Kellan could tell, Westmore's team had taken what had originally been some kind of ancient fortress buried within the heart of the Wasteland and turned it into a nearly impenetrable compound. The location was meant to be top secret, but Kellan had managed to find it, thanks to a large amount of cash he'd unloaded on some unsavory Deschanel vampires who'd heard rumors of the compound's location—and who had no liking for anyone coming into their territory. Kellan had expected the fortress to be hard to get into, which was why he'd allowed himself to be captured to begin with—but it meant the place was going to be just as hard to get out of.

He'd been hoping to find some kind of weakness he could exploit once he was inside…and it seriously pissed him off that he hadn't.

Still, Kellan couldn't complain that he'd been completely unlucky, considering they hadn't killed him. Instead, they'd kept him alive, just as he'd suspected they would, believing he might prove useful when they decided to go after the Dark Markers that the Watchmen had already found. Of course, the Casus had beaten the hell out of him for an entire twenty-four hours, wanting him to admit that he'd come there for the three Markers in their possession, and Kellan had finally given them a false confession. Then they'd thrown him into the same cellblock as Chloe, not realizing she was the true reason he was there.

Kellan didn't know if Westmore's men had constructed the cellblock, or if it'd been part of the original structure, but he'd managed to use his claws to pick the lock on the door. And after that, all that'd been left to do was pull. *Hard.*

"She's starting to wake up," Raine told him. "So as soon as you're finished with that door, I'm going to put myself into a *Transsi.*"

"What the hell's that?"

"It's a kind of light trance state that psychics can go into when we need to rest, but don't want to go fully into a sleep state. So you, uh, don't have to worry about me overhearing anything."

"Overhearing what? I just want to talk to her, Raine. I'm not going to start grilling her for private information.

And if you can 'read' her, it's not like she's got any secrets from you anyway, right?"

"Think about it, Kellan. You need to be ready for what's coming. Her Merrick awakening is in full swing now and she's starving for *fresh* blood. Not to mention sex."

"And what does any of that have to do with me?" he demanded, every muscle in his body going rigid with tension.

A short, heavy silence followed, until Raine snuffled a soft sound under her breath that sounded suspiciously like laughter. "I might not be able to see the future," she murmured. "But something tells me the Merrick witch is going to take one look at you and see more than the guy who's risked his life to save her. Whether she's comfortable with the idea or not, Kell, she's going to see you as the man who can give her *exactly* what she needs."

CHAPTER TWO

THE INSTANT CHLOE MANAGED to crack open her gritty eyelids, she was met with the stunning sight of Kellan Scott standing outside the iron bars that covered the front of her cell.

And while there was a part of her that was amazed she hadn't immediately screamed from shock, the other parts were still too busy taking in his deliciously dark, dangerous good looks.

Even with the fresh bruises healing on his face and upper body, as well as an evil-looking bite wound at the side of his throat, Chloe figured he had to be the best-looking male she'd ever set eyes on. She stared from her place on the cell's spindly cot, her body shivering beneath a thin blanket, while he stared back from the other side of the bars, one wide shoulder propped against the heavy gray rods of metal. He wore nothing but a low-slung, bloodstained pair of jeans, his long feet and broad, kinda sweaty chest completely bare. With his thumbs casually hooked in his front pockets, she had the feeling he was trying to appear as nonthreatening as possible, and it almost made her smile.

Nice try, Lycan. But it isn't working.

No, this was definitely no lamb. Chloe could all but feel the raw force of his masculinity blasting against her, and knew his wicked reputation—the one Raine had told her about when the psychic had "seen" him traveling across the Wasteland as he'd made his way to the compound—had been well deserved. The guy all but oozed an "*I'm a drop-dead gorgeous badass*" vibe with those rugged features, shadowed jaw and what was truly a mouthwatering bod. At least a couple of inches over six foot, he was ripped with hard, corded muscles that were perfectly formed beneath the dark sheen of his skin, the raised veins and long lines of sinew adding to what was an already-stunning physique.

He was more than a little dangerous looking, but he was also sexy as hell.

And the thick-lashed, blue-green eyes… God, they were just overkill.

The drugs they'd given her still had her brain kinda fuzzy, but Chloe lifted up onto an elbow and struggled to form the words she wanted. "How…" She coughed, and tried again. "How long have you been standing there?"

"Just a few minutes. I kept quiet because I didn't wanna startle you while you were waking up." With a ghost of a smile, he added, "It's taken you a good five minutes to get your eyes open."

"I don't understand," she muttered, her forehead scrunching in confusion. "I mean, how did you get out of your cell?"

"I managed to shove the door open," he replied, pushing a hand through the dark, silky strands of auburn hair that almost reached his shoulders, his bicep bulging as the masculine tuft under his arm was revealed.

Chloe rubbed her eyes. "But…the counterweights on these doors are massive! Not to mention the fact that the doors are locked!"

The corner of his mouth twitched, as if he found her reaction kind of funny. "You know I'm not human, Chloe. I don't think they ever planned to hold a Lycan when they built these cells. Either that, or they have no idea how strong we are." His head tilted a little to the side, his gaze focused on her with an unnerving intensity. "The hardest part was picking the lock." He shrugged, adding, "After that, I just gripped the edge of the door and pulled."

"You pulled." Her voice sounded strangely flat, no doubt with shock. "You just pulled what must have been a thousand pounds of counterweight and opened the door."

Something wicked flickered in those thick-lashed eyes, but his tone was deceptively light as he said, "I prefer to use my head when there's a logical answer to a problem. But you can't argue that there are times when some muscle comes in just as handy."

A wry smile touched her lips. "So doing something like that is no big deal to you?"

Another shrug of those tough, massive shoulders, this one a little tense. "I've been traveling in wolf form to get here, so I'm running on excess adrenaline right now."

"Not to mention the fact that you're...huge." She stared at the way his powerful hands rested against the faded denim of his jeans, his thumbs hooked in his pockets, and felt strangely consumed by hunger in a way that she never had before, as if craving were an actual living thing coiling inside her body.

With a hard swallow, Chloe cleared the husky note from her throat and continued talking. "You know, it's probably an odd thing to say to a man I don't even know, but I don't think I've ever seen hands quite as big as yours."

He didn't say anything in response, just used one of those sun-darkened hands to rub the back of his neck, while a warm rush of color crept across the bridge of his nose and his sharp cheekbones. Transfixed, Chloe watched the way his eyes turned kind of heavy lidded, trying hard to remember why she'd been so determined to ignore this guy.

Must not have been thinking straight. He's too beautiful to ignore. It musta been the drugs....

She knew she was probably being rude, but she could *not* stop staring at his hands, mesmerized by them. His fingers were scarred, but beautiful in the way that only something on a guy could be. Not pretty, but long and perfectly sculpted, with short-clipped nails that'd been bleached by the sun.

Then, with her next breath, she remembered the old saying about big hands, big feet, big...

Her gaze took a swift pass over the heavy bulge behind the fly of his jeans...and damn it, now she was blushing right along with him.

"So anyway," he finally rumbled, no doubt saving her from making another embarrassing gaffe, "the reason I'm out here is because we need to talk." The words were deep and deliciously raspy, creating an immediate physical reaction in Chloe's body. She noticed the slightest trace of a British accent in his words, mixed with the harder American pronunciations, an underlying grittiness that no doubt came from the fact he wasn't any more human than she was. If she'd had to describe it, she would have said he had one of those husky voices that sounded like a man saying wicked things in a woman's ear while he surged deep inside her body. The kind of sex-roughened voice that starred in *all* of Chloe's favorite fantasies.

And now this man was here, in the flesh, watching her with the most mesmerizing expression on his face, looking as if he wanted to eat her alive.

I have got to be dreaming....

Raine had told her the Lycan was coming, but Chloe hadn't really believed her. After everything that Raine had been through—traumas Chloe knew were going to haunt the psychic's memories for the rest of her life— she'd worried that the woman was comforting herself with some kind of imagined rescue. Then, two days ago, when Chloe was returned to her cell after an examination by Westmore's doctor, the werewolf was suddenly there, pacing behind the iron bars of his own cell, reminding her of a caged animal. He'd looked like someone who'd just been dragged out of a war zone, but even flying high on their drugs, she'd thought he was...beautiful.

And now Mr. Beautiful had sneaked out of his cell, putting himself in close proximity to her, and *oh...damn*. With a low groan, Chloe suddenly recalled why she'd been trying to ignore him the past two days. Why she'd kept refusing to respond to his questions.

More than once, the Lycan had moved to the front corner of his cell that was closest to hers and tried to talk to her, but she'd never acknowledged him, pretending to be asleep. Of course, with all the drugs they'd been pumping into her system, she *had* actually spent most of the past two days knocked out.

But she was finally awake, and he was obviously done waiting.

And this is a bad, bad idea. I've got a starved Merrick

*inside me, and any second now it's going to wake up
and see something too good to resist.*

As if he sensed her tension, he looked a little grim
as he ran that dark gaze over her blanket-covered form.
"They haven't hurt you, have they?"

"No," she murmured, forcing her sluggish body into
a sitting position. Careful to keep the blanket over her
lower body, since she was wearing nothing but a pair
of panties and an oversize men's dress shirt, she leaned
against the wall and pulled her knees into her chest. The
shirt had been given to her after the last one had gotten
drenched in blood during her captors' failed attempts
to "feed" her through an IV, the panties and bra a clean
set they'd obviously taken out of the luggage she'd been
traveling with when they'd kidnapped her several months
ago.

He narrowed his eyes, studying her face, almost as
if he was trying to determine if she was telling him the
truth about her treatment...or not. "You know why I'm
here, right?"

She took a deep breath—one that filled her nostrils
with his warm, masculine scent—and it didn't help to
steady her nerves. "Yeah, I know. But maybe you should
explain it to me. In your own words."

With a sharp nod, he said, "I came to rescue you."

"But...why?"

Crossing his massive arms over his chest, he spoke in
another dark, sexy rumble that made her shiver. "'Cause
someone had to do it."

"But why *you?* Why risk yourself this way for someone you don't even know?"

He ran a hand over his face, a gritty sound of frustration vibrating in his throat. "If you're looking for a

logical explanation, I can't give you one. All I can tell you is that it's something I had to do."

"Well, I won't leave without Raine," she told him, not knowing what else to say. The guy was clearly out of his mind.

"Neither would I. The three of us are going to get out of this place together. And if we can't find a way out on our own before Friday, then my brother and friends will help us."

Rubbing her palms over her knees, she said, "Raine told me that your brother's girlfriend was able to track you here, and that they're not far away."

He nodded again, and a gleaming lock of auburn hair fell over one of his eyes, making her fingers itch to push it back. For a second Chloe found herself wondering if his skin would be as hot to the touch as it looked, and then she shook her head, forcing herself to pay attention to what he was saying. "They're not going to let us rot away in here. But, I think it's going to be safer for us all if we make it out before then."

She couldn't help the bitter burst of laughter that broke from her throat. "And how are we meant to do that? You might have made it out of your cell, but there are guards all over this place."

"Raine told you about Gregory DeKreznick, right?"

This time it was Chloe who nodded. "She said he's a Casus who wants to kill Westmore. He's even planning to somehow attack the compound."

Watching her closely, he went on to say, "He's also the Casus responsible for your awakening, and the initial reason you were captured."

"I know," she murmured, already familiar with the

fact that each time a Casus managed to escape from Meridian, its return to this world caused the primal blood within one of the Merrick descendants to rise up, kick-starting their awakening. The Casus received a massive power charge when they killed and fed upon a fully awakened Merrick. One so great they could actually pull another Casus across the divide and back to this world, which made Merrick kills a coveted prize. And according to the rules that had been established to keep the monsters in line, they were each exclusively entitled to the Merrick they'd personally caused to "wake up." As far as Chloe understood, it was considered a serious taboo to tamper with another Casus's Merrick.

And that, right there, was why she'd been taken.

"When I was kidnapped, Westmore told me that I'd been taken simply to get back at this Gregory guy for disobeying his orders. Then things changed," she explained, remembering how ill she'd felt when she'd first learned why Westmore intended to offer her as a gift to Anthony Calder. With the death of her older sister, Monica, the Casus monsters had learned that the pleasures they found in raping and killing—an act Raine had told her they called a "blood fuck"—were increased by a Mallory's curse. Now "blood fucking" a Mallory witch who was also part Merrick was considered their ultimate high, which made her a hot commodity to the depraved bastards.

Clearing her throat, she added, "Now they no longer care about taunting Gregory. Instead they've decided to give me to—"

He cut her off, the look on his face disturbingly savage. "I know about Calder," he growled, his eyes beginning to glow with a strange, predatory fire. And then, as if he suddenly realized how angry he'd sounded, he took a few deep breaths, and in a calmer tone, he said, "When Gregory attacks the compound, it's going to create all kinds of chaos, which could give us the opportunity that we need to escape. So you're going to be freed long before their plans with Calder can be put into action."

"You really believe that?"

His voice dropped, the blue of his eyes still burning with that strange glow as he said, "I'm not going to let them hurt you, Chloe."

"So, I guess this means you're pretty righteous, huh?" she asked after several moments of heavy silence, their gazes locked onto each other with crackling intensity. "One of those rare heroes that no one thinks even exists anymore."

He gave a deliciously rough bark of laughter that made her toes curl. "Nah," he drawled, rubbing a palm against his stubble-covered jaw. "I wouldn't go that far. My brother, Kierland—he's the righteous one."

"Then what are you?" she asked, lifting her brows. "The badass?"

"Yeah, something like that," he replied in another quiet drawl, the hunger in those smoldering eyes too sexy to be real. Chloe blinked and rubbed her eyes again, wondering if she was still a little out of it. She *had* to be, because it looked like the guy was actually…interested in her, and she knew that couldn't be right. Raine had been pretty clear about the kind of women Kellan Scott got involved with…and they were *nothing* like her. It would have been like comparing night to day. A flashy red Ferrari to a quirky little Mini Clubman.

Hello? Earth to Chloe, the all-too-familiar voice

of her conscience hissed in her ear. *Are you forgetting about the curse?*

Oh. My. God. For a few seconds there, she actually *had* forgotten, which was ridiculous—but come on. The gorgeous hunk had honestly claimed that he'd risked his life to save hers. What woman wouldn't get a little muddled after hearing something like *that?*

Still, she'd forgotten how careful she needed to be around men, because the instant she started talking to a guy, spending time with him, the curse that had plagued the Mallory witches for centuries would start to affect him. If he had even the slightest casual interest in her, the curse would blow that interest out of proportion, heightening it to an extreme, unnatural level. She'd seen it happen before, and it was happening again…

Right. At. That. Moment.

Chloe had heard things about the Lycan sex drive—not to mention Kellan Scott's reputation. The guy *liked* women, and with all that adrenaline he'd said was burning through his system, he was probably burning on excess mojo, and here she was, cranking it up even higher.

Though every female on the maternal side of her family tree had suffered from the Mallory curse, it had affected Chloe more strongly than anyone else in her family, and she'd never been able to figure out why. Maybe it was because she'd always tried too hard to contain it, determined to control it, that it seemed to work that much harder against her? Or maybe it was just one of those rotten quirks of nature that couldn't be explained?

Whatever the reason, she was like a walking, talking lightning rod when it came to others' emotions. If

someone hated her, like the Casus, then that hatred intensified until they boiled with it.

And the same could be said for desire. For lust. But it
wasn't real. Was just an illusion. Like love at first sight
and happily-ever-afters. At least for her. Chloe had seen
her mother get lucky with Olivia's father, and now Olivia
had apparently found her own dream stud. So that meant
her chances were shot. No way in hell was lightning
going to strike *three* times in one family.

Though it sounded maudlin, she'd always known she
would live her life alone. So, her way of dealing with that
knowledge had been to withdraw from the world, with
the exception of her family and a handful of friends she'd
made in college. She worked at home, running her own
web design company, and made a good living. For safety,
the Harcourt ranch-style family home in Kentucky had
been remodeled into separate living quarters, enabling
Chloe and her sisters to live close to one another, and
yet retain a certain degree of privacy. As her eyes slid
closed, she drew in a deep breath, and for a moment she
could almost smell those familiar scents that reminded
her of home. Smells she missed so much it was a physical
ache inside her heart. Liv's warm sugar cookies baking
in the oven. The smoky blend of Monica's favorite per-
fume. Her niece's strawberry bubble bath.

She missed her family so much she could feel the
pain like a wound. Something torn open, bleeding and
raw, that no amount of time was going to heal.

After the death of their parents, the three of them
had only had each other, and their sisterly bonds had
grown into ones of true friendship. Raine had told her
about what had happened to Monica, but Chloe could
scarcely allow herself to believe it. Her heart broke for

her older sister and for her niece, Jamie, who had absolutely adored her mother. The sorrow Chloe felt over the loss of her sister would have overshadowed everything else—her fear, her anger, her worry—if it weren't for the change building within her. That sorrow could have grown so great that she was consumed by it, but the primal creature fighting to get out of her was determined to keep her focused on survival, refusing to let her give in.

As if summoning it with her thoughts, a sharp burst of heat began to ripple beneath her skin, and Chloe could feel the Merrick stretching within her. Could feel its hunger slithering through her body. Coming on even stronger than it ever had before. She wanted to keep talking, asking Kellan about her family and confirming the stories Raine had told her about Liv and Jamie, but she could no longer focus as the Merrick's presence took command. Words began to tickle the tip of her tongue that she never would have the guts to say. At least not when she was in her right mind. But she still felt panicked, worried the Lycan might be able to read her dirty, sexual thoughts just by looking at her, feeling like they were scrawled across her forehead in bright neon lights.

Nervously tucking her hair behind her ear, she fought to stay calm, painfully aware that she had to do something. That she had to get him to go back to his cell, before she made a complete and utter fool of herself.

If he didn't go, she *was* going to do something embarrassing. It was inevitable. Because the Merrick had finally found something that it wanted, its hunger mounting as it took in the sight of the dark, dangerous-looking werewolf, the need clawing at her insides like a wild animal determined to break free of its cage.

"Kellan," she said shakily, struggling to take in enough air, "you…uh, you need to go back."

"What's wrong?" His rugged features were etched with concern as he stared at her through the heavy iron bars. "You're shaking like a leaf," he muttered, his hands curling around the metal rods in a powerful grip, as if he intended to break them open.

"No!" she gasped, holding up her hands like a barrier. "Please, don't…don't come in here!"

For a moment, he appeared stricken, but then he shook the emotion off with a wolfy roll of his shoulders and head, hardening his expression. "I'm not going to hurt you, damn it. I came to the compound to help you, Chloe."

"I know that," she gasped, licking her lower lip, her Merrick purring with anticipation as he followed the movement of her tongue with his eyes. "It's just that… just that I'm…"

"*What?*" he demanded in an even grittier tone, his hands curling tighter around the bars, and she had the strangest sense that he was trying to hold himself back from her.

"I need…*damn it*. I can't do this. I need…" The words felt strange in her mouth, as if they weren't her own, and dizziness swamped her. Her pulse grew louder, deep and deafening, her heart beating faster…and faster. A wave of blistering heat climbed up over her skin, making the air around her feel charged. Alive.

She couldn't breathe.

Couldn't see.

And then it all built into one stunning, electrifying

moment of awareness, her vision instantly sharpening, her hearing so acute she could count the heavy, ragged beats of his heart—and Chloe knew the Merrick was suddenly sharing her body, as if she had two separate entities living within her.

The cursed, introverted witch who shied away from sexual relationships.

And the primal Merrick who wanted Kellan Scott buried hard and deep inside her, riding her with all the savage ferocity of his beast.

With a throaty laugh, Chloe felt her hands flinging the blanket away as her bare legs slid over the side of the cot. Sinuously moving to her feet, her voice was nothing more than a silky purr as she said, "Break the lock on the door, Lycan. I need you *inside* me. Right now."

The words landed between them with the jarring force of a bomb blast, and they both froze in reaction, their eyes going comically wide.

O-okay. She'd, uh, obviously been wrong. Apparently she *did* have the guts to say those embarrassing words that had been tickling her tongue. Or rather, the Merrick did.

And she'd clearly shocked the hell out of Kellan. His eyes were still round, the color in his face so dark he looked like he'd been fried by the sun. He opened his mouth. Closed it. Finally managed to croak her name. "*Chloe?*"

"I know, I'm sorry!" Each syllable was a struggle to get out, the muscles in her throat constricted with emotion. "I didn't mean to say that. I just…God, it's hot in here, isn't it?" Breathless and burning, she started ripping at the buttons of the shirt they'd given her, revealing the delicate white lace of her bra.

"Shit," he choked out, taking a step back, and then another, while his powerful hands curled into hard fists at his sides, the veins bulging beneath his skin. "You're trying to kill me, aren't you?"

"I don't wanna kill you," the Merrick drawled, fighting her for control. It wouldn't be satisfied until he'd given them what they needed…and it wanted him now. "I just wanna fu—"

"*Enough!*" he snapped, and she flinched from the harshness of his voice, her bottom lip quivering. He looked furious, aroused and worried all at the same time, his chest heaving. The blue of his eyes overtook the green, smoldering with a hot, predatory glow. "You've got to fight this, Chloe. I've learned enough about you to know that this…this isn't what you want."

She tried to make sense of his words, but the fever in her brain was burning hotter…brighter, making it impossible to think. Maybe it was the mix of her Mallory and Merrick blood, or maybe it was simply the fact that she'd been fighting the hunger for so long, but she couldn't control herself. After all this time, she finally had an outlet for the visceral need ripping her to pieces. A tall, gorgeous, mouthwatering hero who'd come to save her—who could give the ravenous Merrick *everything* it wanted.

"Please, Kellan? I need this so badly." She wrapped her arms around her middle, trying to control her shivering, her body flashing from hot to cold. "Please help me."

"Damn it," he growled, while a muscle ticked forcefully in his jaw. "That's just your Merrick talking. The hunger caused by your awakening."

"But it's—"

A loud thud suddenly sounded above them, as if something heavy had been dropped on the floor, and Kellan tilted his head back, cutting a hard look toward the ceiling. There were raised voices and shouts, the commotion growing louder as heavy footsteps followed.

"Get back in bed and pretend to be asleep," he suddenly barked, his dark gaze locking with hers as he lowered his head.

"But what are you going to do?"

"I have to get back in my cell," he told her, his expression grim. "They might be coming down here with our water, and if they catch me out here, they'll separate us. I can't let that happen."

"You're going back now?" she all but sobbed, throwing her arms wide. "You're just going to…to leave me like *this?*"

"Well, I'm sure as hell not going to touch you when there's an audience. I've promised myself not to touch you at all!" he growled, running his burning gaze over the exposed strip of flesh revealed by her gaping shirt. He seemed almost transfixed by the smooth inner curves of her breasts, the white cotton only just covering her nipples. Then he shook himself in another move that looked decidedly wolflike, before muttering something under his breath that she couldn't quite make out.

"Kellan?"

He dared another brief look at her face, then ground his jaw and turned, heading back toward his cell, the heavy door giving a low groan of protest as he pulled it open, then let it close behind him.

Bristling with frustration, Chloe snatched up her pillow and hurled it toward the metal wall that separated their cells, before climbing under the blanket on her cot and pulling the thin wool over her head.

I will not *beg him again,* she vowed, shaking so hard that her teeth chattered. *I* will *beat this*.

Chloe repeated the words again and again, motivated as much by the mortifying way that she'd acted as she was by the pain still tearing through her body. It'd just... it'd just caught her by surprise this time. But next time... next time she'd be ready. If he tried to visit her again, she would *demand* that he leave. Would resist the Merrick's attempts to lure him into feeding her with everything that she had.

You can do it. If you focus and fight, you can *do it*.

After all, they had only a handful of days to live at the most, right? Despite the Lycan's determination, she didn't think they had a chance in hell of actually making it out of there. She could make it that long, no matter how badly it hurt to deny the Merrick its needs.

But as another wave of sharp, visceral craving swept through her, she groaned from the agony, terrified by just how intense the hunger might become.

In the next instant, the scent of blood overwhelmed her senses, and she lifted her hand to her mouth, touching her fingers to her throbbing lower lip. Her fingers came away wet with blood, but she couldn't believe it.

How did I...

Quickly running her tongue over her front teeth, Chloe encountered the source. For the first time since her awakening had begun, the Merrick's fangs had descended.

She had fangs!

Dizzying thoughts of sinking those piercing points into Kellan Scott's strong, corded throat filled her head, and she groaned again, the sound low and keening. Voices could be heard coming from the top of the winding staircase that led down to their cellblock, but she didn't care. All she could focus on was trying to gain control. Trying to keep herself from screaming for the werewolf to come back…begging him to give her what she needed. She'd truly had no idea the hunger could be so demanding, until Mr. Tall, Dark and Delicious had caught the Merrick's attention. Her body's craving for him… God, it was intolerable. A slick, eviscerating acid scraping its way through her veins. Tiny razors slicing at her insides, ripping her to shreds.

You just have to fight it….

Just have to fight….

Curling her arms over her head, Chloe pulled into a tight ball and began to rock—her jaw locked, teeth clenched—while that burning, biting hunger slowly consumed her.

CHAPTER THREE

Sunday evening

ANOTHER DAY OF HELL. Another torturous exercise in self-control that had left Kellan wound tighter than a corkscrew.

He'd paced his cell for hours, trying to wrap his mind around what had happened earlier that day with Chloe. Yeah, he'd known, after obsessing over the photograph Olivia had given him, that Chloe Harcourt was beautiful and that he wanted her. Had thought about her constantly. Dreamed about her in ways that could only be classified as insanely erotic, not to mention dirty as hell. But he still hadn't been prepared for the intensity of the lust that had shot through his system the second she'd lifted her head from that pillow and looked him in the eye.

Pure, one-hundred-proof hunger, in the rawest, most visceral form he'd ever experienced. Potent. Devastating. And the way her mouthwatering scent had wrapped around him... Christ, he was still twitching with the need to get her naked and wet and under him.

Instead of growing familiar, her scent was calling to him in a way that grew stronger with each second that passed by. Tempting him. Daring him to act....

He didn't know what it meant—and he didn't want to

think about it too closely, because nothing good could come from it.

You know that, you stupid son of a bitch!

Yeah, he knew. But now the damage was done. Now he wanted to do a hell of a lot more than have sex with her. What he wanted would have probably scared the holy living hell out of her, if it weren't for the Merrick coming to life inside her.

The Merrick wants what I've got to give, the wolf snarled, its guttural voice rumbling with anticipation. *We play the same little games.*

Running a hand over his mouth, Kellan almost smiled, thinking his beast was either becoming delusional…or succumbing to some heavy wishful thinking.

Chloe wanting the same things as his wolf in its most feral state? Ha. Not bloody likely, no matter how much Merrick was prowling around inside her.

Being a Lycanthrope, his sexual style was aggressive at the best of times, but now…damn it, it was crazy for him to even be thinking about touching her. He knew it was too dangerous—knew he could too easily lose control and actually hurt her. His primal instincts were in full roar after spending so much time in his feral wolf form. So far he'd managed to keep them under control, but he was tempting fate. Try as he might to act within reason, sooner or later, the beast was going to wrestle that control away from him. As the poison continued to wear him down, he would become too weak to fight it. Then all hell was going to break loose, leaving him at the mercy of those dark, predatory desires.

And yet, he couldn't stay away from her. Not when being near her felt so good. So…*right.* When he'd stood outside her cell earlier, the cold, hollow feeling that'd been lingering in his chest for so long had simply faded away. Instead, there'd been a warm, unfamiliar sensation of comfort. Of…peace. And it'd been fucking amazing.

So amazing that he'd had to come back for more.

As he braced his shoulder against the bars at the corner of her cell, her voice reached out to him from the far side of the small enclosure, where she lay on the cot, huddled beneath her blanket. "What are you doing?"

Kellan raked his gaze over her, making sure she was okay. "Not to state the obvious," he drawled, "but I've come to see you again."

"Why?" she groaned, pulling the blanket over her head.

With his hands shoved in his pockets, he moved along the front of her cell, until he'd reached the middle, where the door stood, which was as close to the cot as he dared. The rough gray stones were cold beneath his feet, but his body was burning with heat, the skin he'd washed earlier when the guards had brought each of them fresh water and food already sheened with sweat. "I can hear you groaning from my cell," he rasped, "and it's driving me bat-shit. I can't stop worrying about you."

"I told you I was fine," came her muffled reply. "All twenty freaking times that you've asked me in the past hour."

"Yeah, well, I needed to see for myself that you were okay."

"For the twenty-first time, then, I'm *fine*. F-I-N-E. Now leave, before I embarrass both of us again."

Softly, he said, "You didn't embarrass me, Chloe."

Peeking over the top of the blanket, she cracked open one eye. "Really? Because from where I was standing,

you looked like your grandma had just shucked her panties and asked you to do something that would be illegal
in at least forty-nine states. Not to mention seriously
whacked."

He gave a gritty laugh that rumbled deep in his chest,
finding her funny as hell. "You just took me by surprise,
that's all."

"Ha. I'll bet I did," she snorted, finally moving into
a sitting position on the cot. As she braced her back
against the wall, the flickering firelight from the continuously burning hearth that sat on the far side of the
underground level played over her feminine features, and
Kellan was struck again by how beautiful she was. It
wasn't an in-your-face, porn star kind of look, like most
of the women he'd bedded, but it worked for him. She
had an ethereal, serene kind of beauty, like something
you expected to see in the pages of a fairy tale. She was
small and slim, her fair skin smooth and fine, her mouth
lush in a face that held a dainty nose and slim, sweep-
ing brows that arched over the most mesmerizing eyes
he'd ever seen. They were big and long-lashed, with an
unusual black ring surrounding the smoky irises. Her
hair was so dark, it almost looked blue in the golden
light of the fire, the glossy strands still a little damp
from where she'd washed it.

Want her now, the wolf insisted. *Don't wanna
wait....*

The beast was still working on him, trying harder
than ever to wear him down. It continuously whispered
through his mind in a guttural rasp, the erotic phrases
centered on how desirable she looked. How tender and
pale and soft. It remarked upon the delicate slope of her
shoulders beneath the thin white cotton. The tantalizing

shape of her small breasts. The sensual curve of her throat as she tilted her head to the side.

And it taunted him with image after image of his fangs breaking the surface of that smooth, vulnerable flesh. With the provocative promise of her hot blood pumping over his tongue, slick and warm and delicious.

Not to mention the intensely erotic moment when her own fangs would pierce his throat, her sweet mouth working as she pulled on the wound harder...and harder.

His head started to spin so badly, Kellan couldn't think straight, his resolutions swinging from one extreme to the other with the crashing force of a wrecking ball.

You're killing her by not giving her what she needs.
No!
Yes, it hissed. *Look at her eyes. The dark shadows beneath. So thin. So starving...and desperate.*

Damn it, what in God's name was he meant to do here? He wasn't trying to be a prick, but he didn't want to harm her, either. Yeah, she needed to feed the creature awakening inside her, and he could give her what she needed. But...what if he hurt her more than she was already hurting in the process?

And then there was his less-than-stellar reputation to consider. No matter how he looked at it, Kellan couldn't help thinking that even if he didn't pose a serious danger to her safety because of his wolf, it still wouldn't feel right to touch her when she was so vulnerable. Not when she would have obviously chosen another guy if she had the choice. One who wasn't such a monumental fuckup. Who hadn't nailed so many women, the names could have filled a bloody book.

And the fact that they hadn't meant anything to him, had merely been a means to an end, only made it worse.

Melodramatic idiot, the wolf snarled. *You think she cares where your dick's been? Stop acting like such a sap.*

Kellan growled in response, the guttural sound making her flinch, but she immediately collected herself, lifting her chin, as if determined not to show even the slightest touch of fear in front of him. He thought she'd order him to go away again, but instead, she said, "I overheard your visit from Spark today."

His neck prickled at her tone, and he sensed... trouble.

Spark was an assassin for the Collective Army and one of Westmore's new favorites. Though the two should have been enemies, they were now working together, the partnership between Westmore and the Collective Army yet another strange twist in the war the Watchmen and their friends were fighting. An organization comprised of fanatical humans who were intent on ridding the world of *all* preternatural life, the Collective operated with one goal: to kill those who weren't a part of the human race. It made no sense for them to be partnered up with Westmore and the Casus, but they were.

And all because of greed. Not for money...but for blood.

The Collective had possession of certain items, as well as unlimited monetary and personnel resources, that Westmore wanted to get his hands on, and so he'd gone to the Collective Generals and made them a deal they'd been unwilling to turn down. In exchange for his demands, Westmore had given the Army the secret locations of four Deschanel nesting grounds, with the promise of more clan locations to come. The deal had resulted in the gruesome slaughter of hundreds of vampires, including many women and children. It also meant that a good number of human Collective soldiers were now working directly for Westmore—though Kellan and his friends had heard rumors that the deal was no longer sitting well with the Army, and the Generals were regretting what they'd gotten into. While Westmore had assured the Collective that he would use the Casus to stop a dangerous time of anarchy that was coming to the clans, and then eventually destroy them, it was becoming obvious to all that he'd lied.

And that, Kellan thought, *is what you get when you make deals with the evil and deranged.*

He felt no sympathy for the Collective, and he sure as hell wasn't interested in Spark. She was one of the cruelest bitches he'd ever known, and she was obviously delusional if she thought he would ever actually lay a hand on her.

What was even more obvious was that Chloe hadn't liked what she'd overheard that afternoon.

"What? You think you're too good for me now?" Spark had drawled in a raised voice, after Kellan had refused her offer of sex. "Or is it that you don't want your new little jail buddies here to know that I've already had you?"

When he'd told her to shut up, she'd gotten a sly gleam in her green eyes and had taken perverse pleasure in talking about how raunchy it'd been between them, describing in detail all the things he'd bent her over. All lies, since Kellan had never laid a finger on her, but he knew she'd only been trying to screw with his mind, taunting him with the suggestion that he would sleep with the enemy...since that's exactly what he'd done in Washington. Still, he'd had to be careful how he reacted, lest the assassin pick up on the truth.

The truth being that it bothered the hell out of him that Chloe might believe anything that came out of Spark's mouth. And he'd been right to worry, because it appeared that she had.

"What about the visit?" he sighed, rolling a shoulder.

She shrugged. "I was just surprised. I mean, I knew you got around, but I figured you for better taste than *that*."

Crossing his arms, Kellan braced his shoulder against the bars again and stared her down with narrowed eyes. "Tell me you're not actually buying that bullshit. Come on, Chloe. I thought you were smarter than that."

"How could you think anything?" she asked, her demeanor changing within the blink of an eye. Her face became flushed, her gray eyes glowing like silver fire, and he knew the Merrick was rising back to the surface, as hard and fast as a torpedo. "God, Kellan. We're strangers! You don't know jack about me. I could be a raging bitch for all you know. An idiot. A brainless bimbo!"

Despite his worry and irritation, he snorted, which clearly ticked her off. "Are you...are you *laughing* at me?" she rasped, the low words vibrating with outrage.

"Stop talking nonsense," he murmured, slowly raising one of his brows, "and I'll stop laughing."

That obviously pissed her off even more, because she growled at him. *Actually growled.*

And the rigid state of his dick told him that he'd liked it. A lot.

"And not that it matters," he told her, "but I've never laid a finger on the redheaded bitch. And I sure as hell wouldn't start now."

Rolling her eyes, she said, "Yeah, well, from what I've heard about you, Kellan, a woman's personality isn't exactly high on your list of prerequisites for bed partners. You've always had more valid concerns, like breast size and how long a woman's legs are. And Spark does have one hell of a figure."

He didn't say anything at first. He just pushed away from the bars and started pacing along the front of her cell, his hands shoved back in his pockets, his jaw locked so tight he was surprised he didn't crack a tooth.

"I may be a lot of things," he finally muttered, forcing the graveled words out, "but a masochist isn't one of them, Chloe. I'm trying to change, and I know it sounds like a line of bullshit, but I'm not the jackass I was a few months ago. I try to think with my head these days, rather than my dick. Not that my dick would have ever been interested in that psycho bitch, either. Even *it* has standards, as twisted as they might be."

He didn't look at her as he kept pacing, the seconds ticking out in slow motion, stretching time, the heat of her gaze burning against his body as he moved. He was ready to launch into another spiel about how he was trying to clean up his act, when she finally said, "I get that this is a totally personal question, but do you always talk about your sex organ as if it's a sentient being?"

His own gruff bark of laughter caught him completely by surprise, and he came to a stop, his shoulders hunched as he roughly ran a hand over the back of his neck.

"Well?" she prompted him.

"I, uh, I don't know." With a slow shake of his head, he cut her a wry look from the corner of his eye. "Never really thought about it before."

Smoothing the blanket over her legs, she said, "Just to let you know, you should probably consider stopping."

A grin kicked up a corner of his mouth. "I'll keep that in mind."

She turned her head to the side, but not before he thought he saw her lips twitch, on the verge of a smile. How they'd gone from snapping at each other to smiling again, he didn't know. But it was obvious their moods were all over the place, shifting as swiftly as desert sands.

Pushing a hand through his hair, he said, "Please, just don't listen to Spark, okay? She gets a kick outta messing with people's minds, but it's all a load of crap."

Her fingers plucked nervously at the drab blanket, her profile...sad. Strained. From the side, her lower lip looked a little swollen, as if she'd been nervously pulling it through her teeth, and she swiped it with her tongue before saying, "Listen, Kell, it's really none of my business what you do with Spark, or with any woman, for that matter. I'm not judging you, and if anything, I'm probably just jealous of all the freedom you've had, when that really hasn't been an option for me because of the curse. But that was my choice. The Mallory have always been seen as evil manipulators who twist guys to our whims, and I never wanted to have anyone throw those accusations in my face. Plus, it would hardly be enjoyable to hook up with some guy and spend the whole time worrying he was only interested in me because of some stupid spell." She brought her gaze back to his, her voice a little huskier as she added, "Anyway, I think it'd be better if you just didn't come over here again. At least not until we're ready to die trying to get out of this place."

"Don't say that. You are *not* going to die." He forced the words through his gritted teeth, surprised by the vehemence of his reaction.

Carefully, she said, "I don't want to fight with you, Kellan. So please, just go."

With his jaw locked, he paced along the outside of her cell again before stopping and wrapping his fingers around the cold rods of metal. "I don't want to go," he muttered, holding her with his stare.

Her gaze burned with frustration, but before she could say anything, he continued talking. "I know you feel like crap, and to be honest, I'm not feeling all that great, either. But it makes…it makes me feel better to be with you. And before you ask me to explain what that means, don't. Because I don't have any idea. It's just the way it is."

She studied his face, no doubt noting the ravaging effects of the poison on his system. "You…you don't look well. Are you ill?"

"Nah." He scraped a palm against his stubbled jaw. "It's just some poison I've gotta get outta my system."

"Poison?" she said slowly, the word trembling on her lips. "They poisoned you? When? How?" She started talking faster. "Why would they do that? Is it meant to be some kind of torture? Raine said they still think you came here to steal back the three Dark Markers that are in their possession. Does it have something to do with that?"

Shaking his head, he said, "The poisoning actually happened before I got to the compound."

Her gaze immediately slid to the bite wound burning at the side of his throat, and she visibly swallowed, her pale features stricken with worry. "Is that what the bite's from? An infected Deschanel? I've heard of that, but don't really know much about it."

"It was my own stupid fault," he rumbled, keeping his tone light. "I wasn't paying close enough attention as I was crossing the Wasteland and ended up running into a poisonous vamp named Asa Reyker, who thought I looked tasty."

"So this is another nightmare that can be laid at my feet," she said softly, dropping her head back until it clunked against the wall.

"That's bullshit," he grunted, her reaction reinforcing his decision not to tell her the complete truth about the poison. "You didn't ask me to come here, Chloe. It was *my* choice."

"I'm just so sick of this!" she burst out, thumping her small, fisted hands against the cot as she lifted her head and looked at him. "I want out of this place, but not at the expense of your life, Kellan! I didn't want anyone else to be hurt!"

"I'm not hurt, damn it."

"Yeah? Because being poisoned doesn't exactly sound like something that feels good!"

"I'll be okay," he lied, trying to calm her down, even though he knew damn well that he was dying. "The poison can't kill me, so stop freaking out. It's going to be fine."

"Fine? Look around you, Kellan." She flung the words at him. "Nothing about this situation is fine!"

In another sudden shift, he could see her worry bleeding back into something primal and raw, and she started to shiver. Her eyes became heavy as she stared at him from the cot, her chest rising and falling with swift, panting breaths.

Thickly, he said, "Your Merrick is rising again."

In a gesture he was beginning to recognize as one of the witch's favorites, she rolled her eyes at him again. "Gee, ya think?"

He liked her sassy mouth, though he had a feeling she was more than a little surprised by the things she kept saying to him, as if she hadn't expected to be so brave when faced with a dangerous Lycan.

"Has the blood they've been giving you helped at all?" he asked.

"They've shoved it into my veins," she told him, her voice strained. "Even made me drink it from a cup. But none of it has helped."

"Chloe, I want you to know that I *would* help you with this, if I thought it was the right thing to do. But I know that it's not."

"And I'd stop looking at you as if you were my next meal, but I seem to have this whole split personality thing going on right now that makes that impossible. So you should really just go."

"I know it might not feel like it at times, but you *will* be able to manage the Merrick's hunger until we're out of here," he told her. "I'm not saying it will be easy, but I know you're strong enough to do it."

"Kellan, I'm not kidding," she groaned, obviously struggling to hold it together. "You need to leave. Immediately."

His muscles tensed with frustration. "I don't want you to be alone. Not when you look like you're in pain."

"Damn it, I *am* in pain! And you being over here is making it worse!" Dropping her head forward, she took a deep, shuddering breath and licked her lips, her voice hoarse as she said, "I don't understand any of this. Is it…is it because of the poison? Is that why you won't feed me? Are you afraid of it hurting me?"

Watching the way she was twisting her fingers together in her lap, he forced himself to be honest. "No. A Deschanel nest can become poisonous for any number of reasons, depending on what they've done. For some, it's because they were cursed, and in other cases, because they broke one of the sacred covenants of the Deschanel. There are all different types of poisons and they're not all lethal, though some of them can probably make you wish you were dead. Hell, some can even cause madness, and some just make you feel like you've been put through a wringer. The poison is something that lives in the vampires' bodies, which they can often pass on to their victims, depending on the specific strain—but with most of the infected nests, that's where the cycle stops. The Reykers' strain of poison is one that's no longer contagious once it spreads through their victims. So even though it's inside me, the poison isn't something I can pass on to another."

"Oh." She took another deep, trembling breath. "Then why won't you help me? I mean, I *know* I'm nowhere close to your usual type, but this is…this isn't a normal situation."

He hated that she looked at it that way, as if he ever would have preferred his usual type to her.

"Chloe, I swear I'm not trying to be an ass. The truth

is…" He groaned, wanting to tell her he was afraid of his wolf taking control and hurting her, but damn it, he didn't want her scared of him. So he told her another truth instead. "The truth is that I'd like nothing more than to…to give you what you need, but I can't do that. I'm not the kind of guy you want to get mixed up with, honey. Even for something that's short term." Because he knew damn well that once she learned about all the stupid shit that he'd done…about the way he'd bedded down with one of the Casus females and nearly gotten his friends killed, she'd be disgusted that she'd ever allowed him to touch her, much less take his blood into her body for a Merrick feeding.

Kellan thought it might be more the ragged edge to his words than the actual words themselves that had her lifting her head to look at him. "What do you mean?"

His mouth twisted with a wry smile. "I'm fucked up. Hell, my issues have issues. Big, nasty hairy ones that you really don't want anything to do with."

Her brows drew together in a small V. "Weren't you in here for the beginning of this conversation? I already know about the women, Kellan. Raine said you're known as a playboy of epic proportions. A relentless womanizer."

He couldn't believe the heat burning in his face, as if he was actually embarrassed that she knew about his man-slut reputation. "Yeah, well, that's part of it. Olivia would tell you it's my 'coping mechanism.'"

She suddenly laughed, though the light sound held a brittle edge. "Did I miss something?" he asked.

Shaking her head, she said, "It's just that that's how I look at my lifestyle. The way I seclude myself from other people is my own little 'coping mechanism.'"

Kellan frowned. "And that's funny, how?"

"Well, think about it. We went about 'coping' in completely different ways. You by nailing everything that moves, so long as it was gorgeous and built—while the only things I've been nailing would be pictures on the wall, and all by my lonesome." She snorted, saying, "Of the two of us, I'm betting you've been having a helluva lot more fun than I have."

With a rough burst of laughter, Kellan slowly shook his head, not knowing what to say.

Then her smile faded, and he tensed as she quietly said, "I'm not asking you to marry me, Kellan. I'm not even asking you to be my boyfriend. Aside from the blood, I'm just asking you to give me what hundreds of other women have gotten from you."

He swallowed against the knot of regret lodged deep in his throat, and somehow managed to rasp, "I can't do that."

"Why not?" she asked, clearly baffled by his continued refusal.

"It's…complicated," he muttered, while his wolf roared with raw frustration, the savage sound so loud within his mind that he winced. Though he wanted so badly to give in, Kellan knew that no matter how miserable Chloe Harcourt was at that moment, she *could* get what she needed from one of his unmated friends once they were free…and then she'd be okay. Not to mention a helluva lot safer than if she let him touch her.

"Complicated?" she repeated, her expression a mixture of hurt and genuine bewilderment. "How freaking complicated can it be? It's not like I'm asking you to explain quantum mechanics. If the idea is so repulsive to you, then stop torturing me and just go away!"

By the time the last word had left her lips, she was shaking again, even harder than before, her eyes flashing from gray to silver like sparks of light.

Feeling like a useless jackass, he said, "Just take a deep breath, honey, and try to calm down."

Her eyes narrowed with blazing astonishment. "You don't think I've tried that? God, I thought you were supposed to be some kind of genius with a raging IQ! I thought—" She gasped, leaning forward, her slender arms clutched around her body as she rocked. "Oh, hell," she groaned, gritting her teeth. "This sucks so bad."

Unable to stay away from her, Kellan knelt down in front of the bars that were closest to her cot and reached in with one hand, clutching a handful of the blanket, his hard fist only inches away from her slim little body. "Chloe," he rasped, torn between what he wanted to do…and what he knew was right. "Chloe, honey, look at me."

She didn't say anything at first. Just kept rocking, forward and then back again, and from this close, Kellan could actually feel the potent forces working within her. Feel that mesmerizing rise of power inside her pulsing against him. When she turned her head and pierced him with those glowing silver eyes, Kellan felt her power slam all the way down to his bones. The air felt electric, sizzling against his skin, and he realized that being part Mallory might be having a serious effect on her awakening—one they foolishly hadn't anticipated.

"It's getting worse," she whispered, the sharp points of the Merrick's fangs just visible beneath the sensual curve of her upper lip, "and it's scaring the hell out of me. I don't…I don't think I can control it anymore."

"*Just stop. Please.*" A hoarse, graveled demand.

"If you…if you knew how hard this was for me, Kellan, you wouldn't make me beg." She licked her lips again, her silver eyes glistening with tears. "I can't keep—"

"Just a little bit longer and I'll get you out of here, Chloe. Then we can get you somewhere…" The words stuck in his throat, but he forced them out. "When we're free, you'll be able to find someone to feed from. Someone of your choosing."

"You fed Raine."

He opened his mouth, but before he could explain, she went on. "I'm not complaining. I mean, after everything that she's been through, she needs a champion." Her head tilted a little to the side, her eyes liquid and bright. "I just don't understand why you can't do the same for me."

Westmore had used physical abuse, as well as Raine's family, to force her cooperation, brutally murdering the psychic's younger sister. Her baby brother would have suffered the same fate, if Raine hadn't taken the upper hand, using her "sight" on Gregory DeKreznick to blackmail Westmore into leaving her loved ones alone. But in order to keep her weak, Westmore had continued to starve her, never allowing her to have any blood, only feeding her bits of food. Knowing she needed sustenance or she was going to die, Kellan *had* pushed his arm through the bars of his cell and given Raine his wrist. And while she'd been careful not to take too much, since it would have been obvious to Westmore and the others, Kellan had made sure she'd taken enough blood to dull the pain gnawing at her insides, and to help with the internal injuries she'd suffered.

But that didn't mean he could do the same with Chloe,

because her needs were far more complicated…and it was *Chloe* his inner beast wanted to get its hands on.

"What happened with Raine was different, and you know it," he told her, his deep voice actually shaking with emotion. "All I did was give her my wrist."

And as an awakening Merrick female, Chloe was going to need a hell of a lot more than that.

Tears coursed down her cheeks as she stared back at him, her breath shuddering from her lips as she quietly said, "Give…give me your wrist, then, and I'll do the rest myself. You won't even have to look at me or come inside my cell."

Aw, hell, he thought, her soft words echoing painfully through his head as he swiftly moved to his feet.

Without a doubt, Kellan knew this woman was going to drive him out of his ever-loving mind.

And the danger was only getting deeper by the second.

CHAPTER FOUR

WITH ONE HAND SHOVED deep in his pocket, Kellan shakily scraped his other hand through his hair and struggled to remember his mission.

Find the witch.

Protect the witch.

Save the witch.

Unfortunately, nailing the witch's beautiful little ass to the wall wasn't anywhere on the agenda, no matter how sweetly she begged him. Didn't matter how tempting she was. How desperate he was to touch her. It wasn't gonna happen, because even without his wolf screwing dangerously with his control, Kellan hadn't been lying when he'd said he wasn't good enough for her. Shit, he wasn't fit for her to wipe her friggin' shoes on, much less trust with her body. She was a stunning, white-hot goddess with a sassy mouth and endearing blushes, and he was…well, he sure as hell wasn't a god. Christ, at the moment he was even more animal than man. And he didn't trust the animal to control itself with her. One accidental swipe of his claws or bite from his fangs, and she could be seriously hurt…if not killed.

Which meant that he had to keep his filthy paws to himself…and *off* the delectable, intoxicating little Merrick.

But it wasn't going to be easy. She was too pale, the

bruise-colored smudges under her tear-filled eyes growing darker, and his insides twisted with guilt. Damn it, she needed blood, badly, but it was too dangerous, his beast fighting harder to bust its way through with each second that passed by.

And it wasn't as if blood alone was going to ease her suffering. As an awakening Merrick female, she needed fresh blood...*and* an earth-shattering orgasm.

"This is wrong," he groaned, wincing at the raw, gritty sound of his voice. It held too much of the wolf in it, the animal seething with primitive lust, urging him to forget what was right and wrong and just follow his baser instincts. "You don't wanna do this, Chloe. Trust me."

"Please, Kellan." A vivid blush burned beneath her smooth complexion, and he could tell how much it was costing her to ask him for something so intimate. "I'm *starving.*"

A tremor shuddered through his coiled muscles, a fresh sheen of sweat breaking out over the surface of his skin, despite the freezing temperatures in the cellblock. Knowing that if he gave in he could be putting her in serious danger, he tried again to make her understand why it couldn't happen. "I didn't come here to take advantage of your situation, damn it. I came here to keep you safe."

"You want to do something selfless?" she threw back at him, sliding her slender legs over the side of the cot. "Be the hero? Then give me what I need!"

"It's not that simple!"

She made a choked sound, wiping the tears from her cheeks with her fingers. "If you're waiting for an easier solution, Kellan, there isn't one."

Sounding ragged and on edge and desperate, he carefully said, "A little more time, Chloe, and I'll have you out of here."

"Aren't you listening?" she cried. "I don't have any more time!"

"Damn it, don't say that!"

Sharp, panting breaths slipped past her lips, followed by a stream of soft, unsteady words. "I meant what I said before, Kellan. If you don't help me, I'm afraid of what I'll do." She flicked her tongue against the shiny swell of her lower lip, the brief glimpse he caught of her fangs—the only physical change that Merrick females experienced—just about the sexiest thing he'd ever seen. "And I don't want some other man. Not one of your friends or the people who are helping them. *I want you.*"

Though Kellan had used every ounce of his strength to hold on to his fraying control, those last three words were what broke him, completely shattering his resistance.

Cursing and shaking with lust, he quickly grabbed the keys that hung on the far wall and flipped the switch on the counterweight for Chloe's door. Then he let himself into her cell, dropped the keys on the floor, and crossed the distance between them. In the next instant, he wrapped one arm under her bottom, lifting her against his body as he shoved the cot out of his way, sending it slamming into the iron bars. Then he lunged forward, pinning her against the wall, unable to hear the words he could see her lips shaping over the crashing roar of his pulse. Heat crawled up over his back and shoulders, spreading into his face as his free hand closed around the back of her neck in a dominating hold, his heart hammering to a dark, predatory beat. She stared up at him, her glistening eyes wide and bright and…*hopeful*, and with another sharp curse, Kellan covered her mouth with his, licking his way past those plush, petal-soft lips, seeking the silken warmth within. And God, she tasted delicious. Mouthwatering. Completely addictive, each succulent detail a devastating assault on his senses.

He used every last ounce of his willpower to give her the time to decide whether or not she wanted to go any further with him, but the instant she flicked her tongue against his, he was gone.

"Kellan," she gasped, her slender fingers gripping his hair as she fought to pull him closer, her legs wrapping around his waist. The kiss turned into something savagely explicit, wet and raw and violent, the passion between them dangerously explosive. "*More. Give me more!*"

With a feral growl, Kellan lifted her higher, grinding his granite-hard cock against her mound, his jeans rasping against the soft cotton of her panties. "That what you want?" His voice was dark and rough as he pulled her head to the side so that he could drag his open mouth down the slender column of her throat, the heady taste of her skin making his cock even harder. Her small hands clutched his bare shoulders, her nails digging into the slick, bunched muscles, and he could hear his wolf urging him on as he found her mouth again, kissing her harder…deeper…raw lust searing his veins.

Touch her. Taste her. Everywhere….

A thick animal-like sound rumbled at the back of his throat as he fought the release of his claws and fangs, and he knew he'd scared her when she trembled in his arms. Though the wolf urged him to keep going, enjoying that provocative quiver of fear, Kellan somehow found the strength to break the drugging kiss, and pressed his forehead to hers. "It's okay," he gasped, his chest heaving as he smoothed her hair away from her face with a shaky hand, hoping like hell that what he was saying was true. "I won't hurt you, Chloe."

"I know," she whispered, touching the hot skin of his face with inquisitive fingertips, as if she was learning him by touch, the warmth of her breath pelting against his fevered cheek, layering heat on heat, making him burn. "I trust you, Kell."

"You shouldn't," he muttered, reaching between them and ripping at the buttons on her shirt, unable to stop himself. "You shouldn't trust me at all. Christ, you have no idea how close I am to losing it."

"Then lose it," she urged him, her breath catching as he shoved the lacy cups of her bra down and lifted her higher, hungrily scraping the rough pad of his tongue across a deliciously sweet, tight nipple. Crying out, she braced her arms against his shoulders…and he gave her what she wanted, sucking the tender bud between his lips, trapping it in the wet, scalding heat of his mouth.

As her need grew more intense, her scent became richer, sweeter…the feverish warmth of her skin burning hotter, enthralling him, calling to his wolf, his cock throbbing with each hammering beat of his heart. His breath roughened as he moved to her other breast, his mouth dragging across her chest until another dainty, candy-pink nipple touched his lips. The realities of their surroundings faded away, his entire being focused on his sense of touch…of taste. He needed to touch *all* of her. Needed to taste her pleasure cries in his mouth as he made her come, deeper and longer than she ever had before.

Wrapping his arms around her body, Kellan crushed her against him as he brought her mouth back to his. She nipped his bottom lip, then slid her tongue against his, her rising aggression fueling his own. His gums burned from the pressure of his fangs, his chest vibrating with another primal growl as she reached between their bodies, pressing her hand against the rigid length of his cock. She squeezed him through his jeans, testing his length…his broad width, her breaths coming hard and rushed. Then her hand turned, reaching between her own legs, her hips riding forward in an earthy, sensual need for completion, and he snagged her wrist, jerking her hand over her head as he tore his mouth from hers.

"That's *mine*," he warned in a dark, gritty rumble, locking his hand over her entire forearm, trapping it against the rough surface of the wall. "Next time I'll lay you on a bed and put your hands between your legs, Chloe." She writhed in his hold, her beautiful eyes hazy with lust. "I'll jerk off while I watch you finger yourself, and I'll love every second of it. But right now, it's *my* turn," he growled, pushing his hand inside the front of her panties, his fingers seeking that exquisitely soft, sensitive part of her. And what he found was even better than he'd imagined. She was scalding hot to the touch, the folds of her sex drenched with moisture, the tender flesh already slippery and swollen with need.

"I'm so close," she cried, grinding herself against his palm, her wild, uninhibited pursuit of pleasure nearly sending him over the edge, the building pressure in his shaft bordering on pain.

Have to get in her, he thought, jerking his hand from between her legs. *Want to be all over her. Want every part of her….*

"Put your feet back on the floor," he commanded. The second she'd unhooked her legs from around his waist, Kellan took hold of her shoulders and quickly spun her around, facing her toward the wall. "Now brace your hands against the stone," he grated, his own hands urgently roaming her body, touching every feminine curve and hollow that he could reach.

She followed the husky command, her back arching as she leaned forward, her soft hands flattened against the craggy surface.

Leaning over her, Kellan touched his mouth to the side of her throat, where her pulse thrummed with excitement. With a little catch in her breath, she tilted her head farther to give him better access, her shirt slipping off one smooth, pale shoulder, and Kellan dragged his mouth lower, her skin like silk beneath his lips and tongue and teeth. His hands skimmed over the narrow curve of her waist, gripping her hips rougher than he meant to, and he gritted his teeth, furious at himself for his loss of control.

Calm down, you son of a bitch, he silently snarled, but the wolf was quick to respond.

You want calm? it sneered. *Then get the fuck on with it!*

Kellan wanted to argue with the bastard, but he was too far gone, his ears roaring as he ran a hand over the feminine curve of her ass, his cock so hard it pulsed within the strangling confines of his jeans. With a dark sound on his lips, he ripped the crotch of her panties to the side, and found the slick, swollen entrance to her body. His breath hissed through his teeth as he pushed one long finger inside her…nearly dying from the feel of her muscles closing in on him. So tight…and greedy, they surrounded him with liquid heat and the heavy rhythm of her pulse; the soft, throaty cries spilling from her lips telling him how much she enjoyed his touch.

"God, you feel good," he breathed into her ear.

"Not as good as you," she moaned, riding his finger, her lithe body burning with heat.

As a red, hazy cloud began to fill his vision, Kellan struggled to remind himself of the danger. He knew he shouldn't fuck her. That he should just make her come. Give her the blood that she needed. Damn it, he *knew* that. But it was impossible at that moment to recall the reasons why.

"Can you take two?" he rasped, thrusting deeper, needing to make her ready.

"Oh yeah," she breathed, pressing her firm little ass into his groin.

Twisting his fingers in the damp cotton of her panties, Kellan had just enough sanity left to know that he couldn't rip them off, like he wanted, since she didn't have any others. And no way in hell was he going to have her walking around bare-assed in front of the guards that brought them their food and water. Instead, he pulled the skimpy underwear down her thighs, letting them fall to the floor, then reached back between her legs from the front and thrust two thick fingers into her, jerking a husky cry from her lips. Sliding his other hand inside her gaping shirt, he ran the callused tip of his thumb over a beautifully plump, hardened nipple at the same time he rubbed the base of his palm against the swollen knot of her clit, and she ground her forehead against one of her raised arms, gasping for breath, on the verge of coming for him.

So beautiful. So sweet...

As if he could shelter her against the nightmares that existed around them, Kellan curved his body around hers, surrounding her with his strength, desperate to make her feel safe. To give her pleasure. Give her something those bastards couldn't take away from her, when they'd already stripped her of everything else in her life that mattered.

He was a shitty substitute for her family and friends and home, but goddamn it, he was going to make her come so hard that for those few blistering moments, she didn't care. While that raw, screaming pleasure was pumping through her, breaking her open, she wouldn't care about anything but how bloody good it felt. Wouldn't care about anything but him and what he could give her.

"You want my cock, Chloe?" He whispered the ragged words into the tender shell of her ear, his nostrils flaring as he pulled in deeper breaths of her heady scent. He wanted it covering his skin. Wanted to be drenched in it.

"Yes," she hissed. "I'll take everything you have, Kell. All of it."

"I'm so going to burn in hell for this," he muttered, but he couldn't stop himself from reaching between and ripping open his jeans, a thick sound rumbling deep in his throat as the heavy length of his cock sprang against the satiny curve of her ass. Gripping the broad shaft in his fist, Kellan's eyes nearly rolled back in his head as he bent his knees a little, rubbing the taut crown through her drenched folds.

So hot. So wet.

God, he wanted his mouth on her. Wanted to take her to the floor, spread her open with his thumbs, and memorize every tender, juicy detail. He'd lick her, lapping at her…pushing his tongue inside her until she was screaming and crying and ready to give him everything that he wanted. That he needed.

Next time, he promised himself. *When I get her out of here, I'll spend hours with my face shoved against her, making her come for me again…and again…and again.*

Drunk on lust and seething with his own primitive hungers, Kellan braced his left hand against the wall, just above Chloe's, his right hand running down the center of her back, pushing her forward, then curling possessively around her hip. He was just starting to think that maybe he could master the beast after all…when the deadly claws on his left hand shot free, digging deep into the ancient stone. Flakes of gray floated down to the floor, like puffs of smoke, and he shook his head, stunned that he hadn't been able to control the change in his body. Terrified that he might accidentally hurt her, just like he'd feared he would do, Kellan started to pull away, but she reached down and covered the clawless hand at her hip, holding him against her.

"What are you doing?" he snarled, his entire body shaking with violent, visceral emotion. "My wolf wants at you, Chloe. Goddamn it, this isn't safe!"

"If it wanted to hurt me, your claws would be ripping into my flesh right now, but they aren't. It just needed to let off a little steam," she whispered. And then she shocked the hell out of him by moving up onto her tiptoes and pressing a kiss to the back of his monstrous, claw-tipped fingers, then lower, against the battle-scarred back of his hand.

God, she's too good to be real.

Something suddenly caught at the edge of Kellan's consciousness, like a hand clasping onto him in the dark and trying to pull him back into the light. *Noises? Voices?* His brows drew together as he forced the irritating intrusion away, focusing instead on the breathtaking sensation of her lips against his skin. On the perfect, bone-melting feel of her tender sex sliding against his heavy shaft as he pushed between her legs. Sweat dotted his forehead, a salty drop trailing into one eye as he locked his jaw and fought the urge to reach down, position himself, and ram up into her with everything he had.

No! Can't hurt her. Never hurt her....

Struggling to concentrate, Kellan fought to remember his purpose, but it wasn't easy. Chloe kept kissing her way down his arm, over his thick wrist, the ropy muscles in his forearm, until she was nuzzling the hard, round bulge of bicep. "Bite it," he growled, nudging the muscle harder against her lips, wanting the sting of those sharp little fangs in his flesh. He was more than happy to give up his blood for her, while making her come, no longer able to recall why that was so wrong.

Not wrong, the wolf rasped. *Finally getting what I want. What we need....*

Her small fangs scraped his flesh, just as he bent his knees a little more, the heavy head of his cock nudging inside that small, slick opening nestled within her folds, his breath hissing through his teeth at the blistering contact.

So soft. So tight.

Flexing his hips, he pushed the head of his cock a little deeper into her, working against her natural resistance, the snug, slick kiss of her sex the sweetest, most mind-blowing thing Kellan had ever experienced.

She'd just scraped her fangs across his skin a little harder, getting ready to sink them deep, a low hum of anticipation purring in the back of her throat, her body shivering, on the brink of release…when that invisible hand nudged at him again, warning him there was a problem. He shook his head, hard, trying to focus, and then he caught it. A rumble of voices coming from the upper level. Although they were growing louder, his wolf snarled that it was nothing…to just ignore it. But the voices grew closer, until they were coming from just outside the locked door at the top of the staircase, and Kellan was instantly ripped back to his senses, the reality of the situation crashing over him like an icy bucket of water.

"Son of a bitch!" He took a stumbling step back, his chest heaving while he fought for a deeper breath, his arms trembling at his sides as his claws retracted.

"Kell?"

"Damn it, we can't do this! Not here," he growled, scraping both hands through his hair so hard that his scalp stung. "Not like this. If they find us together, we'll get separated. I can't let that happen."

With a keening sound of frustration, Chloe crumpled against the wall. "You're stopping?" she whispered, her voice cracking as she turned toward him, her expression shadowed with pain and confusion.

"We don't have any choice but to stop." He pushed the words through his gritted teeth, quickly refastening his jeans over the raw, angry ache in his cock. Grabbing her panties off the floor, he tossed them to her, saying, "Get these back on."

She started to argue as she caught them, but he reached out, grabbing her behind the neck and pulling her against him, so that he could take her mouth with another deep, marauding kiss that left her dazed and breathless. Then he lifted her into his arms, kicked the cot back against the wall, and laid her down. Pinning her forearms on either side of her head, Kellan leaned his face close to hers, the panties still grasped in her hand. "I'm not backing out," he grunted, the rough words thick with frustration. "But we have to be smart."

"I don't believe this," she choked out, her eyes suddenly flashing silver as the furious Merrick inside her strained against his hold. "I can't believe you'd do this to me! I was so close!"

"Chloe—" he gave her arms a careful shake "—listen to me, damn it."

"I don't want to listen," she moaned, her neck arching as she fought him, her small fangs glistening in the golden glow of firelight.

He shook her a little harder. "They're coming down here again, and God only knows what they want. Think about it, Chloe. I know you're hurting, but I have a bad feeling about this."

Her body slowly stilled, fear gradually replacing the hunger in her gaze as she blinked up at him. "Oh God," she finally whispered, wetting her lips. "Raine! Do you think they're coming to hurt her again? Westmore's been waiting for her to give him the location for the next Dark Marker, but he's getting impatient."

"I won't let anything happen to her," he promised, tucking a dark strand of hair behind her ear. "Just stay in this bed and pretend to be asleep. No matter what you hear, do *not* draw attention to yourself. I'll keep whoever's coming away from Raine, but I want you to keep quiet."

Knowing he needed to get the hell out of there, before he was caught in her cell, Kellan quickly grabbed up the keys and locked her cell door behind him. Moving with rapid strides, he placed the keys back on their rusty hook and flipped the switch open for the counterweight on her door, then made his way back into his own cell, adrenaline fueling his strength as he wrestled with the heavy door. After making sure the lock didn't show any signs that it'd been tampered with, he headed toward the front right corner of the grim enclosure, his heart still pounding with a deep, resonating beat.

Jesus, the woman had nearly burned him alive, and he hadn't even brought her off. The enormity of what they'd almost done finally started to crash down on him, and he groaned, scrubbing his hands down his face.

A day. He hadn't even lasted one goddamn day before pawing her.

I want you....

Freaking pathetic, the way he'd been drawn in by those three simple words. Kellan could only thank God that he'd been wrenched back to his senses in time. He knew what could have happened. Even though he understood damn well that he should keep his hands off her, he'd been more than capable of taking it all the way. Hell, ten more seconds and he'd have been buried a mile inside her, soaked in that slippery heat, nailing her sweet ass against every surface he could find—and the fact they didn't have anything for birth control wouldn't have stopped him.

A tremor ran through his long frame, and Kellan ran

another shaky hand down his face, a muscle pulsing in the hard set of his jaw.

I don't believe this. You're scared shitless.

He wanted to tell the bastard to shut up, but his wolf had it right. He *was* scared. Of failing her. Of becoming more obsessed with her than he already was. Because the stronger his desire to hold on to her grew, the more this was going to suck when it came to an end. And it *would* come to an end.

Unless he managed to pull a fucking miracle out of his ass, there was no getting around the fact that he was a walking dead man.

The voices grew louder at the top of the stairs, and Kellan pressed his face close to the bars, knowing they had little time. "Raine, you awake?"

She replied immediately, saying, "I'm here," no doubt sensing whoever was getting ready to pay them a visit.

"Be ready."

"I am," she murmured, and then, in a lower voice, she added, "You lied to her, Lycan."

Kellan stiffened with shock, his tone guttural as he said, "I have never laid a hand on that redhead in my life. Spark is just trying to cause trouble."

Raine's voice was soft. "I'm not talking about the assassin. I'm talking about the poison."

Shit, he thought, running his tongue over his teeth. He'd asked Raine to try and get a "read" on Asa Reyker for him, to find out if the bastard's claim of an antidote was true, but when she'd tried, she'd said the vampire's mind was too ravaged by the poison for her to see anything clearly. Still, she was as doubtful as Kellan was, both of them aware that antidotes were practically nonexistent when it came to the strains of poison that existed in the Wasteland. The psychic knew Kellan was dying…and she obviously thought Chloe should know, as well.

"Look," he said, keeping his voice low. "I don't wanna sound rude, Raine. But this doesn't concern you."

"I consider you my friend, Kellan, so yeah, it concerns me. And Chloe's my friend, too. She needs to know the truth."

Like hell she did. The last thing he wanted was to add to her guilt. And he sure as hell didn't want her looking at him with pity or thinking he wasn't strong enough to get her out of there.

"We'll finish this argument later. Right now, we've got company coming. Can you tell who it is?"

"Spark. Be careful and don't do anything crazy."

With a snort, he asked, "You mean like piss the bitch off?"

Raine made a sharp sound of frustration. "That's exactly what I mean!"

"I can't make any promises."

"You should try," she muttered.

"Yeah, but you've seen what I'm like, Raine." Kellan knew there was more than a little of the wolf in his smile as he drawled, "Believe it or not, pissing people off is usually what I do best."

CHAPTER FIVE

CHLOE HADN'T BEEN LYING when she'd told Kellan she was scared, because she was. It was an *out of her freaking skull, breaking out in a cold sweat* kind of terrified…and it was the only justification she had for what she'd done.

Yeah, she'd been desperate. But she still felt like a user, because she knew that when he'd finally caved there at the end, it hadn't been real.

There's just no way he was touching me like that without…help.

The truth was that he'd probably only reacted the way that he had—the desperate, aggressive touching and kissing and make-you-melty sex talk—because of the curse. Because of the way she was jacking up his primal hungers. But what choice did she have? She hated to do it to him, but if he didn't help her, she was becoming truly frightened of what the Merrick might push her to do in its desperation. If she wasn't careful, she feared she might find herself begging for what she needed from whomever might give it to her.

Westmore.

A Casus.

Bile rose in her throat at the nauseating thought, and she drew in a deep breath through her nose as she pulled on her panties, wishing she had more clothes to cover herself with. Restless and worried, she moved to her feet and started pacing from one side of her cell to the other. She could hear several sets of footsteps on the stairs now, and knew there was a group headed down to the cellblock, just as Kellan had feared. Their captors had finally given up trying to "feed" her, and Kellan had already been interrogated at length. Which meant they were most likely coming for Raine. Chloe's heart pounded in fear for the psychic, her palms cold with sweat.

When the firelight caught the gleam of Spark's dark red hair, Chloe felt both a burst of hope—since Spark had never been present during the times Raine had been abused—and a surge of anger, knowing the woman would probably make another move on Kellan. She couldn't stop her lip from curling as she moved closer to the bars, where she could see what was happening, the Merrick in her wanting nothing more than to get its hands on the redheaded she-bitch and teach her a lesson. Having never been one to pick a fight before, Chloe was more than a little surprised by the vehemence of her reaction—but then she'd never known people as vile as her captors.

The assassin's high-heeled boots clicked gratingly against the flagstones as she headed toward the cellblock, a sly smile curving her rouged lips when she cut her green gaze toward Kellan.

At first glance, it was easy to see why so many men had fallen victim to her charms. But if you stared at her closely enough, you could see the cold, calculating killer hidden behind that fiery facade. Though jealousy had gotten the better of Chloe when she'd bought into the woman's earlier attempt to make them think she and

Kellan had been intimate in the past, she believed his denial. Yeah, she knew Kellan's past had been indiscriminate, but she couldn't help but feel that he would have steered clear of Spark.

As the assassin sauntered across the room toward the cells, a group of Casus soldiers fell in behind her, their eerie, ice-blue eyes giving away their species, though they were still in human form. The one named Seton wasn't with them, and Chloe breathed a little sigh of relief. As far as she knew, every time Raine had been sexually assaulted, Seton had been the one running things. He'd also been the one who'd inflicted the most damage.

With her hips swaying in a skintight pair of jeans, breasts showcased in a low-cut black sweater, Spark paused in front of Kellan's cell. "Hey there, pup."

Kellan's deep voice oozed derision as he drawled, "Back atcha, bitch."

"Tell me something, Watchman. When Lycans have babies, do they look human? Or do they come out like cute little puppies? A vile thought. And yet—" a slow grin kicked up the corner of her mouth "—when a guy's hung like you, I'd be lying if I said I wasn't tempted."

"Give it a rest," he muttered, sounding tired. "I told you I'm not interested."

Challenge flickered in the glittering depths of her eyes. "I could *make* you interested, wolf. Trust me. But this isn't a social visit. I'm here for the psychic." Looking toward Raine, she said, "Westmore's done playing your waiting game. He thinks it's time to see if we can get some more out of you."

In a strained voice, Raine said, "I can't tell him what I don't know."

"That's true," Spark murmured. "Unfortunately, we don't trust you. Which is why you're going to be coming with us for a while."

"Don't even think about it," Kellan snarled.

Spark sent him an exaggerated pout. "Sorry, pretty puppy, but you don't give the orders around here."

Chloe could hear him taking a deep breath, no doubt trying to figure out the best way to get through to the assassin, and then he carefully said, "I can't figure you out, Spark. How can you stomach what these assholes do to women? What they've done to Raine? Aren't you meant to be some kind of raging feminist?"

"I take no pleasure in what they do," she replied, her lowered lashes shielding the look in her eyes. "However, there are times when it's necessary to put aside our personal beliefs."

"And you see Raine's rape and torture as necessary?" he muttered. "Huh, you are one sick bitch."

Hatred flared in the human's eyes, a cruel smirk twisting her mouth, while the crackling fire glinted off the flame-red strands of her hair. "Just for that, I think I'll make you watch. Let's see how cocky you are when she's crying for help, Lycan, and there's nothing you can do about it."

One of the Casus reached for a circle of keys hanging on the wall, and Kellan rattled the bars of his cell so hard that the entire cellblock vibrated with his rage. "Leave her the fuck alone!"

"Kellan, don't. I know you're trying to help, but please don't do this," Raine begged, her voice thick with tears. "It's not worth it."

"Like hell it's not," he snarled. "You want to torture someone, Spark, then try me on for size."

The assassin slid him a condescending smile, her bright eyes filled with laughter. "You don't have anything we want."

"Wanna bet?"

The entire group stared at him with snide expressions, as if wondering what he could possibly have to offer.

"Raine might think you're all scum, but she trusts me. Which is why she's already talked to me about everything that she's seen," he told them. "I know—"

"Kellan, stop it!" Raine cried, cutting him off.

Ignoring the interruption, his voice dropped as he said, "I know where Gregory is. And I know where the next Marker's buried."

Ohmygod, Chloe thought. *Is he lying?*

She hadn't actually heard Raine tell Kellan where his friends would be searching for the next Dark Marker, but she knew the answer was within the psychic's power. Using her "sight," Raine had been spying on Saige Buchanan, a female Merrick who was engaged to one of the Watchmen in Kellan's unit, a raptor-shifter named Michael Quinn. An experienced anthropologist, Saige had made a stunning discovery the year before when she'd uncovered a mysterious set of encrypted maps that led to the hidden locations of the Dark Markers. Using an unusual power that enabled physical objects to "communicate" with her, Saige was the only one who'd been able to decipher the maps' complicated codes.

After having been subjected to blackmail and abuse, Raine had already told Westmore what Saige had learned from the last two maps, and the Casus had managed to take possession of the ancient crosses before Kellan's friends could retrieve them. If she'd deciphered another map, and Raine told them where the next Marker could be found, the consequences could prove devastating for the Watchmen.

As Spark moved closer to Kellan's cell, Chloe locked her jaw, fighting the urge to tell the redhead to stay away from him. "You sure you want to do this?" the human asked him in a husky drawl, her gaze a mixture of contemplation, lust and surprise. "Because if you're lying to me, you're going to be sorry."

"I'm not lying. I'll tell you everything, but you leave her the hell alone."

Spark's eyes narrowed with suspicion. "Why do you even care what happens to her?"

"Because I came to this place to find the Markers," he growled. "Not to stand around and watch innocent women be abused."

Spark appeared to be considering his offer, and Chloe's fear took on a new edge as she wondered what the hell he was planning.

"She's already near the breaking point," Kellan added. "Think about it, Spark. Westmore might have sent you down here to do his dirty work, but who do you think he's going to blame if things go wrong and she cracks? Once a psychic as powerful as Raine goes bat-shit, there's no going back."

The human's nostrils flared as she pulled in a deep breath, and then she jerked her chin toward the brawny Casus on her left. "Open his cell. We'll find out one way or another if he's telling us the truth."

"Let's take this upstairs," Kellan grunted, as one of the Casus flipped the switch on the counterweight for his door, while another inserted the key into the lock. After the door had been opened, the other two bastards each clamped a beefy fist on his arms and pulled him out of his cell.

"Bring that chair by the hearth into the middle of the room," she told the Casus who had flipped the switch, before looking back at Kellan. "I'm afraid we'll be staying down here," she drawled. "It sounds like you and I are going to have a little fun, and I happen to like an audience while I work."

He didn't even try to hide his derision as he said, "I knew you were twisted."

The assassin smirked. "Should I let the Casus have a go at you?" she purred, stepping closer and cupping the side of his cheek with her palm, a bulky silver ring encircling one of her fingers. "I mean, really have a go? You're not as pretty as the psychic, but they'll do whatever I tell them."

Kellan jerked his face away from her touch and looked around. "Where are all your clever little Collective soldiers?" he asked, while they pushed him into the chair, then used a set of handcuffs to secure his muscular arms behind his back. "They get tired of taking your shit?"

Shrugging, she said, "Westmore prefers the Casus."

Kellan snickered under his breath. "In his bed? Hell, no wonder he's so eager to break them out of Meridian. Sounds like he's planning the mother of all org—"

Without warning, a meaty fist slammed into the center of Kellan's face, crimson blood spraying as his nose cracked under the bruising force of the blow. Chloe gasped in reaction, but before she could shout at the Casus to leave him alone, Kellan cut her a quick, warning glare. It was the first time he'd glanced in her direction since they'd pulled him out of his cell, and the look in his blue-green eyes made her breath catch as understanding dawned. He was pissing them off on purpose, thinking that if he could keep their anger focused on him, they wouldn't turn to Raine.

"Ya know," Spark said with a low laugh, "that smart-ass mouth of yours is going to get you into trouble one day, puppy."

Kellan worked his jaw. "Feels like it already has," he muttered, his tone dry.

Stepping behind him, she ran her fingertips across the gleaming width of his shoulders. "If you'd just be a good little wolf," she drawled, "this could all be so much easier."

A wry smile kicked up the corner of his mouth. "Yeah, and I'm really concerned about making your life easy."

The look on Spark's face turned icy as she stepped to his side, her tone even icier. "The information about the Marker, Lycan, before I make them fuck it out of her."

Turning his head, Kellan stared her straight in the eye as he said, "You know what they do to women like you in hell, Spark? They string 'em up and peel the skin from their bodies, while letting the demons have their way with them. I guess they figure if torture is what got gals like you off in this life, then it'll serve them well for eternity."

Her mouth compressed to a hard, tight line. "The psychic would be fine, if she'd just learn to cooperate," she told him, walking around to the front of the chair, her body angled so that Chloe could just make out her profile.

"Yeah, let's blame her for not being a cheap sell-out like you." Kellan used his shoulder to wipe away the blood trickling over his chin. "Tell me, you letting Westmore fuck you, too?"

Before the last word had passed his lips, the assassin's hand was cracking across his face, jerking it hard to the side. When he tossed back his hair and glared at the bitch, Chloe could see that the corner of his lip had split open, accounting for the fresh wash of blood covering his mouth and chin. "Is that the best you've got?" he snorted, flashing her a toothy smile. "You hit like a girl."

Stepping back, Spark looked around at the waiting Casus and snapped, "I think it's time the wolf learned some manners."

The Casus smiled with anticipation, two of them releasing their claws, and Chloe tried to cry out for them to stop, but her throat was too tight to make any sound. Tears of rage burned her eyes as she watched claws rip across Kellan's chest, his blood spraying in a wide arc. The sound of crunching bone followed, and she could see that his nose had been broken in a second place.

"Leave him alone!" she finally managed to scream.

"What's this? A little champion?" With a snide smirk, the redhead slid a laughing look from her to Kellan. "I think the witch is smitten."

"Don't touch him!" Chloe hissed, baring the Merrick's small, but deadly fangs.

"Oh, sweetheart," Spark drawled, walking closer to her cell. "Do you honestly think you could be enough for him? He'd probably fall asleep in the middle of it."

Curling her hands around the iron bars locking her in, Chloe smiled and said, "I dare you to come closer."

The assassin actually laughed. "And what are you going to do? Even if I let you out, I don't think you could manage much damage with those little kitten teeth of yours."

"Then get your ass over here. Or are you too scared?"

"Chloe!" Kellan's graveled voice rang out like the crack of a whip. "Shut up and leave it alone!"

Turning her back to Chloe, Spark spun toward the place where Kellan's battered body now sprawled across the floor, the chair he'd been sitting on kicked to one of the far corners. "Enough of the bullshit," she said brusquely, "I believe you had something you wanted to tell me."

Chloe watched as Kellan blinked against the blood and sweat dripping into his eyes, the look on his battered face as he stared up at Spark one of tangible revulsion.

"Now, or the deal's off," she snapped, flicking a quick look toward Raine.

"Fine," he growled, looking as furious as he sounded, the muscles in his shackled arms bulging beneath the gleaming surface of his skin. "It's in Canada. Buried up in the Canadian Rockies. The town's name is Houghton, and the Marker's a few miles north of the town center."

Spark indicated for two of the Casus to pick him up, their claws digging into his muscular arms as they secured him between them. Moving closer, Spark took his blood-covered chin in her hand, her voice deceptively mild as she said, "If you're lying, Kellan, I'll have the Casus cut you into cubes of meat, slow and precise like."

"I'm telling the truth, but it doesn't matter," he rasped. "There's a Watchman unit not far from where the cross is buried, and they'll have already been mobilized. There's no way you can get there fast enough."

"Then we'll steal it away from them."

A deep, guttural laugh shook his bloodied chest and shoulders, the corner of his mouth curling with arrogant humor. "You can try."

"And Gregory?" she murmured.

"What about him?"

The human struck him across the face again with surprising strength and speed, making Chloe wince. But Kellan just looked pissed.

Spitting a mouthful of blood onto the floor near her boots, he growled, "Gregory is going to be here soon."

"How soon?" she pressed.

Curling his lip, he stared her down, saying, "You've gotta explain this one to me, Spark. Because I just don't get it. I mean, I know ol' Gregory is a twisted dickhead and all, but Westmore wasn't afraid of him before. If that'd been the case, he wouldn't have dared to take Chloe. So what's got him so scared of Gregory now?"

Spark snorted. "Like I'm telling you."

"Ah." Kellan gave her a cocky smile. "You don't know, huh? Westmore must not trust you as much as you think he does."

"Shut up."

Pushing her, he said, "You're just his lackey, huh?"

"He tells me everything!" she threw back at him, rising to the bait.

Sounding as if he was starting to enjoy himself, Kellan's drawl became more pronounced. "Obviously not."

Spark practically vibrated with rage as she snarled, "DeKreznick's human host was mortally wounded during that little battle you guys had back in the fall, which meant that Gregory's shade should have returned to Meridian. But he didn't."

"Ah. So Westmore's worried about how he was able to survive. Smart guy. He *should* be worried." Lowering his voice, he added, "You know, maybe you should be worried, too, Spark. I have a feeling ol' Gregory's gonna take a liking to you. You're just his kind of tramp."

Taking two steps back, her voice trembled with fury as she looked at the Casus and gave a single command. "Make him hurt."

The monsters descended on him this time with a violent rain of punches and kicks, his body falling back to the floor as they attacked him. Raine was screaming for them to stop, for Kellan to stop being stupid and fight back, but Chloe didn't make a sound, her nostrils flaring as she plastered herself against the iron bars of her cell and waited for Spark to come closer.

She hadn't gotten the blood she needed from him. And she hadn't come. But at the moment, she and the Merrick were too pissed to care.

As her fury rose, the Merrick rose with it, her senses sharpening until she could smell the blood and sweat that glistened on Kellan's skin, the flickering, maniacal flames of the fire taking on colors and hues that no human eye could ever discern. She could hear the furious pounding of every heart in the room, as well as the muffled groans Kellan was trying to hold back.

Shocking in its intensity, the Merrick's rage was unlike anything Chloe had ever known. More visceral than any anger. More demanding than any hunger. It thrived on the emotions that she'd always tried so hard to keep locked under tight control, but they were seething within her now. She couldn't tap into its full strength without a proper feeding, but she could feel that ancient creature rising up within her, its power pulsing through her body, potent and hot.

When one of the Casus delivered a brutal kick to Kellan's ribs that sent him skidding across the floor, Chloe finally got what she'd been waiting for. Spark took a sudden step back to avoid getting hit, and the Merrick silently howled with satisfaction. Reaching through the bars of the cell, Chloe quickly fisted her hand in the assassin's long red hair and gave it a vicious yank, jerking the human clear off her feet, the back of her head slamming painfully into the iron bars.

Outraged, Spark fought to twist free as she screamed, "Let go of me, you little bitch!"

With her mouth close to the woman's ear, Chloe said, "Who are you calling *kitten* now, skank?"

"Open this cell!" Spark shouted at the Casus, who had stopped beating on Kellan and were now watching the two of them with almost comical looks of shock.

"And what?" Chloe asked with a low laugh, feeling fairly shocked herself. "Westmore will have your ass if anyone touches me."

"She's right," one of the Casus grunted, his blond hair falling over his brow as he nodded.

"See?" Chloe rasped. "Now tell them to undo Kellan's cuffs and put him back in his cell, and then I'll let you go. And before you even think of arguing, you should know that if he gets another scratch on him, I'm going to lie and tell Westmore that you tried to make the Casus rape me. And you can sure as hell bet that I'll make it convincing."

"Screw you!" the human spat.

In response, Chloe yanked on the human's hair so hard, she was surprised it didn't come out.

"All right! Fine," Spark snarled, her voice cracking. "Do it! Do what she says."

Chloe waited until a nearly unconscious Kellan had been uncuffed, then tossed back into his cell. When the Casus had gathered at the bottom of the stairs, waiting, she released her hold on Spark's hair, shoving her away. "Now get the hell out of here."

Cutting her a deadly look over her shoulder, the assassin said, "You're going to pay for that, Merrick."

Though Chloe was sick with fear inside, the Merrick simply smiled and blew the woman a kiss, relishing the look of fury on the bitch's face as she turned and stormed up the winding staircase.

CHAPTER SIX

Monday morning

GUILT SUCKED.

After seeing what Kellan had done to protect Raine from Spark and the Casus, the foul emotion was eating at Chloe's insides like an ulcer. She knew he could have gone wolf and killed every one of those bastards if he'd been alone. As a Lycan, he was deadly enough to do just that. She could only assume that he hadn't because once an alarm had been raised, he wouldn't have been able to get her and Raine out of the compound safely.

But while his beating accounted for a portion of her guilt, there was still the matter of the curse...and the Merrick's hunger.

Chloe had managed a few hours of sleep through the night, but nothing more. Too restless, she'd mostly tossed and turned, torn between wanting to call out to Kellan to make sure he was okay...and the gnawing impulse to break into his cell and take what she needed from him, whether it was wrong or not.

You know it's wrong. No matter how desperate you get, you know using him makes you as twisted as that redheaded bitch.

Shuddering, Chloe pushed her hands through her hair and kept pacing...and pacing, until the soles of her feet were sore. Her confrontation with Spark had left her weak with exhaustion, the Merrick's brief flare of power quickly draining her, making her even weaker. She was operating on nothing more than nervous energy at the moment, her thoughts and emotions as chaotic as the swirling colors in a kaleidoscope.

I can't believe I did that. I almost guilt-tripped the poor guy into having sex with me.

God, what was wrong with her? It was so hard to think clearly when her fears and needs were consuming her—but she should have known better, damn it. Once Spark and the Casus had returned upstairs and her fury had calmed, Chloe had started to see the situation with a bit more clarity, and what she discovered wasn't pretty. When she'd begged Kellan to touch her, she'd taken advantage of a guy who was under the influence of a painful poison, and whose ass was in this horrid place because of *her*. And she'd freaking used him, as if her stupid needs were the most important thing. As if the Merrick's hunger was the only thing that mattered.

There wasn't any chance that Kellan Scott would have been that hot for her under normal circumstances. She knew damn well that she was *nothing* like the women he normally messed around with. And Chloe had a bad feeling that the situation was even worse than she'd feared, because the things he'd said about her had been too personal. She hadn't fully realized it at the time, but seeing him nearly beaten to a pulp had sobered her up real fast. Though he'd told her time and again that he wouldn't touch her, he'd suddenly been all over her, as if she was the most desirable woman in the world, his words and actions flavored with *possession*, rather than mere physical desire.

What if something had happened with the awakening of the Merrick? What if the primal blood inside her was somehow using the curse to project its own hunger onto those around her? As well as cranking up his sexual appetite, was the Merrick somehow *forcing* him to want her as desperately as she wanted him?

Throughout evolution, it'd been proven that species could adapt and change in order to safeguard their existence. Could the Merrick, in its thirst for survival, have somehow keyed into the basic elements of the Mallory curse and twisted them to its purpose? Was that even possible?

Of course it's possible. Anything is possible!

Ever since Chloe had attacked Spark, she could feel the Merrick inside her, lingering, steadily growing in influence. If the Lycan came near her now, she didn't trust herself to maintain control. Even as weak as she was, she'd do something crazy and unforgivable, like attack him. And with that embarrassing image burning in her mind, the absurdity of the whole screwed-up mess crashed down on her, and she pressed her hand against her mouth, choking back a sound that was caught somewhere between a sob and a laugh.

Damn it, this isn't fair! And fate is a cruel, snide bitch I would love to get my hands on!

From the first moment Chloe had been old enough to understand how the curse would impact her life, she'd never been able to stand it when other women bitched and moaned about some big, gorgeous hunk offering them a hot fling...without the promise of a future. It'd always made her roll her eyes and want to shake some sense into the idiots, since they didn't know how lucky they were to even have that choice. To have the freedom to say yes if they wanted to, without worrying that the man was only interested in them because of some stupid curse or that they'd be looked down on as a "user" and a "manipulator." God, she could still remember how cruel a local clan of Saville witches had been to Monica after she'd gotten pregnant with Jamie and her boyfriend had left her, telling Monica that she'd gotten *exactly* what she deserved…and that a Mallory like her was meant to be alone.

If the circumstances had been different, and Chloe had been a normal woman, without this bloody curse hanging over her head, and Kellan Scott had stopped her on the street or in a coffee bar and asked her out, she wouldn't have worried about being too short or too flat-chested or too *anything*. Wouldn't have moaned about the fact that she wasn't the kind of woman who normally caught his eye or who could hold him forever. She would have agreed before the words had even left his mouth and thanked God for the opportunity. Even without expecting it to go anywhere—which she wouldn't have. She would have known he was just using her. But she would have happily been used. She would have enjoyed every moment with him, knowing he'd be worth any regrets that came later.

It was the curse that screwed the fantasy to hell and back—because no matter how badly she wanted him, Chloe couldn't stand the thought of being the user, herself. Not when there was a chance that she was not only jacking up his desire, but creating it in the first place. She was screwing with his head, and it was wrong.

So no matter how desperate I get, I am going to stay in control. And keep my hands to myself!

A sound to her left suddenly made her jump, and she

turned to find him standing inside the open door of her cell, watching her with that overtly sexual, deceptively lazy gaze, like a big hungry animal getting ready to pounce.

She'd been so consumed by her thoughts, she hadn't even noticed him opening the door and coming into her cell. But he was there now, and as she watched, he closed the door behind him, then walked across the floor and turned, leaning his back against the dividing wall, his powerful arms crossed over that broad, muscular chest. Her cheeks warmed, her mind instantly flooding with the memory of the things she'd said to him before Spark had interrupted them…not to mention the things she'd done, but she pushed those thoughts away, focusing on Kellan. He was already healing, thanks to his Lycan genes, but he still looked like he'd been beaten six ways to Sunday. His right cheekbone was scraped raw, the corner of his mouth still a little swollen, his entire torso lined with fading claw marks and mottled bruises.

"You feeling okay?" she asked, nervously running her palms against her shirt-covered hips, wishing there was something she could do to help him.

"Been better." His voice was a little scratchier than usual, a kinda wry half smile shaping his sensual mouth. "What about you?"

"What about me?"

Something in his expression made it impossible for her to look away. "I was pretty out of it at the time," he told her, "but I have a hazy recollection of you giving Spark a smack down."

She licked her lips, her cheeks burning with heat. "I, um, just lost my temper a bit," she murmured, then immediately changed the subject, asking, "Was that a lie about the next Marker being buried in Canada?"

"Yeah. Raine told me that with all the commotion caused by my capture, Saige's work on the maps has slowed down a bit. She still doesn't know where the next Marker's hidden."

"So you lied to them, and picked such a remote location thinking they won't be able to get there and finish their search before Friday, right?"

Another sexy, kinda crooked smile touched his mouth. "That's right. And I hope they freeze their asses off in all that Canadian snow."

Chloe tried to control the tremor in her voice as she said, "You were purposely goading them."

He winced, scraping a palm against the auburn bristles covering his jaw. "I'm sorry you had to see that, but I knew they needed someone to pound on or they wouldn't have been satisfied."

"Is that why you wanted her to take you upstairs? Because you *planned* on getting beaten up?"

The corner of his mouth twitched, his expression as wry as his tone. "Well, I wasn't looking forward to you seeing me get my ass kicked by a girl. I'm trying to build up a big hero reputation, remember?" She choked back a soft laugh, and he added, "Plus, I was hoping to have another look at things upstairs. Raine has given me a good idea of the layout, but it would help to see things with my own eyes."

"I've been upstairs more than Raine," she told him, sitting down cross-legged in the middle of her cot, careful to keep her shirttails covering her panties. "I can tell you a little about what's up there."

"I didn't think you would remember any of it."

With a shrug, she admitted, "Just bits and pieces, really. But I'll tell you what I know."

Over the next quarter of an hour, he questioned her about the floor plan, where she'd seen guards posted and what kind of weaponry she'd noticed. Chloe told him everything she could remember, then asked, "Is Raine doing okay?"

A shadow of anger darkened his gaze. "As okay as she can be after what she's been through. The bit of blood I've given her has helped with her physical injuries, but psychologically..." He shook his head, obviously reluctant to voice his fear that Raine might never get over the abuse she'd suffered.

Quietly, she said, "I wish there was something I could have done to help her all those times they hurt her." She tore her gaze away from his mesmerizing eyes, and stared at the spiraling orange glow of the flames in the hearth. "I can't help thinking that if I were smarter, I'd have figured out a way to stop them."

"Eff that. What's happened to Raine is screwed up, but it's not your fault, Chloe. There's nothing you could have done to stop those assholes."

She thought about what he'd said for a few moments, hoping he was right, and then realized that he'd censored his language. "*Eff* that?" she snickered, bringing her gaze back to his. "Since when do big alpha types like you use words like *eff?*"

"Since a precocious little three-year-old joined the Watchmen, repeating everything we say," he rumbled with a throaty laugh, his eyes crinkling sexily at the corners. "And if you think I sound funny censoring myself, then you should see Ade. He's even bigger than I am."

With a bemused smile, she said, "I honestly can't believe that."

"Believe it," he shot back with a grin, scratching lazily at his chest, and she couldn't help but watch the hypnotic movement of his long fingers, remembering what it'd felt like when they'd been touching her. Buried inside her, hard and rough and wicked.

Clearing her throat, Chloe forced her mind off sex and back to something neutral. "So, uh…is it really true that Aiden's talked Olivia into marrying him? Raine told me they were engaged, but I…I don't think I really believed her."

And she'd had good reason. Trust didn't come easily to the Harcourt women, and Olivia had already been burned once by a complete sleaze of a boyfriend. Chloe couldn't imagine her gun-shy stepsister exposing herself to that kind of risk again.

"It's true," he told her, and she was more than a little surprised to find that she'd been wrong. "Aiden bought her a rock for Christmas that just about blinds anyone who gets too close."

"And what about Jamie?"

His expression softened at the mention of her three-year-old niece, his mouth curving with an easy smile. "They're going to raise her as their own. Ade is already slipping into his role as daddy like he was born to it."

"It seems too surreal that you could actually know our little Jamie," she mused in a soft voice.

"Know her? Hell," he drawled, "we're Disney buddies. I've watched *Hercules* with her probably ten times now."

"Are you serious?"

His smile flashed at her disbelieving tone, revealing

a dimple in one of those carved, shadowed cheeks. "You want me to quote it? Sing one of the songs? Because I probably know 'em by heart by now."

She covered her mouth with one hand as she struggled to hold back her laughter. "Oh, God, I know it's wrong to laugh, considering the circumstances we're in, but I can't help it."

"Hey, Jamie's a charmer," he told her, sliding down the wall until he sat on the floor, the soft denim of his jeans hugging the rigid muscles in his thighs. The pose was casual, his arms resting on his bent knees, his hands hanging loose and relaxed, and yet, she could still sense the wild, crackling energy that was so much a part of him thrumming just beneath his surface. "To be honest," he added, "she has all of us wrapped around her little finger. Especially Noah."

"Noah? Raine mentioned him, as well. Isn't he... doesn't he have Casus blood?"

Since the immortal monsters had wasted away into mere "shades" of the powerful beings they'd once been, after so many years trapped within Meridian, the Casus were forced to take human hosts once they'd escaped. Thanks to Raine, Chloe also knew that Noah Winston, a recent addition to Kellan's Watchmen unit, was descended from a human female who had been raped by one of the Casus before their confinement, which meant that his family could be used as hosts by the escaping Casus shades.

"That's right," he said in response to her question about Noah's bloodline. "It makes him motivated as hell to end this thing. He's determined to keep his family from becoming what he calls 'meat suits' for those Casus pricks."

With more than a little doubt in her tone, she asked, "And you trust him?"

He didn't even hesitate. "With my life."

"And he's good to Jamie?"

"Noah spoils her almost as much as I do."

The slow, sexy smile that accompanied his words was too gorgeous to resist, so she didn't even try. "Well, if Jamie likes you guys, then I guess you're both okay."

"Like?" he scoffed. "That kid adores us. Me especially. She cries like a banshee every time I leave the house."

"Okay, okay, I'm convinced," she said, holding up her hands. "You and Noah are saints. And Aiden, too, for making my sister happy. He does make her happy, right?"

"If he made her any happier," he drawled, "we'd have to soundproof their whole floor, instead of just their room."

Chloe blushed, but she laughed, too. And it felt... good. "I miss this," she sighed, propping her shoulders against the wall at her back.

"What?"

"Laughing."

Sounding strangely fascinated, he asked, "What else do you miss?"

She thought about it for a moment, staring through the bars of the cell again, then said, "Being warm. At night, this place gets so cold, and the fire doesn't give off enough heat."

"I'd give you my bedding," he rasped, "if I had any."

She swung her gaze back to his, her eyes wide with anger. "They didn't even give you a blanket?"

"Nah, but I stay warm."

Chloe started to argue, then recalled the fever-hot warmth of his body when he'd been plastered against her, and realized that was true. "Yeah, I guess you do."

"So tell me what else you miss." His voice was mellow, his eyes sliding closed as he leaned his head back, the shadowed bruises on his face only intensifying his rugged masculinity, rather than detracting from it. "I like listening to you talk."

"Um, well, I guess I miss caramel macchiatos from my local Starbucks and my iPod and my Wii." Wistfully, she added, "I had almost reached professional status in snowboarding with my friend Cara."

He laughed, the rich, rumbling sound making her toes curl. "Who's Cara?"

"She's a friend from college, and a Boudreaux witch. Her specialty is beauty spells."

He cracked an eye open. "She put any on you?"

"Only a hair removal spell. Thanks to Cara, I no longer have to buy razor blades."

"I wondered how you kept them so smooth," he murmured, running his warm gaze over her crossed legs.

"I would have asked her for a boob job," she added lightly, "but she could never manage anything smaller than double Ds, and I was worried about retaining my ability to stand upright if I went for it."

He snorted, then surprised her by saying, "I'm glad you didn't change your body. It's perfect the way it is."

"Uh, thanks," she whispered, her face burning.

"You're welcome," he offered in a soft voice, his mouth twitching with another one of those boyish, lopsided grins, as if he knew just how easily his words affected her.

"So, um, what do *you* miss?" she asked, toying with one of the buttons on her shirt.

Rolling a shoulder, he said, "Not much. I haven't been here near as long as you have."

"No, but with a war going on, I doubt your life has been the same as it was before. So tell me what you miss from back then."

"I guess I miss playing football with my friends in Colorado," he told her, after thinking about it for a few moments. "I miss Ade's pecan waffles and the sound of him playing piano. Hell, I even miss Kierland's lecturing and the Buchanans, and getting my ass kicked whenever I play video games with Quinn."

"You're very close to the guys in your unit, aren't you? I mean, they're like your family."

Dryly, he said, "We sure as hell fight like one."

"And you all live together, right?"

With a nod, he lifted his head, saying, "We have a compound in Colorado called Ravenswing, but for safety, we had to make a quick move to England. Now we're staying at an estate in the Lake District called Harrow House, where Kierland and I were raised by our grandfather."

"What's it like?"

He turned one of his hands over, studying the lines on his palm, lost in thought. Eventually, he blew out a rough breath and said, "It's beautiful, even though it was abandoned for a long time, since neither of us wanted anything to do with it after the old guy passed away. But we're getting the place back in shape. There's a helluva lot of space, if you need it. But, you never feel alone, and no matter how grim things get there's always a lot of laughter filling its rooms."

"I'm glad Jamie and Olivia have that. Since our parents died, it's been hard. And now with Monica gone, they must have felt so alone."

"Well, they're sure as hell not alone any longer. And the same goes for you, Chloe. Once we're out of here, you'll have a home there, same as they do."

With the back of her wrist, she swiped at the tears in her eyes, and decided it was time to get him out of there, before her emotions…or her hunger…got the better of her. "Don't take this the wrong way, Mr. Scott, but you look like you could use some more sleep."

"Mr. Scott?" His forehead creased with a scowl. "Christ, don't call me that. It's not only ridiculous, considering the circumstances, but it makes me feel old."

She shrugged her shoulders. "You're older than I am."

"Barely, Chloe." His dry tone made it clear he thought she was being absurd.

"Really? Wow, I would have put you into your mid-thirties, at least."

He kept those gorgeous blue-green eyes locked on her face, then slowly arched one arrogant brow. "You're messing with me, right?"

Fighting back a grin, she guessed, "Thirty-four? Thirty-five?"

"I'm twenty-six," he forced through his clenched teeth, then paused for a moment, and muttered, "What's the date today?"

Thinking about it for a minute, she said, "I think it's the first tomorrow."

"Shit. That's my birthday. Which makes me twenty-seven. But that's still not old."

A second little shrug of her shoulders, just to mess

with him. "And I'm twenty-four. But in terms of experience, you're aeons older than I am."

His eyes narrowed to hot, glittering slits. "What does *that* mean?"

"What do you think it means?"

Coughing, he kind of choked out, "You're talking about sex, right?" Before she could respond, he shook his head and added, "But I'm not buying it. No way in hell are you still a virgin. Not someone who...*looks* like you."

"Thanks...I think," she murmured, wondering if he'd been thinking *acts* instead of *looks*. Not that she could blame him, since she *had* been all over the guy. "And no, I'm not a virgin. I have experience."

He muttered a heartfelt, "Thank God," scrubbed his hands down his face, then asked a deeply personal question. "How much experience are we talking about?"

Her eyes went wide. "What makes you think I'm going to tell you *that?*"

Without any trace of their previous lighthearted banter, he said, "Because I need to know what I'm dealing with."

"Me, Kellan. You're dealing with *me*."

He just stared, waiting, and she growled with frustration. "God, you are so stubborn. There's been one, okay!"

"Just *one?*" He sounded as if she'd just admitted an unforgivable sin. "Did you date him for a long time, then?"

"I didn't date him at all," she muttered, crossing her arms over her chest. "He wasn't a boyfriend. He was more of a...well, he's my best friend. *Was* my best friend."

"Was? What happened?"

With a roll of her shoulder and a sigh, she said, "Long, boring story."

"I'll be the judge of that." He leaned his head back again, stretching his long legs out before him, and made a *give me more* motion with his hand. "So start spilling."

Chloe thought about telling him to bug off—to eff off!—but knew he was too stubborn to listen. Just wanting to get it over with, she stared down at her lap, and grudgingly gave him the condensed version. "His name is Pete and I've known him since middle school. I had hoped that our friendship might act as a buffer to the curse, which had never really been an issue for us, so we went to bed together. I was eighteen and tired of being a virgin, and being part Fae, Pete liked sex enough to indulge me," she explained, pulling her blanket into her lap, her fingers plucking at its frayed edges. "But the friendship didn't buffer anything, and after a few times, he started acting…differently."

She watched him from the corner of her eye as he frowned. "So you rocked his world in the sack, and it changed the way he felt about you?"

"I hardly rocked his world," she replied, rolling her eyes. "I wasn't experienced, which means I was probably pretty sucky at the whole thing." Agitation roughened her voice. "But whatever enjoyment Pete *did* get out of the act, the curse…well, it blew it out of proportion."

"Ahh. So what did he do?"

Keeping her voice as matter-of-fact as possible, she said, "Since his mother was Fae, she'd heard about the curse. When his parents realized how obsessive he was becoming, they convinced him to leave town. Pete moved to Seattle, met a woman and they got married. They eventually moved back home to Kentucky, but his wife didn't really want him to hang around me anymore. Not that I blame her. I haven't seen him in almost three years now."

"That sucks." He sounded pissed, as if he could tell how much the whole situation had hurt her.

"Yeah, it did," she sighed. "But I've gotten over it."

"His loss," he muttered.

Chloe didn't know what to say to that, so she stayed silent. The whole screwup with Pete was just another pathetic episode in her long list of socially awkward moments, and it would hardly be the last.

"So that's it?" he asked. "Just the one? You never gave another guy a chance?"

Dryly, she said, "After what happened with Pete, I wasn't too keen to ever try it again."

"That's a little extreme, isn't it?"

"Hardly," she told him, pulling her knees to her chest and wrapping her arms around them. "I grew up watching Monica go through one screwed-up relationship after another, and I promised myself I wouldn't do the same thing. I'd thought things might be different with Pete, because we'd been friends for so long, but I was wrong. And if things got so weird with someone I knew so well, imagine how awkward it would have been with someone I didn't know. Plus, we have a really crappy reputation among the other witch clans. They call us the Mallory Manipulators. And though I don't really give a damn what other people say, I've always sworn that I wouldn't ever do anything to prove those judgmental bitches right."

There was, however, one good thing that had come

from the experience. Although she and Pete hadn't exactly set the sheets on fire, Chloe had experienced enough pleasure to believe that the kind of passion written about in romance books could actually exist. To know that it wasn't all just words on a page. All a bunch of overrated hype. With the right partner, she had no doubt that sex could be explosive. Even life changing.

Just imagine what sex with a guy like Kellan would be like.

She scowled, knowing damn well that it was the Merrick who'd whispered that dangerous thought in her mind.

"Stop it," she whispered back too tense to find humor in the fact that she was talking to herself.

But the damage had already been done, because now she couldn't *stop* thinking about it.

Without a doubt, Chloe knew that Kellan Scott was a male who'd been made for pleasure. It practically oozed from his freaking pores, his scent like a mating pheromone, designed to make women plead for his touch. That was how she felt, right at that moment, something primal and wild in her fighting against the woman who was always so cautious and careful.

"It's a strange curse." His voice was low. "Can you tell me how it happened?"

"I can tell you what I've heard, though with the way stories get embellished over time, there's no telling how much truth is in it. But according to legend, there was a Mallory witch who fell in love with a married man. He didn't love his wife, who was a powerful sorceress, and had actually been tricked into marrying her. When the sorceress learned of his undying love for the witch, she cursed the young woman's bloodline, the punishment designed to make it difficult for others to ever be near her."

He cursed under his breath. "So it's meant to make you live your life alone?"

Chloe nodded, studying the coarse weave of the blanket as it stretched over her knees. "And it's damn effective. We have serious trust issues, and we're too exhausting for most men. That's why Jamie's father bailed on Monica. He couldn't handle the way everything was always so over-the-top when he was around her."

"And there's nothing that can…stop it?"

Breath-filled silence, the only sound that of the crackling fire, and then she slowly replied, "It's said that the curse will eventually come to a natural end, but my ancestors have been waiting hundreds of years, and there's been no sign of the curse weakening. But some say…"

"What?"

Her voice was soft. "If you believe in fairy tales, some say that true love can bring peace to a Mallory's life. That it's too powerful for the curse to tamper with."

"Do you believe that?"

Is it my imagination, she thought, *or has his voice grown huskier?*

"Chloe?"

Clearing her throat, she lifted her gaze from the provocative shape of his mouth, staring into those hypnotic eyes, and somehow managed to say, "I probably wouldn't, if I hadn't seen how things were between my mother and Olivia's father. He didn't worship her because of the curse, but he…he loved her. Madly. And it was a healthy love, with ups and downs and the usual disagreements. One that was strong enough to beat that bitch-sorceress's curse into submission."

Gently, he said, "Sounds like they were pretty amazing."

"They were. It nearly killed us when we lost them." Though she'd tried to keep her voice steady, it cracked there at the end.

"I think Olivia mentioned that her father had a heart attack?"

Chloe nodded again. "And my mother died the week after. Monica believed it was the pain of losing him." She paused for a moment, breathing in his tantalizing scent, then slowly added, "I guess I kind of believe that, too."

Her admission stunned her, and she slipped off the cot, walking to the far front corner of the cell. She rested her forehead against the cold iron bars, shocked by everything she'd just revealed. At the honesty she kept giving this guy, when she was usually so guarded and private.

Then again, maybe honesty was exactly what they needed here. God only knew she couldn't trust herself to stay away from him. She had to take action. Implement defensive measures.

"Speaking of the curse," she murmured, keeping her back to him. "I need to tell you that I...I think that's what's happening between us. You need to stay away from me, because you're being affected by it."

Another heavy, breath-filled silence, and then, "You're joking, right?"

Looking over her shoulder, she said, "I'm dead serious, Kellan."

He made a kind of cocky snorting sound. "Bullshit."

Chloe frowned. "You can't just say *bullshit*," she

argued. "I'm right. I've been taking advantage of you!"

"Like hell you have."

"Oh, God." She drew her brows together. "You're not one of those knuckle-dragger types who always thinks he knows more than everyone else, are you?"

He looked like he was trying hard to hold back his laughter. "Knuckle-dragger types?"

Ignoring him, she turned and propped her back against the bars, arms crossed tightly over her chest as she said, "Just hear me out, Kellan. You need sex, and the curse is going to magnify that. And because of the Merrick, I need it, too. What I've said makes sense. There's some kind of wicked mojo going on between us, playing with our bodies, and none of it's real. It's just an illusion."

"And what about good ol' fashioned lust?"

"Between a guy like you and someone like me? Come on," she snapped. "Open your freaking eyes."

The corner of his mouth curled with another of those slow, lazy smiles. "You're cute as hell when you get riled up. You know that?"

A sharp sound of frustration shook her throat. "That's the thing. I'm *cute*. And you're…well, you've seen a mirror. You know what you are. It doesn't add up, no matter how badly I might wish it did. Which means you need to stay away from me and stop coming over here."

"And you just need to take a deep breath and calm down," he countered in an easy drawl.

Her eyes narrowed. "What makes you think I'm not calm?"

"Would you listen to yourself?" He angled his head to

the side, the firelight catching at the crimson highlights in the thick, wine-dark strands of his hair as he stared at her through his lashes. "One second you're begging me to feed you. The next, you're screaming at me—"

"I have *not* screamed," she protested. "Not even once."

He continued as if she hadn't just interrupted him. "—and bitching at me to leave you alone, because you don't wanna take advantage of me." In a deep, whiskey-rough rumble, he added, "You're working yourself into knots, Chloe, and there's no need."

Pulling her lower lip through her teeth, she lowered her gaze. "Between the Merrick and the curse, it's too much. I just…I need you to stay away from me," she said thickly, "because I don't like feeling this way or being this out of control."

"Then I'll go," he said in a low voice.

She blew out a rough breath of air. "Thank you."

"But before I do, there's something I need to tell you."

"What is it?" she asked, lifting her head just in time to watch him getting to his feet, hard muscles coiling and flexing beneath all that golden skin in a jaw-dropping display of power, the cuts and bruises only adding to his raw masculinity.

Pushing his hands into his pockets, he propped a shoulder against the metal wall, and said, "Your sister and some of the others in our unit are starting to think the curse might finally be coming to an end."

Of all the things he could have said, that was the last one she expected. "What? Why?"

"Because of Jamie."

Shaking her head, she said, "Jamie? I don't understand."

"Did Raine tell you about the attack that was made on our group when we were trying to reach Harrow House?"

"No."

He nodded as if that was the answer he'd expected. "She probably didn't want to worry you."

"Why would it worry me?" Her voice was rising. "What happened?"

"We were outnumbered, and things were looking pretty grim. Then your niece went all *X-Files* and started glowing with this strange light, power arcing from her like a generator. Next thing we knew, she'd turned the bad guys against each other, and we were able to escape."

Shock roughened her voice. "She saved you?"

The corner of his mouth kicked up with a wry grin. "Believe it or not, we all owe our lives to the little runt. She is one serious little badass."

"But…why didn't you tell me before?"

"I didn't want you to worry about her," he said in a low voice, rubbing the back of his neck. "She's been fine since that night."

"And you think this means the curse might be ending?" she asked, her heartbeat roaring in her ears.

"That's what the others have speculated. And then there's your awakening."

"I don't understand," she repeated.

"Chloe, if Westmore took you to get at Gregory, then that means his return started your awakening months ago. I know you're in rough shape, but you're still sane. Still breathing. I don't see how that could be possible, unless your true Mallory powers, the ones the curse would have bound, weren't somehow working to keep you alive. They might not be very strong yet, but they've kept you from fading away."

She didn't say anything at first. Just stared at a distant point on the cold gray floor, thinking over everything that he'd said, her chest rising and falling with the slow, deep cadence of her breathing. When she finally forced her gaze back to his, she asked, "Are you attracted to me, Kellan?"

The heat in his eyes should have melted her on the spot. "I'd think that's fairly obvious, considering how I can't stay away from you."

"Then it's still working. It *has* to be."

He pushed away from the wall, frustration riding him hard. "Christ, Chloe. Why are you being so fucking stubborn about this? Is it so hard for you to believe I could want you for *you* alone, without the influence of that bloody curse screwing with my mind?"

"To be honest, yes. It is," she told him, lifting her chin. "And I don't feel any different. If what you've said is true, I think I would have felt the curse weakening, and I haven't."

The thick, ropy muscles across his shoulders and in his arms bunched with tension. "You're also under a lot of stress," he argued, shoving his hands deeper into his pockets. "And the Merrick's giving you so much shit, I doubt you'd be aware of any changes that could be caused by the curse fading."

Refusing to agree with him, she said, "I still say it's the curse."

"Yeah?" His brows lifted with an arrogant arch. "Well, I still say that you're full of it."

"Weren't you leaving?" she snapped.

"Yeah, I'll go, for now—" he moved toward her "—if you give me a kiss."

"You're mad," she said hoarsely, holding her hands up in front of her, while desire settled like a molten flame in the core of her belly. "And I don't mean angry, Kellan. I'm talking off your rocker. One egg short of a dozen!"

Though the corner of his mouth twitched, he didn't laugh, his voice a dark, sexy rumble as he said, "Just a kiss, Chloe."

"Why?" she whispered, forced to crane her head back as he came even closer, her hands flattening against the hot skin stretched over all those rock-hard, breathtaking abs.

The smoldering heat in his eyes stole her breath. "Because I can't stop thinking about how you felt. How sweet you tasted. Because touching you yesterday felt better than anything has felt in…hell, since as far back as I can remember."

She wouldn't have thought it was possible to feel this miserable and excited all at the same time. "That's what I mean, Kellan. It's the curse. It's drawing you to me. *Making* you do things."

He covered the last few inches that separated them, trapping her against the iron bars of the cell, his hands wrapping around the cold metal on either side of her head, caging her in. "If it was making me do things," he said in a rough voice, staring deep into her eyes, "then we both know that I'd be inside you right now, little witch. Because that's where you want me. And it's where I wanna be. But I'm *forcing* myself to settle for a kiss."

"Do you enjoy torturing me?" Hoarse words, almost too soft to hear.

Lust hardened his features, and she felt the tremor that pulsed through all those deliciously hard, ripped muscles. "Trust me, kitten. I'm hurting a helluva lot worse than you are."

"Spark called me *kitten*."

"I know." A low laugh slid lazily from his lips as he pressed them to the apple of her cheek. "I think it's kinda cute."

Chloe started to argue, but he stopped her with his mouth, the kiss raw and deliciously explicit, his tongue rubbing against hers in a way that made some kind of purring noise crawl up the back of her throat, his answering growl the sexiest thing she'd ever heard. It melted her bones, her brain, pulling rough cries up from the core of her body. He ate at the husky sounds, the heavy ridge of his cock pressed hard against her belly. The iron bars dug into her back as the kiss turned rougher… rawer, biting and wet and utterly devastating. Just when she could tell he was on the verge of completely losing it, he tore his mouth from hers.

"See?" he rasped, working hard to catch his breath as he rested his cheek against the top of her head, his hands still wrapped around the bars so tightly, she was surprised they hadn't snapped. "No harm, no foul."

"Do you know what I've never been able to stand?" she asked unsteadily, shaking with hunger and lust and a mass of confusion. "Men who think they know everything. Who get off on making a woman feel weak."

He snorted as he pulled his head back enough that he could look down into her face. "I don't think there's anything weak about you," he murmured, his thumb rubbing the kiss-swollen corner of her mouth as he cupped the side of her face with his hand. "Hell, you terrify me every time you open your mouth. I never know what's going to come out. Another insult? Another demand to fuck you? To leave you alone? You keep my head spinning, lady."

The words suggested frustration, as well as a wealth of irritation.

But the sin-tipped smile on the Lycan's face as he turned to leave almost looked as if he was actually enjoying the ride.

CHAPTER SEVEN

The Auvergne province, France
Monday, 10:00 p.m.

PARTNERED UP WITH TWO bloodsucking vampires.

Friggin' unbelievable.

Six months ago, if anyone had tried to tell him that this was what his future held, Seth McConnell would have told them they needed to get their heads checked. Because six months ago, if he'd come face-to-face with two male vampires in the middle of the night, he'd have done his best to separate their heads from their shoulders, considering that was the only foolproof way to kill a Deschanel. If you got a blade across a Lycanthrope's gut, that would usually do them in—but vamps could more often than not heal from any knife wound. And while burning a witch usually insured they would no longer be around, vamps could survive the flames.

No, if you wanted to kill a bloodsucker, it had to be a swift, clean severing of their head from their shoulders. As a former Lieutenant Colonel in the Collective Army, Seth had made such kills more than once—and he'd have probably kept on making them, if it hadn't been for the return of the Casus.

Though Seth should have been the enemy of those he was now working with, fate had other plans. In an ironic twist, Seth, along with a small group of Collective soldiers who'd remained loyal to him, were now fighting alongside the Watchmen and the Merrick. The disillusioned officer had broken ranks with the Army when he learned that the Collective Generals had made a deal with the Casus and their allies. Because of that deal, Seth's eyes had finally been opened to the ugly truth about the beliefs he'd devoted his entire adult life to—and now he was here, collaborating with two men who drank blood to survive.

It was a surreal situation for the soldier to find himself in, and yet, he'd have been lying if he said he didn't feel more at peace with his actions than he had in years.

After spending the past week in the States, Seth and his second-in-command, Tyler Garrick, had just flown into Brussels that morning, where they'd met up with Michael Quinn, a Watchman Seth inherently trusted despite their complicated history together. While most of the other men in Quinn's unit had headed directly into the Wasteland to meet up with Kierland Scott, who was running surveillance on the compound where his brother was imprisoned, Quinn had stayed behind to help the Granger brothers investigate an important lead. Once they were done, they'd all be heading into the Wasteland together, hurrying to meet up with the others.

When Quinn had met Seth and Garrick at the airport, the tall, dark-eyed Watchman had expressed concern about Seth working with the Grangers, knowing that he'd long held a personal hatred against the Deschanel, since it was a rogue nest of vampires who had slaughtered Seth's family when he was only fifteen—which had been his impetus for joining the Collective. As *Förmyndares,* or Protectors of the Deschanel clan, the Grangers were some serious badasses, but they'd proven their loyalty to the Watchmen's cause in the past weeks, and so Seth had promised Quinn that he would get along with the vampires and wouldn't cause any trouble. A good thing, too, since it looked as if there was already more than enough trouble to go around.

While Ashe Granger, the older brother, had spent the past week helping Kierland Scott and a female Watchman named Morgan Cantrell search for Kierland's brother in the Wasteland, Gideon had been following a disturbing lead on the Death-Walkers.

As if this screwed-up conflict actually needed another element of the bizarre, the Watchmen had discovered the existence of the Death-Walkers back in December, when Aiden Shrader had been trying to protect little Jamie Harcourt from being kidnapped by the Casus. Thanks to Gideon Granger, who'd tapped his connections within the Deschanel Court, they'd learned that when a Casus was killed with a Dark Marker, a portal opened into the part of hell that held the tainted souls of the ancient clans. As Gideon had apparently put it, "Whenever a door opens, there's always the chance that something else might leak out." In this case, those "somethings" were the Death-Walkers, and they were causing a hell of a lot of trouble.

Seth had yet to face off against the vile bastards since they were specifically targeting the Watchmen at the moment, their plan to remove the shape-shifters who kept peace among the various clans and create a time of chaos…then eventually spread that chaos through the world, simply because it sounded like fun to their warped psyches. Their time in hell had demented their minds, and Seth didn't doubt the danger they posed.

A danger that was mounting, now that they'd followed Gideon's lead to this remote human village in the French countryside.

Just before Kierland and Morgan had set off into the Wasteland, Gideon had left word for them that he'd stumbled onto something *big*, saying that he needed to check it out. After following his lead for the past week, he'd finally discovered where some of the Death-Walkers could be found, and so he'd brought Seth and the others to the village with the intent of finding out just what the deranged creatures were up to.

They'd already found forty or so dead bodies strewn along the cobblestone road that led into the rustic village that was buried within acres of farmland, the corpses drained and mutilated with savage bite marks, reminding Seth of rogue Deschanel kills. The village itself, however, appeared to be barren, not a soul in sight, and Seth didn't have a good feeling about what they were going to find. They needed to do a sweep of the streets, but at the moment they were gathered on a small hill that rose at the outskirts of the village, trying to gather more intel before rushing into God-only-knew what kind of situation.

While Seth, Garrick and Quinn waited in the freezing shadows of a gnarled oak tree, the Grangers had climbed up into its sprawling limbs, trying to get a better view into the heart of the moonlit village. The two brothers were similar in appearance, attractive in that cold, deadly way that only a vampire could be, and Seth had no doubt they were popular with females of every species. He could hear them talking as they surveyed the village buildings and streets through high-tech binoculars, searching for any signs of life.

"So," Gideon murmured. "You doing okay, man?"

"Why wouldn't I be?" Ashe replied, his offhand tone suggesting that his focus was clearly on what he was doing and not the conversation.

"Oh, I don't know. Maybe because the woman you've been hung up on for the past decade is now mated to a guy you used to say was the biggest prick you'd ever met? I know you're tough, but hell, Ashe, that has to sting."

Seth inwardly cringed at Gideon's blunt words. The others had filled him in on the turbulent history between Ashe and Morgan Cantrell, as well as Kierland Scott, who had wanted Morgan for himself. Though Ashe and Morgan had been a couple, they'd broken up and remained close friends, and it was actually Ashe who had helped Morgan and Kierland make their way into the Wasteland so that they could track Kierland's brother. During the trip, Kierland had finally admitted his feelings and claimed Morgan as his mate—a fact that Gideon obviously thought was going to have an effect on his older brother.

"You don't know what you're talking about," Ashe muttered, sounding as if he'd rather have bamboo shoots jabbed under his fingernails than discuss what had happened.

"Yeah?" Gideon murmured. "Then enlighten me."

"I love Morgan as a friend." Ashe's words were thick with irritation. "And I'm happy as hell that she's got what she always wanted. So drop it, Gid."

With a sharp sigh, the vampire said, "If that's true, then you're a better guy than I am."

His brother snorted. "Tell me something I don't know."

"So, I guess you're just going to keep sleeping your way through—"

"Not to be rude," Quinn barked at them, cutting Gideon off, "but what the hell are we waiting for?"

With that same deceptively lazy, animal-like grace inherent in all the Deschanel, Gideon dropped out of the tree, landing effortlessly on the balls of his feet beside Quinn. "Remember when I told you we were coming here to confirm a rumor I'd heard?"

"Yeah. But you still haven't shared that rumor." It was clear from the Watchman's tone that he was losing his patience.

Holding Quinn's dark stare, the gray-eyed vampire said, "While I was slumming through the Deschanel Court, hunting down info on the Death-Walkers, I heard something that creeped the hell out of me. Rumors that the Death-Walkers were going to start making their own little army. And down in that village is the proof that what I heard was true." He handed over the binoculars. "Look for yourself."

A handful of seconds later, with the binoculars still plastered to his eyes, Quinn sounded surprised as he demanded, "What in the hell are those things?"

Ashe dropped out of the tree near Seth, his expression as grim as his tone. "Our newest nightmare."

"They look like some kind of…zombie."

"Oh hell." The milky wash of moonlight revealed Garrick's scowl as he lowered his own binoculars. "You've gotta be kidding me. I've seen a lot of strange things in my life, but this kind of shit's just not right."

Grabbing Garrick's binoculars, Seth focused the lenses on the village down below, and felt his heart drop into his stomach. Nearly twenty human males were shuffling down the center of the main road, their skin waxen in the moonlight, mottled with what looked like yellowish bruises. Dark eyes appeared sunken within their gaunt faces, the surrounding skin blackened, almost as if it'd been burned. Their lips were surrounded by similar black markings, their mouths hanging open like gaping maws, lips and chins covered with blood, as if they'd eaten something raw. Instead of struggling to escape, they appeared to be following whatever orders were given, their bodies moving with a slow, sluggish rhythm, their hands bound behind their backs.

The humans were being herded by two Death-Walkers who flanked the group, the spectral beings every bit as grotesque as the Watchmen had described them. The creatures had cadaverously pale, hairless bodies, with small horns protruding from their temples and sinister-looking claws and fangs, their long, unclothed forms floating eerily over the ground. Since the Death-Walkers consisted of all hell-bound clansmen, their original species varied. From what Seth could tell, the two creatures down in the village had once been Deuchar, one of the most violent of the ancient clans, and a mortal enemy of the Shaevan. But while stabbing a knife through their temple could kill the Deuchar, these assholes had been to hell and back, which changed the rules. Though Gideon had been working hard to come up with the answer, they still didn't know how to kill a Death-Walker. They did, however, know that a combination of salt and holy water gave them a bitch of a burn, sending them scurrying for cover, which was why all of his companions were carrying flasks of the solution.

"I hate to say it," Quinn said, still staring through the

binoculars, "but those Death-Walkers look meatier than the last ones I saw."

"What's the plan?"

"We get down there," Gideon replied, "and find out what's going on."

"I was afraid he was going to say that." Garrick's wry tone jerked a grim, breathless bark of laughter from Seth.

Ten minutes later, the group had made their way into the village, keeping to the shadows to avoid detection, though they knew it was only a matter of time before the Death-Walkers scented their presence. As Deschanel, the Grangers could mask their scent, but it was going to be easy for the bastards to pick up on Seth, Garrick and Quinn. As they made their way down a side alley, drawing closer to the place where they'd seen the villagers, Seth caught his first whiff of the Death-Walkers' rotting flesh and almost gagged. He wasn't weak stomached, but their stench was like something left to rot in the bright sun.

"Keep your flasks at the ready." Quinn spoke from Seth's left, while Garrick had taken up position on his right, the vampires having gone around to the other side of the road, so that they could trap the group between them.

"You think they've made us?" Garrick asked in a low voice, and a second later, he had his answer.

"Mmm. I smell company," one of the creatures lisped, lifting its flattened nose to the air.

"Three, at least." The other one's yellow gaze burned with malice as it peered into the shadows that lined the road.

"Have you come to see our handiwork, then?" the

first one called out, motioning for the villagers to come to a stop.

Though he knew it wouldn't do any good against the Death-Walkers, Seth moved the flask to his left hand and drew his gun, not certain what to expect from the grim-looking villagers who clearly had something wrong with them.

"Be ready," Quinn muttered, and in the next instant, the Death-Walkers attacked. Moving more quickly than Seth would have thought possible, they dashed into the alley. Wind rushed against Seth's face as a blurred shape sped past and left his thigh burning from the razor-sharp claws that had slashed clear through his jeans.

"Son of a bitch," he hissed under his breath, tossing the contents of the flask when he felt another blast of wind rushing toward him. He knew he'd hit one of the Death-Walkers when an enraged screech rang out through the darkness and the smell of burned flesh filled his nose. Quinn and Garrick were close by, cursing and snarling as the Death-Walkers kept coming at them, all three working to make their way into the moonlit street, where they could get the creatures into the open. As he moved toward the road, Seth tossed his empty flask aside, switched his gun to his left hand, and used his right to punch one of the creatures in the face as it sped toward him, the moonlight glinting off its pale skin. Satisfaction burned in his veins as his fist connected, cracking its nose, and a thick, black liquid poured down its face.

When the Watchmen had first faced off against the Death-Walkers back in December, they'd said it'd been like striking a gooey mist, their punches and kicks having little effect. But the bastards had substance *now*, even though they were still able to speed through the air like a vapor, and Seth intended to inflict as much damage as he could.

The Death-Walker he'd hit was still coming after him, probably figuring that as a human, he'd be one of the weakest links in the group. With its jagged fangs bared, it swiped at him with its long claws. Arching backward, Seth managed to narrowly avoid the deadly claws, quickly twisting and bringing his right leg around in a bone-cracking roundhouse that slammed against the Death-Walker's jaw. Both of the vampires had joined the fight, and the creature staggered toward Gideon, who had already released his talons. The vamp swiped at its chest, pulling a thick spray of black mist that covered Gideon's front. While it was still reeling from the blow, Seth tucked his gun into the back of his jeans and whipped out his handcuffs. Wrenching the Death-Walker's arms behind its back, he slapped the cuffs on its wrists and slammed it against the nearest building.

"The other one just took off," Ashe muttered, using his sleeve to wipe away a spray of black slime that had caught him in the face during the fight. "I don't think they were expecting us to be able to hurt them."

"Make sure the villagers don't move," Quinn said to Garrick, who still had his weapon drawn, before moving closer to the Death-Walker Seth had captured. "What's up with the changes in your bodies?" he demanded harshly.

"We've been feeding," it growled, struggling against Seth's grip as he held the creature pinned against the front of the village church, his long fingers clenching its throat. "Every time we've made a kill, we've gotten stronger."

"We saw the bodies of your victims on our way into the village," Gideon said, standing beside his brother. "Thought you assholes were only meant to be hunting the Watchmen."

"Oops," it lisped, its lips spreading in a wide, maniacal smile. "I guess when we explained our purpose to your friends we left out a few important details."

"Ya think?" Gideon snapped, jerking his head toward the tethered humans.

"You might be getting stronger," Seth growled, tightening his grip on the creature's throat, "but now we can get a hold on you."

"True," it laughed, its yellow eyes bright with madness. "But you still can't kill me."

Seth squeezed until he felt something snap. "Tell us what the hell this is about."

"Fuck you," it wheezed, though it didn't seem to be struggling for air. Hell, for all they knew, the Death-Walkers didn't even need to breathe.

"What did you want with this village?" Ashe demanded in a deep, guttural snarl of words, coming a little closer. "Why bother with the humans, when you're meant to be coming after the Watchmen?"

"Our bites only work on humanity." The Death-Walker grinned, which made it even uglier. "But first we needed to get a little meat on our bones. You can't give new life to something until you have some substance yourself."

"New life?" Quinn grunted, pointing toward the villagers. "You've killed those people!"

"No. Just borrowed them, really."

"You mean destroyed them."

Humor danced in the yellow depths of its eyes.

"Would it help if I said we had no choice?" it asked with a rusty laugh.

Seth slammed the back of its head against the building, and it laughed even louder. "Okay. All right. The plain and simple truth is that your side is just taking too long. The Merrick are moving too slowly against the Casus, and there's too few of us to do what needs to be done. So we had no choice but to start building ourselves a little army."

Seth considered pointing out the fact that things were only going to move slower if these assholes kept killing off the Watchmen, but before he could say anything, Quinn came a little closer, his tall, muscled form shaking with rage. "What the hell did you do to them?"

"We bit them. Our bites, while ineffective against the clans, have an interesting effect on humans."

"So you've what? Turned them into your own little zombie soldiers?"

"What are they meant to do, anyway?" Seth demanded. "They can barely move, much less fight."

"Their name is the *Infettato*, or the Infected, and they're not meant to fight. They're meant to *eat*. And like their makers, the more they eat, the stronger they'll become," it explained in that grating, lyrical voice. "It's genius, really. Just imagine the kind of chaos an army of flesh-eating humans will cause!"

"You're even worse than the Casus," Ashe said, enraged. "They might be a group of sadistic assholes, but at least they have something they're fighting for. You... you're just outta your fucking mind."

"Oh, yeah?" it snapped. "Try spending an eternity in hell, vamp, and see what it does for your mental stability."

"Where are the women and children?" Quinn's question drew the Death-Walker's attention. "The bodies out on the road are all males."

"That's because this village, while human, has ties to the Shaevan clan through a marriage. They keep a constant lookout for things that prowl the night. When they saw we were coming, it was the men who came to fight. But most were too weak for our needs. The strongest…well, you can see for yourself." It sent a pointed look toward the villagers.

"You didn't answer my question," Quinn snarled, forcing the words through his clenched teeth. "Where are the children?"

With wide eyes, it asked, "Is that a rhetorical question?"

"Oh, hell no," Gideon growled, while the rest of them cursed.

"Where are they?"

It laughed, the moonlight glinting off its bald, misshapen skull. "Why would we want baby soldiers?"

"You murdered them?" Quinn seethed, sounding ready to kill—and Seth knew exactly how the Watchman felt.

In response to the question, the Death-Walker's jagged teeth flashed in a taunting smile.

"That's it. Talk time's over," Ashe muttered, pulling a small vial from the front pocket of his jeans. "Everybody move back. I'm done with this fuckhead."

"What is that thing?" Seth asked, releasing his hold on its neck and stepping away with the others.

"After going up against these bastards in the Wasteland, I decided to try something new. This is a modified sparkler—a weapon that can be used to kill rogue

Deschanel." Sliding a wry smile toward Seth, the vampire added, "One we've made sure the Collective never learned about. It won't harm any of us, but I'm hoping that the combination of the blast and the salted holy water will be enough to kill this asshole."

"You really think it'll work?" Quinn asked him, casting a doubtful look at the innocuous glass vial.

Ashe rolled his shoulder. "Nah, but it's worth a shot. Until we discover a way to kill 'em, we've got to keep trying new things."

Raising his clenched fist high in the air, the vamp hurled the vial against the ground, and to Seth's surprise, it detonated in a massive explosion of power and sound, and what had to be close to fifty gallons of salted holy water slammed against them with enough force to knock them all on their asses. Wiping the water from his eyes, Seth watched as the Death-Walker writhed against the wall, violent screams pouring from its throat, its skin melting like rivers of wax trailing down the sides of a candle. The handcuffs slid off its wrists, dropping to the ground, and it bent forward, curling its arms over its head, fragments of skull showing where the skin had been burned away.

"This isn't over!" it screamed, and in the next instant, it shot straight into the air, disappearing into the starry night with a furious burst of speed.

Scraping his wet hair from his face, Gideon was the first to break the shocked silence that followed with an eloquent, "Shit."

"I guess it pisses them off," Quinn said. "But it doesn't kill them."

Standing up, Seth walked over and scooped his handcuffs off the ground. "Might not have killed it, but it won't be coming after us anytime soon. Should give us enough time to get to where we're heading without any trouble."

"I've been thinking," Quinn murmured, pushing himself to his feet.

"Yeah?" they all grunted in unison.

"This plan the Death-Walkers have to create chaos among the clans…" The Watchman rubbed at the back of his neck. "If that bastard wasn't lying when he said this village has ties to the Shaevan, then that means the clan is going to be protective of those who live here. And the Death-Walkers have made it look like those corpses out on the road were Deschanel kills."

Ashe cursed. "If the Shaevan find out, they're going to be looking for revenge."

Quinn nodded. "Which is exactly what the Death-Walkers have been after all along. They want to turn the clans against one another, and with the Watchmen busy fighting a war, we're not going to be able to keep the peace. The conflicts are going to escalate. Especially now that they're targeting humans, as well."

Seth shoved his hands into his pockets, saying, "And if that happens, things are going to become harder to contain. If we're not careful, there's a damn good chance the media's gonna catch wind of something it shouldn't."

"Not to mention what could happen if the Death-Walkers keep making their gruesome little army of human zombies."

"There's no telling how bad this could get." Gideon's voice was rough. "The world's not ready to know about the clans. Jesus, they can't even handle different belief systems. What do you think they'd do if they knew there were nonhumans walking among them? We're talking a war of biblical proportions."

"We need to get word out, warning the others of what's coming," Quinn said. "Not all of them will listen, but we need to do what we can."

"Not to change the subject," Garrick called out, "but we still have the *Dawn of the Dead* crew over here."

Scrubbing his hands over his face, Quinn asked, "Got any ideas?"

Seth shook his head. "I wouldn't even know where to start."

"Ashe, you got anything?" the Watchman asked.

"A headache," the vampire muttered. "But that's about it."

They spent the next few minutes discussing what to do with the "infected" villagers, and finally agreed that they should learn more about what had been done to the men before trying to kill them, in case there was a way for the victims to regain their humanity. Quinn made a call to a nearby Watchmen unit that agreed to guard the so-called *Infettato* as well as take care of the bodies out on the road. When the last of the zombies had been herded into one of the village barns, Garrick barred the door, locking them inside. Then everyone stood silent and still beneath the heavy weight of the chilling darkness, listening for any sounds from inside, but all they could hear was a low, eerie groaning noise that made Seth's skin crawl.

"Those poor sons of bitches," he muttered, surprised by how easy it had been to trap the villagers in the barn. They'd been disoriented, their muscles too weak to make them a danger to anyone. But he didn't doubt they would grow stronger with time, just like the Death-Walker had claimed. "Think they'll try to fight their way out?"

"Who knows?" Quinn responded, sounding tired. "But to be safe, we'll wait until the unit's here before heading out."

Propping his shoulder against the ancient barn, Garrick asked, "And then what?"

"We keep to the original plan," Ashe answered, "and meet up with Kierland and the others in the Wasteland."

"And after that?" the soldier asked.

"We just keep doing what we've been doing," Seth told him, hunching his shoulders against the brutal wind, the cuts in his leg starting to hurt like a bitch.

"And what exactly have you been doing?" Gideon asked, lifting his brows.

With a grim smile, Seth met the vampire's curious gaze. "Whatever the hell it takes to survive."

CHAPTER EIGHT

*The Casus/Kraven compound, the Wasteland
Tuesday afternoon*

THEIR TIME HAD RUN OUT.

Ever since Raine had told him that Gregory DeKreznick was coming for Westmore, Kellan had been hoping the Casus would hurry up and make his move, so that they could use the attack as a diversion while making their escape. But they couldn't wait any longer. That morning, Raine had let him know the Casus was finally closing in on the compound…and that he wasn't alone. According to the psychic, there was a shadowy presence traveling with Gregory that she hadn't caught before and couldn't get a clear read on. Kellan didn't like this new development, uncertain what it meant for Chloe… or how it would affect Raine's ability to keep a "read" on Gregory, and it had put him even further on edge.

Then there'd been the visit from Westmore.

It'd happened an hour or so after Raine had told him about Gregory. He'd been pacing the floor, trying to work things out in his head, when Westmore himself had suddenly made an appearance. Though Kellan had expected him to be a big brute of a man, the guy was actually quite average in appearance, his build slight, his head not even reaching Kellan's shoulder. But what the bastard lacked in stature, he more than made up for in sheer, perverse evil. With pale brown hair and ruddy cheeks, Westmore could have passed for any human male walking down the street—but he wasn't human.

And he wasn't Casus, either.

Despite his determination to see the monsters freed from Meridian, Westmore wasn't one of them. He was actually a Kraven, the offspring of a Deschanel female who'd been raped by a Casus many generations ago, before the clan's imprisonment. Viewed as an abomination by the Deschanel, the Kraven had been kept a secret for centuries, their existence only recently revealed to the Watchmen.

From the moment they'd first learned of his plans, Kellan and his friends had wondered exactly what Westmore hoped to achieve by bringing back the Casus, but his goals remained unclear. The Deschanel had been the Kraven overlords for centuries, and some thought that perhaps the Kraven had decided to trade the "protection" of the vampires for that of the more powerful Casus. It was no secret that the Kraven hated the vampires, who regarded them as little better than slaves. But if that was Westmore's plan, Kellan had no doubt he was going to be sadly disappointed, considering the Casus cared for no one but themselves.

Of course, if Kellan ever actually got his hands on Ross Westmore, the guy was going to be more than just disappointed; he was going to be dead. And after what he'd heard that morning, Kellan was ready to make the event as slow and as painful as possible.

When the Kraven had first come down to the cell-block, Kellan had feared that Westmore had come up with some new plan to "feed" Chloe. But that hadn't been the purpose of the bastard's visit. Westmore had basically come to gloat, and his news had left Kellan chilled to the bone.

Instead of saving Chloe for Anthony Calder upon his escape from Meridian, Westmore had decided to placate the pissed-off Casus leader with an early gift—that gift being *Chloe*. The Kraven was actually going to try to send her into Meridian during the full moon on Wednesday night. Westmore believed that if he could transport Chloe directly into Meridian, then Calder would be able to use her murder to acquire enough power to fully regenerate, negating his need for a human host once he returned to this world. He would rape her, then consume her flesh, all for a power kick. And the harder she fought him, the more power the sick son of a bitch would take from the feeding.

Just the thought of it made Kellan's fangs burn to be released, his claws pricking at the tips of his fingers.

Can't let it happen. Won't let it happen….

Determined to do everything he could to keep her safe, Kellan had finally settled on a plan of action, which was why he'd just sneaked back into Chloe's cell a few minutes ago. Expecting her to be a nervous wreck, he'd frowned when he found her sleeping, knowing her exhaustion was a bad sign. The Merrick was obviously wearing her down, draining her more with each hour that went by. After what they'd recently learned from Westmore, she should have been far too anxious to sleep.

Standing beside her cot, Kellan eyed the silken tangle of dark hair spread out over her pillow, and couldn't deny that he wanted to touch it, caress its silken warmth, sift those gleaming strands through his fingers. Her palm was curled innocently in sleep beside her face, and he stared…unable to do anything else. He wanted to kneel down and lay his cheek against her pale, perfect skin. Breathe in a deep lungful of her warm, precious scent and let it ease him, relaxing the tight clench of tension and fear that had his insides twisted into knots.

How did she manage to look so beautiful in the middle of such a nightmare? Words bottled up in his throat, choking and dry, fighting to be said. There were so many things Kellan wanted to tell her. Crazy, possessive things that he'd never said to anyone before. But they were words that had no place between him and this woman. Ones better left locked inside, where they couldn't complicate what was already one hell of a shitty situation.

Damn it, what was the point in making promises he would never have the chance to keep? And even if he wasn't running out of time, he would still have had a battle on his hands, convincing her he was worthy of her trust…much less any kind of deeper emotion. He would have had to fight tooth and nail just to get her to believe in him once she'd learned about the vile, inexcusable mistakes he'd made. The danger he had put his friends in. And yet…it was a challenge he would have gladly accepted.

Impossible to explain how furious it made him that he didn't have that choice, and as Kellan clenched his fists, he found himself wishing that fate were a physical thing he could get his claws into, ripping it to pieces, just like it was doing to him.

For months now, he'd been jealous as hell of what his friends had found, wishing he could find it for himself. That sense of rightness and peace, knowing that no matter what life threw at you, you were no longer alone.

Yeah, he might have been surrounded by family and friends back at Harrow House, but they hadn't been *his*. Most of them had already found that one perfect woman who could make them complete, and had become a part of something new. And now that he'd found the same thing, he couldn't have it. Couldn't have *her*. Fate was just taunting him, damn it. Playing with him. And it pissed him off.

But I can have this, he thought, running his gaze over the sweet, feminine shape of her body beneath the coarse blanket. He *had* to, because there was no longer any question that she needed to build her strength. That they no longer had the time to wait.

Kellan hated the danger he could still pose to her if he failed to control his wolf, but he felt oddly comforted by the fact that the beast was now as worried for her as he was. The animal had been stunned by what they'd heard from Westmore, its feral hunger not softened, but now matched by its fear for her safety. Not a better situation…but perhaps one he had a chance of controlling. Both animal and man understood that the stakes had just been raised. Now the escape was going to be even more dangerous than he'd feared, which meant that Chloe was going to need to be as strong as possible.

And God forbid, if something happened and they got her away from him, Kellan needed to know that he'd given her every advantage she could have against these bastards, so that she could kill them before they killed her.

So let's do this thing, the wolf growled. *Let's give her what she needs.*

With his heart beating to a hard, painful rhythm, and

his pulse thrashing in his ears, Kellan reached down and touched the side of her face. "Chloe, honey. Wake up."

She moaned, nuzzling her cheek against his palm, her breath soft and sweet.

"That's it," he whispered, lowering himself to his knees beside the cot. "Come on, kitten. Open your eyes."

Her eyelids fluttered, and then he was staring into luminous pools of deep, smoky gray, her lashes thick and dark, casting shadows against her cheeks. "Kellan? What are you doing over here?"

"You know, you're always asking me that same question."

The corner of her mouth twitched with a soft, sleepy smile. "That's because I keep telling you to stay away."

He forced a grin, but she must have been able to sense the tension thrumming beneath his surface, because she asked, "What's going on?"

"Come on, Chloe." His voice roughened as he said, "You know why I'm here."

She blinked, and her eyes went wide. "I do?"

"You heard what Westmore said today." His voice was unsteady, a rough edge to the words that made him sound more guttural. "We're going to have to go ahead and make our move tonight, fighting our way out. There's no other way, and I need you…I need you strong for that."

Her eyes went even wider. "You mean…"

"Yeah." She started to say something, but he pressed his fingers across her lips. "Please," he whispered, "just hear me out. I know I started out fighting this tooth and nail, but only because I thought it was best for you. I still don't think I'm fit to touch you, and before you ask, we're not going to talk about why. The truth is that what I think doesn't matter anymore. This *has* to happen."

"But—"

He cut her off again, a grin kicking up the corner of his mouth as he said, "Don't even try it. Didn't anyone ever tell you that you can't argue with a guy on his birthday?"

She snuffled a soft laugh under her breath and looked away, her profile beautiful in the hazy glow of the fire. "I'd forgotten," she said in a quiet voice. "Happy birthday."

"Thanks," he rasped. "But don't even think about calling me old."

Another soft laugh, and she brought her gaze back to his, staring so deeply into his eyes, he felt like she was trying to see into his soul. "Are you sure you want to do this, Kell?"

It would have been impossible to hide the lust that thickened his voice, so he didn't even try. "I've wanted to do this for what feels like forever."

Kellan could tell she didn't believe him—that she was thinking about that bloody curse—but she was going to understand just how hungry he was for her the second they got started. If it was the last thing he did, he was going to make sure this woman understood exactly how much he wanted her.

"What's Raine doing?" she whispered, her breath starting to come a little faster. A rosy flush of color warmed her cheeks, her heady, provocative scent filling his head, rising with the heat of her body.

She was waiting for an answer about Raine, and he somehow managed enough brain function to scrape out,

"She's put herself in a light trance, since it's going to be a long night."

With a careful brush of her fingertips against his bruised cheek, she whispered, "You've had a heck of a birthday, haven't you?"

"It's getting a helluva lot better," he rumbled in a rough, husky slide of words. Taking hold of the blanket, Kellan shoved it to the side, needing to see her body... desperate for her sweet, delicate curves. Her eyes closed as he reached for the buttons on her shirt, his breath quickening as he swiftly got them undone, pushing the sides apart and pulling down the cups of her bra, revealing all that smooth, pale skin and her perfect breasts.

"Christ, you're beautiful," he groaned, leaning down and touching his tongue to a tight, plump nipple. Her back arched as he drew the pink bud between his lips, sucking and licking, wanting to eat her alive. Her legs moved restlessly against the cot, her hands tangling in his hair as he moved to the other breast, working the succulent tip against the roof of his mouth, her throaty cry making him see red.

Ripping off her panties, Kellan lifted her into his arms and turned to sit down on the cot. Her eyes opened as he pulled her over his lap, cradling her shoulders in his left arm, his right hand settling low on her belly. "What are you doing? I thought we were going to—"

"Shh. Just let me take care of you."

"Take care of me?" She choked out the words, "I thought we were going to have sex!"

Settling his hand on the inside of her thigh, Kellan shook his head. "I'm worried I might not hear someone if they come down here. I need to try to stay as focused as possible. But I can still give you what you need."

She started to argue, but he cut off the words again, this time with his mouth, swallowing the sounds as he slid his tongue deep, rubbing it against hers. Her taste jolted his system, lush and sweet, and he kissed her harder, nipping at the tender swell of her lower lip as he whispered, "Open your legs for me, Chloe."

She trembled, but she did as he said, parting her thighs, revealing her glistening sex, and Kellan's breath hissed through his teeth as he spread her open with his thumb and his forefinger. He stared, rapt, his breathing becoming rougher as he studied all the deliciously pink, delicate details—and that was when he felt the Merrick rising within her, its power blasting against him like a hot wind, searing his flesh. Her eyes opened wide, and he could see her fear as she struggled to cope with the Merrick's presence, the sensation of having it there inside her probably more like his wolf than he would have guessed.

"It's okay," he whispered, stroking his fingertips against her soft, slippery folds. "It's going to be all right, Chloe. Don't fight it. We're gonna give the Merrick everything it needs."

Moaning, she arched herself against his hand, her legs spreading wider as he touched that most intimate, exquisitely tender part of her. She was hot and slick, and he gritted his teeth, forcing himself to be gentle as he pushed inside, sinking one long finger into her. "*So tight*," he groaned, carefully pulling his finger out. It gleamed with her juices, and he pushed in two, working them into her while he pressed his thumb against her clit, rubbing the swollen little knot of nerves in a slow circular motion that pulled a husky cry from her throat. "You got those little fangs out?"

"Yeah," she groaned, her eyes dilated with hunger beneath the heavy weight of her lashes, her breath coming in ragged gasps.

"Let me see 'em." She opened her mouth, and he could just catch the delicate points of her fangs glistening beneath the sensual curve of her upper lip, her lips becoming redder…fuller. He made a thick sound in the back of his throat and touched his lips to hers, running his tongue over one of those sharp points, and the ache in his shaft doubled, his blood rushing hard and fast.

Need her fangs, the wolf seethed, prowling beneath his skin as Kellan lifted her against his chest, her face nuzzling against the side of his throat, where the wound made by the poisoned Deschanel had finally healed. *Need her strong.*

"Do it," he growled, wanting it so badly he could taste it. "Make the bite, Chloe."

She groaned in response, flicking her tongue against his hot flesh, then sank her fangs deep, the piercing sensation shooting all the way to the head of his cock. Kellan choked back a rough shout, fingering her deeper, her inner muscles pulling on him tighter…and tighter. She cried out against the side of his throat, her body tensing as she fisted her hands in his hair, and then she crashed full force into a violent, shattering orgasm, the deep, rhythmic clenching around his fingers damn near pulling him right along with her. His fingers were soaked with her juices, and he kept pumping into her, her mouth pulling hard and sweet against his vein, greedy for the hot rush of his blood. With his jaw locked, Kellan ground his thumb against her clit, prolonging the shivering spasms, and the cot began to shake beneath him as if they were in the middle of an earthquake, a hot, fiery wind rushing through the chilly cell, whipping at their hair. The air became charged with the power of the Merrick, thick and electric, as if there was a physical current in the room that pulsed against his skin, raising all the hairs on his body.

With a sharp gasp, she pulled her fangs from his throat, her back arching over his arm as she shuddered and rocked, jerking her hips against his hand, riding his thick, drenched fingers, lost in sexual abandon. Kellan groaned, low and deep, at the stunning sight, thinking she was the most beautiful thing he'd ever seen. He tightened his arm, pulling her against the furious pounding of his heart, his eyes squeezing shut as he buried his face in her silken hair, fighting the urge to push her to her back and shove himself inside her until he was so deep he could feel her soul. At last, the clenching spasms of her orgasm eased, and he pulled his fingers from the exquisite clasp of her body, her inner muscles struggling to hold on to him, protesting the loss…making it that much harder for him to stop before he went too far.

Wrapping both arms around her, Kellan held her tight as he struggled to get it together, his control devastated by the raw, chaotic rush of emotions tearing through him.

You're being pathetic, you bloody idiot. Stop dicking around and make sure she's okay.

Right. Damn it, he could do this. For once in his fucking life, he could be selfless and ignore his own needs, doing what was right for a change. With a few deep, shuddering breaths, Kellan finally relaxed his hold, until she was lying in the cradle of his left arm again. "How do you feel?" he asked, pushing her hair away from her face with a shaky hand.

"Incredible." She stretched in his arms, her voice a low, provocative purr. "It's like someone opened the top of my head and filled me up with warm, sizzling energy."

"That's good, honey." He tried for a normal tone, but couldn't quite pull it off, his voice too gritty. Too strained. "I'm...glad you feel good."

"I feel better than good," she murmured, smiling up at him. "It's like my whole body has been filled with some kind of shimmering light. I'm surprised I don't have sunbeams shooting out from my fingers and toes."

He started to laugh, but she wiggled...and the feel of her firm little ass rubbing against his cock pulled a graveled curse up from his chest.

She stilled instantly, concern mixing with the plea-sure-glow burning in her eyes. "Kellan?"

"Just..." A muscle pulsed in the side of his jaw, his forehead dotted with beads of sweat. "Just don't move for a second, 'kay?"

WATCHING HIM CAREFULLY, Chloe could see that Kellan was in bad shape, his muscles coiled with tension, bulg-ing beneath the burnished glow of his skin. Deep brack-ets were etched into the sides of his mouth, his eyes fever-bright beneath the dark slash of his brows, and she realized that while the Merrick might have gotten what it needed...Kellan hadn't.

"What about you?" she asked softly, settling a little deeper against his massive erection, the denim of his jeans straining around the thick, rigid bulge.

"Don't worry about me," he said in a rough voice, one hand gripping her hip to hold her still. "I'll live."

"Are you serious?" She couldn't believe what she

was hearing. "Come on, Kellan. If you're going to let yourself get used, you should at least get something in return."

He caught her wrist in a firm grip, stopping her as she tried to reach for the button on his jeans. "I'm going to say this one last time, so make sure you're listening, Chloe. You are *not* using me. What just happened between us…yeah, you needed it. But don't think for a second that I didn't want it to happen. I wanted *everything* that happened between us, and a helluva lot more than that."

"Then let me touch you." She pulled her wrist from his grip and climbed off his lap, settling onto her knees at his side, then reached for his fly with both hands, desperate to get to him. He cursed something raw and gritty, but she knew he'd given in when he leaned back, bracing his shoulders against the wall. With his chest heaving, he watched as she clumsily yanked at the button and zipper, her fingers trembling with anticipation, her vision going hazy with lust as she got her first good look at him.

His cock was dark and heavy, thicker and longer than she would have imagined, even in her dirtiest fantasies, but she wasn't complaining. How could a woman complain about something so evocatively male and impossibly beautiful? He made a thick, groaning sound as she wrapped her fingers around him in a greedy hold, the Merrick practically purring with excitement.

"Oh, wow," she whispered, licking her bottom lip. "I didn't get a good look at you on Sunday. But this…*just wow.*"

He let out a husky bark of laughter that made her smile, her heart pounding to a furious beat as she carefully explored him, mesmerized by the deliciously masculine details. A heavy knotwork of veins was mapped beneath the suede-soft skin that'd been stretched tight over the granite-hard shaft, and as she held him in her hands, Chloe could feel the powerful beat of his heart pulsing against her palms.

"Shit," he said thickly, his hands fisting in the cot's thin blanket. "Tighter, Chloe. You won't hurt me. Squeeze it as hard as you can."

She did as he said, and it was sexy as hell, the way he started lifting his hips, thrusting his cock through the tight grip of her hands. She'd tried not to let herself think about how it'd felt on Sunday, when he'd put just the head inside her before pulling away, knowing she'd drive herself crazy. But now she couldn't stop, her body contracting, wanting so desperately to be filled.

His lips pulled back over his teeth, revealing the sharp tips of his fangs, and unlike hers, those suckers were long and thick…and insanely sexy. Chloe could feel him getting thicker in her grasp, proving that yet another one of the rumors she'd heard about Lycan males was true. She could also scent him, so warm and masculine and wonderful, that mouthwatering mix of sex and sweat and musk spiking her own arousal. She stroked her tongue across her lower lip again, desperate for the touch and taste of him. Unable to fight it any longer, Chloe gripped him firmly at the broad root and just went for it, his rough shout filling the cell as she bent over him and ran her tongue over the wet, straining head.

"Son of a bitch," he groaned, his voice shaky and hoarse, and she would have smiled if she could have, loving that she was giving him pleasure. She was intoxicated by his taste and the feel of his rigid flesh against her tongue, thrilled by the way he fisted a hand in her hair, holding it back so that he could watch. She didn't have a clue what she was doing, her experience in this department a pathetic zilch, but it didn't matter. Giving herself up to the Merrick, Chloe moved wholly by instinct, her movements sensual and feline, as if she had primal animal instincts working within her, as well.

"Damn it," he growled, shaking so hard he nearly knocked her off the cot. "Chloe, Jesus. I can't…I can't take it."

She tightened the suction of her mouth, silently telling him that he'd have to, and he pulsed in her grip, so sexy and gorgeous and impossibly male, she couldn't stand it. His eyes burned as he watched her. She could feel the delicious intensity of his stare like a physical touch, and wondered if it was a werewolf thing…or a Kellan thing. She didn't know…but she loved it. Loved the rush that it gave her, pleasure thrumming beneath her skin, enthralling and dark.

"I'm not gonna last," he rasped, his voice shaking, his thighs and abs so rigid, she could see the outline of every breathtaking muscle. "You sure you're ready for that?"

Chloe answered by sucking him even deeper, and he came in a rush of power and scalding heat, the intensity of it unlike anything she could have ever imagined, drowning her senses in pleasure. She waited until the sharp pulses had finally stilled, then pressed a tender kiss to the taut, swollen crown and lifted her head, staring up at him. He reached down, rubbing his thumb against the corner of her mouth, his heavy-lidded eyes hazy with satisfaction as he rumbled, "I think you just made this my best birthday ever. There's not even a close second."

She laughed, but the soft sound faded and she looked away, blushing.

"*Now* you blush," he murmured with a husky laugh, stroking her hair.

She swallowed, wanting to say something…anything, but not knowing which words to choose. The silence stretched out, the air prickling against her skin, and she could feel the heat of his stare as he ran his gaze down the front of her body, everything on blatant display between the gaping sides of her shirt.

When she started to shiver, he finally broke the tension by saying, "I wish I could stay in here with you. Just hold you and sleep through the night."

"Me, too," she whispered, wishing they were anywhere in the world but there, painfully aware that the next few hours might be their last. She hadn't let herself think about what Westmore had told them earlier, knowing she would freak if she did—but she couldn't help worrying about Kellan and Raine, terrified they'd be hurt when the three of them tried to escape.

The irresistible muscles in his abs bunched when he sat up, his voice a low, throaty rasp as he said, "We're heading out at about 4:00 a.m., since that seems to be when there's the least security. We shouldn't see anyone before then, but if something happens and anyone comes down here, don't let them see that you've fed."

"Right."

"I mean it, Chloe."

"Don't worry," she murmured, pulling her shirt together as she curled her legs to the side. Wanting to make him smile, she lowered her lashes and teasingly said, "You'd be amazed by how well I can fake it."

He was laughing as he leaned toward her, putting his face close to hers, his big hand curling around the back of her neck. "You weren't faking it, honey, and I've got you all over my hand to prove it. And if we were somewhere safe right now, someplace private, it'd be all over my face."

"You're so full of it," she snickered, knowing damn well that he'd probably never touch her again, now that the Merrick had been fed. But that didn't mean that her desire for him was any less intense.

Her skin heated beneath the warm touch of his lips, and she knew he could hear the increase in her heart rate as he whispered into her ear, "You'd like to be full of me, wouldn't you, Chloe? You'd like to know what it'd feel like to have me packed deep inside you, where I could feel every shiver and pulse when you came apart. Isn't that right, sweetheart?"

The Merrick silently purred with hunger, and she knew she was close to losing it. "If you...if you don't want to have sex," she said unsteadily, "then you need to get away from me, Kell."

"I'll go, but only because I know that's what's best for you." He pressed a tender kiss to the side of her throat, then pulled away from her, moving to his feet as he did up his jeans, and her breath caught as he slid her a smoldering stare. "But once we're out of here, you won't be pushing me away anymore. I'm gonna be fucking you every chance we get."

Whoa. The guy's sexy was insane. Just hearing those words slide from his sensual lips had nearly made her come. Chloe squeezed her thighs together, trying to hide her reaction, knowing he was right about it not being the time or place, with Westmore and his minions liable to walk in on them at any moment. And with the thought of their enemies, her arousal fled, replaced by anger and fear and repulsion. She wished she were the kind of witch who could wield magic like a weapon, because she would have loved nothing more than to fry Westmore's smarmy ass.

"Kellan!" she called out, as he headed across the cell.

Looking back over his shoulder, he said, "Yeah?"

"If we die, I just…I want you to know how much I appreciate what you've done for me and my family."

His brows drew together over eyes the color of a Caribbean sea, the firelight playing beautifully across the wine-dark strands of his hair. "We're not going to die," he said in a low voice.

"I'm sorry. I don't mean to sound rude. I know you'll do your best, but if there's one thing that I've learned during the past few months, it's that nothing's ever a given."

He stared at her across the distance of the room, his expression a mixture of frustration…and something that looked incredibly like soul-deep determination. "You don't have a lot of faith in me, and I get that. I mean, I've never been the kind of guy who instills a lot of faith in people. But that's changed. I'm not going to let you down, Chloe. I'm something you can count on, and it's going to be okay. It's going to be better than okay. You get that?"

Feeling as if she was in a trance, she nodded, watching

him as he made his way back out of her cell—and despite the freezing temperatures, the heat of his gaze stayed with her long after he'd gone.

CHAPTER NINE

The Watchmen base camp, the Wasteland
Tuesday, 9:00 p.m.

"DEKREZNICK IS FINALLY getting ready to make his move on the compound."

Kierland Scott dropped down from the thick branch he'd been using for pull-ups, and turned to face Aiden Shrader, one of his oldest friends and a fellow Watchman from Kierland's unit. Taking the towel Aiden offered him, he wiped the sweat from his face and asked, "How soon?"

"We reckon he'll hit them sometime between 3:00 and 5:00 a.m."

There was an edge of strain in his friend's voice that Kierland knew came from more than just the news about Gregory DeKreznick. Aiden had left Olivia and Jamie Harcourt, the two most important females in his life, back at the safety of Harrow House in England, and come on his own. Leaving his girls behind had been a tough decision for the Watchman to make, but Ade had promised Olivia that he'd be there to help get her sister to safety.

Of course, the fact that the spells cast over the region made technology ineffective and rendered cell phones useless within the Wasteland only made Aiden that much more frustrated, since he couldn't call home to check on them. It also meant that everyone there at base camp was completely cut off from the rest of the world, making it impossible to contact Quinn and the others.

"Are you sure it's Gregory?" Kierland asked, rubbing the towel against the back of his neck.

The tiger-shifter's mouth was curved with a smile, but it was one that only Aiden could pull off, kind of mean and happy looking all at the same time. "I'm sure."

Anticipation rippled along Kierland's nerve endings, and he fought to keep calm. The past few days had just about killed him, as he and Morgan had waited for Kellan to escape the compound with the Merrick witch. They'd been watching for Gregory, after it'd been reported that a Casus matching his description was traveling through the region, and assumed that DeKreznick had decided to make his own move against Westmore, since the Kraven had tried to have him sent back to Meridian. Knowing how his brother thought, Kierland had no doubt that Kellan would use the Casus's attack on the compound to make an escape—and when that happened, they'd be there, ready to help him.

"When do you think we should leave?" he asked, heading toward the full-size tent that he shared with Morgan. They had a surveillance station set up on a high ridge a few miles southeast of the compound, which they used to monitor the fortress, but the base camp was farther south, ensuring them more safety. Grouped around a cabin that was used by the *Förmyndares,* tents had been set up for individual use in the camp, leaving the cabin to function as a central meeting area.

Following him into the tent, Aiden said, "We should plan to head for the compound in a few hours. We'll have to hold position until Gregory shows, but the snow will help cover our scent."

"Sounds good." Kierland pulled off his sweaty T-shirt, tossing it into the bag they'd set aside for laundry. "Can you ask the others to get ready?"

"I already have," Aiden drawled, his expression eager, as if he was actually looking forward to the coming fight.

In addition to Aiden, they also had Noah Winston and a young Lycan named Jamison Haley there, as well as the help of the exiled Sabin family who resided in the Wasteland. Juliana Sabin had recently befriended Kierland and Morgan, and the vampire had offered them her full support, even using her personal guards as scouts so that they could gather more intel. And if they were lucky, Quinn and Seth would be joining them soon, along with the Granger brothers, which meant their numbers would be even greater. Together, they were going to mount one hell of an offensive against Westmore and his men, but it still felt like they were missing something without Kellan there.

Using her powers, Saige Buchanan had gone through Kellan's things in his room back at Harrow House when he'd first disappeared, trying to see if she could learn anything about where he'd gone. The female Merrick had sensed Kellan's restlessness with his life and his desire to redeem himself, as well as his worry for all of them, which had made Kierland and the others feel like shit. They'd been giving him a hard time ever since his screwup in Washington, and all along, he'd been even harder on himself. Now, looking back, Kierland couldn't help but feel that he should have been more supportive, instead of such a belligerent hard-ass. If he had, Kellan might have confided in him about his plans to rescue Chloe Harcourt and the brothers could have worked together, instead of Kellan taking off on his own and putting his life in the hands of a madman.

"I heard about Gregory," Morgan suddenly said, pulling Kierland from his thoughts as she came into the tent, her warm, lush scent instantly hitting his system, easing his tension with ridiculous ease. She headed straight for him, and his heart stuttered the same damn way that it always did when she came into a room. Considering he'd always been a man who worked to keep perfect control over his emotions, he might have actually been worried about the female Watchman having such a powerful effect on him, if he hadn't been so crazy in love with her. As she nestled against Kierland's side, she looked toward Aiden, saying, "It's a good thing you brought several of the Markers with you. With any luck, we're gonna take care of that bastard once and for all."

"There's something else," Aiden rumbled. "Juliana just received word from her scouts that Seth, Garrick and Quinn are in the Wasteland. They spotted them from one of the mountaintops. It looks as if they're still a few hours away, but they should make it here before we have to head out."

Sensing Morgan's tension, Kierland pulled her closer against his side, his arm curved around her waist in a possessive hold. "Ashe and Gideon aren't with them?"

Aiden shook his head, and for the next ten minutes the three of them discussed what needed to be done before they could head out, then Aiden left to coordinate with the others, leaving Kierland and Morgan alone.

Catching her troubled expression, the Lycan asked, "What's wrong, angel?"

Her long hair spread over her shoulders as she shook her head. "Nothing."

"Tell me," he coaxed, pulling her against his chest.

She closed her eyes for a moment, then opened them and said, "The truth is that I'm scared."

Kierland ran his hand down her spine in a soothing motion, while his wolf tensed with agitation, hating to see her upset as badly as the man did. "What are you scared of?"

"At the moment," she sighed, her gray eyes troubled and dark as the words poured out of her in a breathless rush, "it feels like everything. I'm worried about Kellan and about what has happened to Ashe, since he isn't with Quinn. I'm worried about how everyone is doing back in England. But mostly I'm worried about *you* and this war and the Markers and what you're planning on doing with them once we finally have them all."

Biting back a smile, he said, "I love it that you worry about me—but, honey, if it turns out that the Markers really are the keys that will open the gate into Meridian, like you suggested last week, then we don't have any choice about what to do." He lifted his hand, tucking a dark lock of hair behind the delicate curve of her ear. "We'll use them to get into Meridian and kill the bastards, the way they should have been killed before."

"But we don't even know where Meridian is," she pointed out in a quiet voice.

Utterly confident, he murmured, "We'll find it."

She lowered her gaze to his chin and took a deep, shaky breath. "Then you should probably know that I'll be going with you."

Over my dead body, he thought, his jaw hardening as she lifted her gaze and he read the determination burning in her eyes. "I'm not even happy about you going with me tonight," he growled. "So trust me when I say there isn't a chance in hell I'd let you go into Meridian to face off against the entire Casus race!"

She lifted her chin in that defiant way that always made him hard and aching, even though he knew she was going to be stubborn as hell. "We can argue about it all you want, Kier, but it won't make any difference. I plan on being there to keep an eye on you, and there isn't anything you can say to change my mind."

"It *won't* happen," he rasped, secretly loving that she was strong enough to stand up to him, even though it sometimes drove him out of his ever-loving mind. "I'm fully prepared to fight you on it, Morgan."

Her soft lips curved with a slow, provocative smile. "I'll still win."

Like hell you will, he thought, leaning down to claim her mouth with a hard, dominating kiss, but she stopped him with the press of her hands against his chest, and Kierland could tell from her expression that she'd suddenly seized onto a new worry.

Taking a deep breath, he waited as she asked, "What do you think the Consortium will do, once they realize what your plan is?"

The Consortium was a kind of preternatural United Nations comprised of leaders from each of the remaining ancient clans, their purpose to govern the clans and to keep peace—and it was the Consortium the Watchmen actually worked for. Lately, however, the Consortium had become too bogged down in politics and bureaucracy to do what needed to be done. Although they should have been heading the war against the Casus, they'd actually decided to turn a blind eye to the situation, and tensions between the leaders and Kierland's Watchmen unit remained high.

Answering her question, he said, "To be honest, they'll probably fire my ass."

"That's not fair!"

"I don't think fairness is something that really concerns them," Kierland pointed out in a dry tone.

Frustration laced her words as she said, "But I just don't get it, Kier. Why won't they take action against the Casus?"

"Because they're worried about their own asses?" he drawled, shrugging his shoulders. "Waiting to see who comes out on top? Hell, at this point, who knows what they're thinking?"

"They're idiots," she muttered. "The entire situation is ridiculous."

"I'm beginning to think the same thing," he admitted in a low voice.

She stared into his eyes, studying his expression. "I know that look. What are you thinking, Kier?"

Wondering how she was going to take what he was about to say, since she'd devoted her entire life to the Watchmen cause, Kierland exhaled a shaky breath. "I just have doubts about the role we're playing. The Consortium has become something different than it was meant to be."

"Ohmygod." Understanding dawned in her eyes, and she lifted her brows. "Are we going to start a revolution?"

He loved the sound of that *we*, knowing she would always be there to stand beside him, through good times and bad. "We need to talk to the others, but it might be time that we break ties and go our own way. Hell, we're not following their orders as it is. And we have the funds to keep us going. We might as well take control."

"Kellan's never going to believe it," Morgan murmured with a grin. "His perfect brother planning a mutiny. I've always known that deep down you were a rebel."

Kierland laughed, wrapping her in a tight hug, and she nestled her head under his chin, her tone turning serious as she said, "I know I was the one who talked you out of stopping him from going through with his plan to get captured, but I want Kellan out of that place."

"Me, too," he told her, resting his chin on the top of her head. "I hope to God he's ready."

"He'll be ready. I just wish we could go after him *now*."

Cupping her sweet little ass with his hands, he said coaxingly, "You know, since we still have to wait for a while, I think I should do something to help you relax."

She shivered, her breath coming a little faster, the warm, sensual scent of her desire flooding his senses. "Do you always like to make love before heading into a fight?" she whispered, and he could hear the smile in her voice as she stroked her hands down his back, his muscles twitching beneath her touch.

"You know me," he breathed into the tender shell of her ear. "I'll take every excuse there is to get my hands on you."

Wrapping her arms around his neck, she went up on her tiptoes to bring her mouth close to his, her gray eyes heavy with lust and with love. "You don't need an excuse, Kier."

"But I need *you*," he groaned in a dark, husky slide

of words, lifting her into his arms and laying her down on their pallet. "I need you more every goddamn day, Morgan."

"Then it's a good thing you've got me. Question is, what are ya going to do with me?"

He reached for the front of her jeans, his wolf chuffing with excitement as he ripped them off her body. "We could talk about it," he growled, pushing his hand inside her panties, his pulse thrashing when he found her hot and slick and wet, "but I think I'd rather just show you instead."

"Mmm. I do love the way you think," she moaned, smiling up at him, and with a low, wicked rumble of laughter, Kierland lowered his body over hers....

CHAPTER TEN

The Casus/Kraven compound, the Wasteland
Wednesday, 4:00 a.m.

WHY DID SOME WORDS come so easily, while others
were so difficult?

As they readied themselves for their escape, there
were so many things Chloe would have liked to say to
the Lycan pacing her cell—but the words were all locked
in her throat and she couldn't get them out.

Any minute now, they were going to make their break
for it. Kellan had spent hours talking her and Raine
through the plan, covering one contingency after another.
He'd also briefed them both on how to kill the things
they would likely come into contact with while making
their escape. Since the Kraven could only be killed by
a wooden stake through the heart, he'd torn her cot into
pieces, breaking the wood into sturdy spikes that could
do the job. It'd been a jaw-dropping sight, watching the
muscles across Kellan's arms and shoulders bulge and
flex from the physical work, moving beneath the sweat-
slick surface of his taut, golden skin, and for those few
blissful moments Chloe had actually forgotten her fear.
It'd come roaring back, though, when he'd started talking about the Casus. Even though a Dark Marker was
the only way to destroy a Casus's soul, the host bodies

they occupied could be killed, sending the Casus's shade back to Meridian. But they were still incredibly strong, and the odds were high that the monsters would release their deadly claws and fangs at the first sign of trouble, or even completely shift into their true Casus form.

To make matters more complicated, Raine had warned them that Gregory would soon be making his move—the news setting Kellan even further on edge since Raine still couldn't get a clear read on whoever was traveling with the Casus. Their only consolation was the fact that Raine had seen Kellan's brother and friends closing in on the compound, as well, which meant they'd have some badass warriors fighting on their side when things got ugly.

Knowing these were most likely the last moments of privacy she and Kellan would have, Chloe finally took a deep breath and forced out the words she wanted to say. "I've been thinking about what you said yesterday, and there's something I want to tell you."

"Go for it." He wore his usual cocky smile, his stance casual as he stopped in the middle of the floor and shoved his hands in his pockets, but she could see the tension that tightened the muscles in his face, as if he were mentally bracing himself for a blow.

Forcing herself to hold his sharp, glowing gaze, she said, "You're wrong about not inspiring faith in people. You might have been self-centered in the past, but that's not who you are anymore." A grin twitched at the corner of her mouth as she watched a wave of shock play across his expression, his eyes burning brighter within the shadowy darkness. "Somewhere along the way, I think you grew up, Kell. And you did a nice job of it, too."

He kept staring at her, his expression constantly

shifting, and she could tell he wanted to say something...
but couldn't quite get it out, as if the words were difficult
for him, as well. Eventually, he gave a wolfish shake of
his head, as if throwing off the moment, and reached
down, grabbing the blanket he'd fashioned into a makeshift sack to carry the wooden spikes. "You ready to get
out of here?" he asked in a low voice, slinging the sack
over his head and shoulder, so that it hung diagonally
across his back.

Chloe nodded, and he walked to the door, asking,
"Raine, you ready?"

"Oh yeah," the psychic murmured from her cell.

Kellan shoved the door open and Chloe quickly made
her way toward the roaring fire in the hearth, curling
up on the cold floor a few feet in front of it. Using the
keys, he opened Raine's cell, and in the next second,
the psychic started shouting for the guards standing
outside the door, calling for help. As soon as the door
opened, Kellan moved into the shadowed corner nearest the bottom of the stairs, waiting as the men came
thundering down. Thanks to Raine, they'd known two
Collective soldiers were on duty that night, and despite
their training, the humans were no match for a full-
blooded Lycan.

"The Merrick is out of her cell! Call for backup!" the
first soldier shouted, heading toward her, but Kellan was
already reaching for the guy's head. With a swift jerk,
he twisted the guard's head and broke his neck. The
second guard started to raise his gun, but Raine ran up
behind him and smashed her water bowl over his head.
Although the blow didn't knock him out, it stunned him
for the few seconds Kellan needed to kick the gun out of
his hand. With a snarled curse, the soldier reached for

the knife strapped to his thigh, but before he could free his blade, Kellan quickly grabbed his head and twisted, breaking his neck as easily as he'd done with the first.

Snatching up the guards' guns, Kellan tucked one into the back of his jeans, keeping the other in his hand. "Come on," he grunted, jerking his head toward the stairs. "Let's go."

It was unbelievably quiet as they made their way up the stairs and into a dark corridor, the only lighting coming from dimly lit sconces that lined the passageway, their flames casting eerie shadows against the pale stone walls. Chloe was just starting to breathe a little easier, thinking they might actually make it out without any problems, when the sudden blast of gunfire and pounding footsteps stopped them in their tracks. Kellan shoved her and Raine against the wall, putting his body in front of them, his gun raised and ready to fire.

"What's happening?" she whispered.

Kellan listened for another half minute, then shook his head. "I don't fucking believe it."

"What?"

"Sounds like Gregory's here."

"He's right," Raine said, her frail body covered in nothing more than a thin slip, her big eyes dark with exhaustion. "It's him."

"Can you get a read on where he's at?" Kellan asked the psychic, keeping his attention focused on their surroundings.

Raine closed her eyes, her forehead scrunched with concentration. "He's attacking from the west." The compound was actually shaped like a cross, the underground level where they'd been kept located in the south arm, which meant that Gregory wasn't far from their current position.

"Then we'll go east," Kellan said in a low voice. "Come on. We've got to hustle."

They changed direction, running through what seemed a never-ending maze of corridors. Gunfire continued to echo through the compound, coming from every direction now, and Raine told them that Kellan's friends had entered the fight. They'd just made another turn into a wide, low-ceilinged hallway when they ran into a group of Westmore's men, and Chloe knew from their ice-blue eyes that at least three of them were Casus. The other one had eyes that were burning like blood-red embers of fire, and Kellan reached for the stakes slung on his back.

"Get behind me!" he barked, just as the Kraven came at him, its fangs dripping with saliva, and blood sprayed as he stabbed one of the wooden stakes through the center of its chest. As the Kraven's body fell to the floor, the Casus released their claws and attacked. Kellan managed to shoot one of them straight through the center of its forehead, before another one knocked the gun from his hand. Chloe watched in shock as he released his own fangs and claws, digging them into the monster's throat and ripping it out. Then he spun, ready to take on the last Casus, blood dripping from his claws and coating his upper body. She should have been terrified at the sight of such brutal violence, but the Merrick part of her was too proud for such a wimpy, human reaction. It gloried in the primal savagery of the Lycan's protection, hungrier than ever for him.

He was still embroiled in the battle when another Kraven came from the opposite direction, its red eyes glowing with bloodlust as it attacked Raine, tackling her so hard that she slammed to the floor. Gritting her teeth, Chloe grabbed one of the wooden stakes that were now scattered on the floor and ran for the bastard as he crouched over Raine, her Merrick in full force as she let out a bloodthirsty cry and drove the wood deep into his back, aiming for his heart. He slumped over the psychic, pinning her to the floor, and Chloe was still trying to shove him to the side when Raine shouted out a warning that there was another Kraven behind her. Before she could turn, the Kraven grabbed Chloe's arm, nearly wrenching it out of the socket as he jerked her around, his sadistic grin revealing the tips of his fangs as he pulled her against his chest.

"I've been watching you." His rank breath nearly made her gag.

"Westmore will kill you if you touch me!" she snarled, keeping one eye on Kellan, who was still trading vicious blows with the last Casus.

"If I kill you when I'm through," the Kraven said with a low laugh, "then Westmore will never—"

His gloating was cut short when Chloe jerked her knee up as hard as she could, aiming right for the bastard's groin.

"You little bitch!" he roared, backhanding her across the face and sending her skidding across the floor. Tasting blood in her mouth, she pushed her hair out of her eyes just in time to see Raine sink a stake into the creep's back, exactly like Chloe had done moments earlier when she'd killed the other Kraven. Footsteps thundered overhead, the sound of gunfire growing louder as Chloe pushed herself to her feet and looked for Kellan. As their gazes met, Chloe tried to call out to him, to let him know she was okay, but before she had a chance the entire compound shook with a violent tremor, the terrifying roar of an explosion coming from right over their heads, and the ceiling gave way between them. She started to scream his name, but a blinding flash of light filled the corridor, and the next thing Chloe knew she was flying through the air, a deafening blast of sound filling her head.

In a daze, she rolled over, squinting against the clouds of dust as she struggled to see. "Oh, God. Please be okay," she whispered, terrified that Kellan and Raine might have been harmed by the blast. They hadn't been as close as she had, since they were at the other end of the corridor, but she knew how unpredictable these things could be. Staggering to her feet, she'd only just managed to make it upright when rough hands gripped onto her arms. "No!" she screamed, fighting to break free, but her captor was too strong.

"Shut up, you little bitch," the man grunted, knocking the wind out of her as he tossed her over his shoulder. She pounded her fists against his back, trying to inflict as much damage as she could, while shouting at the top of her lungs, but her screams were choked off in a painful fit of coughing when he ran into a thick wall of smoke.

"Grab the Markers," she heard a few minutes later from a voice that sounded like Westmore's. "Then meet me in my private office."

The man holding her asked, "What do I do with the Merrick?"

"Lock her in the library with the archives. I don't want her getting killed before we're ready to leave."

Chloe continued to pound against her captor's back

as he set off at a loping run through the smoke-filled hallways, more earsplitting blasts shaking the compound as he threw open a heavy wooden door and tossed her inside. Moonlight filtered in through a series of high windows, illuminating a book-filled room with a vaulted ceiling and dark furniture, the familiar scents of paper and leather lingering in the air.

Ignoring the pain in her hip, Chloe scrambled to her feet as soon as the lock clicked, and immediately started looking around for anything that might be useful. She was confident that Kellan would be coming for her—but in the meantime, she needed to find something she could use as a weapon. If Westmore came back for her before Kellan could reach her, she intended to be prepared. The Merrick's power was weakening, the morning's events already taking their toll on her strength, but no way in hell was she letting them drag her out of there without a fight.

LUB-DUB. LUB-DUB. LUB-DUB.

The deep, resonant beat of his heart filled Kellan's head, strangely disorienting as it drowned out all other sounds. Cracking open his eyes, he saw that the blast had knocked him clear off his feet, slamming him through the crumbling side of the hallway, until he'd hit the floor and slid across what appeared to be an empty room.

He couldn't believe the compound had been rigged to blow. His left shoulder felt like fire and he knew, without looking, that he'd been badly burned. Not that he gave a shit. All he cared about was making sure that Chloe and Raine were okay. Moving to his feet, he felt a sharp pinch in his side and looked down to find a five-inch piece of shrapnel piercing his skin. Gnashing his teeth, he grabbed the jagged steel and yanked, a thick, guttural sound ripping from his throat as it tore free. Blood seeped from the wound, but he ignored it, picking his way over the debris, until he'd made it back into the corridor, where a mound of rubble now stood between him and the place where he'd last seen Chloe.

Screaming her name, Kellan threw himself at the wall of debris, fear clawing at his insides as he tore at the crumpled stone with his claws, his chest heaving with sharp, ragged breaths.

"It's okay, Kell. She's alive." Raine's hoarse voice came from somewhere off to his right, and he turned, trying to find her through the thick, choking cloud of smoke. "The blast didn't kill her. But...Westmore's men...they've taken her."

Furious that Chloe had been captured, Kellan followed the sound of Raine's voice and fought the wolf for dominance as it tried to take over, knowing that if he gave in to it now he would lose all sense of reason, consumed by his rage. A sharp curse left his lips when he found Raine's small body crumpled on the cold floor. Her right arm was badly burned, a deep gash across her temple seeping blood. Just as Kellan retracted his claws and dropped to one knee beside her, someone moved into the corridor, and he snarled, showing his fangs, ready to rip the bastard to shreds, when a familiar voice shouted, "Whoa, damn it. It's me!"

"Oh, shit," Kellan cursed, realizing it was Seth Mc-Connell. "I've never been so happy to see you, you son of a bitch."

"Your brother and most of the others are with me," Seth told him, coming closer, "but we got separated when things started exploding. Looks like Westmore had this place set to blow, and he doesn't give a shit if his own men get taken out in the process."

"Is everyone okay?" Kellan asked, thinking that the soldier was looking harder these days. Meaner. His once-shaggy blond mane was now shorn close to his scalp, his dark green eyes shadowed and tired.

"The others are fine, but—" the soldier crouched on the other side of Raine's body "—damn, Kell. What happened to your witch?"

"This isn't Chloe," he explained, looking down to see that Raine had lost consciousness. Checking her pulse at her wrist, he quickly said, "Her name's Raine. She's the psychic Westmore has been holding prisoner."

Rubbing a hand over his mouth, Seth asked, "She get caught in a blast?"

"Yeah, and I got separated from Chloe. Do you have someone who can get Raine out of here for me?"

"I'll take her," the soldier told him, his expression dark as he looked over Raine's battered body. "We're meeting up in the woods northeast of the compound. I can get her there."

Uneasiness settled along Kellan's nerve endings. He knew the reason Seth had joined the Collective Army at the early age of fifteen was because his entire family had been brutally slaughtered by a nest of rogue vampires—and it was Seth's hatred for the Deschanel that had fueled his commitment to the Army until his recent defection.

Blowing out a rough breath, Kellan muttered, "I don't think that's such a good idea."

The soldier's gaze locked with his. "Why the hell not?"

"Seth, man, it's not that I don't trust you. But she's part Deschanel."

"She's a vamp?" the soldier muttered, his brow knitting as he held Kellan's stare.

"Yeah. One who's been through hell, so...she doesn't—"

"How old is she?" Seth grunted, cutting him off. "She doesn't look any more than nineteen."

Wondering what the hell her age could matter, he said, "She's twenty-six."

Seth started to pick her up, and Kellan reached out, grabbing hold of his arm. "It's okay," the soldier said in a low voice. "I'm not gonna hurt her, Kell."

Letting go, Kellan stood up and pushed his hair back from his face, his voice gruff as he said, "Just be gentle with her, man. Like I said, she's been through hell."

"Those fuckers hurt her?" Seth growled, carefully putting her over his shoulder so that he'd still be able to hold his gun.

Kellan responded with a grim nod, impatient to get on with his search for Chloe. "Have you seen Gregory?" he asked.

"Not yet. But something weird as hell is going on around here."

"What do you mean?"

"I've run across about twenty Casus so far who look like they were just cut down, one after the other. How the hell is Gregory doing that on his own?"

"I don't know," he muttered, reaching for the gun tucked into the back of his jeans and checking the clip. "But I've gotta go find Chloe. The blast separated us, and Raine told me that Westmore's men have got her."

Seth shook his head. "You know, it's a sad day when a guy can't keep track of his own woman."

Eyeing the hole above his head that had been made when the ceiling caved in, Kellan said, "Piss off. You don't even have a woman."

"Not true. I have several," Seth murmured. "Just not interested in keeping any of them."

As he tucked his gun back into his jeans, Kellan pinned the soldier with a hard glare. "Look, I get that you're trying to keep me here until backup arrives, but it's not gonna happen. I don't have time to wait."

Seth's eyes narrowed with frustration. "Come on, man. You're in rough shape, and you're not even dressed for the weather out there. If we stay together, there's a pack of supplies stashed outside the compound that we can give you. So be smart and wait for the others."

"There's no time. I didn't even give her one of the guns," he growled, knowing what those bastards had planned for her. No way in hell was he going to let them send her into Meridian to be Calder's plaything. Climbing up onto the rubble, Kellan reached for the jagged edge of the hole in the ceiling, saying, "If I haven't met up with you in the woods in the next thirty minutes, promise me that you'll come back for Chloe."

"Damn it, Kellan. You can't—"

"Just promise me!" he shouted.

Kellan waited until Seth had given him a curt nod, then pulled himself up, his injured shoulder aching like a bitch as he swung his leg up onto the ledge, heaving his body onto the floor of what looked like another smoke-filled corridor. He hurt like hell from his head to his toes, but he ignored the pain, forcing himself to his feet, determined to find his woman.

She'll only be yours when you've claimed her, the wolf snarled, seething with frustration.

"Shut up," he muttered, grabbing his gun and firing a round of bullets into two Collective soldiers who suddenly rushed him from his left. He'd been trying to conserve bullets before, but he didn't have time to waste fighting the bastards now. Searching for Chloe's scent, he moved around the gaping hole that'd been blown through the floor, stepping over the mangled bodies of what looked like more Collective soldiers, and set off at a run. The place was a maze of hallways, the smoke from the explosions making visibility damn near impossible, not to mention the way it was screwing with his sense of smell.

Get her out alive, he thought, his mind consumed with the hunt. *Just have to get her out of here.*

To Kellan, that was all that mattered. Yeah, there were a few things he'd have liked to add to that list, such as taking out Westmore and Gregory DeKreznick. But if he had to settle on one last accomplishment before he bit the big one, it was going to be making sure that Chloe got out of that hellhole in one piece.

He could feel the wolf's power surging through him—that visceral, primal instinct that pushed him to succeed at any cost. Knowing the animal's senses were sharper than his own, Kellan let the beast rise to his surface, right up to the cusp of a full change, and allowed the predator to hunt for her. As he turned down another hallway, he caught a faint whiff of her scent, as well as the distant sound of a scream, and a low growl vibrated in his chest, his muscles burning as he pumped his legs down the passageway. When he reached an intersection with another corridor, he searched for her scent, but couldn't find it beneath the acrid clouds of smoke lingering in the air. Then his ears picked up a noise to his right, and he started running again, following a distant sound of voices that led him to a closed door at the end of the hall. Bursting into the room, he found Westmore standing in front of a wall safe, shoving money into a leather satchel, whoever he'd been talking to already gone. Grabbing the Kraven by the throat, Kellan shoved him against the wall, his lips pulling back over his fangs as he snarled, "Where's Chloe, you son of a bitch?"

"Where's Raine?" the Kraven shot back, spittle spraying from his lips, his red eyes burning with madness. "Is she alive? I can't believe that little bitch didn't tell me Gregory wasn't alone. Where *is* she?"

Ignoring his questions, Kellan slammed the Kraven against the wall so hard the back of his head split open, blood dripping down the pale stone in meandering rivulets. "Tell me where Chloe is," he seethed, "or I'll make you hurt in ways you can't even imagine."

"You can't hurt me," the Kraven sneered, pulling on Kellan's wrist, but he was no match for the wolf's strength.

Tightening his grip on the bastard's throat, Kellan released the tip of his thumb claw, pressing it against Westmore's jugular. "You think you've got a monopoly on pain? Think again, asshole."

With an arrogant laugh, the Kraven said, "You're wasting your time, Lycan. The Markers are already gone."

"I don't give a shit about the Markers," he growled. "All I want is the girl."

That obviously hadn't been what Westmore was expecting to hear, his eyes narrowing with disbelief. "You're lying. Why would you care about the Merrick?"

"My reasons aren't any of your goddamn business. Just tell me where she is!" he roared, slamming him into the wall again. "Way I see it," Kellan snarled, getting right in the guy's face, "I can beat you so senseless, you'll be easy pickings for Gregory when he finds you. Or you can tell me what I want to know and I'll walk away *before* breaking your legs. Your choice."

"All right!" the Kraven sputtered, rage darkening his face to a deep crimson. "Release me, and I'll tell you!"

Relaxing his grip, Kellan allowed Westmore to slide down the wall until his feet touched the floor, then lowered his hand and took a step back, the savage look on his face warning the Kraven that he'd better not dick around with him.

"She's in the library," Westmore said, rubbing at his reddened throat. "It's in the north arm of the compound."

"Take me there."

The Kraven's eyes went wide. "With Gregory out there? You must be—"

"Take me to her," Kellan growled, his chest heaving as he fisted his hands at his sides, "and I'll let you walk away. But no way in hell are you getting away from me before I've got her."

"Fine," Westmore snarled, grabbing the leather bag he'd dropped on the floor and hooking it over his shoulder. "I should've killed you when I had the chance," he grumbled under his breath, heading out into the hallway. Kellan stayed right on the Kraven's heels as they made their way to the north wing, finally stopping in front of a heavy wooden door.

"Give me the key," he demanded, after trying the handle and finding it locked.

Gunfire sounded from the floor above them as Westmore curled his lip, saying, "I don't have it."

Chloe suddenly shouted his name from inside the room, and Kellan turned his back on the Kraven, no longer even caring about the bastard, only dimly aware of Westmore running away as he pressed both hands to the door, his fingers clenching against the dark wood. "Chloe!" he called out. "I need you to move away from the door, honey. I'm coming in."

"Got it!" she shouted. "I'm getting out of the way!"

Moving to the other side of the hallway, Kellan charged the door shoulder first, slamming his weight against it. The wood splintered with a loud crack, groaning in protest, and his next try broke it open. With his heart pounding, Kellan rushed into the room, searching for Chloe, and then she was there, throwing herself into his arms, his heart damn near bursting its way out of his chest.

"Kellan!" she cried, trying to hug and kiss and inspect him all at the same time. "Oh, God, I was so scared. Are you hurt? Oh, crap. Your shoulder!"

"It's nothing," he growled, running his hands down her arms and sides, trying to touch every part of her that he could. "But what about you? Are you hurt anywhere?"

"No. No. I'm okay."

"Thank God," he groaned, pushing her hair away from her face, unable to believe he'd found her and she was unharmed. "You scared the hell out of me, lady."

"Where's Raine? Is she all right?"

"I ran into one of my friends," he told her. "She's with him."

"Will your friends be able to help us get out of here?"

Wishing he had better news, Kellan shook his head. "With all the explosions that have ripped this place apart, I don't even know if they'll be able to reach us, and we don't have the time to wait for them." Taking hold of her hand, he started toward the door, saying, "We've got to make it out on our own."

"Kellan, wait! We can't go yet."

He looked back over his shoulder. "What's wrong?"

"There's an old safe on that table over there," she told him, pulling him toward the back of the room, the safe illuminated by a thick, flickering candle that sat beside it. "I think the archives are locked inside."

Shock roughened his voice. "You mean the ancient archives?"

"That's exactly what I mean."

The archives, which had been created by the original Consortium, had been lost during the years of war that followed the formation of the Collective Army, not long after the Casus had been imprisoned. For centuries, the new Consortium had searched for the ancient documents that were believed to contain valuable information about the clans, but last fall, Kellan's Watchmen unit had learned from Seth that the Collective had already found the archives. In fact, they believed it was Westmore's desire to have access to the ancient documents that had been the main motivation behind his partnership with the Collective.

"As much as I'm sure the others would love to get

their hands on them," he said quickly, casting another glance toward the safe, "we'll have to come back for them. I need to get you out of here."

He could tell from her expression that she didn't agree. "But the Casus might come for them before we make it back, and we can't let that happen."

Struggling for patience, he said, "Chloe, they've already read them."

"But we haven't," she argued, pulling her hand from his as she started pacing in front of him. "I...I don't know how to explain it," she said in a low voice, looking toward the safe, "but I can feel something in there, Kell." She shivered and brought her gaze back to his. "It's like there's something in there that's calling to me. We need to try to break it open."

He quietly cursed. "Look. Whatever's in there, it's not worth risking your life over."

She shook her head, wetting her lips. "If it's going to give us answers about the Casus, then you're wrong."

Bracing his hands on his hips, Kellan worked his jaw, a thick sound of frustration rumbling in the back of his throat. "I don't like this, Chloe."

"You sound a little spooked," she murmured, staring at the safe again. "And I don't blame you, Kell. To be honest, I'm a little spooked myself."

"Anything ever happen like this before?"

"No, but the Merrick—" her voice got a little huskier "—it, uh, only just got fully charged yesterday, so maybe that's had some kind of effect on me." Looking back at him, she said, "Can we at least try? I know we don't have a lot of time, but I can't shake this feeling that we're meant to have what's in there. And Raine told me that you're supposed to be some kind of genius when it comes to things like this."

Choking back his growl, Kellan moved closer to the antique cast-iron safe, the above-average height of the table making it easier for him to get a good look at what he was dealing with without having to crouch down.

Moving beside him, she asked, "Can you open it?"

"Have you found anything I could use to get in here?" he asked, pointing to the small keyhole situated in the middle of the safe's door.

"Here," she said, reaching into her shirt pocket and handing him three paper clips. "I found these when I searched the room, along with some matches and the candle."

"Perfect." Setting one of the clips on the table, Kellan straightened out the other two, then leaned close and inserted their tips into the keyhole.

"How do you know how to do that?" she whispered, watching him maneuver the metal as he carefully manipulated the inner mechanisms of the lock.

"What can I say? I'm just naturally good with my hands," he replied in a lazy drawl.

She snuffled a soft laugh under her breath, and he hid his grin. A few minutes later, a loud snick echoed from the lock, and the front of the safe cracked open. "Nice work," she told him, and he could hear the quiver of excitement in her quiet words.

"Okay, let's see what we've got." Reaching inside, Kellan pulled out what appeared to be a thick stack of papers wrapped in some kind of ancient oilcloth.

"Huh. To be honest," she murmured, watching as he set the bundle on the table, "I was expecting something a little bigger."

Pulling his hand down his face, he let out a husky laugh that had her questioning him with a look. "I'm sorry. It's just that I'm really happy I've never heard those particular words on a woman's lips before. Especially when I'm the only man in the room with her."

Chloe rolled her eyes. "Haha. You're so funny."

"Come on," Kellan drawled, sliding her a lopsided smile. "You threw that one right in my lap."

The corner of her mouth twitched, but her grin faded as she turned her attention back to what he sure as hell hoped were the true archives, considering the time they'd wasted to get them. "Do you mind if we open them up quickly?" she asked. "I know it sounds crazy, but I want to see if there's a journal inside."

Knowing they'd already wasted too much time, Kellan choked back a curse, tempted to just toss her over his shoulder and start running. "Can it wait until we're out of this place?"

At her beseeching look, he sighed and peeled back the oilcloth, rifling through the yellowed pages until he pulled out a thin leather volume with frayed edges. "This is the only one I could find."

She reached out, laying her hand on the small journal, then quickly nodded. "That's it. That's the one!"

"Great," he muttered, wondering what the hell was going on as he slipped the journal back inside the oilcloth. Casting a quick look around the library, Kellan grabbed a backpack that had been left in the corner and quickly slipped the archives inside, then hooked one of the straps over his shoulder. Jerking his chin toward the door, he said, "Now let's get the hell out of here."

"I know you must think I'm crazy, Kell, but thanks for doing this for me." She started to turn away from the table, then suddenly swayed, catching herself against the edge. "Whoa."

"You okay?"

"Yeah," she whispered, pressing her hand to her fore-head. "Sorry. I'm just…I got a little dizzy."

Dropping the backpack, Kellan moved closer and tipped up her chin, studying her eyes. They no longer glowed with the power of the Merrick, the gray darkening like a bank of storm clouds rolling in on the horizon. Damn it, he could see how weak she'd grown, the strength she'd gained from the feeding he'd given her already drained after everything she'd been through. The Merrick, starved for so long, was obviously going to need another feeding before it was at full strength— and Kellan needed her as strong as possible if they were going to make it out of there alive.

You know what you have to do, the wolf whispered, its guttural voice coaxing and soft. Running his tongue over his teeth, Kellan wanted to argue with the animal, but damn it, the bastard was right.

"What's wrong?" she asked unsteadily. "You look like you're about to tell me my dog just died."

Locking his jaw, Kellan told her to pick up the candle and grabbed her other hand, pulling her through a connecting doorway and into what looked like a private study, the candlelight flickering against the high, book-lined walls.

"I don't understand," she whispered, setting the candle on a gleaming mahogany desk that sat in the center of the room. "Why did we come in here?"

"Because I broke the door in the library," he explained in a raw, gritty rasp, shutting the door and twisting its lock, before turning to face her. She stared back at him, her gaze clouded with confusion, waiting for the rest of his explanation. "We're going to have to run for it, Chloe, and you can barely stand."

"I know." She ran her tongue over her lower lip as she leaned back against the desk. "I'm sorry. I'll—"

"Shh. Stop apologizing. It's not your fault. But…" Kellan swore under his breath, rubbing a hand over his eyes, and forced out the thick, rough-edged words. "Christ, I hate like hell to put you in this situation, but you need another feeding. A strong one."

She blinked, understanding dawning with a dark flush of color in her pale cheeks. "You mean…right now?"

With his gaze locked on hers, Kellan crossed the room to her. "I don't know what we're gonna run into out there, and with Gregory already here, we can't take any chances."

She wet her lips, her expression a mixture of so many emotions, he couldn't tell what she was thinking. Feeling like a total ass, since anticipation was searing through his veins, his cock already hard and aching, Kellan cupped her cheek, rubbing his thumb across that fever-glow burning beneath her fair skin. "Chloe, I'm sorry."

"Don't be," she whispered, taking a swift breath. And then she shocked the hell out of him by pressing her hands against his chest, going up on her tiptoes and touching her lips to his. "It's okay," she said against his mouth, her soft breath warm and sweet. "I'm ready, Kell."

Then she kissed him again….

CHAPTER ELEVEN

SHE WANTED HIM.

Gripping Chloe's upper arms with shaking hands, Kellan pushed her back until he could see her face. The warm glow of candlelight illuminated heavy-lidded eyes and moist, parted lips, her chest rising and falling with her shivering breaths. He'd seen the signs enough times to know what it meant—but it had never mattered to him like it did in that moment. Chloe *honestly* wanted him, and he was suddenly trembling harder than he'd been with his first woman.

Quietly, she asked, "Do you...do you want me to turn around?"

Knowing she was thinking of how he'd faced her toward the wall in her cell that first time he'd touched her, Kellan shook his head. "Not this time. I want to be able to watch your eyes."

She smiled, and the look of happiness shining in her gaze hit him like a punch to the gut. His beast wanted her, desperately, but this crazy thing between them was about so much more than lust. More than just her sexy little body and that seductive scent that made him want to eat her alive. He wanted to take her blood inside him and feel her spilling through his system, claiming ownership over every part of him, making him hers—and his beast wanted the same. Already, the animal's fangs were heavy in his mouth, but he struggled to pull them back, not wanting to frighten her. Of course, he'd forgotten the fact that this woman didn't scare easily.

Staring at the sharp points visible beneath his upper lip, she grinned, not an ounce of fear in her voice as she said, "Your fangs are bigger than mine."

He let out a surprised bark of laughter. "Just give me a sec, and I'll be able to pull them back in."

"You don't have to."

His gaze, which had drifted to the provocative hollow of her throat, shot back up, and her grin bled into another dazzling smile as she studied the look on his face. "It's okay, Kellan. I'm not afraid of your fangs. You can do whatever you want to me." Her fingertips touched the feverish heat in his brow, her touch tender as she brushed back his hair. "I have a feeling I'm going to like it all."

"Damn it, don't do that, Chloe." A muscle pulsed in his hard jaw. "You don't want to tempt the beast out of its cage."

Her eyes sparkled. "Sure I do. I love animals."

"Oh, God," he groaned, his hands settling onto her slim hips as he leaned over her, resting his forehead against hers. For a moment, Kellan wondered if she was trying to off him with a heart attack, his pulse rushing so hard and fast, he couldn't think straight over the loud, thrashing noise. Taking a deep breath, he ran his tongue over his lower lip, struggling to remember the things he needed to tell her. "I…I won't hurt you."

Softly, she said, "I know that, Kell."

"And I, uh, don't have any rubbers." The low, hoarse rasp settled heavily into the space between their bodies, and he braced himself for her withdrawal.

But it never came.

Instead, she sounded like she was choking back a laugh. "Gee, Kell. I'm really shocked you aren't better prepared. I mean, why on earth didn't you just pop down to the local drugstore last night and grab us a box of condoms?"

The light, teasing tone was so unexpected, it jerked another gritty sound from his chest, and he drew back his head to look down at her. "I can't carry any diseases, just so you know. But I still…I've always used a condom, in the past."

Her head tilted a little to the side, her eyes dark with emotion, while her provocative scent rose with the heat of her body. "Me, too. But you should know that I'm not on the Pill or anything."

"I'll pull out." Kellan forced the guttural words past his clenched teeth, struggling to control that primal part of him that wanted *at* her. That craved spilling his hot seed deep within her body, getting her with child. A head-spinning, completely *WTF* kind of thought right there—but one he couldn't deny. If his future were his, Kellan had no doubt he'd be doing everything he could to bind this woman to him in every possible way, intertwining their lives until they couldn't be torn apart.

"Not to sound bossy," she whispered, "but you need to get a move on with this thing, because I'm about two seconds away from attacking you."

With another husky rumble of laughter, Kellan lifted her onto the sturdy desk, the height perfect for what he had in mind. His heart was beating like a friggin' jackhammer as he reached for the gun tucked into his waistband and set it on the desk, his hands shaking even harder as he went to work on the buttons of her shirt, the once-white fabric now streaked with blood and soot.

They probably looked as though they'd only just survived some kind of natural disaster, but he still thought she was the most beautiful thing he'd ever set eyes on.

"I didn't want it to be this way for you...for our first time." His tone was almost regretful as he pulled down the cups of her bra and swept his thumbs over her swollen nipples, before helping her work her panties over her hips, then pulling them off her legs and letting them drop to the floor. Pressing between her sleek thighs, he ground his jaw as she settled her palms against his chest, her fingers exploring the cut of muscle beneath his sweat-slick skin, and he told her to lean back and lift her heels onto the edge of the desk. She followed his ragged command, spreading and lifting her legs as she settled back onto her elbows, the explicit pose blatantly erotic, and as Kellan stared down at her dark curls and the deliciously pink flesh that was already gleaming with her juices, the pain in his cock doubled...and he knew that he'd never been so hard in his entire life.

Her hungry, clouded gaze followed the movement of his hands as he reached for the button on his jeans, working the zipper down, his cock surging from the strangling confines of denim as he shoved the jeans low on his hips. His pulse roared in his ears as he gripped the heavy, ruddy shaft in a tight fist, the color darkening as he squeezed. With a low groan on his lips, he ran the taut, swollen head through her folds, then pressed against that tender entrance, working his way inside, the feel of her hot, slippery juices soaking his naked dick damn near stopping his heart. He tightened his muscles, needing to thrust hard and deep—the wolf in him clawing at his insides, demanding it—but she stiffened beneath him with a sharp gasp, and he cursed under his breath.

"Damn it, this is too dangerous. You have no idea how close the wolf is to taking over."

"I probably have a better idea than you think," she murmured, staring up at him through the thick veil of her lashes. "I can see it glowing in your eyes. Hear it in your voice. And it doesn't bother me, Kell."

His muscles quivered, his body covered in blood and ash and sweat. He had no doubt he looked crazed...wild, his hunger for her predatory and raw, unlike anything he'd ever known, pushing him to a place he didn't trust. "Damn it, Chloe." He shook his head, fighting to get the words out. "I know you need to feed, but you don't know what the fuck you're getting into. I...I don't wanna be the thing that hurts you."

"Kellan, look at me." She waited until he'd locked his burning gaze with hers, then said, "I might not have your colorful past, but I'm not an innocent. I'm a grown woman."

"Who's had one bloody lover," he snarled, trapped in a physical hell—too afraid to push deeper...and unable to drag himself away.

Narrowing her eyes, she said, "I'm not a child, Kellan. So stop freaking out. You're not going to scare me."

"Don't wanna hurt you, either." Rough, guttural words that had more of the animal in them than the man. Not that she seemed to care.

"Yeah, well, some good things are worth a little pain," she offered in a gentle voice, a grin playing at the corner of her mouth. He didn't know if the words were hers, or the Merrick's, the primal creature rising within her, burning in her luminous eyes, but that heart-melting grin was *all* Chloe, and it broke him, shattering his restraint.

"Can't...can't hold it," he gasped...shaking...his control slipping away....

With a soft, devastating look of trust glowing in her bright eyes, she lay back, pressing a soft palm against the hammering beat of his heart, and simply said, "Then don't."

In the next instant, Kellan threw back his head and roared, a guttural snarl ripping from the depths of his chest as he dug his fingers into her hips and slammed into her, shoving over half of his thick, vein-ridden shaft into the depths of her body. He cursed something dirty and raw, pulling back his hips, then drove himself even deeper, working more of his length into her, the pleasure so intense it bordered on pain.

"God, Chloe. The way you hold me... I swear it's never felt this good before," he groaned, and she flinched in reaction, not from any physical discomfort...but from his words, and he knew she was thinking about that bloody curse. "Damn it, don't do that."

"Do what?"

Bracing his elbows on either side of her head, Kellan leaned his face close to hers, pumping into her, thrusting with hard, heavy lunges, until he'd finally buried every inch of his cock inside her. Then he forced himself to hold deep and still, letting her get used to the heavy penetration as he told her, "This is real, Chloe. As real as it gets...and I've wanted it since I first laid eyes on your photograph." He lowered his head, pressing his lips to the corner of her eye, then the apple of her cheek, his damp hair brushing against her face. "And the more time I spend with you," he growled, pressing his hips tighter against hers, loving the way she caught her lower lip in her teeth, "the more I want it. Not because of some curse, but because you blow my fucking mind. You understand me?"

She nodded, her breaths coming faster, and he caught the way she flicked her gaze over the vein in the side of his throat, his blood pumping hard and strong. Pulling back his hips, he gave her a deep, grinding thrust, and rasped, "You see something you want, little one?"

As she licked her lips, her fangs flashed in the soft glow of the candle, and Kellan nearly came then and there. Curving his hands under her arms, he pulled her up with him, the pebbled tips of her breasts brushing the heavy slabs of his chest, and he angled his head to the side, offering her his throat. She groaned, exhaling a soft breath against his hot skin, and Kellan fisted one hand in the back of her hair, pressing her mouth tighter against him, while the other hand gripped her hip, bracing her as he lost the ability to keep it slow, his hips slamming against her. She flicked her tongue against his skin, then she sank her fangs deep, piercing the vein, and the second his blood hit her tongue, she started to come, those lush muscles convulsing around him, pulling him deeper and deeper. She drank greedily, a choked scream trapped in her throat, and just like before, that same fiery wind swarmed around them, the Merrick's power pulsing against his body, searing across the surface of his skin.

Losing control, Kellan pulled her away from his neck and pushed her down onto the desk, his own fangs dropping hard and fast, his claws slipping from the tips of his fingers. With a thick growl that sounded dangerously like "*Mine*," he sank his claws into the desktop, gouging the wood, pumping his cock into her harder…faster, the swollen shaft thickening even more, until he could barely move within the narrow, cushiony walls of her sex. "Damn it," he grunted, his voice rough…breathless. "You feel so good. I don't want it to end."

"Next time," she moaned, arching beneath him, her small hands fisted in his hair. "Next time you can stay in me all night."

"I'll hold you to that," he whispered against her cheek, and then he couldn't talk anymore, the pressure in his shaft too much to withstand. With his lungs locked in a vise, Kellan shoved into her once, twice, then wrenched himself free from the tight, liquid depths of her body. Retracting his claws, he grabbed his slick shaft, spurting across her hip, the thick, jaw-grinding pulses going on and on under the blistering heat of her gaze as she watched him fist his cock.

"Wow," she whispered unsteadily, when it was finally over.

"Sorry," he gasped, fighting for air as he braced his hands near her shoulders. "Christ, I didn't mean to drench you."

A soft smile touched her lips. "Don't apologize, Kell. I'd be lying if I said it wasn't criminally sexy."

"You think?" he asked, his chest vibrating with a gritty laugh.

"Oh yeah."

"Damn," he groaned, shaking his head as he leaned over to his right, pulling open the top drawer in the desk, hoping to find something he could clean her up with. "I've never come so hard in my life."

"I'll, um, take that as a compliment."

"It was definitely that," Kellan rumbled, finally finding a small pack of tissues. Wanting to kiss her, but not trusting himself to stop at just that, he quickly took care

of the mess he'd made and handed her back her panties, then buttoned up his jeans while she refastened the
front of her shirt. Casting a quick glance around the
book-lined study, he ran a trembling hand over his face.
"Hell," he groaned, "I'm never going to look at books
the same way again."

"Me either," she admitted with a shy smile.

"I think there's also a damn good chance I'm liable
to get hard every time I catch the scent of old paper."

She gave a delicate snort. "You'd do well to avoid
libraries, then."

"You're probably right," he drawled with a wry smile,
loving that they could be easy with each other after
something so raw and violent and terrifyingly good.
"And as much as I'd like to keep you in here with me
forever, we've got to get moving. How do you feel?"

She slid off the table and stretched, her voice a low,
seductive rumble of pleasure as she said, "Like I could
take on the entire Casus race."

"That's good." Kellan silently prayed it didn't come
to that. "Now let's get the hell out of here."

CHAPTER TWELVE

THE GUY HAD BLOWN her freaking mind.

A cheesy way to describe what had happened between them, but the best Chloe could come up with while her head was still reeling. She'd thought she had a good idea of what truly incredible sex would be like, but she hadn't had a clue. It was so much richer and deeper. Rougher and hotter and rawer than she'd ever imagined, the pleasure so intense it felt like something burning and bright searing its way through your body, melting you down from the inside out. She loved how Kellan had felt inside her. Loved his rough breath in her ear. Those gritty animal sounds that he made at the back of his throat, and the rich, intoxicating taste of his blood slipping across her tongue. *So hot. So good.*

She'd never felt so charged and full of life, but now that the feeding was over, it was clear to Chloe that the power thrumming through her system had come at a price. Barefoot, bare-chested and battered from his fights, Kellan Scott looked like the perfect example of sex-on-legs bad-boy style, but she could see that the poison inside his body was taking its toll. Deep grooves bracketed his beautiful mouth, while grim shadows darkened his eyes…a visceral pain etched into the rugged lines of his expression. Either the fighting or the sex had caused the poison's effect to become more severe, and she felt a sharp stab of guilt that she'd found so much pleasure in an act that might well have weakened him.

Taking her hand, he dragged her back into the library, a delicious ache still pulsing between her legs that would have made her smile, if she wasn't so worried about his health. As Kellan snatched up the backpack that held the archives, he told her they would be meeting up with his friends in the woods outside the compound, then pulled her with him into the hallway. They hadn't gone more than twenty yards when two Casus stepped around the corner, still in human form, but with their claws and fangs fully released.

"Chloe, get back!" Kellan roared, releasing his own claws as he blocked the attacking Casus. He took down one of the monsters, but a third Casus came at his back, and she felt a low growl vibrate in her throat, the primal power of the Merrick surging through her veins. Moving in what seemed like a strange, slow-motion kind of blur, Chloe wrenched one of the heavy iron sconces from the wall and hammered it into the Casus's skull, knocking it unconscious.

She was still holding the heavy iron sconce in one hand, standing over the monster's fallen body, when Kellan finished off the other one and turned back to her. She didn't know how he would react, but she wasn't expecting the slow, sexy smile that curved his mouth, his deep voice husky with pride as he said, "There's my girl. You're a first-class little badass now, aren't you, honey?"

She laughed, tossing the sconce aside, and they quickly took off down the hall again, passageways turning and twisting until she had no idea what direction they were heading, though Kellan seemed confident they were going the right way. After a few minutes, they entered a part of the compound that seemed even older than the rest, with weathered wooden beams running down the center of a narrow corridor, holding up what appeared to be a wattle-and-daub ceiling. The corridor shook from time to time as explosions continued to rock the fortress, though she and Kellan were too far away from the main part of the compound now to hear any gunfire. Eyeing the uneven ceiling and beams warily, Chloe wasn't paying much attention to the rooms they passed, until something strange caught her eye as they ran past an open set of double doors. "Wait," she called out, tugging on Kellan's hand. "I just saw something."

"Honey, we don't—" The gruff words trailed away when she tugged him in front of the doorway and he caught sight of the candlelit altar that climbed up the far side of the room. "What the hell?"

"What do you think it is?" she whispered, her skin crawling as she looked over the strange structure that appeared to be made of some kind of dark metal, intricate designs etched into every inch of its glittering surface.

"Those markings look similar to the ones on the Dark Markers," he said in a low voice.

Chills swept over the back of her neck. "That's creepy."

His gaze fell on the bowl that sat on the floor at the base of the altar amid a cluster of thick candles, what appeared to be bloody entrails hanging over the bowl's wide rim. "Looks like they've been making blood sacrifices. I guess Gideon wasn't lying when he told Kier that the Markers were mixed up in some evil shit."

"What do you mean?"

He quickly explained, telling her how the Watchmen

had recently learned, thanks to a vampire named Gideon Granger, that after the original Consortium had imprisoned the Casus within Meridian, the leaders, desperate for a way to destroy the immortal monsters, had actually gone into hell in order to find the materials they'd needed to fashion the powerful crosses. The Deschanel believed there was duality in all things—aspects of both good and bad, the light *and* the darkness—and they viewed the Markers as a perfect example of that conviction. Though it was an eerie concept, Chloe figured it made sense when you thought about it, considering the Dark Markers could protect life…as well as take it away.

"Kellan," she murmured, tightening her grip on his hand. "If the markings on the altar are the same as the ones on the crosses, then this altar must have something to do with the Casus. It might even be the way Westmore communicates with Calder in Meridian. Like some kind of paranormal telephone."

"Could be," he grunted, tension vibrating through the hard lines of his body. "Come on. I want you the hell away from that thing."

"Yeah. Me, too." Chloe let him pull her along as he started back down the corridor, and was still thinking about what he'd told her about the Markers, when Kellan's guttural curse made her jump, and the next thing she knew, he was tossing the backpack onto the floor and shoving her behind his back. His shoulders and arms bunched with rock-hard muscle as he released his claws once again, a low snarl rumbling in the back of his throat.

Wondering what kind of monsters they'd run into now, Chloe peeked around his broad shoulder, a sliver of fear slipping down her spine as she spotted a man and woman standing at the far end of the narrow passageway. The man was tall, with thick, sun-streaked brown hair and the ice-blue eyes of the Casus—but it was the woman who caught her attention. She was petite, barely reaching the Casus's shoulder, with masses of curly golden hair that reached all the way to her hips, the thick locks tangled and wild around a face so thin, she looked as if she were nothing but skin and bones. At one time, the woman had likely been beautiful, but now she was nothing more than a shell, her expression void of emotion, as if she felt nothing at all.

"I'm sorry to interrupt your little escape," the Casus drawled, "but you have something that belongs to me, Watchman."

Realizing that this was *Gregory*, Chloe pressed closer to Kellan's back, fear twisting her stomach into a painful knot.

"That's where you're wrong," Kellan growled. "The Merrick is *mine*."

Prowling a step closer, the Casus lifted his brows. "You're just a pup. You really think you'd stand a chance against me?"

"I'm ready to die trying."

Gregory lifted his nose and sniffed the air, then slid Kellan a hard, knowing smile. "I can smell the poison in you, Lycan. You're already as good as dead."

"Then what do you have to fear?" Kellan snarled, his deep voice raw with fury as he started toward the Casus.

"Take care of the canine problem," Gregory murmured to the blonde. "As much as I'd enjoy teaching him a lesson, I just don't have the time."

The woman lifted one of her hands, her fingers up, her palm pointing right at Kellan, and his powerful body suddenly slammed to a stop, then flew face-first against the wall, his muscular arms pinned at his sides. "What the fuck is this?" he roared, the tendons in his neck straining, while the muscles in his arms and back quivered beneath his dark skin. He was obviously trying to move—but be couldn't. It was as if he'd been locked in place, and Chloe's fear tripled, nearly doubling her over.

"Chloe, can you move?" Kellan shouted, while the Casus's ice-blue gaze raked over her body, and she shuddered, wishing she had on more than underwear and a shirt. "Chloe, damn it, answer me!"

"Yes," she whispered, trying to choke down her stupid fear so that she could think of something to do. She couldn't just stand there like an idiot, waiting for Gregory to kill them.

Kellan's voice shook with rage. "Then get the hell out of here!"

"I'm not leaving you," she told him, and the Casus slid her a slow, provocative smile. Kellan was roaring for her to run, but she stood her ground, refusing to leave him, her complete attention focused on Gregory.

She couldn't believe *this* man was the reason she'd been taken. If the look in his eyes hadn't been so evil, he would have been gorgeous, like one of those models in the Armani ads that they put in all the fashion magazines. Not as good-looking or as well-built as Kellan, but not the kind of guy you'd expect to be a ruthless, cold-blooded monster, either—and it was easy to understand how these bastards had been able to lure their human victims into trusting them. When they were hidden inside human hosts who looked likc this one did, it no doubt made it easy for them to prey on the unsuspecting.

He started toward them, jolting Chloe into action, and she quickly grabbed the gun that Kellan had tucked into the back of his jeans. She had no idea how many bullets were left, but she planned on making every single one of them count as she pointed the weapon at Gregory, taking a single step forward.

"Stop her," the Casus told the witch, slowing his steps.

The blonde raised her skeletal hand again, but nothing happened. Chloe took another step forward, ignoring Kellan's curses as she moved past the next support beam that held up the ceiling, an idea suddenly coming to her.

"Why is she still moving?" Gregory snarled over his shoulder.

The woman lowered her hand, her brow furrowed as she said, "She's a witch."

"One without any power!" He flung the words at the woman, his face turning red with fury, and yet, the blonde's expression never changed.

Studying Chloe with her pale, emotionless eyes, she simply said, "No. That's not true."

Still straining against his invisible bonds, Kellan growled, "So she's the reason you've been able to survive the Wasteland, isn't she, Gregory?"

With an arrogant roll of his shoulders, Gregory seemed to throw off his anger, sliding Kellan a sharp smile. "She's amazing, isn't she? My own little one-woman army."

"Are you blackmailing her?"

The Casus gave a low, rusty laugh, pressing one hand to the center of his chest. "Is it so hard to believe she might actually champion my cause?"

"Whatever he's promised you," Chloe said, cutting a quick glance toward the blonde, "it's a lie. You can't trust him."

Gregory casually crossed his arms over his chest, a smile still curving his mouth as Chloe came a little closer, her two-handed grip on the gun surprisingly steady, considering her palms were damp and her heart was beating like a bitch.

"You can shoot me," he offered in a smooth drawl, sounding as if he was actually enjoying himself, "but she'll only heal me again."

"Move back!" Chloe snapped, jerking her chin toward the end of the hallway. "I'll go with you, but we're leaving Kellan here."

Eyeing her with a speculative, hungry gaze, the Casus followed her command, taking a single step back.

"Another one," she ordered, praying her plan would work, her inspiration born from the events that had taken place about an hour ago. She moved past a second support beam, hoping she'd put enough distance between herself and Kellan. Another five steps brought her to the next beam, the Casus standing not fifteen feet away. Taking a deep breath, she searched within her body for any new, unfamiliar spark of power, curious after the witch's words—but there was only the Merrick, and so Chloe relaxed the hold she'd had on the primal creature, unleashing its visceral fury as she turned and buried the gun's remaining bullets into the beam. The wood cracked, and she turned the gun in her hands, using everything she had to slam the butt against the groaning support. It started to bow, only seconds away from giving out, and Chloe quickly turned, running back toward Kellan as fast as she could, while Gregory roared with outrage, his heavy footsteps pounding against the floor as he came after her.

"It's coming down!" the blonde screamed, and Chloe looked back over her shoulder just in time to see the woman grabbing hold of Gregory's arm, then yanking him back with surprising strength. They hit the dusty floor, and before DeKreznick could regain his feet, the beam snapped and a portion of the ceiling caved in, crashing into the passageway in a mass of rubble and dust. Though she didn't remember falling, Chloe found herself sitting on her bottom in the middle of the corridor, and she pushed her hair out of her eyes just as Kellan broke away from the wall, the witch's spell obviously broken.

"I don't even want to know what the hell you were thinking," he growled, yanking her back on her feet.

Coughing, she said, "I was thinking I was saving your ass."

He grunted, then snatched up the backpack and grasped her upper arm, pulling her back the way they'd come, the air still thick with dust, making it difficult to breathe. "We have to hurry," he muttered. "That's not gonna hold him for long."

"How do you feel about climbing out through a window?"

Looking down at her, he snapped. "Where?"

Chloe jerked her head in the direction they'd just come. "That last room we passed."

Without a word, Kellan turned back, and within minutes they'd stacked the room's furniture into a makeshift platform that allowed them to crawl out one of the high windows that lined the far wall. It was about a ten-foot drop to the ground on the other side, but Kellan braced himself in the open window, lowering Chloe as far as he could, before dropping her into a bank of snow. Without shoes and proper clothing, she was freezing, the shocking blast of cold that tore into her lungs making her cry out, but Kellan lifted her into his arms as soon as he'd dropped onto the ground beside her, his landing one of perfect animal grace that she would have been tempted to compliment, if she wasn't so miserably frozen.

Chloe had been unconscious when she arrived at the compound, so she hadn't yet seen what the Wasteland looked like. Glancing around as Kellan carried her toward the place in the woods he said his friends would be waiting, she couldn't help thinking that the strange, moonlit region was seriously messed up. Trees, which should have been barren, were still heavy with leaves, swaying in the icy breeze. The moon shone so brightly, it reminded her of a lavender twilight, the shimmering beams of light glinting against the snow-frosted ground.

"Does the s-sun ever shine h-here?" she stammered, her teeth chattering so violently she could barely talk.

"Not much, even in the summertime," he rumbled huskily, the chilly wind whipping at the auburn strands of his hair. "The spells that trap the exiled Deschanel inside also dim the sunlight."

"But how can everything still g-grow? There are trees everywhere."

"You're applying the natural laws of science to this place, but it doesn't work that way. There's so much magic at work here, you never really know what you're going to run into."

"I wish they could have d-done something about the wind."

Holding her tighter against his chest, his earlier anger seemed to soften as he murmured, "Just a few more minutes and I'll be able to get you warm, honey. I can scent Seth close by, and he'll have some clothes for us."

"Who's Seth?"

"The guy who took Raine out of the compound for me. She got banged up pretty badly in that blast and lost consciousness."

As if impervious to the brutal climate, Kellan's body radiated heat as he carried her into the thick forest, and sure enough, within minutes they came across Seth and Raine. The blond-haired, green-eyed male had wrapped a thick blanket around the unconscious psychic, her small body curled on top of another blanket that'd been laid over the ground. A butterfly bandage had already been placed over a gash in her temple, a thick sweater draped over her left arm and torso, while Seth knelt at her side, wrapping some kind of gauze around her injured right arm, an open first aid kit lying beside him. As Kellan called out a greeting, the good-looking blond pulled a flare gun from a nearby pack, then fired it into the air.

"What was that for?" Kellan asked.

"To let the others know I've got you," Seth explained, flicking a quick look over Chloe, before lifting his hard gaze back to Kellan. "Now we can get started back right away, without having to wait for them."

Lowering Chloe down to the edge of the blanket, so that her feet didn't touch the cold ground, Kellan wrapped his arms around her from behind, sharing his body heat as he asked, "Where's my brother?"

"He and Morgan were just here," the human replied, returning his attention to his task, the creases of strain at the corners of his dark green eyes evidence that he was trying to be as careful as possible, "but once they saw the two of you dropping out of that window, and knew you were okay, they took off to follow Westmore's trail."

"Who else came with you?"

"Aiden, Quinn and Garrick, as well as Noah and Jamison, but they'll head back to the base camp now that they've seen the flare."

"What about the Buchanans?"

Seth shook his head. "Saige stayed behind to work on the maps, and Molly and Hope have been helping her, so Ian and Riley are watching over them. Plus, they're also looking out for Olivia and Jamie, since Ade wouldn't trust any outside security with the job, and no way in hell was he bringing those two into the Wasteland."

Finishing with Raine's arm, Seth moved to his feet, and Chloe was surprised to see that he was nearly as tall as Kellan. Seth slid his curious gaze over her face, and Kellan said, "Chloe Harcourt, meet Seth McConnell, former Collective badass."

She stiffened with shock as Seth reached out and shook her hand, his mouth curved with a wry smile as he noted her wide eyes. "Don't worry, Chloe. I'm a badass for your side now."

"So you, uh, saw the light?"

With a gritty laugh, he drawled, "Something like that." Reaching down, he grabbed one of several packs that sat on the blanket and handed it to Kellan. "These are some things that Morgan put together for you. There are shoes and clothes for both of you, as well as some water, food, a knife and a gun with five rounds of ammo."

Taking the pack, Kellan replied, "Thanks, man. You're a lifesaver."

"Did you hit any trouble on your way out?" the soldier asked, while Kellan opened the pack and handed Chloe a pair of jeans and a sweater.

"We ran into Gregory right there at the end, along with some woman who's helping him." Looking at Chloe, he asked, "Do you have any idea what she was?"

Pulling on the jeans that he'd just given her, she said, "Some kind of witch, I think."

"Why couldn't she freeze you in place the way she did with me?"

"I'm not really sure." Chloe quickly pulled on the thick sweater, then sat down beside Raine's legs so that she could slip on a pair of heavy woolen socks that felt like heaven on her cold toes, followed by the sturdy hiking boots that Kellan found at the bottom of the pack. "But…"

"Yeah?" he prompted, when her voice trailed off into an uncomfortable silence.

Hoping he didn't make more out of it than he should, she shrugged, saying, "It's just that there are some witch clans whose power doesn't work when going up against a more powerful witch. But it wouldn't make any sense, in this case, because the Mallory curse binds any power I might have otherwise had."

His gaze locked on hers, dark and intense, smoldering with something that looked strangely like triumph. "It would make perfect sense, if the curse is finally coming to an end," he drawled in a soft rasp.

Knowing she needed to tell him he was crazy, Chloe took a deep breath, ready to launch into her argument, when Seth interrupted them, jerking his chin toward the backpack that Kellan had set on the ground while he dressed. "What's in the bag?" the soldier asked.

Kellan held her stare for a moment longer, warning her that the conversation wasn't over, then looked at Seth. "We found the archives," he told his friend, quickly slipping on a black jacket and reaching for the backpack, then slinging it back over his shoulder.

"Do you have the journal that was with them?" Seth grunted.

Kellan's eyes narrowed, his voice a little gruffer as he said, "How do you know about the journal?"

"After you disappeared, my men got their hands on a Collective officer back in the States. I flew back last week to talk to him. Took forever to get anything out of the guy, but he finally broke. Couldn't tell us anything about this compound, but he did tell us about a journal that Westmore had found with the archives. Evidently, it's how the Kraven found out about the maps that lead to the Markers."

Chloe sent the Lycan a smug look as she moved back to her feet. "I told you that journal was important."

He answered her look with a slow, bone-melting grin that did wonders for her core body temperature. "I guess you were right."

"I'm glad you found it," Seth said in a low voice, kneeling down to dress Raine in the sweater that'd been draped over her chest. Chloe knelt down on the psychic's other side to help him, both of them trying not to jar her injured arm. "I was hoping we'd come across the journal in the compound, but I hadn't even had a chance to tell everyone about it," he added. "The second Quinn, Garrick and I hit Kierland's camp, we set off for this place."

"Why didn't the three of you travel into the Wasteland with Aiden and the others?"

"We had to make a quick detour with the Grangers, so they came in ahead of us," the soldier replied, thanking Chloe for her help before packing up his supplies.

A few moments had passed before Kellan eventually said, "Uh, Seth, you know the Grangers are vampires, right?"

Seth's tone was dry. "Believe it or not, that *did* occur to me."

Scratching his chin, the Lycan asked, "And you're okay with that?"

As he moved back to his feet, the soldier slid Kellan a wry look. "I'm not up for an hour on the couch at the moment, but yeah, I'm okay with it. I won't say I'm completely comfortable with the situation, but the Grangers seem like good guys. It's too bad they missed the action here. We could have used them."

"Where are they now?"

Seth caught the edge of concern in Kellan's deep voice and snorted. "Christ, I didn't off them," he offered in a rough drawl, sliding the bag with the first aid kit onto his back. "They had something personal come up that they had to take care of, and when that's done, they're meant to be joining us back at the base camp. Which is where we need to be heading, the faster, the better."

"Is it safe there?" Chloe asked, helping Kellan to fold

up the blanket that had been spread over the ground after Seth had lifted Raine into his arms, the psychic's honey-colored hair spilling over his arm in a long, tangled fall.

As Seth settled Raine's slim body against his chest, his jaw grew tight, and Chloe couldn't help but notice that his expression looked somewhat…pained. "It's not Fort Knox," he finally said, answering her question about the base camp, "but it's safer than any other place we could reach today."

"Then the base camp it is." Kellan grabbed the last pack, took hold of Chloe's hand, and they set off together, the silence of the forest a blessed relief after the traumatic morning. Despite the fact that the Wasteland was a deadly place and their lives were still in danger, a sense of security settled into her system, and Chloe couldn't deny that she felt safe with Kellan there by her side. He'd fought for her, fed her with his body and his blood, his touch as possessive as the hot stares he kept sliding in her direction.

She just wished she knew if his hunger was real.

And if it was…how long would it last?

CHAPTER THIRTEEN

The Watchmen Base Camp, The Wasteland
Wednesday, 5:00 p.m.

IT TOOK A LONG-ASS time for the group of four to reach their destination, Kellan and Seth taking turns carrying Raine throughout the long hours of walking, but they finally made it to the base camp late in the afternoon. While they'd traveled, Seth had told Kellan and Chloe about the confrontation he'd had with the Death-Walkers on Monday night, explaining that the creatures were growing stronger from their feedings. He also told them about the humans the Death-Walkers had killed in the French village, as well as the ones they had infected with their bites, the gruesome news sending a shiver of unease down Kellan's spine.

Since Chloe had never heard of the Death-Walkers before, Kellan told her everything the Watchmen had learned about the vile creatures, even touching on their concern that for every Casus killed with a Dark Marker another Death-Walker was released from hell. When she asked if they needed to worry about a Death-Walker attack in the Wasteland, Seth had told her that the others didn't think the creatures would be so bold as to try again. Apparently, the Death-Walkers had been scared out of the region the week before, when they'd tried to

come after Kierland and Morgan. But just to be safe, the
soldier handed both Kellan and Chloe a flask of salted
holy water, saying that it was better to err on the side of
caution.

Kellan also asked how Seth, Garrick and Quinn had
managed to reach the base camp so quickly the day
before, considering it'd taken him days to travel through
the Wasteland when he'd been trying to reach Westmore's compound, and Seth had explained that there
was a Deschanel vampire named Juliana Sabin who was
helping Kierland and Morgan. Apparently, Juliana had
shared some important geographical shortcuts with the
Watchmen, and Ashe Granger had been able to pass that
information onto Seth and the others before heading off
with his brother, Gideon.

After the harrowing events of the morning, and such
a long, grueling day of travel, the poison was wearing
Kellan thin, but he fought to hide it from the others when
they finally reached the camp, doing his best to put on a
smiling face as he was reunited with Aiden and Quinn.
While most of the group was a bit singed from the ex-
plosives Westmore had set off, they'd been lucky and
managed to avoid any serious injuries—and although
Kierland and Morgan were evidently still chasing down
Westmore, Noah and Jamison had returned to the base
camp, but were running patrol on the camp's perimeter.
Kellan couldn't believe his friends had allowed Jamison
Haley to come with them, considering he was still learning to cope with his newly acquired Lycan traits, but
according to Aiden, there'd been no stopping the guy.

Seth took Raine, who was still unconscious, to the
tent that had been set up for his personal use, and Juliana Sabin, the dark-haired Deschanel whose family had

been exiled to the Wasteland, went to help him treat the psychic's injuries. After Kellan had introduced Chloe to everyone, the group all gathered around a roaring bonfire that didn't produce any smoke—thanks to a special powder Juliana had sprinkled over it—eager to hear how the two of them had managed to make it out of the compound.

"Did you run into Gregory?" Quinn asked, handing Chloe a steaming mug of coffee, while Kellan popped the top off the beer Aiden had just offered him.

Enjoying the cold burn of the brew as it slid down his dry throat, Kellan nodded, saying, "We came across him just before we made our way out, and he wasn't alone. Had some blonde with him."

Aiden slid him a sharp look of surprise. "A woman?"

"Yeah."

"Christ," the tiger-shifter grumbled, pulling a tattooed hand down his face. "He's got some psycho girlfriend now?"

Kellan took another swallow of his beer. "I'm not sure why she was there," he explained, wiping his mouth with the back of his wrist, "but she was definitely helping him."

"Was she Casus?" The question came from Seth's second-in-command, a brawny soldier named Garrick, who was sitting on the other side of the fire, between Aiden and Quinn.

Shaking his head, Kellan said, "We think she's probably a witch. She used some kind of power to lock me in place. Plastered me against the wall and I couldn't move my arms or my legs."

Aiden let out a rough curse, and Quinn murmured,

"So that must be how Gregory managed to cut his way through the compound. The witch was simply immobilizing anyone who got in their way."

"The thing is," Kellan added, pushing his hair back from his face, "I think this power of hers only works if she can see a person, because the instant the ceiling caved in, separating us, the spell was broken and I could move again."

"Why did the ceiling cave in?" Garrick asked, throwing another log on the fire.

Kellan slid a lopsided grin toward Chloe, his voice a deep, husky rasp that brought a flush to her cheeks despite the bitter chill of the wind. "Because the little Merrick here collapsed the ceiling's support beam and ended up saving my ass."

Aiden tipped his beer toward her, a sharp smile on his lips. "You Harcourt women may look gentle," he drawled, "but God help anyone who pisses you off."

Everyone shared a low rumble of laughter, the moonlight providing a silvery glow to the rustic setting, while the firelight cast golden shadows over the formidable group of warriors. As the laughter faded, Quinn ran a hand over his shadowed jaw, saying, "I wonder why the scouts working for Juliana didn't see this woman, or witch, when they spotted Gregory heading toward the compound."

"If she's powerful enough," Chloe murmured, sitting cross-legged on the ground beside Kellan, her coffee mug cupped in her palms, "she might have been able to camouflage her presence with a spell."

"Did the psychic know about her?" Garrick asked, sounding as exhausted as the rest of them.

Kellan shook his head again. "When he got closer

to the compound, Raine could sense that someone was traveling with Gregory, but she couldn't get a clear read on who it was." His voice roughened, his gaze piercing as he looked around the group. "We need to stay sharp, because there's a good chance the bastard will be coming after us."

Garrick looked confused. "But won't he go after Westmore?"

Finishing off the last of his beer, Kellan set his bottle on the ground beside his hip, then braced his arms on his bent knees. "Depends on who he decides he needs first," he grated.

Aiden's tawny brows drew into a scowl. "What the hell are you talking about?"

"What Kellan's trying to say," Chloe explained, her soft voice edged with strain, "is that Gregory DeKreznick is the Casus who caused my awakening."

A heavy silence settled over the group, and then Aiden cursed as he shoved his tattooed fingers back through his hair. "Shit, this is all we needed."

"I think there's a good chance that Westmore is going to be coming after us, as well," Kellan added. "He isn't going to be happy about losing Raine and Chloe." Struggling to get a grip on his anger, he explained how the Kraven leader had planned to send Chloe into Meridian, which pulled another round of creative curses from the group, some of them phrases that Chloe had probably never even heard before.

"But won't Raine be able to tell us if Westmore's following Chloe?" The question came from Seth, who'd just made his way over from his tent, his grim expression evidence of the fact that Raine's condition hadn't improved. The soldier stood on the outside of the circle, one broad shoulder propped against a thick-trunked pine, his long arms crossed over his chest.

In response to Seth's question, Kellan explained that Raine's powers didn't work on Westmore, and Quinn asked, "What other blind spots does she have?"

"From what I understand," Kellan told them, "it's hard for her to see the ones she's closest to, like her family."

"Damn," Garrick grunted. "That's got to be frustrating."

"Can she see the ones who attacked her?" Seth asked, the guttural words brimming with violence.

Sliding the soldier a questioning look, Kellan gave a slow nod, but before Seth could say anything more, Aiden muttered, "So even if ol' Gregory *does* go after Westmore first, he'll be coming after Chloe next. Like Kellan said, we need to stay sharp and be ready for whatever he might have planned."

"We will be," more than one of them said in response.

"The Wasteland is a treacherous place, even for those who know their way around," Juliana Sabin murmured, suddenly joining the group and taking a place by the fire. Turning her gray gaze on Kellan, she asked, "How did you manage to reach Westmore's compound without encountering any trouble?"

Wincing, Kellan scraped a palm over his whiskered jaw. "It wasn't exactly easy," he admitted. "When I ran into some vamps from the Reyker nest, I—"

"You crossed the Reykers' land?" Juliana gasped, her gray eyes wide with surprise. "But…how did you manage to survive?"

"I, uh, made a deal with them," he offered in a low

voice, wondering just how much the female Deschanel knew about the Reykers...and wishing he'd kept his effing mouth shut.

"What kind of deal?" Kierland's deep voice came from just behind him, and Kellan choked back a few choice words at the crappy timing, knowing damn well that he was about to get grilled.

Looking over his shoulder, he sent a hard grin up at his brother. "'Bout time you showed up."

Kierland slid a curious look toward Chloe, then arched one arrogant brow at Kellan. "You gonna introduce me or just sit there on your ass?"

"I missed you, too," Kellan muttered in a dry tone, getting to his feet, then reaching down for Chloe's hand and helping her up.

"Ignore him," Morgan murmured, jerking her head at Kierland. "He's just pissed because we lost Westmore, after chasing him all damn day." With a warm smile on her beautiful face, the female Watchman threw her arms around Kellan's neck, giving him a fierce hug as she wished him a belated happy birthday, then turned to Chloe and gave her a hug, too, chatting with her as if they'd been friends forever.

While the women talked, Kellan ground his jaw as he waited for his brother to lay into him, but instead, Kierland shocked the hell out of him when he said, "You got Chloe out, and from what I just heard on my way into camp, managed to find the archives, as well. You did good, Kell."

"Was that actually a compliment?" he croaked, and Morgan choked back a laugh at his shocked expression.

"It might not have been pretty," Kierland said,

slapping him on the shoulder in a masculine sign of *good job*, "but you accomplished what you set out to do."

Feeling as if he'd slipped into some kind of alternate reality, Kellan took a deep breath and struggled to process the fact that his brother actually looked…*proud* of him, but it was impossible. He remembered only too clearly the look on Kierland's face when the others had ratted him out every time Kellan had screwed up in the past. Not to mention his brother's reaction when he found out about the monumental cock-up in Washington.

Probably sensing that he didn't have a clue how to deal with Kierland's praise, Morgan slid Kellan an understanding smile, then grabbed hold of his brother's arm and made him take a seat by the fire. "Now, what was that you were saying before we interrupted?" she asked, sitting beside Kierland while Kellan and Chloe sat down again, as well.

Tossing beers to Kier and Morgan, and then a second one to Kellan, Aiden said, "Kell was getting ready to tell us what kind of deal he had to make with some nasty vamps while on his way to Westmore's compound."

Figuring it was best to offer up at least a measure of the truth, Kellan cleared his throat, then said, "The deal was pretty simple, really. In exchange for allowing me to cross their land, I had to let one of the Reykers feed from me while in *were* form. I guess it, uh, gives them a real power kick."

More muttered curses filled the air, and Juliana turned a worried look toward Kierland, saying, "The Reykers are relatively new to the Wasteland, but they're said to be even more vicious than the Carringtons. Not to mention extremely poisonous. If bitten, a poisoned

victim can't pass the strain on through their blood, but
they…"

"They what?" Kierland grunted, his deep voice thick
with concern. "What does one of their bites do to a
Lycan?"

"It just made me feel sick as hell," Kellan interjected,
before the Deschanel could finish her explanation. "But
that was all. It's wearing off more every day."

Juliana sent him an odd look, and he gave a furtive
shake of his head, silently warning her not to say anything more. She frowned, but didn't contradict him, and
Kellan quickly changed the subject, saying, "So Seth told
me about the Death-Walkers, but what else happened
while I was gone?"

While Quinn made another pot of coffee, Kierland
brought Kellan up to speed on the things that he'd
missed, ending with the story of how Noah had been
attacked a little over a week ago, in the village just south
of Harrow House. Since the human was still healing
from his injuries, they'd tried to talk him into remaining behind with the Buchanans, but like Jamison, he'd
refused. Of course, Kellan wasn't surprised they hadn't
been able to get Noah to stay in England, knowing the
human was worried as hell about his family. With the
way the Casus were pouring out of Meridian these days,
it was only a matter of time before someone in Noah's
family was used as a host, and he knew his friend was
determined to keep that from happening.

"If Noah was heading into the village to find a
woman," Kellan said, finishing off his second beer,
"then why didn't he just take Jamison with him? That
way they could have watched each other's backs."

"He tried," Quinn murmured, "telling the kid it would

be good for him, but Jamison wasn't interested. I think he's still not sure about…you know, the whole wolf thing when it comes to sex."

Jamison Haley was an academic colleague of Saige Buchanan, and the two of them had often worked on digs together in the past, since Saige was an anthropologist and Jamison an expert in archeology. When Saige had discovered the second Dark Marker in Brazil, she'd asked Jamison to take the powerful cross to Colorado for her, but Spark had captured him before he reached his destination. The assassin had handed Jamison over to Westmore, who'd allowed Gregory DeKreznick, who'd been working for the Kraven leader at the time, to torture him for information about Saige and the Watchmen. Jamison had refused to talk, and by the time the Watchmen had found him, he was nearly dead. Left with no other choice, Kierland had bitten the human, turning him into a Lycan in order to save his life.

"Has he made his first complete change yet?" Kellan asked, knowing Kierland had been working with Jamison, trying to teach him how to give himself over to the power of the wolf.

"Oh, yeah," Aiden answered with a grin. "You'll hardly recognize him. The change must've put an extra fifty pounds of pure muscle on him, not to mention a few inches in height."

Kellan said he couldn't wait to see it, and after they shared a quiet laugh, Kierland returned to his update. "With the help of the Watchmen units we've been loaning the Markers out to," his brother went on to explain, "some of the newly awakened Merrick were able to take out a few more Casus."

"Doesn't that mean that more Death-Walkers are

going to come through?" Chloe asked, sounding more than a little worried.

"It does, but we can't let that stop us from taking down as many Casus as possible," Kierland explained. "We've got to think about this war in two stages. The first stage is to wipe out the Casus. Then, when that's accomplished, we'll find a way to deal with the Death-Walkers."

"Among other things," Kellan muttered. "Seth told me about the villagers in France. I've got a bad feeling this thing with the infected humans could get out of control before we've even gotten a handle on it."

"Maybe there'll be something in the archives that can help us figure it out," Quinn offered, looking at Kellan and Chloe. "We owe you both a hell of a thank-you for getting your hands on them."

"Does this mean we have to actually be nice to the kid now?" Aiden grumbled, causing everyone but Chloe and Morgan to laugh. Flashing Kellan a cocky smile, the shifter said, "Who would have ever thought the fuckup would finally get something right?"

Kellan was ready to tell Aiden to lay off, not in the mood for his ribbing, when Chloe took the situation into her own hands. "You have no right to talk about him that way," she snapped, her voice cracking with anger, and everyone stopped laughing, their expressions ranging from surprise to curiosity to approval. "You have no idea what Kellan went through in that place, or what he endured to keep me and Raine from being harmed. If anything, you should be praising him, instead of sitting there acting like a complete and utter ass!"

"You're right," Aiden murmured, looking both chastened and impressed, the corner of his mouth twisted with a wry little grin. "I apologize. I just like to give the kid a hard time."

"In case it's escaped your notice, he's not a kid. And if you don't want me telling my sister what a jerk you're being, I suggest you find another way to entertain yourself."

Aiden's amber-colored eyes went wide. "You'd rat me out to Liv?"

Chloe lifted her chin, looking like a determined little Amazon. "In a heartbeat."

With his grin melting into a slow smile, and his deep voice thick with admiration, Aiden said, "Then I guess I'd better watch what I say."

"You do that," she muttered under her breath, the low words immediately followed by a sharp gasp as she noticed that everyone was staring at her. She blushed and jumped to her feet, but Kellan stood up and grabbed hold of her hand before she could rush off. No way in hell was he letting her get away from him. His emotions were still too on edge to talk to her about what had just happened, his heart beating like a friggin' jackhammer, but he was content just to walk beside her, holding her small hand in his.

As he led her away from the bonfire, leaving the others staring after them, she asked, "Where are we going?"

"When we got here, I asked Quinn if he could arrange to have a bath heated for you," he replied in a low rasp. "Thought you might enjoy it."

Chloe thought a bath sounded wonderful, so long as she could have some privacy. "Where? I don't even have a tent, much less a bathtub."

"The others have been using the cabin for meetings,

but it's ours for the night, until we all clear out in the morning." There was a smile in his voice as he added, "So it's bath time for you, little one."

"But won't the others be annoyed?" she asked, eating him up from the corner of her eye as they headed toward the cabin, loving the way the moonlight played over the thick, windblown strands of his hair and his rugged profile. "We haven't even told them about what I read in the journal." Every time they'd stopped to take a short rest during their journey to the camp, Chloe had pulled out the small leather journal and read from its yellowed pages.

"If they've waited this long," Kellan told her, opening the door to the cabin and pulling her inside, "they can wait a little longer. You deserve some downtime."

Her gaze settled on the copper tub placed before the roaring hearth, steam billowing from the hot water in a warm, sensual cloud, and a rush of pleasure slipped through her veins. "Kell, that looks incredible. It makes me feel sleepy just staring at it."

"If you let me wash your back," he coaxed, stroking his thumb against her palm, the simple touch seeming somehow painfully intimate, "I can promise to make sure you stay awake."

Chloe snuffled a soft breath of laughter, and pulled her hand from his. "Thanks, but I can bathe myself."

With his own low laugh, he pushed his hands in his pockets, his beautiful eyes glittering with mischief. "You don't trust me?"

"Let's just say that I bet you can be fairly distracting," she murmured wryly. "And seeing as how I was locked in that cell for months, unable to ever get completely clean, I plan on taking this bath pretty seriously."

A slow smile touched his mouth, and he lifted his hands in a playful sign of surrender. "In that case, you've got an hour. Then it'll be time for dinner." She nodded, and Kellan started to head for the door, when she said his name. "Yeah?" he asked, looking back over his shoulder, thinking she was the most adorable, beautiful thing he'd ever seen, standing there in front of the steaming bath with shining eyes and a shy smile.

Quietly, she said, "In case I forgot to tell you earlier, I wanted to say thank you."

"For what?"

Her smile spread a little wider. "For everything."

The soft sound of her voice seared through his system, and Kellan had to force a graveled response from his tight throat. "An hour, Chloe. If you're not out by then—" he paused, lowering his gaze to the sweet, provocative curve of her lips "—I'm coming in after you."

"That tub's only a single," she teased as she tilted her head toward the bath.

"Not a problem." His smile turned downright wicked. "I'll let you be on top."

She was laughing as he closed the door behind him, the soft, sexy sound still playing through his mind as Kellan shoved his hands back in his pockets and walked away. The full moon burned down on him with a heat that rivaled that of the sun, calling to his wolf, and he knew he'd be even more aggressive than usual tonight... but it wasn't going to stop him. He'd do whatever it took to control the beast, because he had to. *Not* touching this woman simply wasn't an option.

No matter how insane this thing was that he'd started, he couldn't end it now.

Right or wrong, Kellan was seeing it through to the end.

CHAPTER FOURTEEN

Wednesday, 9:00 p.m.

IT HAD, WITHOUT DOUBT, been the longest day of Chloe's life. And yet, she wasn't ready to sleep, her head still buzzing with everything that had happened. She'd been surprised that Kellan hadn't bailed on her once they'd reached the safety of the base camp, assuming he'd want to put some distance between them—but he'd stayed right by her side throughout the evening, whispering in her ear whenever there was something he wanted to tell her, his body warm beside hers, his tempting scent filling her head.

After she'd bathed and they'd gathered around the fire again, Kierland and Quinn, who had looked over the archives before dinner, told the others that their previous assumptions that Westmore had learned about the Dark Markers from the ancient documents were, in fact, correct. According to the archives, the Dark Markers were not only the keys that opened the spellbound, heavily fortified gate to Meridian, they also formed a map that would lead to the hidden prison. That explained why Westmore was so eager to get his hands on them, since the Markers could be used to locate Meridian, open the doors and bring about the flood, freeing all the Casus at once. Unfortunately, the pages explaining how the crosses were meant to form the map and be used as keys had been removed. They knew those specific pages had been taken because a notation had been made in the front of the archives, along with a notation for the removal of another journal. They also suspected that the removed pages might have explained how to contact the Casus in Meridian, perhaps even giving instructions on how to bring the shades across the divide, which had prompted Kellan to tell them about the strange altar he and Chloe had found just before they'd run into Gregory.

Then Chloe had shared what she'd discovered in the pages of the journal that she and Kellan had found. Everyone had been shocked to learn that it was a Reavess witch named Alia Buchanan, descended from a dormant Merrick bloodline, who had created the maps in the early 1800s. According to the journal, Alia's father had been a Merrick scholar who had secretly headed the new Consortium's search for the ancient archives. And although he never found them, it seemed that he discovered something even more important: the place where the original Consortium had hidden the Dark Markers. Fearing the powerful crosses would be sought by the same men who had murdered her father, Alia and her husband, a shape-shifter named Rhys, had hidden them around the world. However, they'd also believed that a time would come when the Markers would be needed, and so Alia had created the encrypted maps, burying them with one of the Markers in Italy—which was exactly where Saige Buchanan had found them.

As she'd read, Chloe had felt the deep emotion written into every page of the small journal, and she couldn't help but wonder if that's what had drawn her to it. Had the mix of her awakening Merrick blood and the Mallory curse somehow turned her into an emotional beacon? Or did her strange connection to the journal have something to do with Kellan's belief that the Mallory curse could finally, after all these years, be coming to an end? If so, had her Mallory powers, previously bound by the curse, drawn her to it? Or was it simply because she was a Merrick, like Alia? Whatever the reason, Chloe had been fascinated by the breathtaking love that Alia had held for her husband, their story made more poignant by the fact that he'd never felt he was good enough for her... while Alia had always seen him as the most remarkable man she'd ever known.

After Chloe had finished telling the others what she'd learned, they'd discussed the idea that Alia Buchanan could have been the one responsible for gifting the Buchanans with the strange powers that had helped the siblings during their Merrick awakenings, as well as in their search for the Dark Markers.

"The way this has worked out for the Buchanans, it's almost as if this Alia woman actually planned it," Quinn had murmured. "I mean, look at Saige's gift. It not only helped her to find the maps, but it's enabled her to decode them."

"But how did she know Saige would be the one who found them?" Garrick had asked.

"Who knows?" the Watchman had replied. "All I can think is that she must have been one hell of a powerful witch."

Taking another drink of his beer, Aiden had scratched his chin and spoken up. "So Westmore learned how to contact the Casus...and how they could send a shade back to this world, as well as everything he knows about the Dark Markers, from the archives. But it was this journal that told him about the Markers being hidden around the world and the maps that lead to their locations?"

Chloe had nodded. "That's right. From what I've read in the journal so far, I don't know that Alia ever fully understood what the Markers could do. But after what happened to her father, she recognized the need for them to be kept out of the wrong hands."

They'd talked for a while longer, but eventually the group had headed off to bed, except for a few who had taken up guard duty, and Kellan had brought her back to the cabin, the others agreeing that they should have a night of comfort after what they'd been through. And now they were alone. Chloe fidgeted nervously, painfully aware that she was falling harder for the sexy Lycan with each moment she spent with him. With each passing increment of time. But there didn't seem to be anything she could do to stop it.

"Your friends are great," she murmured, watching him from the corner of her eye as she moved closer to the fire.

"They're a bunch of smart-asses," he drawled, raking his fingers through the dark strands of his hair. He'd obviously found somewhere to shave and bathe earlier, and someone had loaned him some more clean clothes, like her own borrowed sweater and jeans.

"They enjoy riling you." She turned fully toward him, wrapping her arms around her middle. "But it's also obvious that they love you."

Rubbing the back of his neck, he gave a little shake of his head. "I still can't believe Aiden apologized to you. He's not a guy who offers apologies often."

"I'm sorry if I embarrassed you," she told him,

wishing she could calm the frenzied rush of her pulse, "but he really pissed me off."

The Watchman gave a low, husky rumble of laughter that was almost as sexy as his smile. "You didn't embarrass me, honey. And it was priceless, seeing Ade's reaction. He's scared shitless you're gonna rat him out to Liv."

"I'm tempted," she murmured, managing a small grin before she asked, "Do you know why Juliana Sabin is here?"

He shook his head again. "I asked Kierland, but he said he didn't have any idea."

"She seems nice. What do you think she did to end up exiled in the Wasteland?"

Rolling his shoulder, he took a seat at the foot of the bed and started unlacing his boots. "She might not have done anything. Sometimes, if the wrong person gets pissed off, entire families can be condemned because of the actions of a single member."

Chloe frowned. "That's hardly fair."

"Fair or not, I've heard of it happening. Once her name was entered into the *Book of the Exiled*, then the spells that govern this place will hold her in whether she's guilty or innocent."

Shuddering, she asked, "Do you trust her?"

"From what Seth told me," he replied, toeing off his unlaced boots and removing his socks, "she helped save Morgan's life. Kierland trusts her, so that means I do, as well."

She angled her head a little to the side as she said, "Speaking of Seth, I still can't believe you didn't tell me that you're working with a former Collective officer."

"You were already skittish enough about Noah," he

rumbled, sliding her a sheepish grin. "I didn't see any point in freaking you out, when I knew there was nothing to worry about. Despite his former occupation, Seth's a good guy."

"We should offer to let Raine feed tomorrow, or do you think he'll give her the blood she needs?"

WATCHING THE WAY THE firelight glinted off the dark fall of her hair, Kellan wondered if she was talking to keep him from touching her. Or was she simply nervous? If she was, Kellan didn't blame her. Not when his wolf was prowling so close to his surface, the full moon setting the predatory beast even further on edge.

Scrubbing his palm against his freshly shaven jaw, he answered her question. "To be honest, I can't imagine Seth allowing any vamp to sink fangs into him. Hell, I'm still amazed that he's letting Raine stay in his tent and helping Juliana with her."

"Maybe he feels sorry for her," she said softly, and Kellan dug his fingers into the edge of the mattress, struggling for control, when all he really wanted was to launch himself across the room and take her to the floor. Hold her against his body, until he could soak her into his skin…breathe her into his lungs. Everything about her was just so damn soft and tender and sweet, and yet, she had a backbone of steel that only fueled his hunger. She'd fought for him that day, stood up for him in front of the others, and it'd softened his heart even more, while making other parts of his body impossibly harder.

Still, Kellan knew he should get out of there and find some other place to bed down for the night. Her color was high, the power of the Merrick all but thrumming through her. She didn't need another feeding; for the moment, she'd gotten what she needed from him. If he touched her now, it would be for no other reason than his own selfish desires. Just one more sin to add to so many.

For her sake, he should walk away.

But he couldn't.

Instead, he stared at the way the firelight shimmered against the burnished length of her hair, the dark strands falling over her shoulders, the sweater Morgan had loaned her lying softly against the delicate shape of her breasts, and knew he was about to do his worst. Knew he was going to fuck her harder, longer, than he'd ever taken any other lover. And he was going to savor every dark, devastating second of it.

"You like those jeans?" he asked, the gruff words damn near sticking in his throat.

"Well, yes," she replied, looking down at the jeans, before meeting his gaze once again, this time with a slight smile on her lips. "I mean, they're *clean*. Right now, that ranks alongside designer couture in my book."

"Then take them off."

She blinked, her face warming with color. "You want me to undress?"

"If I get my hands on them," he growled, "those clothes are gonna be ripped off you in about two seconds flat, Chloe. So lose the jeans."

A feverish glow burned in her cheeks and her eyes, but she reached for the hem of the sweater and pulled it over her head, letting it fall to the floor as she asked, "Are we going to have sex, then?"

"I sure as hell hope so," Kellan groaned, rubbing a

hand over his mouth. "If not, there's a damn good chance you'll see a grown man cry."

"And here I've been worrying that you'd give me that speech again," she murmured, taking off her bra, her sweet little nipples already hard and thick. "You know, the one about how you're not good enough for me?"

"I'm *not* good enough for you," he admitted with a shrug, the easy gesture completely at odds with the visceral burn of hunger searing through his veins, his heart hammering to a hard, painful beat as she pulled her lower lip through her teeth…her fingers lingering on the top button of her jeans. "But I can't stay away from you. So I guess I'm going to shut up and appreciate my good fortune until you finally get smart and tell me to get lost."

"You don't care that you only want me because—"

"Don't say it," he snapped, his voice thick…rough. "I'm in a good mood, and that's only going to piss me off."

She seemed to be thinking over his warning for a moment, and then the corner of her mouth twitched in that adorable way that he loved. "So then what you're saying is that I should just shut up and appreciate my good fortune until you finally get smart and tell *me* to get lost?"

A slow, deep breath filled Kellan's chest, and he gave a slow shake of his head. "No. If I'm smart, Chloe, then I'll stick as close to you as possible, for as long as I've got."

"You make it sound like you don't have long." Her words no longer held their teasing edge, her delicate brows drawn into a troubled vee.

His mouth twisted with a wry smile, his hot gaze

glued to her perfect breasts as he said, "We're in the middle of a war, honey. Things are only going to get uglier from here on out."

"But you'll be careful, right?"

"I always am," he said a little too easily, and she scowled as she crossed her arms over her chest, covering what he figured was the closest view of heaven he was ever going to get.

"Damn it, I'm serious, Kellan." Rough, shaky words that held an unmistakable edge of fear. "Promise me that you'll be careful. That you won't do anything reckless."

"I promise that I won't do anything that's not absolutely necessary." She started to argue, but he cut her off, saying, "Didn't I mention you should lose the jeans?"

She took a few trembling breaths, obviously debating whether to keep arguing with him...or to get on with more enjoyable activities. He felt a sharp surge of relief when she finally reached for the button on her jeans again, then paused, sliding him a sultry look through her lashes. "What about you?"

"What about me?" he asked, watching the way she pulled her lower lip through her teeth again. For as long as he lived, Kellan knew he'd never forget what it'd felt like when she'd taken him into her mouth when they'd been at the compound. And now he couldn't wait to return the favor, needing her taste on his lips so badly he wanted to howl with the hunger.

"I'll take the jeans off when you take off yours," she told him, the enticing scent of her body mingling with the warmth of the fire, pushing his hunger into something that was even darker than he'd feared it would be. But he couldn't fight it.

Just need to take it slow. Need to stay in control for as long as possible.

Moving to his feet, Kellan repeated the mental commands as he ripped off his sweater, then reached into one of the back pockets on his jeans and pulled out a string of foil-wrapped condoms.

"I don't believe it." A soft burst of giggles spilled from her lips. "Where on earth did those come from?"

With a sharp smile, he tossed the rubbers onto the rug in front of the fire, not far from where she stood. "I stole them from Seth."

"You didn't!" She laughed, her shoulders shaking as she covered her mouth with her hand. "Don't you think he's going to miss them?"

"Nah. It's not like he needs them right now. And we do."

"Are you sure you got enough?" she snorted, glancing down at the long strip, before lifting her sparkling gaze back to his.

"Actually, this is only part of what I took," he confessed with a slow, sin-tipped grin. "I figured we could save the others for tomorrow."

She was still laughing and shaking her head when Kellan started undoing his fly, though her laughter faded into a sharp, breathless silence the instant she realized what he was doing. Locking his jaw, he shoved both boxers and jeans over his hips, pulling them off together before flinging them toward a nearby chair.

"Unbelievable," she whispered, staring right at the heavy length of his cock, the plum-shaped head already dark and slick with moisture....

"Unbelievable?" A rusty bark of laughter rumbled up from his chest, and he ran a hand over the back of his neck. "I think I'm almost afraid to ask what you mean by that."

"Sorry," she offered in a hoarse voice, her gaze moving up and down his body with greedy, provocative strokes that felt like physical touches, her chest rising and falling with the quickening rhythm of her breath. "It's, uh, just that this is the first time I've seen you completely naked and you're, uh…well, you're pretty breathtaking, Kell."

His face burned with heat, and he closed his eyes, fighting for control. It was crazy that such a simple declaration could have such an extreme effect on him, but damn, the ache in his dick doubled, and he covered his face with a hand.

"Are you blushing?" she asked, and he could hear the smile in her voice.

"Guys don't blush," he muttered, lowering his hand and sliding her a mock glare.

"You *are* blushing! Oh, God, that's too funny."

Completely charmed, Kellan found himself standing there with the unlikely combination of a massive hard-on and a goofy-assed grin, and in that moment, he finally realized just how dangerous this woman could be to his heart. Not to mention just how deeply it was going to cut when he lost her. But Christ, how could he not go sappy over her? She made him laugh. Put her trust in him. Stood up for him. For the first time in his life, he was going to bed down with a woman who saw him as something more than a good fuck, and it made a difference. One he'd never been able to comprehend until that moment.

"Come here," he rasped, finally allowing himself to

reach out and snag her hand, unable to wait a second more to feel her in his arms.

Need her under me, the wolf snarled, prowling the confines of his body, but he fought against its feral pull, terrified he'd scare her away before they even got going.

"Is your shoulder okay?" she asked, while he pulled her closer.

"Honey, of all the things hurting on my body right now—" rough, gritty words that made it sound like he'd gargled with gravel "—my shoulder is the least of my worries."

"I'm serious, Kell."

"Look," he told her, twisting his upper body to the side so that she could see for herself. "It's nearly healed."

Their gazes locked, something sharp and electric passing between them as she said, "Are you sure this won't make you feel bad?"

"What do you mean?"

She drew an unsteady breath. "I'm worried about how the poison's affecting you."

Brushing her hair back from her face, he said, "Don't worry about the poison, Chloe. I'm fine."

A shadow of suspicion darkened her gaze, making him feel like a total jackass. "Gregory said something about you—"

"God," he grunted, cutting her off as he settled his hands against the tender curve of her waist. "Don't give any credence to what Gregory said. He was just screwing with us."

"And why didn't you tell me that you'd let yourself get bitten as a part of a deal with the Reykers?"

"That was only because I don't like to even think

about it, much less talk about it. But I wasn't trying to keep it from you," he lied, pulling her tighter against his body as she shivered. "Cold?"

She nodded, wrapping her arms around his waist, her cheek pressed against the hammering beat of his heart, and Kellan lowered his head, touching his lips to the tender shell of her ear. "Then I guess I'd better get you warm." He was determined to give her something better to think about than Gregory and that bloody poison. Lifting her into his arms, he laid her on the rug that spread out over the floor, the heat of the fire washing over her delicate skin, painting her body with shimmering waves of warm, luminous gold.

"You're so bloody beautiful," he groaned, hungrily taking a tight, sweet nipple into the heat of his mouth, loving the way she dug her fingers into his hair as his hands ripped at the fastenings on her jeans. Within seconds, he had her stripped, his weight braced on his arms and knees as he caged her beneath his body, his breaths coming in a hard, ragged rhythm while he stared down at her, wanting to be everywhere at once. "God, Chloe. I'm gonna fuck you so hard tonight."

She shivered, her eyes growing heavy in response to his graveled words, while her cheeks burned with color, and Kellan lowered his head, hiding his smile against her breast, thinking she was the most adorable thing he'd ever known. Not to mention the sexiest.

"Why are you making me wait?" she gasped, her hands stroking his shoulders and chest. "Why...why not now? Damn it, you should already be inside me!"

"Because there's something I've gotta do first," he said in a dark, husky drawl, wedging his knees between her legs as he kissed his way down her body, loving the way she tasted…the intoxicating scent of her skin. "I want your knees spread as wide as they'll go," he growled against the soft, dark curls at the top of her mound, and she cried out as he slid his thumbs through the thick, drenched flesh between her thighs, opening her…spreading her, wanting it so badly he could feel the hunger pulsing in every cell of his body, his cock so full and thick he thought he might burst.

Unable to hold himself back a second more, Kellan pressed his open mouth against the soft, voluptuous heat of her sex, and in a stunning jolt of discovery, he realized she was even more addictive than he'd feared. He made a thick, raw sound in his throat, then went wild, licking and lapping at her silky flesh, his tongue lashing against the swollen heat of her clit as he pressed a thumb inside her, pumping it into that deliciously tight, plush sheath. Hot. Wet. Mouthwatering. She was the most exquisite thing Kellan had ever known, and he couldn't get enough of her, every swirl of his tongue across her moist flesh pulling a guttural snarl from his lips. She tasted like something that *belonged* to him, damn it. Something that was his to own, *to possess*, and as he pressed his face harder against her, his body burning with heat, shuddering with need, he knew his control was slipping away….

And there wasn't a bloody thing he could do to stop it.

CHLOE HAD ALWAYS WONDERED what oral sex would feel like, and as Kellan went at her with another raven-ous stroke of his tongue, all she could think was that nothing in her entire life had ever felt better.

Lifting her head, she reached down to him with a

trembling hand, brushing the thick, damp strands of his hair away from his face. "Kellan," she whispered in between her panting breaths. "Open your eyes."

He shook his head, his brow creasing as he squeezed his eyes shut even tighter, his mouth eating at her with a primal, hungry avidity that told her just how much he enjoyed what he was doing.

"Please, look at me," she moaned, knowing she wasn't going to last much longer. "I want…I want to see your eyes when I come."

He cursed under his breath, then slowly opened his eyes, staring at her through his lashes, and she understood then why he'd closed them. He hadn't wanted her to see the glowing blue irises that held so much more of the wolf than they did of the man, the unearthly color smoldering with a dark, dangerous hunger that should have scared the hell out of her—but didn't.

"It's okay," she whispered, stroking the side of his face as if she was trying to soothe a wild animal, her fingertips cool against the feverish heat of his skin. The corner of her mouth twitched with a smile, and she told him, "Stop struggling so hard. Your wolf can come out and play if he wants to, Kell. I'm not afraid."

He made a thick, guttural sound, holding her heavy-lidded gaze as he took another slow, deliberate lick, his tongue soft and wet and deliciously warm, then pulled away. "You're playing with fire," he growled, his breath jerking from his lungs in rough, ragged gusts as he leaned over her, bracing his weight on his arms. His powerful biceps bulged, his forearms roped with muscle and sinew, every part of his body hard and rugged and outrageously beautiful. "It isn't safe to push me, Chloe. To tempt me to lose control."

"I don't care," she whispered, pushing her hands into
the thick locks of his hair, the damp strands like heavy
silk. "I can't stand to have you hiding from me, Kell. I
just…" Her voice turned softer…huskier. "I want every
part of you."

The Lycan's molten gaze drilled into hers with a wild,
visceral intensity, burning with lust, and he worked his
jaw, his breathing getting louder…rougher. Without another word, he reached for the condoms that lay on the
floor off to his right, ripping open one of the foil packets
and unrolling the latex over the dark, vein-ridden length
of his cock. Then he lowered himself over her body
again, bracing his weight on one hand, while he reached
down and fisted his other hand around his cock, giving
it a rough squeeze. A surreal sense of rightness flowed
through her, and Chloe touched her fingertips to the
swollen heat of her sex, then lifted the glistening digits
to his parted lips as she spread her legs wider, offering
herself up to him…fearlessly tempting the beast. The
firelight cast shadows across the hard, masculine angles
of his face, his eyes dilated with savage, primal lust,
and he growled as he licked her fingers, the mesmerizing blue of his eyes burning brighter as his nostrils
flared. She could feel the predatory animal prowling
within him, demanding its freedom, and he started to
look away, turning his head, when she reached for him.
"No, look at me," she whispered, cupping his cheek in
her hand, refusing to let him hide from her. "I want to
watch your eyes when it happens. When you come inside
me."

Some kind of dark, primitive sound tore from his
throat, his muscles bulging beneath his golden skin
as his long fangs dropped hard and fast—and then he

was driving into her, shoving all those incredibly hard, thick inches inside her, and Chloe dug her nails into his biceps, needing to anchor herself in the breathtaking storm of sensation that tore through her body. She was stretched impossibly tight around him, straining to accept his broad width as he worked his hips against her, giving her more…and more…until she'd finally taken all of him. She knew there should have been pain that came with such a deep, heavy penetration, and yet, all she could focus on were the lush swells of pleasure that pulsed through her as he started riding her body, giving her slow, grinding lunges that turned into hard, hammering thrusts, the broken curses falling from his lips the most erotic sounds she'd ever heard.

Chloe wanted that sweet, inexorable climb to last forever, but she couldn't hold back the devastating rush of ecstasy that consumed her body, the deep, rhythmic clenching growing stronger…tighter, until she screamed and thrashed, pushing her hips up against him, desperate for everything he could give her. He drove himself into her with one last deep, shuddering thrust, his feral gaze locked on hers, his magnificent body burning with heat, straining above her. And then he broke with a guttural roar, his shaft pulsing inside her…becoming harder… thicker, until Chloe found herself lost in another wrenching blast of ecstasy that crashed over her so hard, everything went dark and dreamy and silent. She floated… weightless…loving the way he'd collapsed against her, still slowly thrusting his hips, as if he couldn't bear to stop.

"I don't believe it," she whispered sometime later, when the world had finally come back to her and she was able to open her eyes, her breaths as soft and even as a calm sea after the raging, violent fury of a storm. "I thought I'd died, but I'm still alive."

"Speak for yourself," he muttered into her hair, his sweat-slick body heavy against hers, though she could tell he was trying to keep most of his weight on the bent arms he'd braced on either side of her head.

"I've never thought about doing anything like this on the floor before," she admitted with a smile in her voice, enjoying the way his big body shivered as she ran her fingertips down the sleek, muscled length of his back. "But I'd be lying if I said it wasn't fun."

"Get used to it," Kellan rumbled, his voice pleasure-slurred as he reached down and grabbed his cock, holding the condom in place as he tried to pull out of her body, while her inner muscles fought to hold on to him. "God, I love how that feels," he muttered under his breath, finally managing to pull free, then kind of collapsing onto the floor beside her.

Unable to repress what had to be an idiotic smile, Chloe rolled toward him, resting her cheek on her folded hands. "Why should I get used to it? You got a thing for floors?" she asked with a soft laugh.

He rolled onto his side and reached out, sifting his fingers through her hair, the look of sleepy satisfaction in his beautiful, heavily lashed eyes making her toes curl. "I've got a thing for *you*. One that apparently makes me insane," he said in that dark, velvety voice that always made her melt, his fangs no longer showing. "Can't always promise we'll make it to a bed."

Chloe started to make some teasing reply, when her inner conscience suddenly caught hold of his words, and the sensual, blissful warmth that had been slowly drifting through her body went instantly cold. "Please, don't say things like that," she whispered, almost dizzy from the sudden flare of guilt that seared through her system.

His eyes narrowed with concern. "Why not?"

Her stomach knotted with tension. "Well, you know how we've talked about the curse?" She lowered her gaze to his chin.

His tone was almost painfully dry. "You mean the way you've spent the past few days harping at me about it?"

Ignoring the chorus of voices in her head that were screaming for her to shut up and simply enjoy him for as long as she could, she forced herself to say, "Yeah, well, the thing is, there's something I didn't tell you."

With a sharp, explosive sigh, Kellan rolled onto his back, one hand tucked beneath his head as he stared up at the wooden rafters. "What now?"

Chloe took a deep breath, then spoke in a quick, rambling rush. "What I didn't tell you before was that, well, I think I might be projecting my emotions onto you. That the Merrick might somehow be corrupting the curse, twisting the spell's power for its own purpose. See, I've never wanted anyone as much as I want you, and I think…actually, I'm *terrified* that the Merrick might somehow be using the force of that desire to get what it wants from you."

Popping his jaw, he slowly turned his head toward her, the look in his eyes a volatile combination of fury and frustration. "Damn it, Chloe. That's not how the curse works and you know it."

"But I'm not a pure-blooded Mallory," she argued, sitting up. "Who knows how the Merrick might affect the curse? And if I'm right, then it's an even grosser manipulation of your emotions than the original curse. I could be *forcing* you to do this, Kellan. Don't you see that?"

His eyes narrowed to a hot, angry glow, his big body vibing with tension. "Bullshit."

"All I'm saying is that you should think about what this means. Maybe you don't even want sex. Maybe the Merrick's power is making you want it!"

"Look, I'm going to say this one last time, so make sure you're listening. I do *not* want you because of a curse. I want you because you make me hot as hell," he growled, the muscles in his abdomen bunching as he rolled up and grabbed hold of her. Then he pulled her against him and he kissed her, making it impossible for her to argue. And, God, did he know how to kiss. His mouth worked over hers, the kiss rich and drugging and deliciously explicit, damn near melting the few brain cells that had managed to survive those mind-shattering orgasms.

"I wasn't trying to make you angry," she whispered against his lips, unable to get enough of his taste.

"Then forget about that bloody curse." He gave her another hard, eating kiss, before letting her come up for air.

"You know," she panted, "before we get carried away again, I should probably point out that the bed over there looks awfully cozy."

"If I carry you over there," he murmured against her mouth, nipping at her bottom lip, "then you'll owe me."

"What do you want?" she asked, drawing back so that she could read his expression.

A slow smile touched his lips, too sexy to be real. "Let's see if you can guess."

"You know," she snickered, grinning back at him, "for a werewolf, sometimes you are *such* a guy."

With a gritty laugh, he got to his feet and took care of the condom. Chloe couldn't help but enjoy the view as he moved through the room, his body like some decadent, alluring work of art, all long, beautiful lines and tough, powerful muscle. After pulling back the covers on the bed, he grabbed the condoms, scooped her up off the floor, then carried her over, laying her down on the soft, cool sheets, before snuggling in beside her. She knew she should have tried harder to make him understand her concerns about the curse—knew that she'd given in too easily—but damn it, she only had so much willpower. And she wanted so badly to believe that what he'd said was true.

"So," he murmured in another one of those dark, rumbling drawls, "you've never wanted a guy as much as you want me?"

"I should have known *that* was the one thing you'd take from that conversation," she snorted, rolling her eyes.

"HEY, I'M NOTHING IF not an attentive listener," Kellan rasped, leaning close to kiss her, but she stopped him at the last second with her hands pressed against his shoulders, her eyes going wide. "What's wrong?"

"Your eyes," she whispered with a shiver of fear. "The blue is turning red."

"It's okay. It's just a Lycan thing," he lied, silently cursing, knowing damn well that his eyes were turning because of the poison. While Chloe had been bathing,

Kellan had managed to pull Juliana Sabin aside for a quick talk without any of the others noticing. Though the vampire thought he was making a mistake by not being honest with the others, she'd agreed not to share what she knew about the Reykers' poison. She'd also warned him that she'd heard the poison was fast acting, and that after it had changed his eyes to red for the first time, he would have a week left, at the most. Fortunately, his eyes would return to their natural color...but they could still change from time to time as the poison continued to weaken his system.

"If it's a Lycan thing, then what does it mean?" Chloe asked, pulling him from his thoughts.

"Just that I'll need to hunt soon."

"Oh." Her voice was soft...and a little unsteady. "I was afraid it meant something was wrong."

"I should have told you," he said, feeling like a total jackass. "Should have explained how the wolf can affect my body so that you wouldn't be caught by surprise."

"You mean like the way you keep getting thicker when you come?" she asked, reaching down and curling her fingers around his cock, which was already growing hard for her again.

"Uh, yeah." He slid her another sheepish smile. "I'm sorry I didn't tell you about that before, but the change has never been quite so intense as it is with you."

A myriad of questions swam through her eyes, but she didn't ask them. Instead, she simply said, "No need to say sorry. I like it, Kell."

"Yeah? What else do you like?" He reached down, covering her hand with his, showing her that she could squeeze him as hard as she wanted and it wouldn't hurt him.

"Everything," she whispered, her beautiful eyes going heavy with desire, "which is an awful thing to say, because it's only going to inflate your ego. But I like the way you smell. The way you kiss me. Touch me." She ran her thumb over the moisture easing from the crease in the tight, swollen head of his cock, and he gritted his teeth, her voice a little huskier as she said, "And I really love the way you feel when you're inside me."

"Damn it," he groaned, quickly reaching for the strip of condoms, knowing he had to be inside her again… or risk going out of his ever-loving mind. The instant he had himself sheathed, Kellan pulled her on top of him, positioning her so that she straddled his hips, her sweet little sex warm and wet against his shaft as he pulled her down for a deep, ravaging kiss that left her trembling and breathless. Then he nudged the heavy, bruise-colored head against her soft entrance, tearing a low moan from her kiss-swollen lips. "You like that, don't you, Chloe?"

He pushed a little deeper, feeding himself into her slick heat, and her eyes nearly rolled back in her head as she gasped, "What's not to like?"

With a husky laugh on his lips, Kellan curved one hand around the back of her neck and pulled her closer, her soft, silky hair falling around them like an intimate veil. "God, you make me happy," he groaned, unable to hold still. Hunger gnawed at his insides as he gripped her hip with his free hand and started pushing up into her, working himself deeper…and deeper, until he was snugged up tight in her, soaked in her heat. "I know we're overdoing it, but I can't stop. You feel too perfect."

"So do you. And I feel wonderful, so stop worrying."

"Not too sore?"

"Only in a good way," she told him with a sweet, provocative smile. "I think being a Merrick must make a difference. I know I should be in some serious pain right now, but instead, I feel amazing. It's like…magic."

Kellan could tell by the way her voice had trailed away there at the end that she was thinking about that bloody curse again, and he hated that she thought he wanted her because of some centuries-old spell. He wasn't some inexperienced idiot, damn it. He knew his own emotions. Knew that what he felt for her was unlike anything that had ever happened to him before.

With his body buried deep in hers, he rolled her beneath him and grasped her hands, pressing them into the bedding as he put his face close to hers, staring deep into her eyes. "This is real," he growled, giving her a deep, heavy thrust. "No matter what happens, Chloe, I want you to remember that this is as real as it gets. You understand me?"

She nodded, her eyes hazy with passion, and for long moments afterward, Kellan set about showing her just how much he wanted her, his rhythm hard and demanding as he took her on the bed, then against the headboard with his knees digging into the mattress, their bodies burning and slick with sweat. Their kisses eating and hungry and wild. She accepted every part of him, no matter how dark or aggressive, and he relished the bite of her nails and her husky cries. Relished the beautiful way that she arched against him in complete, breathtaking surrender. And in the quiet hours of the night, when she finally fed from him again, taking his blood into her body, the sensation was so intense he had to bury his guttural shouts in her hair, his cock nearly turning itself inside out as the devastating pulses of pleasure wrenched through him.

Kellan knew, damn well, that the more he touched her, the worse the pain was going to be in the end—but he couldn't keep his hands off her. He was setting himself up for a major catastrophe, rolling more and more boulders down the side of the mountain, and he wouldn't be able to get out of their way when they reached the bottom. When the end hit, it was gonna shatter him into a million fractured pieces and crush him into dust, the agony more destructive than anything else he would have to face in the coming days. Hell, it was going to be worse than dying. But he didn't care.

Whatever the consequences…his time with the witch was worth it.

CHAPTER FIFTEEN

Thursday morning

KELLAN'S HEAD WAS STILL spinning, and he couldn't make it stop.

As the Lycan walked through the crisp morning air toward Seth's tent, leaving Chloe with Morgan, who was telling her the story of how Olivia had fallen in love with Aiden, he tried to think of an adjective that would do the night justice, but they were all blurring together. *Mind-blowing. Bone-melting. Breathtaking.* Impossible to pick just one. The brutal, violent warrior in him was sneering with embarrassment, but hell, it wasn't as if he'd ever spent the night buried inside a fiery, impossibly sweet, white-hot goddess before. A guy was bound to get a little sappy after something so freaking amazing.

He knew Chloe would never believe him, considering his reputation, but the sex had truly blown his mind. When he was inside her, Kellan had a feeling of…of what felt like peace, as if everything was finally as it should be. She'd made him realize how cold sex had always been for him, just a physical act that got him by, but never really touched him. Never satisfied the ache. He'd had raunchy sex. Aggressive sex. Dirty sex. But none of it had ever meant anything, until he'd found himself sinking inside Chloe Harcourt, pushing his body into hers, becoming a part of her. And God help him, he couldn't wait for the day to be over, so that he could lose himself in her all over again, driven to make the most of the time they had together.

He refused to think about how brief that time was, his jaw tightening as he forced the bitter thought from his mind.

Spotting Seth standing outside his tent, Kellan nodded his head in greeting. After a few hours of sleep, his eyes had thankfully returned to their natural color, and he squinted against the soft rays of dawn as he headed toward the soldier. "How's Raine doing?" he asked.

Seth hunched his shoulders against the biting wind, his hands shoved deep in his pockets. "She's still pretty groggy, but she's finally starting to come around."

"She feeling okay?" he murmured, noting that Seth looked tired and grim, as if he hadn't slept well.

"I think so. Juliana said she's healing more slowly than a Deschanel normally would, but that she'll eventually be okay. It's just going to take some time." With a stiff roll of his shoulder, he added, "She's pretty skittish, though."

"What do you mean?"

Seth cut his hard gaze toward the surrounding forest as he explained, his deep voice grittier than usual. "When she opened her eyes a few minutes ago and I started talking to her, she looked scared as hell of me. That's why I came outside."

"Well, that's not too surprising," Kellan drawled, trying to lighten the soldier's mood. "I mean, have you ever looked in a mirror? You *are* pretty scary looking."

"Fuck off," Seth grunted, and as he lifted a hand to

his face, rubbing it over his mouth, Kellan caught sight of the bandage wrapped around the soldier's right forearm. Recalling the conversation that he'd had with Chloe, he wondered if Seth had actually allowed Raine to feed from him…using the bandage to cover up the mark.

Deciding it was better to leave the subject alone, since the guy was already vibing with tension, he said, "I'll talk to Raine. Tell her she doesn't have anything to fear from you. Explain you really *are* one of the good guys."

"I'd have thought rescuing her from the compound might have done that," Seth muttered, his tone as dry as autumn leaves being raked off the ground.

"For most guys, yeah. But then, you're not like most guys, are you?"

"Why do I get the feeling there's something you're not telling me?" The soldier's voice was little more than a graveled scrape of sound, his green gaze suddenly locked on Kellan's with piercing intensity.

"There's probably a lot I'm not telling you," Kellan replied in a wry drawl. "But if you're talking about Raine, I don't think I've left anything out. You already know she's psychic."

Seth nodded. "You told me yourself that Westmore used her to keep an eye on Saige, so he'd know where to send the Casus to search for the Markers."

"That's right," Kellan continued, sensing that Seth hadn't quite understood what he meant. "But maybe I didn't explain it all that well. See, the way she was able to do that was by getting inside Saige's mind."

Seth's green eyes went wide. "Are you telling me that she can…what? Read minds?"

Pushing his hands into his pockets, Kellan gave a

slow nod. "Yeah, with a lot of people, she can read their minds, as well as see into their pasts. And in your case, man, I'm guessing there are a few things in there that would make a woman who's half Deschanel a little uncomfortable."

Another rough curse left the human's lips, and as he lowered his gaze, Kellan noticed there was a muscle pulsing hard in his jaw.

"Just so you know," the Lycan murmured in a low voice, "I think Westmore's going to want her back."

"Because of her power?" he asked, staring at the snow-crusted ground, his tall body still radiating tension.

"Not just that," Kellan admitted. "It was the way he would look at her. Westmore never touched her, as far as I know, but I think he was working up to it. Though that didn't stop him from letting the others have at her."

Seth's green eyes burned with anger as he lifted his gaze. "The Kraven bastard can try, but he's not getting her back."

"I know that, man. But if you're going to be helping take care of her, I thought you should know."

"Take care of her?" The soldier's chest shook with a grim, breathless bark of laughter. "Get real, Kell. After what you've just told me, I doubt the woman is going to want me anywhere near her."

"Like I said, I'll talk to her," he murmured, then jerked his chin toward the tent. "Now let's see how she's doing. There's something I need to ask her."

Seth cursed something foul under his breath, but he followed Kellan as he headed into the tent. Raine was sitting up against a pile of pillows on the pallet in the far corner with one hand held over her eyes, as if the soft glow of the candle Seth had left burning was too bright. "Hey," Kellan rumbled, keeping his voice soft as he moved toward her. "How you feeling?"

She lowered her hand, her gaze shadowed with worry and pain as she asked, "Is Chloe okay?"

"Yeah, we all got out fine. I'm just sorry you got so banged up."

"I'll be okay. But…"

"What is it?" Kellan asked, noticing the way she kept stealing glances at Seth, who had remained near the entrance.

"Now that we've escaped," Raine said, twisting her hands in the pallet's blankets, "I'm worried that Westmore will try to harm my family again."

"Do you know where they are?"

She nodded, saying, "They're staying with one of my uncles in Italy."

With his hands shoved in his pockets, Seth finally stepped forward. "I could send Garrick to them," he told her. "He could take them to one of the Watchmen compounds, where they'd be safe."

"You'd do that?" Raine whispered, surprise showing in her eyes as she stared up at the man who now stood at Kellan's side.

"Of course," he grunted. "It wouldn't be a problem."

Kierland came into the tent before Raine could say anything more, and Kellan introduced his brother to the psychic. After Kierland told them the group would be setting off soon, Kellan said, "We found the archives, Raine, but there's record of a journal having been removed from them. I was hoping that maybe you could tell us something about it. Or even where the journal might be."

Rubbing her bandaged arm, she gave a small shake of her head. "I'm afraid I don't know anything about a journal."

"Could you try to use your power?" Kellan asked. "Maybe tune into someone who's read it? I know you can't read Westmore, but we're hoping that maybe someone else has it."

"All right. I can try," she said softly, pushing her honey-colored hair back from her face as she closed her eyes, a small crease forming between her brows, and Kellan could have sworn that she looked a little paler than she had a moment before.

Beside him, Seth muttered, "Maybe this is something you could bother her with later, Kell. I don't think Raine should be doing much of anything right now but resting."

Thinking the soldier sounded surprisingly protective of the vampire, he said, "I wouldn't bring it up, but that journal could be important."

"And her recovery isn't?" Seth grunted, cutting him a dark look.

"Please, don't argue," Raine murmured, her eyes still closed in concentration. "I...I can see that there's a journal in Spark's possession. She calls it the 'death' journal. Westmore didn't find it important, since it didn't list anything about existing clan species that he didn't already know, so he let her take it."

"Why does she want it?" Kellan asked.

Lifting her lashes, the psychic gave a small shrug of her shoulders. "I don't see her very clearly, but I think she just found it interesting. There's information in the journal about species that don't even exist here, but she likes reading about them." With a frown, she added, "As an assassin, I think she finds death kind of fascinating."

"Kellan, last week, on the night that I found you with Spark and her men, but you sent me away so that they would bring you to the compound," Kierland said quietly, "I saw Spark reading a small leather journal."

"Yes. That's it," Raine told him. "That's the journal that was taken from the archives."

Running a palm over his chin, Kellan stared down at Raine, thinking over everything that she'd just told them. "You said it holds information about species that don't exist here. What exactly does that mean?"

"Species that aren't a part of our world, but exist in others."

Kierland slid him a significant look, as if to say, *You thinking what I'm thinking?*

"Has she read anything about the Death-Walkers?" Kellan asked.

For a moment, the pain in Raine's gray-blue eyes was overshadowed by exasperation. "Don't you think I would have told you if she had?"

"Then there's nothing about them in the journal?" he pressed, pushing his hand back in his pocket.

Rubbing at her bandaged arm again, she said, "I don't know. From what I can tell, Spark only picks the journal up every now and then, leafing through its pages. If something about the Death-Walkers is written inside, I don't think she's gotten to it yet."

"Can't you just tap into whoever else has read the journal?" his brother asked.

Raine shook her head. "As far as I know, Westmore's

the only other person who might have had access to it, and I can't read him."

"What about someone in the Collective?" Kellan questioned, running a hand over the back of his neck. "It is possible that they read it?"

"Maybe," she replied, "but I wouldn't even know where to start."

"What about the Casus or the Kraven? Can you see what they're doing?"

She shook her head again, her long hair tumbling over her shoulders. "I don't think so."

"Can you try?" he asked, the rough words thick with impatience. "What about Gregory? Do you know where he is?"

"That's enough," Seth cut in, his tone flinty. "Stop pushing her."

"You're right." Blowing out a rough breath, Kellan scrubbed his hands down his face. "I'm sorry, Raine. I didn't come in here to act like an ass."

"And I don't mean to be difficult." She looked miserable, the shadows under her eyes becoming darker... deeper, as if her strength was draining right before their eyes. "It's just that...my powers don't seem to be working that well at the moment."

"What do you mean?"

She looked away, her eyes glistening with tears of frustration. "I'm only getting glimpses of things, but nothing's really clear. I'm sorry. I know you need information, but I don't know how much I'll be able to give you."

Feeling like a jackass, he muttered, "Christ, don't be sorry. You haven't done anything wrong."

A low laugh slipped from her lips, and she lowered

her gaze to her lap, where her hands were twisted together into a knot. "You know that's not true, Kell."

"Raine, we know you were only trying to protect your family," Kierland told her, his tone one of easy reassurance. "No one here blames you for the things you told Westmore."

"They don't need to." Her voice was soft, tight. "I blame myself."

Moving around Kellan, Seth crouched down beside the pallet and reached out, looking as if he was going to push the heavy fall of Raine's hair back from her face, but she flinched, and he quickly stood up again, heading back outside. Kellan and Kierland said that they'd give her some privacy so that she could get ready to leave with them, and then joined Seth, who was pacing outside the entrance to the tent, his face set in a hard scowl.

"I think you should find someone else to look after her," he muttered, as soon as Kierland had closed the tent flap behind them. "She's scared to death of me."

Choosing his words with care, Kellan said, "I wouldn't say she's afraid of you, man. More like she's just being cautious."

Seth cut him another dark look. "I know when a woman's scared, Lycan. Don't fucking patronize me."

Kellan rolled his shoulder. "All I'm saying is that she's skittish around everyone right now. You remember what I told you yesterday, right? Those bastards beat and raped her I don't know how many times before I reached the compound. Hell, Seth, after what she went through, I'm amazed she doesn't scream her head off whenever any man goes near her."

"I'm trying not to think about what happened to her,"

the soldier growled. "Whenever I do, I…Christ, that Westmore bastard needs to pay."

"We'll deal with Westmore later. Right now," Kellan told him, "it's important that we get Raine back on her feet. Just stay mellow with her, because she needs someone like you to keep a close eye on her. I meant what I said about Westmore coming after her."

Before Seth could respond, the three of them caught sight of the Granger brothers heading into the camp, talking to Aiden and Quinn, who had been running the early-morning patrol. "It's about time you got here!" Kierland called out, heading toward them, while Kellan and Seth followed. Kellan had never actually met the two Deschanel *Förmyndares* before, but he recognized Ashe Granger from Morgan's photographs, and assumed the tall, dark-haired vamp walking beside him was his brother—Gideon's hair was a bit longer than Ashe's, but their features and builds remarkably similar. Kierland made the introductions, then asked, "Where the hell have you two been? Seth told us some kind of family business came up, but he didn't know anything more."

"We got a call from one of our cousins and had to meet up with him before we could head here," Ashe replied, slipping his heavy pack off his shoulder. "I'm sorry we weren't able to help at the compound. Quinn was just filling us in on what happened."

"This thing with your cousin," Kierland said, crossing his muscular arms over his chest as he held the vampire's pale gray gaze. "Would it have anything to do with that family trouble you refused to tell me about last week?"

"Don't worry," the vamp evaded with a sharp smile. "It's nothing we can't handle."

Kierland looked frustrated, but he let the subject go. "Did you hit any trouble on your way here?" he asked Gideon, who was pushing his dark hair back from his face, the uplifted position of his arm revealing the gleaming Sig he had holstered under his jacket.

"Didn't hit any trouble," the vamp drawled, his deep voice holding a hint of a Scandinavian accent. "But there are a few things we need to tell you. And let me just preface by saying the news isn't good."

"What's happened?" Kellan asked.

"Just before we came into the Wasteland, we heard from an uncle who's been living in the States. A story has just broken on the news over there. From what he told us, it sounds like the American media have caught wind of some kind of supposed paranormal activity taking place in a rural town somewhere in Texas. We don't have confirmation yet, but we think the Death-Walkers might be taking another shot at building up that little army of theirs."

"Son of a bitch," Kierland cursed, his green eyes burning with a hot, angry glow. "I don't effing believe it."

"The Consortium's trying to do damage control," Ashe added, "but they've sat around for too long. This thing is gaining momentum. Even if they get a lid on things in Texas, who knows what will happen next time?"

"What about the Collective?" Quinn asked, sliding his gaze toward Seth.

The Collective Army had always done their best to hide any proof of the ancient clans that fell into their hands, even going so far as to devise a chemical compound that would destroy any evidence of their kills.

From what Kellan understood, the Army didn't want other human vigilante groups to interfere with its hunting, but he also suspected that the Collective enjoyed working outside the laws of any government.

"From what I hear from my sources," Seth replied, "the Army's basically in chaos right now, and the threats of revolt are growing stronger. I don't think they're in any position to help contain anything, much less put a stop to it."

Kierland cursed again, and Aiden rolled his shoulder, saying, "With the way things have been moving, it was only a matter of time before something like this happened."

"Doesn't mean I have to like it," Kierland grunted. "If the humans find out about us, how understanding do you think they're gonna be, Ade? You think Jamie will be safe? Your fiancée might be human, but what about your daughter?"

The tiger-shifter scowled, his amber eyes bleeding to gold. "You think I don't know how dangerous this is?" he growled. "But what the hell are we supposed to do? Christ, we still don't even know how to kill the bastards!"

"But we might have a lead," Kellan cut in, quickly explaining what Raine had told them about the death journal.

"I'm afraid that isn't the only bad news we've got," Gideon went on to say. "We've also heard that the Shaevan have attacked the Deschanel in retaliation for the village in France. Looks like the Death-Walkers' plans to create chaos are working, and now all hell's breaking loose."

Quinn scrubbed his hands down his face. "God," he muttered, "this is turning into a friggin' bloodbath."

Just then, Juliana Sabin walked over, her delicate features etched with strain as she joined the group between Kierland and Ade. "I'm sorry to interrupt," she said, "but we…" Her words trailed off as she caught sight of the Grangers, but she quickly tore her gaze away from them and cleared her throat, focusing on Kierland as she said, "We have a problem. The scouts I sent out this morning to make sure our way would be clear to my family's compound have just returned. None of them were killed, but they were attacked by a group of Death-Walkers. Apparently, the Walkers wanted them to deliver a message."

Kellan sensed that things were about to get a helluva lot worse. "What's the message?"

"They wanted you to know that the Infettato enjoyed the Watchmen…and now they're ready for more."

"Shit," Quinn snarled, his dark eyes burning with fury. "The humans who'd been infected in the village must have killed the unit I called in to watch over them."

"But how?" Seth asked, his deep voice edged with disbelief. "They were so weak they could barely stand."

"They must have gotten stronger." Quinn forced the words out through his clenched teeth. "Just like that bastard we talked to said they would."

"So what are we gonna do?" Aiden asked, a deep scowl seated between his tawny brows.

"Actually, it's not the Death-Walkers that we need to worry about." The husky words were Raine's, and everyone looked toward Seth's tent, where the frail psychic stood just outside the entrance, her pale face pinched with an expression that was equal parts discomfort and determination. "They've already left the Wasteland, but they brought the Infettato here. The infected humans are to the southwest of us."

"Then they're blocking our way to the Sabin compound," Juliana murmured.

Catching Raine's gaze, Kellan asked, "Are you sure?"

"My sight is hardly working well at the moment, but I saw this clearly just now. The Infettato are coming for us, tracking us by scent."

Chloe joined the growing group with Morgan, and while the female Watchman threw her arms around Ashe Granger's neck in a friendly hug and demanded to know where he'd been, Chloe made her way to Kellan's side. "What's going on?" she asked him, her expression showing her concern.

Though he knew she was waiting for an explanation, Kellan could only stare at her, momentarily lost in how beautiful she looked in the dusky morning light, the pale shades of sunshine playing softly over the dark strands of her hair. She'd been through hell the past few months, and yet, she hadn't once complained. Instead, she'd kept herself busy that morning helping with whatever tasks she could find, fitting into the group as if she'd been a part of it forever, and taking the time to personally thank everyone for coming to the Wasteland to make sure Kellan made it safely out of the compound. He could tell they were all charmed by her, and although he read the slight wariness in her gaze, as if she was still worried about how the Mallory curse would affect the group, Kellan hadn't seen any signs to make him think that the curse was influencing anyone. She'd explained to him, during one of their quiet conversations in the middle of the night, how the curse could affect large groups of people, telling him about a time that her sister Monica had won tickets to a Colts game and taken Chloe for her birthday. They'd been having a wonderful time, until they realized the people around them were becoming increasingly aggressive as the Colts fell a bit behind on the scoreboard. By the third quarter, when the Colts were only down by a touchdown, a violent fight had broken out, and the sisters had been forced to crawl through the aisles in order to escape.

"Kellan?"

He jerked back to awareness as she said his name, stunned that he'd actually zoned out there for a few seconds, considering they were in the middle of a crisis. Ignoring Aiden's muffled laughter, he cleared his throat and said, "The Infettato are on their way here."

"Ohmygod," she whispered, and he grabbed her hand, aware of his brother's curious gaze. "What do we do?"

Giving her hand a reassuring squeeze, he said, "We're going to have to fight."

"Maybe not," Juliana murmured, drawing everyone's attention.

"You got an idea?" Seth asked.

"There's a small mountain range that begins on the eastern side of this forest," Juliana explained. "A waterfall runs down the face of the mountain, completely covering the entrance to a series of caverns."

Kierland nodded as he grabbed hold of Morgan, who had finally stopped hugging Ashe, and pulled her close. "I've seen the waterfall when I was running patrol."

"Yeah, me, too," Aiden added. "It looks like it feeds into some kind of hot spring."

The wind whipped at the long strands of the Deschanel's hair as she said, "If we poured some of the holy water you brought with you into the spring, it might be enough to keep the Death-Walkers from following us, should they change their minds and head back in our direction. I'm thinking that if we can make our way through the falls and into the caverns, then we could travel beneath the mountains, and actually come out not far from my family's compound."

Gideon, who had been silently observing the interchange, asked, "And what about the Infettato?"

"If they're tracking us by scent," Juliana replied, "then the water should cover our trail. They'll have no idea where we've gone."

"Considering we don't know how to kill them," Quinn grumbled, "this might be our best option."

"Maybe," Ashe muttered. "But I hate running from a fight."

"We're not running," his brother pointed out with a crooked smile. "We're strategically postponing."

"Right," the vamp snorted, curling his lip. "Now why didn't I think to look at it that way?"

"Can't help it if you're slow," Gideon drawled, his gray eyes glittering with laughter, and Kellan could tell that the guy got a kick out of riling his brother.

"Considering all the shit we have coming after us," Kellan said, keeping a tight hold on Chloe's hand, "we need to put survival before our desire to kick ass."

"The only downside I can think of," Juliana added, "is that it's going to make our trip a little longer."

"So long as it's safer," Kierland said, sliding a warm

look toward Morgan, "I don't give a damn how long it takes."

"Does anyone else know about these caverns?" Aiden asked, his black sweatshirt printed with white letters that read: "Come over to the dark side... We have cookies."

"I can't say for certain," Juliana said in response to the shape-shifter's question, "but I assume that the Sabins aren't the only ones who've discovered them."

"Then we'll need to stay sharp," Quinn muttered.

Aiden gave a husky bark of laughter and lifted his brows. "Aren't we always?"

"He said *sharp*, not sarcastic," Chloe drawled, and Kellan grinned, thinking again about how perfectly she fit in with his friends.

Crossing his muscular arms over his broad chest, Ashe Granger suddenly turned his piercing gaze on Juliana, his voice a little rougher as he said, "You really think you know what you're doing?"

Taking a deep breath, she lifted her chin and answered his question. "I think I know this land better than you do."

Ashe arched his brows and snorted. "That's because between the two of us, honey, you're the outlaw."

"Go to hell," she growled, spinning on her heel and storming away, while everyone in the group turned to stare at Granger, including his brother. Not that he noticed. Instead of acknowledging their curious looks, the vampire kept his dark gaze locked on Juliana Sabin... and Kellan could have sworn the guy was staring at her ass as she walked away.

CHAPTER SIXTEEN

Thursday afternoon

Though Kellan had been more than a little skeptical, Juliana's plan to throw off the Infettato had actually worked, and it had been a surreal experience as they'd made their way through the waterfall that hid the entrance to the caverns. While the waterfall itself had been freezing, the pool had been wonderfully warm, heated by natural hot springs that Juliana said spread beneath the mountain, warming the route they were using to reach the Sabin compound. And thanks to the waterproof bags that Quinn had brought in case of a heavy snowfall, they'd been able to keep their belongings dry; the kerosene lanterns that Juliana's scouts had provided lighting the way as they traveled deeper into the mountain.

While the situation was hardly ideal, Kellan couldn't help but feel that they were off to a good start, a bit of luck finally going their way. Still, they remained on high alert, knowing it paid to be cautious. After everyone in the group had made it into the first cave—aside from Garrick and two of Juliana's scouts, who were taking a treacherous shortcut out of the Wasteland so that the soldier could reach Raine's family—Raine had sensed that the Infettato had lost their scent. But the infected humans hadn't given up, driven by their insatiable hunger, and according to the psychic, were still searching for a new trail to follow. And despite the fact that the Death-Walkers had already left the Wasteland, Kellan and the others had still emptied a gallon of salted holy water into the pool, just to be safe, which had nearly wiped out their travel supply.

Never one to particularly like tight, enclosed spaces—something he had in common with Morgan—Kellan had been relieved to find that the caverns were larger than he'd expected, with a ceiling of at least twelve feet and a width of thirty feet or so in most places. He was currently walking with his brother and Morgan, while Chloe walked up ahead, talking with Juliana. Every now and then, the Merrick witch would look over her shoulder and smile at him—and every time she did, that simple act of connection hit him like a punch to the gut, sucking the air right out of his lungs. Though he was trying to give her some space, and sensed that she was doing the same for him, Kellan knew it was only a matter of minutes before they would gravitate back to one another, talking about everything from movies and music to their favorite authors and sports teams. Innocuous subjects, but ones that allowed them to tread carefully into the other's life, like roots slowly tunneling into the ground, until the seeds of friendship could intertwine themselves with the shoots of what was already a full-blown affair. Only, it was a friendship unlike any that Kellan had ever known, flavored by the need to unravel her, piece by piece, until he was able to get inside and explore every part of her, each intimate detail dazzling to him in a way that he still didn't fully understand. All he knew was that he wanted to break her open, but not with malice or harm. He just wanted to take her apart so that he could gather the scattered pieces into his soul... and be the thing that bound her together.

But it was a double-edged sword, because it meant he had to break, as well. Meant he would need her to bind him back together, when Kellan knew damn well there was nothing she could do to keep him in one piece. He was already broken in a way that couldn't be undone. That couldn't be fixed.

And I'm a bastard for taking this thing further, he silently growled, disgusted with himself. He knew they were heading for a nasty, ugly collision with a brick wall, the outcome inevitable. And yet, he couldn't make himself stay away from her. Chloe Harcourt was like his own personal brand of crack that had him completely hooked, and while there were actually times that he wished he could blame his obsession on the Mallory curse, Kellan knew it would have been a lie. What he felt...it was *real*. He just wished he knew how to prove it to her.

"You know, I've been watching you all day," Kierland suddenly rumbled at his side, "and all the while, you've been watching the witch with this hungry look in your eyes that I've never seen you have before. She has you hooked, doesn't she?"

Kellan arched a brow, deciding to turn the tables on his brother by saying, "I've been meaning to ask you the same thing about Morgan."

Instead of reacting with a sarcastic comment, like he'd expected, Kierland actually gave a husky bark of laughter and reached out, pulling Morgan tight against his side. "She's got me hooked, all right," his brother murmured, leaning down to press a warm kiss on Morgan's smiling mouth.

"You know," Kellan drawled with a slow, shit-eating grin, "if you think about it, Kier, you actually *owe* me for getting you into this mess."

Kierland immediately shot him a dark glare, his muscles coiling with tension, but Morgan simply patted his chest, soothing the Lycan's anger as she slid Kellan a wry smile. "I know you love pushing your brother's buttons, but be careful, Kell. He still wants to wring your neck for scaring the hell out of him with your crazy-assed plan to get captured."

Kellan accepted the warning with a jerk of his chin, then quietly said, "You know, the two of you still haven't told me what you went through to get here. I imagine it was a pretty rough trip."

For the next half hour, Kierland told him about how he and Morgan had traveled into the Wasteland with Ashe Granger, after Kellan had disappeared, his brother's voice getting rougher when he admitted that he'd almost lost Morgan the night he'd gone out on his own to find Kellan, determined to stop him from going through with his plan. Morgan had followed him, and had been attacked by a group of Death-Walkers. She'd been badly injured in the attack, before Ashe and the Sabins managed to scare the creatures away, and it was only the healing power of Kierland's mating bite that had saved her life. The bite had marked her as his brother's for all eternity, and Kellan couldn't have been happier for Kierland, knowing the guy had been crazy about Morgan for years.

Kellan had just finished thanking the couple for everything they'd gone through to help him, when ahead of them Ashe started walking beside Juliana, who was still talking to Chloe. They couldn't hear what was said between the two Deschanel, but within thirty seconds Juliana's spine had stiffened and she'd quickly crossed to the other side of the tunnel, putting as much space between her and Granger as possible.

"What's the deal with those two?" Kellan asked, glancing at his brother.

With one arm draped around Morgan's shoulders, Kierland shrugged. "No one knows, but they've been like that since they met last week. I guess she just rubs him the wrong way."

"Looks like the little vamp doesn't care for him eith—"

Kellan's words suddenly trailed off as Gideon Granger took Juliana's place beside Chloe, the dark-haired, good-looking vamp walking so close beside her that their arms touched as he said something that made her laugh.

"Gid," Ashe muttered. "Move away from the witch, bro." The vampire cast a quick glance back at Kellan, who had his hands fisted at his sides, and added, "The sooner the better."

Gideon turned his head toward his brother. "There a problem?"

"Just do it," Ashe grunted, "or the Lycan's going to have your bloody head."

Without even bothering to glance in Kellan's direction, Gideon gave an arrogant snort. "He can try."

While Chloe sent a curious look over her shoulder, Kellan heard Ashe mutter, "Not the time or the place, Gid. So get the hell away from her."

Something in his brother's dark look must have convinced him to heed the warning, because the vamp gave an irritated roll of his shoulder, then turned his attention back to Chloe, his deep voice laced with irritation as he said, "Sorry, sweetheart. I guess you're currently off-limits."

Kellan couldn't hear what she said in response, but as Gideon moved away from her, he could sense that the bastard was still interested. "I hate to cause trouble," Kellan muttered under his breath, "but I think I'm going to have to kill your new friend."

"Aw, don't mind Gideon," Kierland rumbled. "He won't push it too far. He's just yanking your chain."

Kellan ran his tongue over his teeth, his voice a little grittier as he said, "I don't give a shit what he's doing. He stays away from her, or he's done."

Aiden came up on Kellan's other side, whistling under his breath as he whacked him on the shoulder. "I never thought I'd see the day you were actually jealous, pup. Are we going to be brothers-in-law, then?"

"Shut up, Ade."

"I'm sorry, brother," the tiger-shifter drawled, clearly enjoying himself, "but this is family business. Seeing as how I'm marrying her sister, it's only right that I suss out your intentions."

"My intentions are none of your goddamn business," Kellan growled, but the words had little effect. The ribbing continued throughout the long day of trekking through the meandering string of caverns, until he was ready to wring Aiden's bloody neck. By the time they'd made camp that evening and settled down around another one of Juliana's smokeless fires, he was wound up and aching, the poison eating him raw inside. Juliana continued to send him questioning looks, as if wondering how long he was going to keep the truth to himself, but he responded each time with a curt shake of his head, and she would look away again. But even now, the vampire was talking to Chloe as the two of them kept company with Raine, and he couldn't help but worry that she would say something he didn't want said.

"The Merrick likes you," Morgan murmured, pulling him from his private thoughts as she sat down beside him.

"Of course she does." Kellan slid the female Watchman a wry smile. "I got her out of that place. That probably makes me her most favorite person in the world."

With a roll of her gray eyes, Morgan said, "It's more than gratitude, Kell."

"Then what do you call *that?*" he asked, watching as Chloe left Juliana and Raine to make her way over to Jamison, who was sitting by himself on the top of a boulder, reading a book. Acting as if they'd been longtime friends, Chloe sat down beside the Lycan and started chatting with him. Jamison quickly set his book aside, giving her his full attention, and Kellan felt something raw and possessive settle in his gut, his nostrils flaring with aggression.

"Is she trying to make you jealous?" Morgan asked uneasily.

"That sneaky little witch," he muttered under his breath, watching as Chloe leaned a little closer to Jamison. "I don't friggin' believe it."

Morgan's tension mounted. "Are you going to tell me what's going on, or leave me hanging in the dark?"

Kellan popped his jaw, fighting to control his temper. "She's testing her theory."

"Her theory on what?" his brother rumbled from

behind them, obviously eavesdropping on their conversation. "How to piss you off?"

"Not the time," he muttered, his patience already spread thin. "So back off, Kier."

"Kellan," Morgan said gently, "does this by any chance have something to do with the fact that Chloe's a Mallory witch?"

With a sharp nod and a low curse, he moved to his feet…and headed toward his prey.

MAKE A PASS AT ME. Put your hand on my knee.

With her muscles tensed to the point of pain, Chloe repeated the mental commands, the pressure in her head so tight she was surprised her skull hadn't split in half. Jamison Haley was a nice guy, but her little experiment didn't seem to be working. Even though she was certain she'd caught him watching her earlier with a gleam of male interest, which the curse should have been cranking up now that she was focusing her attention on him, nothing was happening. If anything, Chloe seemed to be scaring the hell out of the poor guy as she moved a little closer to him, his worried gaze starting to flick toward the place where she knew Kellan was sitting.

Kellan had told her the horrible story about how Jamison had been captured by Spark and tortured by Gregory DeKreznick. He'd been dying when the Watchmen had found him, and Kierland had bitten him to save his life, changing him to a werewolf. After everything he'd been through, she hated playing with his emotions, but she didn't know what other choice she had. She needed to test the curse, and she was too afraid to try her theories out on any of the other men in their group. The situation sucked, but she had to make some kind of play for a reality check, because it was becoming painfully clear that her feelings for Kellan Scott were out of control.

Last night, Chloe had fully expected him to be furious over her admission about the curse and her suspicions that her Merrick blood could be affecting it, but instead, he'd made love to her again and again throughout the surreal hours of darkness, drowning her senses in wave after wave of devastating, erotic pleasure.

And the day had been even more unsettling, because every time she got close to him, she found herself falling for him a little harder. A little deeper...

God, there was so much danger here. Not from Kellan himself, but from how much she was starting to like him. Enjoy him. She wasn't even talking about the sex, though it was un-freaking-believable. It was just being with him, spending time with him. He was funny and protective and smart. Arrogant, but humble, as well. The guy was simply too good to be real, and Chloe knew she needed to get a grip now, before she was so far gone she started begging him for more than sex. No way in hell could she let that happen, because as incredible as he was, Kellan Scott had never once made mention of any kind of future relationship between them, as if their time together was limited to their escape from the Wasteland. If she wanted to be able to walk away from this thing between them with her heart still in one piece, she *had* to remember that he was only in this for the physical, and not the emotional.

Suddenly checking his watch for the fifth time in just as many minutes, Jamison said, "It's, uh, getting pretty late."

Taking pity on the poor guy, Chloe finally gave up her scheme and told him good-night, her thoughts mired in chaos as she headed for the small cave where Kellan had told her he would be setting up their tent.

Could it be true? she wondered, feeling even more lost than before. *Is the curse truly fading?*

It seemed crazy, but Chloe couldn't deny that she was afraid to believe the curse had finally come to an end. Terrified, actually, of getting her hopes up, when she'd gone into this thing with Kellan with her eyes wide open, knowing it was only short-term. But, God, that had been so much easier to accept before she'd spent so much time with him. Before she'd…before she'd lost her freaking mind and started falling in love with the complicated alpha.

Nearly stumbling over her own two feet, the truth of that statement hit her system with the stunning force of a nuclear explosion, and she took a deep breath, pressing a trembling hand to her fluttering stomach. Shivering with confusion, Chloe had almost reached the cave that held their tent, a small fire flickering within, when Gideon Granger stopped her. They talked for a few moments, and then she went inside, thankful for the privacy the cave provided, wanting a bit of time alone with her thoughts.

"What did he say to you?"

Unaware that Kellan had followed her in, Chloe spun around with a gasp. "Who?" she asked, lifting her hand from her stomach to press it against her pounding heart.

"The vampire." He forced the words through his gritted teeth as he came to a stop a few feet away from where she stood, the small enclosure accentuating his height and muscular build.

Licking her lips with a nervous flick of her tongue, she said, "Gideon? He told me good-night."

"That's it?" he asked, his dark eyes burning with accusation.

Refusing to be intimidated, Chloe took another deep breath and crossed her arms over her chest. "Not that it's any of your business, Kell, but he said that I reminded him of someone he'd known a long time ago."

"Be careful around him," he warned her, pushing one hand back through the thick, auburn strands of his hair. "His reputation's even worse than mine."

Choking back a breathless laugh, she said, "I honestly find that hard to believe."

He took a step closer, his voice dropping to a dark, husky rasp. "And what about that little stunt you were pulling with Jamison?"

"What stunt?" she asked lamely, the heat in her face telling her she was blushing like an idiot. Chloe could tell by the look in his eyes that he'd been watching her the entire time.

His hair tumbled over his brow as he stepped even closer. The rich, delectable scent of his skin filled her head, their bodies nearly touching as he stared into her upturned face. "Are you trying to test me?" he demanded, the words soft, but rough, his chest rising and falling with each of his hard, ragged breaths. "Because I can tell you right now, it's a bad idea. You're gonna find yourself with a pissed-off wolf on your hands, and all he's gonna care about is making sure you understand just who your little ass belongs to."

"Oh? And who's that?" she snapped, finding it strange that she could be so irritated and turned on at the same time.

"For now, it belongs to *me*."

Her eyes went wide. "For *now?* God, Kellan. Do you have any idea how chauvinistic that sounds?"

Ignoring her question, he said, "I know what you were doing back there. And it didn't work, did it?"

"I was just talking to him. Is that a crime?"

"You were flirting with him," he snarled, taking hold of her shoulders. "Testing him. Christ, Chloe, I thought we settled this shit about the curse last night!"

Choosing her words with care, she stopped evading… and gave him an explanation instead. "This is a dangerous game we're playing, Kellan. So yeah, I was testing him. I know it was wrong, and I'm not proud of it, but I need answers. After everything that's happened, I'm too keyed up to just keep screwing around with you like this. I can't explain why, but I feel like we have an axe hanging over our heads. Like something bad is going to happen."

"The only thing that's going to happen is you're going to get stronger, because we're going to make sure the Merrick keeps getting what it needs."

"So you're only here with me because of the Merrick?" she demanded with a burst of outrage.

"I'm here because I can't keep away from you," he growled, yanking her closer and suddenly covering her mouth with his. The demanding kiss was flavored with violence, stealing Chloe's breath…stealing the troubled thoughts from her mind. With shaking hands, he ripped off their clothes and took her into the tent, quickly putting on a condom before pressing her down on the pallet. His hands were hard on her body, the man reduced to his raw, animal instincts, but she loved it. Loved the rough, graveled sound he made as he ran the damp heat of his mouth along her jaw and down her throat, kissing his way across her chest. With his tongue swirling across a sensitive nipple, he rolled to his back, pulling her on top of him…then pulling her higher up his body. Chloe's heart jolted into her throat the instant she realized his intention, but before she could stop him, she found herself straddling his face, his tongue lapping hungrily through her folds, and pleasure arced through her body with such stunning force that she had to cover her mouth with her hand to muffle her scream.

"Kellan," she panted, when she could finally draw enough air to speak, barely able to hold herself upright, the hot glow of ecstasy melting her bones. "It's too much…"

"Too bad," he rasped, his rough breaths rushing against her sensitive flesh. "This time, Chloe, I'm not stopping until you're coming in my mouth."

"I can't take it," she sobbed, trying to hold herself together, but it was impossible. Anger melted into hunger, her worries into craving, and she lost herself, coming hard and fast, her arms curled over her head as hoarse cries spilled from her lips. Her body pulsed with blinding points of light and heat, and he growled with visceral satisfaction, keeping at her with his lips and tongue, his mouth deliciously greedy, letting her know that he got off on the explicitly intimate act every bit as much as she did. She was still coming, hard and sweet and heavy, when he tightened his hold on her hips and lifted her with ridiculous ease, the power in his muscular arms making her breath catch. Then he stole her breath completely when he pulled her down his body…and straight onto the throbbing head of his cock.

"Take me, Chloe. All of me," he groaned, his fingers

biting into her hips as he waited, jaw clenched, for her to work her way down all those thick, vein-ridden inches. A choked gasp shook her chest when she'd finally sheathed him, her body stretched to its limits, her face tingling, blood pulsing in her earlobes and her breasts…in her fingers and her toes. Curving his hand around the back of her neck, he pulled her against his chest and rolled over, reversing the position of their bodies, his hips slamming against hers, shoving his cock so deep, she felt like he was in every part of her, taking up space in every cell of her body. His hand fisted in her hair, holding her, his eyes fever-hot and wild with need, glowing an unearthly blue, the sheer intensity of his gaze making it impossible for Chloe to look away. Watching her closely, he pulled back his hips, then rammed in, shoving himself deep, the slick, blistering friction too good to endure. He was going to kill her with pleasure, but she didn't care. She just wanted to soak in every second of bliss, her fingers tingling as she ran her hands down the muscular length of his back, loving that animal-like play of muscle beneath his sweat-slick skin as he started riding her in a rough, grinding rhythm.

He made a hard, thick sound in his throat, and then his mouth was covering hers, the kiss raw, drugging her senses with pleasure. She climaxed, screaming, and he swallowed the keening sound, the orgasm catching her in an explosive rush, crashing over her in another shattering wave of ecstasy.

"You didn't come?" she whispered against his throat, when she could finally catch her breath, realizing he was still hard inside her, feeling even bigger than before.

"Not yet," he growled, wedging his hips tighter between her thighs. His soft lips touched the apple of her cheek, as if tasting the heat of her skin, his muscles locking the instant he found the hot trail of tears slipping from the corner of her eye. "What the hell, Chloe?" He drew back his head so that he could see her face. "Did I hurt you?"

She shook her head, taking a shivery breath, trying to get it together.

"Then why are you crying?"

"Because it shouldn't be this good!"

At first he didn't say anything, a tremor moving through his big, muscular body as he held himself hard and still, packed deep inside her. And then he quietly asked, "Why?"

Chloe turned her face to the side, wishing that she'd never said anything, because now that the conversation had started, she knew it wasn't going to end anywhere good.

"Damn it," he growled, losing his patience. "Answer me."

Quietly, she said, "This isn't real, Kellan."

"You're wrong." Bracing his weight on one forearm, he touched her chin, demanding she look at him, his eyes smoldering in the flickering shadows cast from the distant fire. "I told you before, this is as real as it gets."

"You're giving me your body," she whispered, unable to stop her tears, "but…that's it."

His brows drew together over the burning blue of his eyes, his heart thudding heavily against hers. "What the hell is that supposed to mean?"

Chloe licked her lips. "You're holding yourself back from me."

For a moment, he looked stunned, and then a grim,

breathless rumble of laughter shook his chest. "You've gotta be kidding me."

"I wouldn't joke about this. And you're wrong if you think I don't know this sounds crazy. I mean, we only just met. I know that! And I know this wouldn't be considered a normal conversation for a couple who only just started…doing whatever it is we're doing, but damn it, nothing about this situation is normal."

"Yeah, well, this doesn't feel like holding back to me," he grunted, his voice a guttural mix of anger and lust as he gave her another deep, devastating thrust, her body melting around him, clinging to his shaft.

Drawing an unsteady breath, she somehow managed to say, "I'm not talking about holding back when it comes to sex. I'm talking about holding back when it comes to *us*. I mean…look at us, Kellan. You've never once said anything about us continuing to see each other once we're out of the Wasteland. How hard would it be to say 'Hey, when this is over, maybe we should go out on a date sometime?' But no. All you're willing to give me is *this*," she told him, wiggling her hips, "and that's why I think it *has* to have something to do with the curse. Because I might not have your experience, but I'm not stupid. Men don't make love to women the way you make love to me then talk about it only being for the moment. *For now.* That's not how it works."

"Christ, Chloe. In case you didn't notice, this isn't a bloody social outing. We're on the run for our lives. It's not like I've got time to sit and come up with a fucking five-year plan."

"That's not what I'm asking for," she argued, shoving against his chest.

His nostrils flared, a muscle pulsing in the hard line of his jaw. "What do you want from me?"

"I don't know," she burst out. "I just...I need to understand what's happening. Where this is going—or if it's even going anywhere, so that I can prepare myself for what's coming. Because if I'm not careful, Kell, I'm going to get in too deep. And I can't help feeling that I'm the only one treading water here. That maybe we should step back a little and ease things off."

Fear shook him.

"No. I can't...I can't do that. I don't want to lose you, Chloe. Damn it, I *won't* lose you. Not yet." The ragged words trembled with emotion, and he took her mouth, pouring everything into the kiss that he couldn't put into words. She lay still beneath him for a heartbreaking span of seconds, then moaned, finally kissing him back, her arms wrapping around his neck, and his wolf silently howled with triumph, his fangs getting heavier in his gums, burning to be released.

God, he wanted to bite her so badly it was a physical ache in his gut, the wolf punching against his insides, demanding he do it. As if she were already spilling down his throat, he knew exactly how perfect her blood would be against his tongue...how hot and sweet and achingly addictive.

Since the moment Kellan had first met her, his feelings had been wrapped up in utter chaos—his cravings and fears battling for dominance. But now they'd coalesced into one seething entity. One fired by a hunger to have her and claim her that was unlike anything he'd ever known.

Possession.

He wanted every man out there to know exactly who her sweet little ass belonged to. Wanted it so badly he could taste it. It was only for Chloe's sake that Kellan stopped himself from making the bite, because he couldn't do that to her—couldn't tie her to him when the odds were strong that he wouldn't be around much longer. If he bit her, she would still feel the pull long after he'd gone. Spend the rest of her life aching for something that she couldn't have. That was no longer within her reach.

Fighting the primal pull of the beast with everything that he had, Kellan pushed himself up on his straightened arms and raked his gaze down her slender, beautiful body, until he reached the intimate place they were joined. With hot eyes, he watched the way his cock stretched her, the heavy shaft gleaming with her juices as he thrust into her with deep, penetrating lunges, keeping the pace grinding and slow, knowing it would drive her crazy. Lifting his gaze, he watched the breathtaking swirl of emotion in her glowing eyes, needing that intense connection. Pressing deep, he held hard and tight inside her, loving the warm flush of color in her cheeks…the white flash of fang beneath the curve of her upper lip; their breaths ragged and loud, as if the air was too thick for their lungs; their bodies shuddering…pulsing, held on that knife's edge of sensation. And then a low, predatory sound tore from his chest, and he broke, his fingers biting into her hips as he leaned back, pulling her over his spread thighs, pumping into her with a raw, savage rhythm that would have scared the hell out of most women, his wolf so close to his surface he had no doubt she could see it in his eyes.

"Touch your clit," he growled, thrusting into her

harder…faster, the slick, erotic friction so good it nearly killed him. She flushed brighter, but followed his gritty command, and the instant she grazed that swollen little knot of flesh with her fingertip, a scalding orgasm burned through her, sharp and explosive. Her power filled the tent, rushing against his body, searing and strong, and he gave a guttural roar as she screamed, her climax dragging him right along with her, milking him…draining him, until he collapsed over her, completely destroyed.

Kellan had no idea how long it took before he could finally find the strength to pull away and take care of the condom. "You drive me over the edge every time," he muttered a moment later, lying beside her on the pallet, wishing she would open her eyes and look at him. "I promised myself I was going to be gentle with you tonight, but I was too rough again."

"No you weren't." With a yawn, she turned so that her back was against his front, then nuzzled her sweet little ass against his groin. "Regardless of how I feel about the curse and what's happening between us, I like your wolf, Kellan."

"What the hell are you talking about, Chloe?"

"You're always so worried about hurting me or scaring me," she said in a soft voice, sounding thoroughly exhausted, "so I thought I'd go ahead and make it clear that I like it when your wolf takes over and you lose control. I think it's sexy as hell."

Christ, this woman completely blew his mind. She was so sweet, accepting every part of him, no matter how rough-edged or difficult, with open arms. And in return, he gave her half-truths and lies. Ones he had no chance of escaping, much like his fate. The way his eyes had turned red the night before was proof that the poison was gaining the upper hand. Proof that he was losing the fight.

I'm such a bloody bastard, he thought, knowing it was wrong for him to be there with her, when she was only going to end up hurt. Knowing she deserved so much more than this. And yet, he didn't have the strength to get up and walk away.

Silently cursing his weakness, Kellan took her into his arms and pulled her against the heat of his body, simply needing to hold her as close and as tight as he could… for as long as it lasted….

Until his time ran out.

CHAPTER SEVENTEEN

Friday afternoon

OUT OF THE FRYING pan…and into the fire.

They'd only just made it out of the mountains an hour ago, and already there was trouble. Having been on the move since the early morning, the group had finally stopped for lunch, and had been in the process of packing up when the scouts that Juliana had sent up onto a high ridge, where they could get a clear view of the forest that spread out for miles below them, reported back with grim news. Not only had they spotted a sizable force coming toward them from the northeast, they'd also reported activity heading their way from the northwest, which meant their group was being hunted on two separate fronts. Since the mountain range formed a kind of J shape, they'd actually come out south of the Sabin compound. Their only option was to go north…right between the two oncoming groups…and there wasn't enough time to reach the compound before they were caught in the middle.

The situation was the last damn thing that Kellan needed, considering he felt like death warmed over. His condition had been growing worse all day, his body ravaged by the poison coursing through his system, but he ignored the pain, determined to hide any signs of weakness, hoping like hell that his eyes wouldn't turn red in front of the others. Though his body was working to counteract the poison, he was losing strength with every passing minute—and it was only a matter of time before his healing abilities were useless.

We need to find the Reyker bastard, the wolf snarled. *Find him…and fight him for the antidote, just like we agreed to do.*

Get real, he growled back, refusing to encourage the animal's hope, knowing damn well that the odds were slim he could defeat Asa Reyker in his current condition, and even slimmer that an antidote actually existed. And that wasn't taking into account the fact that he'd have to find Gregory first, wanting that bastard taken down so that he'd no longer be a threat to Chloe. It was a fucking mess, but he didn't have time to worry about it now. He refused to leave Chloe's side until she was safely secured within the Sabin compound—and that wasn't going to happen unless they figured out a way to survive the afternoon.

Knowing they needed answers, and quickly, Kellan glanced around the small glade where the group had stopped to eat. He wanted to talk to Raine, but he didn't see either her or Seth, and he knew they'd be together. Despite the palpable tension that remained between them, Seth continued to watch over the psychic, often carrying her when she was too weak to walk. Her body was still trying to heal from the trauma she'd suffered at Westmore's compound, and Kellan was worried that she might never fully recover. Her power remained unstable, but while she hadn't been able to get a clear read on where Gregory was, she *had* managed to provide the group with several important pieces of information…

and he was hoping to get more. "Does anyone know where Raine is?" he asked, interrupting the others as they discussed what should be done next.

"Seth is with her," Noah replied, his black hair falling over his brow as he stood at the edge of the group, his shoulder propped against one of the surrounding trees. "He said she needed some sleep before we start moving again."

"Where the hell did they go?"

Noah jerked his chin toward a tangle of broken tree limbs that sat on the far edge of the glade, and after making sure that his brother was keeping an eye on Chloe, Kellan headed in that direction, his tension ramped up more than ever. Earlier that morning, Raine had told them the Infettato had managed to track Kierland's scent along the route he'd taken earlier in the week when he'd traveled from the Sabin compound to the base camp. Considering the direction they knew the Infettato were traveling, Kellan had little doubt that they were the group closing in on them from the northeast, and it was obvious that the Watchmen had underestimated how quickly the infected humans could track.

Raine had also told them that Spark had heard rumors of the Infettato traveling through the Wasteland, and had started searching the "death" journal for information about them, though she hadn't yet found anything. Though he figured it was probably a long shot, Kellan needed the psychic to try to check in on Spark again, in case the assassin had recently opened the journal and found something useful.

As the Lycan moved around the snarled tangle of stumps and broken branches that Noah had directed him toward, he found Seth sitting on a bit of dry ground, his back propped against one of the fallen tree trunks. The soldier was whittling at a piece of wood with his pocketknife, while Raine slept curled up on a blanket beside him, still looking too gaunt and pale, her body healing far more slowly than it should have been, despite the blood she'd been taking from Juliana. Knowing damn well that Seth was going to give him a hard time, Kellan cut right to the chase. "We need to wake her up."

Closing his knife, Seth slipped the blade back inside his jacket pocket and lifted his head, his shadowed gaze making it difficult to read his mood. "We heading out already?"

"Not yet," Kellan replied, quickly telling the soldier about the report Juliana's scouts had just given them. "I need to know if Raine can see anything new with Spark."

"You know, every time you ask her to use that power of hers," Seth grunted, moving to his feet, "it drains her a little more. Don't you think she's been through enough already?"

"Look, I don't like it any more than you do, but she might be the only chance we've got."

Seth cursed, but he didn't argue as he turned and dropped to one knee beside the sleeping Deschanel. She came awake with a small gasp the instant he touched her shoulder, and Kellan could tell that Seth was trying to keep his tone as gentle as possible as he told her what had happened…and what they needed. Despite the fact that she really did look like she needed the sleep, the bruises under her eyes even darker than they'd been the day before, she didn't argue or complain as she sat up and pushed her long hair out of her face. Kellan moved a little closer when she closed her eyes, her forehead scrunching with concentration as she tried to focus her power. It seemed like he waited forever for her to finally open her eyes again, the gray-blue depths shadowed with frustration as she stared up at him.

"I'm sorry I couldn't see it before," she told him, "but Spark is leading the group closing in on us from the northwest. Westmore sent her to get me and Chloe back, and they've heard rumors that the Sabins are helping the Watchmen. That's why they *were* heading for the Sabin compound, but I think the Casus she's commanding must have caught our scent, because they seem to be heading straight for us now."

"Since the Casus are naturally able to home in on the Merrick, they're probably tracking Chloe," he muttered, fighting to keep a tight hold on his rage, knowing it wasn't going to help solve anything if he lost his temper. "What about the other group? The scouts said there was something moving in from the northeast as well."

"That's definitely the Infettato."

"Great," Seth said with a rough sigh, shoving his hands in his pockets. "More effing zombies."

"What about the journal?" Kellan asked. "Can you see if Spark has read anything more?"

Raine said she would try, and the men waited as she turned her focus inward, the only sounds that of the wind blowing through the trees and the distant murmur of voices coming from the glade. "Okay," she finally said, after nearly five minutes had passed. "Spark has found something in the journal about the Infettato and she gave it a quick scan about an hour ago. According to the journal, the infected humans become stronger over time, and the way they gain that strength is by consuming flesh. They eat everything in their path, but can be given a specific scent to follow and will become completely locked on it. The only things they won't eat are the ones who made them. It seems the Death-Walkers have complete control over them."

Swearing softly, Seth asked her, "Can they be turned back to normal?"

She shook her head. "I'm afraid these types of things don't usually work that way. Once life has been taken away, it can't be given back."

"But aren't they still living, at least in some way?" Kellan asked, ready to reach out and lend her a hand as she tried to get to her feet, but Seth beat him to it, taking hold of her elbow and helping her off the ground.

As soon as she was standing, she seemed to flinch at Seth's nearness, so he immediately moved back a step, the soldier's expression even more severe than before. Looking Kellan right in the eye, Raine shivered as she answered his question. "I'm afraid not. They're literally the walking dead, Kell. The best thing you could do for them would be to put them out of their misery."

"And how the hell are we meant to do that?"

The wind whipped the long strands of her honey-colored hair around her shoulders as she huddled within the thick coat that Morgan had given her. She looked like a lost little girl, but for the grim shadows darkening her eyes. "They can be killed, but it isn't pretty," she said in a thick voice. "You have to take their beating hearts from their chests and burn them. Only then will their spirit leave their bodies and finally be able to move on."

Kellan thanked her for the information then headed back to the others. Noticing that Chloe was looking more than a little worried, he moved close to her side, then told everyone to gather around and quickly relayed what he'd just learned.

"So what's the plan?" Quinn asked, his dark gaze locked with Kellan's. "I can see those wheels spinning in your head, Kell. You've got an idea, don't you?"

With a grim smile, he said, "I'm actually thinking that if we're smart, we can kill two birds with one stone. Or rather, let the birds kill each other."

"You mean turn the Infettato against Spark and her crew?" Kierland looked surprised…but interested.

Aiden gave a low whistle and slapped a hand on Kellan's shoulder. "That's downright diabolical," he drawled, his amber eyes glittering with excitement. "I like it."

Shifting his gaze toward Quinn, Kellan asked, "How's your wing?"

As a raptor-shifter, Quinn had the ability to fly, thanks to the wide, powerful set of raven-colored wings that normally lay hidden within his back—but one of his wings had been badly injured during a fight against the Casus several weeks ago, and he hadn't been able to take to the air while it was mending.

"It's fully healed," the shifter replied. "Why?"

Looking around the group, Kellan explained his plan. "If we each give up some blood, Quinn can get in the air and head toward the Infettato. When he finds them, he can scatter a trail of blood that will lead the Infettato to Spark's unit. Once the humans attack and are busy feeding, then we'll launch our own attack and destroy them, one by one."

"It's risky," Kierland muttered, "but it could work. What do you think, Quinn?"

"The trees should give me some decent cover," he

murmured, scraping his palm over his chin. "I think the kid's got a helluva plan."

Kellan turned his gaze on Aiden. "Yesterday, you said something about having brought some equipment with you from Harrow House. Any chance you brought my tech kit?"

"Just the small one," the Watchman told him, walking over to his bag and rummaging inside, then returning with a small leather case. "What are you thinking?"

"I'm thinking you're a saint."

Aiden gave a rough bark of laughter. "Hardly. But this shit won't work out here," he said, handing over the case. "I only brought it because I thought you might need it once we're out of the Wasteland."

"Won't matter," Kellan murmured, opening the kit. "If we use one of the tracking chips I designed, the signal will kick in when it leaves the Wasteland. We should be able to pick it up on my computer, once we're back at Harrow House."

"Who are we going to put the chip on?" Chloe asked, her husky tone a mixture of both curiosity and surprise.

Kellan slid her a slow smile. "Who do you think, honey? Westmore's little pet assassin."

Jamison, who'd been quiet till this time, started choking. "We're gonna tag Spark?" he wheezed, after Noah had whacked him hard on the back.

Kellan nodded. "We're gonna need those Markers that Westmore has. If we tag Spark, then we'll be able follow the signal when she meets back up with him. It'll save us a helluva lot of time tracking him down, since we have no idea where he might run to."

Aiden gave another gruff bark of laughter. "That's genius."

"Can't Raine just keep an eye on her?" Jamison muttered, clearly not looking forward to getting anywhere near the woman who'd been responsible for his capture the year before.

Shaking his head, Kellan kept his voice low as he said, "Raine's still in pretty rough shape, and her powers are too spotty after what she's been through. We can't put that kind of pressure on her. Our best bet is to tag Spark and follow the signal."

"Wait," Morgan said, her gray eyes troubled as she looked from Kierland to Kell. "If Spark's with her crew, won't the Infettato attack her, as well?"

Kellan shook his head again and smiled. "Not if we grab her first."

IN THE END, Kellan's plan had been even easier to orchestrate than he'd hoped, everyone working together so that it went surprisingly smoothly. Using the Deschanel's ability to mask their scent, the Granger brothers had managed to kidnap Spark as she and the Casus made their way through a heavily wooded area of the forest, and bring her back to the camp. At the same time, Quinn had left the trail of blood for the Infettato to follow, the trail leading straight to Spark's unit, which he'd managed to douse with blood while using the treetops for cover. Following the scent, the infected humans had attacked the Casus with vicious ferocity, overpowering and killing all of the Casus but the few Kellan, Kierland and Ade had taken down. Then, while the Infettato were caught up in the mindless frenzy of feeding upon their kills, the three Watchmen had used their claws to rip the humans' hearts from their chests, one by one, while Quinn had been in charge of burning them.

By the time Kellan and the others had cleaned up and made it back to the glade, where Seth, Noah and Jamison were standing guard, Chloe and Juliana had already skimmed through Spark's journal, which she'd been carrying in her backpack, and had found the pages that confirmed what Raine had told Kellan about the Infettato. While the Grangers kept an eye on the assassin, who had been knocked unconscious when the brothers had taken her, the women had also found the pages in the journal that talked about the Death-Walkers, but were only able to read the part that explained who the Death-Walkers were. Unfortunately, the part of the passage they assumed contained the information on how to kill the creatures appeared to be written in some kind of archaic language. One that looked similar to the strange markings etched into the surface of the Dark Markers.

The group was still in the midst of discussing the frustrating news, when Gideon called out to say that Spark was starting to come to. As they headed over to the place at the far edge of the glade—where the assassin had been left lying on the ground, her hands bound behind her back—Kellan walked beside Chloe. She had a death grip on his hand, and he knew she'd been worried about him while he'd been gone, the knowledge putting a kind of warm feeling in his gut, as if he'd swallowed something soothing and hot.

"Does it make me a bad person that I want to kick her while she's down?" Chloe asked in a husky voice, and Kellan laughed, while Morgan patted her on the shoulder.

"Nah," the female Watchman drawled with a sweet smile. "She just has that effect on people."

With a low groan, Spark managed to slowly maneuver herself to her feet, then leaned against the tree at her back, while the group fanned out around her in a wide half circle, making it clear that she wasn't getting away. "Huh. To what do I owe this auspicious honor?" she drawled, pulling back her shoulders in a brazen pose, though Kellan could scent her unease and knew she wasn't as indifferent as she tried to sound.

"We'll be the ones asking the questions," he grunted, the fury he felt toward the bitch making his voice hard. "Not you."

"Well, if it isn't the puppy and the little kitten," she murmured, sliding her calculating gaze over him and Chloe. "How cute. I won—"

"What are you and your men after?" Kierland asked, cutting her off.

"What do you think? Westmore sent us to collect his little playthings." She tilted her head toward Chloe and Raine. "He wants them back, and trust me when I say he isn't going to give up anytime soon."

"By the way," Quinn rumbled, sliding the redhead a sharp smile. "I'll be sure to let Saige know you had your front teeth replaced. She'll be eager to knock them out again."

Chloe snickered, and the assassin narrowed her eyes, before slowly looking over the rest of the group. When her green gaze landed on Seth, shock widened her eyes, a wry smile twisting the rouged curve of her mouth. "Well, well, well, if isn't the turncoat."

Seth locked his jaw, his expression one of pure disgust

as he held Spark's taunting stare, while Raine stood a little ways off to his left.

"You know, Raine, you should really have a go at him. He might be human, but he fucks like an animal," the assassin drawled, giving the psychic a sly smile, before flicking her gaze back toward Seth again. "It's such a shame you had to turn, McConnell. I would have enjoyed another go."

"Kell, what the hell are we waiting for?" the soldier growled, looking as if he'd enjoy nothing more than to get his hands around Spark's pale throat and wring her psychotic little neck. "I want her the hell out of here."

With a low, throaty laugh rumbling on her lips, Spark cocked her head a little to the side as she slid her gaze over the group. "Is this the part where I'm meant to believe you'll kill me?" she asked. "Come on, guys. If you'd wanted me dead, I wouldn't be standing here talking to you, now would I?"

"We want you to deliver a message to Westmore," Kierland told her.

"Do I look like a messenger pigeon?" she shot back, arching one slender brow.

"You look like a heinous bitch, but that's not the point," Aiden drawled, crossing his brawny arms over his chest. "The point is that you can either deliver the message, or we can kill you now. Your choice."

"You wouldn't kill a woman," she scoffed, though the scent of her fear was becoming a little more noticeable.

Morgan took a step forward and held open the front left side of her jacket, revealing the Walther PPK holstered under her arm. "They might not be able to stomach it," she said with a wide smile, "but I would. So don't tempt me."

The assassin held Morgan's glittering stare, obviously trying to decide if she dared to go up against her, then muttered something under her breath. "Fine," she snapped, tossing her hair over her shoulder. "What's the message?"

Placing his hands on Morgan's shoulders as he stood behind her, no doubt ready to push her out of the way if Spark tried to make a move, Kierland said, "Tell Westmore that we know what he's planning, and we'll do whatever it takes to stop him."

"And if he wants to live," Aiden added, "then he'll hand over the Markers that are in his possession. The exchange will take place at noon, two weeks from today, at the base of the Eiffel Tower. This will be his only chance to do this peacefully. If he doesn't show, then we'll come after those three Markers with the full force of the Watchmen."

Another throaty laugh spilled from the assassin's lips. "Are you serious?"

"It's his choice," Kellan replied, wrapping his arm around Chloe's waist and pulling her closer to his side. "But remind him that we've found him twice now. If he tries to hide, we'll only find him again."

"Fine. I'll deliver your message," she muttered, her green eyes burning with fury. "But I need my hands unbound, and I want my pack back."

Gideon quickly sliced through the ties that had been wrapped around her wrists, and Ashe tossed her the backpack, which contained the tracking device they'd hidden inside while Spark had been unconscious, quickly sewing it inside the lining of the front pocket.

"Now get moving," Kierland grunted, jerking his chin toward the forest that stretched out behind her.

She took a quick glance inside the backpack then looked around the group with an arrogant sneer on her face. "You've taken my journal. Not to mention my weapons! Do you honestly intend to send me off into the Wasteland without a way to protect myself?"

Quinn gave her a cocky smile. "The journal is ours now. And since we don't want the Deschanel offing you before you deliver our message, we've left you a weapons pack a mile north of here. You'll find it buried under a pile of rocks in the middle of a meadow."

"Bastards," she whispered, but she didn't argue, slipping the pack over her shoulder before turning and getting the hell out of there. They watched the flash of her dark red hair until she'd disappeared from sight, then gave a collective sigh of relief.

Raking his hair back from his face, Kellan asked, "You think she bought it?"

"Who knows? But either way," Seth muttered, "I'm glad to be rid of the bitch."

"Now all we have to do is make it to the compound," Juliana said. "We should get moving as soon as possible."

As the group headed off to collect their gear, Raine asked if she could talk to Kellan for a moment. While Chloe excused herself to go help Morgan, Kellan joined the psychic, who was still standing near Seth. "What's up?"

"You're not going to like it," she told him, hugging her elbows, "but I suddenly have a feeling that Gregory is heading our way."

"Shit," he groaned. "How close is he?"

"I'm sorry, Kell, but I'm not sure. All I know is that he's tracking Chloe. But his hunger's so strong, it's over-shadowing everything else."

Choking back a string of curses, he braced his hands on his hips and lowered his head, staring at the ground with burning eyes. His nostrils flared as he took a deep breath, but he managed to thank the psychic for telling him, before she walked away with Seth, leaving him standing there with his thoughts…and his anger. He could feel his heart rate rising, his pulse roaring in his ears as the wolf seethed beneath his skin, snarling with fury and frustration. It didn't like Chloe being in danger any more than he did. Didn't like the fact that Kellan would be forced to make his move against Gregory that night.

The Lycan had hoped that he could give himself another day with Chloe, once they reached the Sabin compound. Had hoped he'd be able to spend a little more time with her, soaking up every moment that he could while giving his body a chance to rest, before heading out to track down DeKreznick, and then the Reykers. But now there wasn't time. With the bastard so close, he needed to eliminate him as soon as possible.

Knowing he needed to talk to Chloe before she heard the news about Gregory from someone else, Kellan had just turned to pace back toward the group, when he caught sight of Kierland heading his way, the look on his brother's face telling him that he'd just been told. Bracing himself for what he figured was going to be a sticky conversation, Kellan stood his ground. But the first words out of his brother's mouth weren't about the Casus. Instead, Kierland's expression shifted from worry to shock as he snarled, "Your eyes have turned red!"

Kellan choked back a groan, thinking that his body's timing couldn't have been crappier. Blowing out a rough breath, he forced a casual expression onto his face and shrugged his shoulders. "There's no need to freak, Kier. It's just the poison flaring up. I think my body is trying to kick the last of it out of my system."

Kierland's pale green eyes narrowed with suspicion. "What's going on, Kellan?"

"Nothing," he muttered. "Let it go, Kier."

"Like hell I will," he bit out, forcing the words through his gritted teeth. "I'm tired of the bullshit and secrets and never knowing what the fuck is going on with you anymore. It stops now, Kellan!"

"I told you it was nothing. And we've got bigger problems than my damn eyes at the moment."

For a long minute, Kierland just held his stare, his chest rising and falling with rough, choppy breaths. "If you're thinking about going after DeKreznick alone," he finally rasped, the low words vibrating with anger, "then you can forget it. We still don't even know how to deal with that witch he's got with him. The best thing we can do is get Chloe to the Sabin compound and take the time to figure out a plan. But you *cannot* go running after him. It would be suicide!"

With his nostrils flaring, Kellan took a step forward, getting right in his brother's face. "And what would you do?" he demanded in a guttural snarl. "If he was after *your* woman, what would you do, Kier? She's his goddamn Merrick! You know what that means. What he'll do to her, if given the chance. You think I'm gonna just stand by and let that happen?"

Kierland's brows drew together, forming a deep ridge above his nose, his voice little more than a whisper as he cursed something gritty and soft. "I don't believe it. You're…Christ, you're in love with her, Kellan."

The *L* word him hit like a brutal punch to the gut, and he blinked, fighting to hide his reaction.

But the damage was done. Kierland was right.

I've known all along, his wolf snarled, and Kellan knew, instinctively, that the son of a bitch was telling the truth.

It was impossible to describe the specifics, the man in him unable to fully comprehend the workings of the wolf, but the animal had known the first moment he'd seen Chloe's photograph that this woman would change his life. And after he'd met her, Kellan's fascination had grown…and his heart had followed. He *was* in love with her, damn it. The head-over-heels, rip-out-his-beating-heart-and-lay-it-at-her-feet-in-devotion kind of love. Why else would he have let Westmore slip through his grasp when he finally had him at the compound? Why else would he have done half the crazy shit he'd done since meeting her, or have been able to keep on breathing when he was already half-dead inside, just so he could keep her protected?

His gaze slid past Kierland and across the glade, until it'd found her. She was standing beside Morgan, smiling at something the Watchman was saying, the dusky light playing softly over the delicate beauty of her face. But it was more than just her looks that drew him in. It was the way she laughed and smiled and teased. The way she stood up for the things she believed in, and refused to give in, even when she was afraid. It was the way she looked at the world. The way she looked at *him*.

Yeah, he loved her. So much that it felt like a friggin' knife had been slammed into his heart every time he looked at her, knowing he couldn't keep her. But he wasn't admitting a damn thing to Kierland.

Pushing his hands deep in his pockets, he blew out a rough breath of air as he slowly drew his gaze back to his brother. "Even if I did love her, it wouldn't make a difference. Chloe deserves better than me."

"That's such a crock of shit," Kierland growled. "If you love her, Kell, then don't do anything drastic. Anything that can't be undone. Because she's a helluva lot better off with you by her side, than without you."

The corner of his mouth twitched with a bitter smile, and he snorted. "Come on, Kier. I know you, of all people, don't believe that. You might love me, but deep down, you've always thought I was a fuckup."

His brother's expression looked pained, and he ran a shaky hand over his mouth, before clearing his throat and saying, "Look, Kell. I know I've given you a hard time, and I'm sorry about that. I should have been more understanding, but—"

"No, you've been right about me all along. And you've been better to me than I've deserved."

His brother's eyes went tight, the pale green burning with emotion. "Damn it, Kellan. Promise me that you're not planning anything stupid."

A gritty bark of laughter stuck in his throat, a crooked smile twisting his lips. "I won't do anything without talking to you first," he lied, knowing damn well that if he weren't careful, Kierland would spend every waking moment watching him like a hawk.

From the other side of the glade, Morgan called his brother's name, and Kellan sent up a silent thank-you for the reprieve. "This isn't over," Kierland said, giving him a hard look, as if trying to see inside his head, before letting out a sharp sigh and turning toward his woman.

Kellan watched as his brother made his way across the snow-crusted glade, wishing like hell that he could tell him the truth. About Chloe. About what was happening to him. What he was going to have to do. But he choked back the impulse, knowing it was wrong. If he told him what was happening, Kierland would move mountains to try to help him, endangering his own life even more than he already had, and Kellan refused to let that happen.

The lies he'd told had been made to protect the ones he loved, and he could live with that.

What he couldn't live with was putting them in danger. Taking them down with him.

No matter what lay ahead, this would be a battle he had to fight on his own.

CHAPTER EIGHTEEN

The Sabin compound, the Wasteland
Friday night

DESPITE ITS LOCATION, the Sabin compound was a warm, comfortable environment, Juliana and her family doing everything they could to make their haggard group feel welcome. After being shown to their rooms, they'd all cleaned up and gathered in the dining hall, enjoying a meal of roast chicken and vegetables, which Kellan knew was a rare luxury for those who lived within the cold, desolate realm. He enjoyed the food and beer, laughing as Aiden shared stories about some of their past adventures, and was still a little taken by surprise by how comfortable Chloe seemed with the group, considering he knew she'd always considered herself a bit of a loner.

But as much as Kellan enjoyed the easy, relaxed atmosphere, there was a bittersweet edge to the evening, since he knew it was likely the last he would be sharing with his family and friends. The Sabin compound was safe and secure...and although he'd hoped to get Chloe all the way to the border of the Wasteland before leaving her in Kierland's care, there simply wasn't time—but at least he knew that while he was hunting down Gregory, she would be safe within Juliana's home.

Kellan also knew that Kierland would think he was crazy for carrying out his plans alone, but he couldn't see any other way. With the witch at his side, Gregory would have no trouble taking the group apart, no matter how many of them there were. His best bet was to go in alone and sneak up on the pair, catching the witch unaware and taking her out before she could use her power on him, then facing off against DeKreznick man-to-man. The Lycan was prepared to fight as dirty as necessary to get the job done, and then, once the bastard was dead, he'd find the Reykers and deal with that issue…and Chloe would be safe.

Kellan was thinking over everything he needed to put in the letter he planned to leave behind for Kierland, since he wanted his brother to make sure that Chloe was looked after, when Quinn slid forward in his chair at the far end of the table, a sly smile on the Watchman's lips as he looked toward Seth and said, "So, there's something I've been meaning to ask you, McConnell."

"Great." The soldier's mouth compressed into a thin line as he set his beer bottle down on the table. "I wondered when you were going to get around to it."

With laughter glittering in his dark eyes, Quinn drawled, "So you and Spark, huh?"

"This is *not* something we need to talk about," Seth grumbled, flicking an uncomfortable look toward Raine, who had been determined to join the group for dinner, her spirits lifted after the scouts who had taken Garrick to the border had returned with good news, saying that the soldier had made it safely out of the Wasteland. However, the grin Raine had been wearing had faded, her attention focused on her plate as she pushed at a piece of broccoli with her fork. Though she didn't appear to be listening to the conversation, Kellan had a feeling the psychic was riveted on every word that'd just been said.

Earlier, Raine had told him that her powers had become so weak, she could hardly get a clear read on anyone—which meant she couldn't just sneak into Seth's mind for the details of the story.

"You're a brave man," Quinn murmured.

"I was hardly brave," Seth muttered, his lip curling. "Just drunk."

Aiden threw back his head with a husky bark of laughter, then slid Seth a wide smile. "I wouldn't think there's enough alcohol on earth."

"Trust me," Seth grunted, rolling his shoulder in a stiff, uncomfortable gesture. "There is."

Eager to get Chloe alone, since he knew the minutes were counting down before he had to leave, Kellan finished his beer and grabbed her hand, saying, "We're gonna call it a night."

They said their goodbyes and thanked Juliana for her hospitality, then got up from the table. Kierland gave him a long look as they crossed the room, and Kellan forced a smile, hoping like hell that his brother couldn't read the truth on his face. They'd talked again, not long after reaching the compound, and by then his eyes had thankfully returned to their normal color, which he knew had been a big relief to his brother. When Kierland had asked him about Gregory, Kellan had told him that he wouldn't be making any decisions about what he wanted to do until they'd gotten Chloe safely out of the Wasteland, hoping the lie would keep Kier from watching him too closely.

As they made their way through the candlelit halls,

Kellan felt a shiver move through Chloe's arm, down into the slender hand he still held, so he pulled the little witch closer to his side, wondering if she was cold…or nervous. Though heavily fortified, he supposed there was a certain spooky element to the Sabin compound, especially since they'd been warned not to pay any attention to the screams they might hear in the night, since Juliana's brother, Micah, was imprisoned in one of the distant wings. According to Kierland, who'd filled him in on the story, Micah had been poisoned by a rogue female vampire after the family had been exiled to the Wasteland, and while the poison wasn't fatal, like the one Kellan had been infected with, it tormented Micah's sanity, dragging him into feral bouts of madness that made him a danger to others. Though Kierland, Morgan and Ashe had encountered some trouble with him the week before when they'd been trying to find Kellan, Micah was now being held in a heavily secured room that Kierland himself had inspected, so Kellan felt confident the vampire wouldn't be a danger.

They walked in silence now, lost in their thoughts, but they'd talked a lot throughout the long afternoon, as they'd made their way to the compound. Chloe had been full of questions, and Kellan had done his best to answer them, even telling her the grim story of how his father had murdered his mother in a jealous rage when he and Kierland were young, which was why they'd been raised by their grandfather at Harrow House, the estate his Watchmen unit was now using for their base of operations, its moat filled with salted holy water, which safeguarded the house from the Death-Walkers. And yet, despite all the hours of conversation, there was still one topic that they'd stayed clear of, but that he wanted to get out in the open before he took her to bed.

The wind howled against the windows as they made their way to the wing that held their chamber, the compound's cold stone walls decorated with colorful tapestries that must have been in the Sabin family for centuries, while priceless rugs covered the hardwood floors. When they finally reached their room, Kellan bolted the door behind him, a fire already roaring in the hearth, sending out melting waves of warmth. He watched as Chloe walked to the side of the bed, her cheeks flushing in that tantalizing way they did when she knew he would soon be kissing her. Touching her. She looked a little tired, and while he knew she would need another feeding before he left, he was trying hard not to think about who would be feeding her once he was gone. Instead, Kellan simply watched as she slipped off the Marker he'd insisted she wear, setting the cross on the bedside table, the firelight glinting against its metallic edges. As she sat down on the snowy white bed and leaned over to unlace her boots, he said her name, and she looked at him from behind the heavy curtain of her sleek, dark hair, the mesmerizing color of her eyes so beautiful that it almost hurt to look at them.

Clearing his throat, Kellan propped his back against the door and held her heavy-lidded gaze, his voice a deep, husky scrape of sound as he said, "Before I touch you tonight, there's something I want to tell you."

"What is it?"

He raked one hand through his hair, his voice roughening as he said, "I'm not some oversexed kid who doesn't understand lust. I know the difference, Chloe. The hunger that I feel for you, it's…Christ, it's more powerful than anything I've ever felt before, but that doesn't mean that I'm a slave to it. It might drive me past the bounds of my control when I get you under me, but it doesn't control my will. I can think apart from it. I don't know why I'm not affected by the curse—but the simple truth is that I'm not. Maybe it's a Lycan thing, and I'm simply better at fighting off the curse than other species. Or maybe the curse is weakening, like we've suspected. To be honest, I don't give a shit why it's the way it is. For one night, I just want…I want you to trust me to know what's real. Can you do that?"

She slid her gaze toward the roaring flames in the fireplace, the plump swell of her lower lip caught in her teeth, then slowly nodded her head. The breath Kellan hadn't even realized he was holding released with a quiet whoosh, his hands shaking at his sides. "Good," he rasped. "Because I've wanted to fuck you since I first laid eyes on your picture, honey. Before I was anywhere close enough for that bloody curse to go to work on me."

She swept her tongue over her top lip as she moved to her feet, her breath coming a little faster as she locked her beautiful gaze with his. "Is that really true, Kell?"

Crossing the room to her, he took her face in his hands and leaned over her, pressing his forehead against hers. "I know it makes me sound like a pig, considering you were in danger and all I should've been thinking about was your safety. But yeah, it's true. From that first day that I saw your picture and Olivia started telling me about you, I went to bed every night thinking about you. Dreaming of finding you and being able to touch you and kiss your soft lips. Of being able to undress your sweet little body." He pressed a warm kiss to the side of her throat, his hands sliding over her shoulders and down her back, until they settled possessively on her heart-shaped little ass. "God, I spent days thinking about what it would be like when I could finally get you against my mouth, Chloe. When I could finally get you under me."

She gave a soft moan in response, her body shivering, but didn't say anything, the only sound that of the wood crackling in the hearth and their quietly soughing breaths. Though their previous encounters had been like violent storms crashing against a rocky shore, Kellan forced himself to go slow this time, wanting to savor it, drinking in each moment with care, so that he didn't miss a single drop of sensation. He undressed her with shaking hands, each pale curve of feminine flesh drugging his senses with pleasure. Her breasts were dainty and small, but beyond beautiful, her skin so smooth and pale it reminded him of shimmering moonlight, softer than anything he'd ever known. As he picked her up in his arms and lowered her to the bed, Kellan stared at her lithe body draped across the snowy linens with hot, smoldering eyes. His heart beat in a deep, painful rhythm, hammering against his chest, and he couldn't stop himself from imagining what she would look like lying there, with their child cradled against her body, nursing hungrily at one of those creamy breasts. The vision was so powerful, it made him tremble, a low groan spilling from his lips as he flexed his fingers, his gaze raking over every inch of her body as he started unbuttoning the shirt he'd worn down to dinner, before returning back to those sweet, delectable breasts.

Following the line of his gaze, she flushed, her voice already a little breathless as she said, "I'm sorry they're so small." A grin touched her soft lips, her eyes suddenly shining with laughter. "Maybe I should have said to hell with being able to stand upright and let my friend Cara work her magic on them."

Kellan's chest shook with a husky rumble of laughter as he sheathed himself in a condom and climbed onto the bed, caging her beneath his body, his weight braced on his hands and his knees. "I meant what I told you before," he whispered, nuzzling his nose against one of those plump, candy-pink nipples that always made his mouth water. "You're perfect the way you are."

"Hardly," she scoffed, brushing her fingers through his hair. "But you're sweet to say so."

Lifting his head, Kellan stared deep into her eyes, willing her to believe him. "I mean it, Chloe. I wish you could see yourself the way I do. I wouldn't change anything about you. Not a single thing."

Touching her hand to the side of his face, she pulled her lower lip through her teeth again in that provocative way that he loved, her eyes full of mysterious shadows and heat. "I want you inside me, Kell."

Unable to resist, he touched his mouth to hers, sinking his tongue into that sweet, warm well, and lost himself in her succulent taste. When he finally came up for air, he kept his face close to hers, watching her eyes as he said, "Before this night is over, I'll be so deep inside you, you won't be able to remember what it was like not to have me filling you up. But I'm not going to rush it. Not tonight."

It wasn't easy, but Kellan called on the raw, breathtaking depth of emotion he felt for her to bind the wolf into submission, forcing the animal to heed his commands. Then he spread Chloe's thighs and opened her with his fingers, touching her…studying her…taking the time to be awed by every slippery, deliciously pink detail, the puffy cushion of her sex the sweetest, most beautiful thing he'd ever seen, not to mention the most luscious. A primal, visceral pleasure jolted through his veins as he covered her with his mouth, hungrily licking and lapping, unable to get enough of her. He kept at her with single-minded intent, lashing her clit with his tongue until she crashed over the edge, coming in an intoxicating rush of warmth against his face. Then he rose over her trembling form and claimed her mouth with a dark, devastating kiss at the same time as he forced his body into hers, shunting thick and deep. The pleasure was blinding, like a fevered kind of madness that burned through him, making a raw animal sound vibrate in his chest. He couldn't stop kissing her. Couldn't stop stroking and thrusting, rubbing his tongue against hers as he rode her body in a deliciously slow, thick rhythm, every grinding push and pull forcing husky little cries from her throat that only made him harder…and more desperate.

They rocked together in a deep, sensual glide, like waves slipping over the top of an ocean, their hunger building in a sweet, inexorable climb, while their breaths shortened, heat layering on heat as their bodies turned slick with sweat. Kellan touched his mouth to the delicate edge of her jaw, his hands greedily roaming her body as he kissed his way down the slender column of her throat, over the hammering beat of her heart, until he took one nipple into his mouth, her inner muscles clasping his cock in a wet, pulsing grip that made him growl. His fangs started to slip his gums, and he locked his jaw, fighting it with everything that he had as they came together on a long, surreal wave of pleasure that just kept going…and going, until he felt like he'd pumped out his very soul.

"Christ, I can't get enough of you," he breathed out in a low voice, clutching her against his body as they lay on their sides afterward among the crumpled bedding, her head tucked under his chin, their legs tangled in a sensual mesh of limbs.

"You know," she whispered, nuzzling her mouth against his chest, "when a man says something like that, it's usually followed by something more, Kell."

He stiffened with that familiar tension and closed his eyes, holding her a little tighter than before, as if she was suddenly going to slip away from him. "I wish like hell that I could give you more—" he swallowed, choking on the bitter taste of regret "—but I can't."

"Can't? Or won't?"

Kellan knew damn well what she wanted to hear, but he couldn't do it. He'd seen his friend Ian Buchanan, the first Merrick to be awakened, make a jackass of himself when he'd tried to keep away from his woman, refusing to feed from her until he'd almost lost her. The same could be said for his brother during all the years Kellan had tried to avoid his true feelings for Morgan Cantrell.

In Ian's case, he'd been terrified of accidentally killing Molly, and Kierland had feared what his jealousy would drive him to do. But Kellan's situation was different. He already had a fairly definite handle on his future—one that didn't look good. He couldn't make Chloe promises that he might not be around to keep, and he couldn't tell her the truth about the poison, worried about what she might do to try to help him.

So with a deep breath, he choked out the hoarse words that needed to be said. "No matter how badly I wish things were different, the truth is that I'm not good enough for you, Chloe. I'm damaged goods, in more ways than one. The last thing you need is to start getting intense about me."

She pushed against his chest, and he forced himself to let her go as she pulled away from him and sat up. Locking his jaw, Kellan propped himself up in the bed, resting his back against the carved headboard. She gathered the sheet into her hands, holding it against her breasts as she turned to face him, her eyes glistening with unshed tears as she wet her lips and said, "I don't mean to pressure you, Kellan. I mean, I know how crazy I sound—but then, this whole situation is crazy. I just…I don't understand what you want from me."

"I want…" *Too many things*, he thought. But to Chloe, he simply said, "Tonight, I want to pretend that I'm the kind of man you could be proud to have at your side. The kind you could want for something more than just a hot time in the sack."

"You *are* that kind of man," she told him, clutching the sheet tighter against her chest, the gray of her eyes darkening with emotion.

With a bitter, breathless bark of laughter, he scrubbed his hands down his face. "I'm not even close," he muttered, bracing his arms on his bent knees, his hands shaking with slight, almost imperceptible tremors. "Christ, I've been a fuckup my entire life, Chloe. I think you could do better. Hell, I *know* you could do better."

"That's not—"

"If you knew the things I'd done then you'd understand. It's not just the women. A shitty reputation I could get over, by proving to you that I've changed, but some of my mistakes were big ones. Ones that hurt my friends. That almost got them killed."

She started to argue, but he cut her off again, his voice dropping as he said, "A few months ago, I almost got an innocent woman killed because I was screwing one of the Casus females while I was working up in Washington with Riley Buchanan. The woman was Riley's fiancée, Hope, and that Casus bitch almost got to her because of *me*."

Her eyes went wide with shock, and Kellan knew that Raine had been telling him the truth when she'd promised to keep what she knew about his time in Washington to herself. "Did you…did you know what she was?" she asked. "The Casus, I mean."

"No, but it doesn't excuse what happened," he growled, that old, familiar guilt coiling through his insides, twisting him into knots as he dropped his head back against the headboard, closing his eyes. "And it sure as hell doesn't mean I'm not to blame."

SHE MIGHT NOT HAVE possessed the Lycan's incredible senses, but Chloe could recognize his shame. The raw, painful emotion blasted against her like a hot wind, and she longed for the right words to soothe him. "Mistakes happen," she said in a soft voice. "A bad choice doesn't make you a bad person, Kell."

His face tightened, his voice so guttural, it barely sounded human. "There aren't good people who do bad things, Chloe. There are just *bad* people."

"That's not true. Look at *us*, Kellan. Look at what you've done for me. You were willing to throw it all away, and for what? A stranger. Someone you didn't even know."

"You're wrong," he argued, lifting his head, and the look in his dark, glittering eyes stole her breath. "I knew a lot about you before I ever even set foot in the Wasteland. I talked to Olivia about you every chance I got. I knew you were smart and honest and loyal. Funny and sweet and sometimes a little shy, but courageous as hell. And everything I learned just made it that much clearer to me that I had to get close to you."

"And now you're close to me," she whispered, fighting to hold back her tears. "But I still can't have you, can I?"

"Don't," he rasped, his eyes burning a bright, unholy blue.

"Why not? It's true, isn't it? You're just using these excuses to keep—"

"You're wrong," he snarled, and the next thing she knew he was across the bed and pressing her into the mattress, pinning her beneath his heavily muscled body as he took hold of her wrists, trapping them above her head. "Not making you promises about the future," he growled, his deep voice breathless and rough. "Not talking to you about the future… Christ, Chloe. It's the most unselfish thing I've ever done in my life!"

"So it's all for my own good?"

"Yes!"

"That's such bullshit!" she snapped, unable to hold back the hot spill of tears as she struggled against him, the power of her Merrick rushing through her blood, but its strength was no match for the Lycan's. He simply pressed the hard, solid length of his muscular body more heavily against hers, trapping her beneath him.

"Please, Chloe, just listen to me," he groaned, burying the rough, fractured words in her hair. "I don't want to lose what time we have left. Just…just know that if I could, I'd give you everything."

"Kellan, I—"

"Damn it, just shut up and listen!" he barked, drawing back his head so that he could look down at her, his expression one of raw, tormented agony. "If I could, I'd make you every promise that can be made between a man and a woman. Every goddamn one," he growled, forcing the words through his clenched teeth. "But that's not an option. I wish like hell that it was, but it's *not*."

"Oh, God," she whispered, fear suddenly slicing through her like a blade. "There's something going on, isn't there? Something you're not telling me. Something bad."

He took a deep, shuddering breath, then managed to say, "Nothing's wrong, Chloe. I just…I just want you to be safe. I want you to have a good life, and that's not… that's not something I can give you."

He sounded sincere, but every instinct she possessed was screaming that he was keeping something from her. Something important. She could see the truth burning in his eyes. Feel it tremoring through his body.

She just didn't know if it was something they could get through together.

Or something that would tear them apart…

CHAPTER NINETEEN

The Wasteland, north of the Sabin compound
Saturday, 3:00 a.m.

THIS WAS IT. Crunch time.

Careful to avoid Juliana's sentries, Kellan had managed to slip away from the Sabin compound without detection, the crushed juniper leaves he'd rubbed into his skin successfully masking his scent, helping him to blend in with the surrounding forest. Determined to make sure that Chloe would be cared for no matter how his night ended, he'd left behind a letter for Kierland, explaining that he wanted her to be given his portion of their inheritance, as well as a place to live at Harrow House for as long as she wanted. There was so much more that he'd needed to say, but in the end, Kellan had simply finished the letter by telling Kierland that he loved him and wished him all the happiness he could find, since there was no one who deserved it more. Then he'd slid the envelope beneath his brother's door, and though he'd wanted to go back to his room and look in on Chloe one last time, he'd forced himself to leave.

For over an hour now, he'd been stalking through the wind-chilled forest, on the hunt for Gregory, and he needed to concentrate, but he couldn't get Chloe out of his mind. After their heated argument over her suspicions that he was keeping something from her, he'd spent long, breathless minutes coaxing her to relax. Tempting her to give in to the provocative burn of pleasure so that he could lose himself in her sweet, warm body...blocking the brutal reality that lay on the other side of midnight. And once she'd surrendered, he'd taken her into that rich, rushing darkness again...and again, his body already addicted to the way that she moved and tasted and came. Their time together had been nothing short of mind-blowing, the sex so explosive he was surprised they hadn't set the bed on fire. And after she'd taken another feeding, drinking deeply from his vein, she'd slipped gracefully into a heavy, exhausted slumber. Kellan had dozed with his cheek pressed against her stomach, two fingers buried deep inside her, just needing that connection with her. Needing to be a part of her, for as long as he could.

And now that he'd left her, he was in even worse shape than he'd feared he would be. The hold he'd had on the wolf during their lovemaking was slipping away from him, the animal howling with fury, enraged that he'd walked away without staking their claim, marking her as *their* woman. But then, the beast still believed they were going to make it out of this alive, while Kellan knew better.

Still, he'd come prepared. The heat of the Marker Chloe had left on the bedside table burned inside his pocket, thrumming with power. He wasn't just going to kill Gregory's host body and send his shade back to Meridian, where the Casus could eventually escape again. No, he wanted the bastard gone for good, which meant he had to use the cross and blast DeKreznick's ass straight to hell.

He was currently making his way across a moonlit meadow, thinking he might have just caught a faint trace of Gregory's scent, when the hair on the back of his neck stood on end. *Shit*, he thought, spinning around, searching the milky rays of moonlight for the source of his apprehension. A movement off to his left caught his eye, and he shifted in that direction, choking back a roar of frustration as, one by one, Reyker males began to stalk out of the surrounding forest, their pale gray eyes burning like sinister sparks of light.

And right in the center of the group stood Asa, the son of a bitch who had poisoned him.

Because they were Deschanel and could mask their scent, Kellan hadn't been able to detect the vampires' approach. And now it was too late. Cursing his monumentally crappy luck, the Lycan choked back a visceral snarl, knowing he would have to tread carefully with the Deschanel if he was going to continue on with his hunt.

"What do you want?" he asked, settling his sharp gaze on Asa Reyker's tall, rangy form.

The vampire's silver eyes burned with maniacal fire, his expression as bloodthirsty and mad as it'd been the last time Kellan had seen him. Hard to believe that it'd been little more than a week ago, when so much in his life had changed since then.

A week spent dying, and yet, they'd been the most meaningful days in Kellan's entire life.

And everything he was losing, he was losing because of Asa—that sudden realization making him want to throw himself on the vamp and rip his bloody head off.

Not the time, he silently snarled, struggling to control his temper. *Have to deal with Gregory first.*

"What do you think I want?" the Deschanel finally replied, the husky words revealing a trace of a Scandinavian accent, reminding Kell of the way Gideon spoke. "We had a deal, Lycan. One you've failed to honor."

Keeping a careful eye on the other eight members of the Reyker nest who were spreading themselves around the edges of the meadow, Kellan curled his hands into tight fists, his voice little more than a guttural rasp. "What the hell are you talking about? The deal was that I had to come and see you before I left the Wasteland. And I'm still here."

Asa lifted his shoulders in a casual shrug, the long strands of his chocolate-colored hair blowing across his hard-featured face. "But the poison is breaking you down, and you won't be any good to me dead, now will you?" he drawled, stalking across the meadow, until no more than a handful of feet separated them.

"I'm not dead *yet*," Kellan muttered, while his wolf snarled with aggression, eager to tear into the bastard. "And I have every intention of honoring the deal. Just not at this moment."

Asa hooked his thumbs in his front pockets, his tone eerily relaxed, as if they were merely discussing something as mundane as the weather. "I'm afraid that's not possible. We settle it now."

"Like hell we do," Kellan argued, wanting to wipe the vamp's smug expression right off his face. "There's something I have to do first."

"The terms of our deal were simple," Asa murmured, clearly not listening to him. "You wanted to cross my land, and I wanted to feed from you in your *were* form.

Not attack you—but simply enjoy taking your blood while you were bowing down before me, all obedient like. But since my bite is lethal, I offered you a deal that you were foolish enough to accept. If you survived your time in Westmore's compound, then you were supposed to come back to me and fight me for the chance to survive. If you won, I'd give you the antidote to the poison burning through your system. And if you lost, I'd be allowed to finish the feeding, draining you dry." The vampire lifted his brows. "And if you failed to show, then there would be dire consequences. Or did you forget?"

"Goddamn it!" he snarled. "I was coming back! But there's something I have to do first."

Rubbing his jaw, Asa said, "You're probably talking about that Casus who wants your woman, but I'm afraid I can't let you run off and get yourself killed."

Kellan took a deep breath, then slowly let it out, his head pounding as he tried to think of a way out of this. "How did you even manage to find me?" he asked, stalling…racking his brain for a solution.

"I'm afraid that juniper won't work on me," Asa offered in response to his question. "You can cover your scent as much as you want, but I'll still be able to track you. See, I'm one of those special breeds who can blood-track, just like your brother's mate."

A shape-shifter with an unusually eclectic bloodline, Morgan also possessed the ability to bloodtrack—honing in on the location of those she'd taken blood from—which was how she and Kierland had managed to track down Kellan in the Wasteland. Worried that he might not be able to get Chloe out of the compound on his own, Kellan had gone to Morgan before he'd left England and asked her to take his blood, knowing she'd be able to lead Kierland to him, so that they could be there to help if there was a problem.

It seemed a testament to Kellan's shitty luck that Asa could do the same damn thing.

"Listen," he muttered. "I'm telling you the truth. I have every intention of coming back to you, once I've dealt with Gregory."

The vampire smiled, slow and cruel...and *hungry*. "I'm afraid I don't believe you. Nor do I particularly care." Glancing at the others, he ordered, "Surround him."

Realizing they were making a ring with their bodies, standing shoulder to shoulder, Kellan seethed with fury, his wolf rising within his body on a great wave of raw, predatory violence. He welcomed the change, knowing the beast would fare better against the powerful vampires than the man, considering the shape he was in—but he couldn't make the complete shift into his *were* form. The poison had already wreaked too much destruction, and he only managed to release his claws and fangs. But he wouldn't let it stop him, damn it.

"Then have it your way," he snarled, flexing his long, sinister claws at his sides as he narrowed his gaze on Asa. "I'll fight you, you fucking bastard."

"Oh, I'm afraid that opportunity has passed now," Asa murmured, a crooked smile touching his mouth. "You've forfeited, Lycan. And now your ass is mine." Looking at his kinsmen, his voice hardened to one of guttural command as he said, "Get him down."

"You son of a bitch!" Kellan roared, fighting with everything he had, clawing and biting like the savage animal he was, but there were too many of them. The

Reykers descended on him all at once, like a devastating wave of darkness, spreading him out over the ground and holding him down, several pairs of hands gripping each straining limb. The silvery glow of moonlight shone at Asa's back, leaving his face in shadow, his glowing gray eyes smoldering with insanity, and Kellan knew, in that moment, that his doubts about the antidote had been true. If the Reyker nest was in possession of such a thing, surely they would have used it on this twisted bastard, the poison clearly having warped his mind, much like the strain that had infected Juliana's brother. As Asa sank down onto his knees beside him, the wolf seethed beneath Kellan's skin, punching against the insides of his body, but no matter how ferociously it struggled, it could *not* get out.

Swiping his tongue over his upper lip, Asa leaned over him, his talons digging deep into the ground as he growled, "Turn his head to the side."

The order was followed, and then Asa went for the bite, his long fangs tearing into Kellan's throat. The vampire fed with savage aggression, pulling at the wound in deep, ravenous gulps, draining him more…and more, until the fight slowly left the Lycan, his body no longer straining. No longer struggling.

Instead, Kellan found himself filled with a sinking sensation, his arms and legs too heavy for the cold, hard ground to support. It was as if he was simply melting into the earth, leaving behind nothing but skin and bones. Eventually, the vampires released their hold on his lax body, his limbs growing numb as his blood was drained from his veins. He was on the verge of slipping away, when at the hazy edges of his consciousness, he caught the sound of a commotion at the far end of the meadow, a new voice ringing out with fury, shouting Asa's name as it came closer...*closer*.

"Damn it, Asa! Let him go! I can't believe you came after him behind my back. We had a deal about you handling this situation fairly!"

With a guttural snarl, the vampire tore his fangs from Kellan's ravaged throat and surged to his feet. "He's done, anyway," he muttered, delivering a vicious kick to Kellan's ribs that sent his sluggish body tumbling over the cold ground, his limbs flailing, as useless and limp now as a rag doll's. As he struggled to draw in a gasp of air, the Lycan wondered how much blood still pumped through his veins.

Not enough, he realized, when his body refused to follow the simple commands being relayed by his brain. And whatever was left was now more poisoned than ever. He was dying...fading away, the ground no longer quite so cold as he lay there, the surreal sense of numbness spreading, slowly eating away at the pain.

"You broke your word," the female accused, her voice shaking with anger as she continued to berate the vampire.

Asa snickered. "Wasn't the first time, little sister. And I dare say it won't be the last."

Sister? Kellan tried to remember if he'd seen a female when he'd run into Asa the week before, but he couldn't recall. Not that it mattered. If her plan had been to help him, she was too late. He was already on his way out.

The argument continued, but he stopped listening, no longer caring what they said, his last thoughts turning to Chloe. Despair filled him at the realization that he would never see her again. He'd known it was coming, but he'd hoped that he would at least be able to destroy

Gregory for her, and he hadn't even been able to accomplish that.

Fucking pathetic, he thought, managing to open his eyes enough that he could watch Asa turning and heading back into the thick, snow-covered forest. The rest began following after him, and Kellan gnashed his teeth, somehow finding the strength to roll to his front, no longer even feeling the chill of the snow against his flesh. He knew he was dying, his body almost completely drained of blood. Resting his cheek against the hard ground, he concentrated on pulling in each breath, one after another, while listening to their voices as they left him to die. Then the wind blew over him, the scents of the surrounding forest filling his head, and he caught it....

Gregory!

Choking back a guttural groan, Kellan somehow managed to lift his head, his nostrils flaring as he searched for that scent, and he found it again, his upper lip curling back over his fangs. The bastard was out there...so close he could taste it.

Then get up off your ass and let's get him, the wolf snarled, vibrating with rage, refusing to accept defeat.

It was, as he'd heard Noah call them, one of those *sharp moments*. The kind that would be the make-or-break of his pride. He could do what was easy and lie down and die—or do what was hard and keep fighting for the woman he loved.

And damn it, he *did* love her. With everything that he had. He might be as good as worm food, but he wasn't going to give up on her until he'd finally drawn his last breath.

Digging his claws into the snow-crusted ground,

Kellan pulled his body forward, pain tearing through his system like a knife, excruciating and sharp. Tears burned at the backs of his eyes, but he gritted his teeth and managed to drag himself another foot over the ground, determined to somehow find the strength to deal with Gregory.

"Lycan, stop."

Kellan cursed at the sound of the soft words and kept going.

"Damn it." The female's voice was closer this time, coming from his right. "Stop crawling away from me. You're only going to weaken yourself even more, and I intend to help you."

"Help me?" A bitter laugh scraped against his throat. "Oh, Christ. How effing stupid do you think I am?"

"I could care less about your intelligence," she snapped. "I'm just trying to save your life."

Wondering what the hell she was up to, he stopped, and the female—Asa's sister—knelt beside him, quickly taking something out of the pack she slipped off her shoulder. The next thing he knew, she'd pushed him to his side, ripped open his sleeve, and injected a needle-tipped syringe into his vein.

"What are you doing?" he snarled, his arm suddenly burning with heat, the skin around the needle throbbing with pain.

She kept her focus on his arm, her brow knitted with concentration as she said, "I'm helping you, just like I said I was going to."

Kellan's thoughts spun with confusion, whatever she was injecting into his system chasing away the cold that had settled into his veins, and replacing it with a slick, scalding heat that had beads of sweat breaking out over his face. "Why?" he wheezed, trying to focus his wavering vision. "Why…help me?"

"I don't know. Maybe I'm just crazy." She sounded irritated as she flung the words at him, her gaze still focused on the place where she had the needle imbedded in his vein. "Now shut up, relax and let the antidote do its thing, or you're not going to do that woman you're so set on protecting a damn bit of good. You get me?"

"You're lying," he growled, struggling to sit up, but she plastered one hand against the center of his chest and pushed him back against the ground, his body still too weak to offer any resistance.

"You really need to work on your trust issues," she muttered, her gray eyes glittering with frustration as she glared down at him. "And for God's sake, learn to have a little faith. I get that you probably piss a lot of people off and make your fair share of enemies, but not everyone in the world is out to get you. Just trust me, okay? I'm golden, I swear."

Kellan wanted to tell her to shut up, but the cocky little vamp was right. He *had* lost his faith. Or maybe he'd just given up, months ago, when he'd realized what a fuckup he'd become…and slowly allowed his guilt to hollow him out inside. Allowed it to turn him into a man who'd been willing to accept his fate, no matter how shitty, instead of fighting against it.

It was unforgivable, when you thought about what he had to fight for. His family and friends, not to mention the woman who had laid claim to his heart and now owned his soul. Instead of focusing so much on what had happened in his past, he should have been moving mountains to sort out his future. And Christ, who gave a shit if he wasn't good enough for Chloe? None of that crap mattered. All that mattered was that he became the kind of man she *could* be proud of. One who was worthy of her—who cherished her the way she deserved.

You should have listened to me. I told you we'd find a cure, the wolf chuffed, and Kellan realized there'd be no living with the animal now. It would be gloating about this for years, holding it over his head whenever they disagreed.

Eyeing the syringe the vampire was slowly decompressing, feeding what looked like a thick, golden liquid into his vein, he said, "So then your brother wasn't lying when he told me there was an antidote for the poison?"

"Asa might be a bastard, but he's an honest one. At least sometimes," she added dryly.

Kellan's heart began to pound a little faster as he realized he was actually going to have the chance to throw himself at Chloe's feet and beg her for a second chance, but he took a deep breath and pushed the breathtaking thought to the back of his mind, knowing he had to keep his focus on Gregory before he could go running back to her.

"What's your name?" he asked, cutting his gaze back to the vampire's sharp little face.

"Everyone calls me Gabby."

"I'm not trying to sound ungrateful for what you're doing, but why didn't you help me before? On the night that Asa poisoned me?"

Her short brown curls brushed against the sides of her face as she depressed the plunger all the way down, emptying the contents of the syringe into his vein. "To be honest," she murmured, slipping the needle from his arm and dropping it back into its case, "I didn't see anything worth risking my neck to save. See, my brother and I both have special…talents, I guess you could say. While Asa can bloodtrack, mine are more intuitive."

"You're psychic?" he asked, while she gave him a shot that she explained would help his blood supply regenerate.

"No. I just…I see things. All kinds of things. Truths. Lies. And sometimes I can see inside a person's heart. Kind of like…like reading an aura." As she finished zipping up her pack, she looked down at him as she added, "You've changed this past week. The anger you carried inside of you has been replaced with love, and that's something I'm willing to take a risk for."

He grunted in response, gritting his teeth against the blistering heat sliding through his veins, the sensation as scalding as if he'd been injected with liquid fire, the antidote literally burning the poison from his system. When the pain finally started to recede, he asked, "Why haven't you given the antidote to your brother?"

With a frown, she explained, "Although this antidote will work on the Reykers' victims, I still haven't managed to create one that can purge the poison from its carriers."

"How did he get infected in the first place?"

"How else?" she muttered with a soft snort, rolling her eyes. "He and a cousin of mine made a mistake that affected every male in the family."

"So you're not poisonous?" he asked, managing to sit up as she moved to her feet.

"Nope, I'm in the clear," she replied, slipping her nylon pack back over her shoulder. "Only the males were cursed with the poison. I'm also not condemned to the Wasteland."

Moving first to his knees, Kellan waited until his head had stopped spinning before taking the small hand she offered and letting her help him to his feet. She was a tiny thing, like Chloe, barely reaching his shoulder, but she had a look about her that said she was anything but delicate. More like a pint-sized Doberman dressed in jeans and a heavy, cable-knit sweater. "If you're not exiled," he said, "then what are you doing here?"

"Some witch friends of mine have been helping me formulate the antidote, and we only just came up with a workable sample last week. I'd brought the news of the antidote to Asa on the day that he poisoned you."

Using his sleeve to wipe at his bloodied throat, he said, "That explains why the Sabins didn't know about the antidote."

Gabby lifted her brows. "It's true that we haven't exactly spread the word around, but I'm surprised the psychic you've been traveling with couldn't tell you that the antidote was real."

Kellan winced. "Raine's in bad shape after her time at Westmore's compound. Her powers are weak right now, and when she tried to get a read on Asa for me, his mind was filled with too much violence for her to see anything clearly."

"That sounds like my brother," she muttered under her breath, and he could sense the pain that roughened the edges of her words.

"You mentioned Asa and your cousin made a mistake that brought about the curse. What was it?"

Her knuckles turned white as she gripped the strap that crossed her shoulder. "Her name was Merol, and she's a prickly sorceress. One who likes to play with men as if they were her personal toys, but expects utter devotion in return. Needless to say, they screwed with the wrong woman when they got involved with her."

"Haven't we all?" he grunted.

"And yet, fate has granted you a gift in the witch," she told him. "I still hope the same can happen for my brother."

"I'd tell you you're wasting your time," he rasped, reaching out to brace his hand against a nearby tree as a wave of dizziness swept through him, "but since I have a brother, I understand."

She responded with a slight nod, then seemed to take a moment to study his eyes. "If you just give it a minute, the dizziness should fade."

Clearing his throat, he said, "Listen, I know I acted like a dick at first, but I owe you for—"

She waved away the words with her hand. "You didn't ask for my help, therefore you owe me nothing. This was my choice."

"Will your brother be angry with you?" he asked, pushing his hair back from his face with a shaking hand as he fought the nausea twisting through his stomach.

The vampire shook her head. "I can handle Asa. Just get the hell out of the Wasteland as soon as you can. And whatever you do, *don't* come back."

Eager to get on with his hunt for Gregory, Kellan thanked her for her help, then turned and headed into the woods, searching the forest for that faint trace of the Casus's scent that he'd picked up on earlier. Though his head was still spinning, he knew that the sooner he dealt with DeKreznick, the sooner he could make his way back to Chloe, throwing himself on her mercy. He was thinking about what he would say to her when he realized that Gabby was following him, and he cut her a sharp look over his shoulder. "What the hell are you doing?"

"Helping you finish it." Wearing a determined expression, she hiked her pack higher on her shoulder and lifted her chin. "The way I see it, the sooner you're done here, the sooner you're gone. And I really don't want to keep worrying about Asa coming after you again."

"Just be careful," he muttered, figuring she'd earned the right to follow him wherever she wanted, considering she'd just saved his life. Some light snow flurries were beginning to fall from the slate-gray sky, screwing with his sense of smell, so he headed north, which was the direction he'd caught the Casus's scent coming from earlier. Kellan estimated they were already at least a few miles north of the Sabin compound, and with each step he took, he could feel the antidote fighting to destroy the remnants of the poison, his healing abilities slowly returning to full strength, working hard to replenish his blood supply with the help of the shot that Gabby had given him. He was still a long way off from being at a hundred percent, but he was no longer knocking on death's door, and his thoughts turned to the coming fight.

"You need to mask your scent," he told Gabby, hoping like hell there was still enough juniper on his skin to disguise his presence. "The Casus has a witch with him who can lock their opponents in place. My only chance against him is to take the witch out first."

"Lycan," she murmured, her tone signifying a problem, and he caught the scents in the next instant, fear and frustration searing through his veins.

"Goddamn it," he snarled, running toward the source, powering his way through the moonlit forest as he dodged low-hanging limbs and jumped over fallen logs. Gabby was right on his heels as he burst into a small clearing a few minutes later, unable to believe his friggin' eyes.

They were all there, except for Raine. His brother and his friends and their allies. Every single bloody one of them.

And Chloe Harcourt was standing right in the center of the group.

CHAPTER TWENTY

OH SHIT, HE THOUGHT. *This* cannot *be happening!*

Kellan quickly blinked his eyes, certain he must be imagining that Chloe was standing there between his brother and Morgan. But no…she was real. Jesus, had Kierland lost his bloody mind? Kellan had trusted him to take care of her, and instead, he'd brought her out into the open!

"Get her out of here!" he snarled, his wolf on the verge of breaking free as he advanced on his brother with long, furious strides. "What the hell were you thinking?"

Kierland's green eyes burned with his own fury. "I could ask you the same thing," he shot back, getting right in Kellan's face.

"You stubborn bastard!" His voice cracked as he shoved hard at Kierland's shoulders, a flare of satisfaction burning through his veins when he managed to knock the powerful Lycan back a step, his body becoming stronger by the second. "I trusted you to take care of her! Not offer her up to Gregory like a goddamn sacrifice!"

"You didn't leave us any choice," Kierland argued, his words biting and sharp. "After Chloe woke up and found you gone, she came to me and we found your letter. So what exactly was I meant to do, Kell? Sit around and wait for you to get yourself killed?"

"You were meant to trust me to handle my own life, you bloody control freak."

"Kellan, please calm down," Morgan murmured. "You know Kier only wants you to be safe."

"I don't wanna hear it," he growled, cutting her a hard look of warning. He knew damn well that she'd used her bloodtracking ability to lead the group to him, which put her at the top of his shit list at the moment. The only reason he'd had Morgan make the damn bond was to ensure Chloe's safety—not his own!

From the corner of his eye, Kellan noticed that Aiden and the others were fanning out around him, and he couldn't help but wonder if they planned to drag him back to the Sabin compound kicking and screaming.

If that's their plan, he thought, his nostrils flaring with rage, *then they'd better be ready to get bloody, because I'm not going without a fight.*

"Did you honestly expect me to leave you out here on your own?" Kierland rolled his shoulder in a hard act of aggression, as if he was getting ready to throw a punch.

"I expected you to keep her safe," Kellan muttered in disgust. "But I guess I should have relied on someone else."

Kierland flinched, but before he could say anything to defend his actions, Chloe moved toward them, her soft voice thick with emotion. "Your brother asked me to stay behind, Kell, but I refused. So if you're going to be angry with anyone, it should be me."

Ignoring her, Kellan kept his furious gaze locked on Kierland's rigid features. "If Gregory finds us like this, the witch will have us frozen in place within seconds. We'll be as good as dead." Rough, gritty words that vibrated with anger. "So I'm going to make this very clear. Turn around and get your asses back to the compound."

"He's right," Gabby murmured. "You don't have any time to lose."

"Who the hell are you?" Kierland demanded, his pale gaze landing with blistering animosity on the petite vampire.

It was Juliana who answered. "I can tell by her scent that she's from the Reyker nest."

"Leave her alone," Kellan barked, stepping between his brother and Gabby when Kierland's expression turned deadly. "She's not an enemy. She helped me tonight."

"Why would she help you?" Juliana asked, her forehead scrunching with confusion. "The Reykers only ever look out for themselves."

Gabby moved out from behind him, sliding Juliana a wry look. "Asa might be a bastard these days, but we're not all bloodthirsty savages, Sabin. You think your family's the only one who landed here because of a bad choice?"

"What are you talking about? What bad choice?" Ashe demanded, obviously hoping to find out why the Sabins had been exiled, but Kierland cut him off.

"Just what exactly was your plan for the night, Kellan?"

Furious that he was having to waste time on this shit, Kellan scrubbed his hands down his face, then said, "I figured if I was on my own, I had a chance of sneaking up on Gregory and taking out the witch first, then the Casus. And after that, I'd promised Asa Reyker a fight."

"But my brother found Kellan before he could track down the Casus," Gabby explained, "and that's where things went wrong. Though he was meant to give Kellan the chance to fight him for the antidote to the poison, Asa attacked him instead."

"Antidote?" Kierland's eyes went almost comically wide. "What antidote?"

"The one I've already given him," Gabby replied. "It was close, but he got it in time to make a full recovery."

"You're not dying?" Kierland rasped, his deep voice choked with tears as he locked his bright gaze with Kellan's. "In your letter, you said...that the poison was killing you. And when I confronted Juliana, she admitted that the Reykers' poison is fatal to *all* species."

"What I said in the letter was true at the time," Kellan told him, stunned by the depth of Kierland's reaction. "But I'm okay now."

For a moment, Kierland simply stared at him, his expression shifting between shock and relief, and then he seemed to snap back to the moment. "You said the antidote was what Kellan would have won if he beat your brother in the fight," he rasped, sliding his stormy gaze back toward Gabby. "But what would have happened if he'd lost?"

"If he'd lost, my brother would have been allowed to finish the feeding, draining him completely. Which is what almost happened."

Chloe gasped, while his brother blanched. "It would have hardly been a fair fight when Kellan's been fighting off a lethal poison!"

Gabby frowned. "I didn't say it was fair. I said that's what Kellan agreed to. And he had every intention of honoring that deal."

"How do you know what Kellan intended to do?" Morgan asked, eyeing Gabby with a wary gaze.

"I know because I happen to possess the ability to see the truths in a person's heart. Even though Kellan believed Asa's promise of an antidote was most likely a lie, he would have kept his word and met Asa's challenge."

Kellan listened as Chloe took a deep breath, his heart stuttering with fear as she moved closer to him, her tear-dark gaze first settling on the bite wound Asa had left on the side of his throat, before lifting to his face. "Is all of that true, Kellan?"

He shrugged, and she shook her head in disbelief, a flush of heat beginning to burn beneath her fair skin. "So this is why you wouldn't talk to me about any kind of future between us? Because you were *dying?*"

His jerky nod only seemed to make her angrier.

"God, do you have any idea how ridiculous that was? Why not just tell me the truth?"

"I didn't want to hurt you." He swallowed, wishing like hell that he could take her into his arms, but knowing that it wasn't the time. "Didn't want you worrying about me or feeling guilty about something that was *my* fault. If I hadn't stumbled onto the Reykers' land last week, I never would have been poisoned."

Frustration glittered in her eyes, her fangs visible beneath the curve of her upper lip as she argued, "And what about Gregory? What if you'd found him? Did you think it wouldn't bother me when I learned that you'd gone off and gotten yourself killed while trying to protect me?"

He clenched his jaw. "I was *trying* to do the right thing."

"Damn it, Kell. Don't you get it? You don't have to kill yourself for me!"

"Worth it," he grunted, working his jaw. "I'd do anything to keep you safe."

"No, it's not worth it, you damn idiot!" She trembled, more furious than he'd ever seen her, and he could feel the power of the Merrick rising up within her, burning behind those beautiful, stormy eyes. "It's not worth it if it means I lose you. I want a partner. Someone to spend my life with. Not a goddamn memory!"

"Damn it, we don't have time for this," he muttered, raking both hands through his windblown hair. Her dark eyes were full of worry and fear, as well as a wealth of hurt that he couldn't allow himself to think about. Not then. Not when her bloody life was still in danger. "Gregory's too close! You need to get out of here!"

"If that was true," Quinn offered in a rough voice, "Jamison would have sounded a warning. He's running a perimeter on the clearing."

"No. The Lycan is right," Gabby murmured, lifting her nose to the whispering breeze as she released her talons from the tips of her fingers. "The Casus isn't far."

Accepting that they were out of time, Kellan forced down his rage and pulled the Marker from his pocket, slipping it over Chloe's head before shoving her behind him. As he scanned the surrounding woods with a sharp gaze, searching for any sign of the bastard, she whispered his name, and he told her, "Stay quiet."

Ashe pulled in a deep, searching breath, then released his talons at the same time as Gideon. "The Reyker female is right. He's here."

A hawk screeched in the distance, a cold breeze slicing through the trees that whipped viciously at their hair, and then Gregory waltzed out of the thick shadows on the far side of the clearing, a body slung over his broad shoulders. For a split second, Kellan thought it might be the golden-haired witch he was carrying, the darkness making it difficult to see—but then she stepped out of the trees, as well, standing a little off to the Casus's right.

"Tell me," Gregory called out, his long hair slicked back from his chiseled face as he slid a glittering look toward Kierland, "was this your pathetic attempt at a guard dog?" Lifting the body over his head, he tossed it into the center of the clearing, a gleaming shaft of moonlight revealing Jamison's bruised face, his torso a bloodied, pulverized mess. With a slow smile, the Casus said, "As you can see, I went right for that tender underbelly. Works every time on you Lycans."

Kierland, Quinn and Aiden roared with fury as they rushed toward the Casus, but the witch lifted her hand, freezing them each on the spot. Kellan felt her power lock his own body in place, and knew the same had been done to everyone but Chloe, who was clutching the back of his shirt with shaking hands, her breaths coming in sharp, shallow pants, while his friends growled and cursed, struggling against the invisible force that bound them.

"He would have stopped you, if you'd given him a fair fight," Kierland snarled in a savage voice. "But you had the witch freeze him, didn't you? You fucking murdered him!"

"Yes, well, I'm afraid honor escapes me at the best of times. And when I'm tracking my Merrick…" His voice trailed away as he shrugged. "I'm hardly going to allow something as insignificant as honor stand in my way."

"I'm surprised you didn't go after Westmore first," Kellan forced through his gritted teeth, "considering how badly you want him."

A crooked smile touched the bastard's mouth. "I *do* want him. And I'll get him, too, right after I've filled myself up on the little Merrick."

"She's wearing a Marker," Kellan growled, his own fangs dropping hard and fast. "You won't be able to touch her."

"Sure I will. With the right persuasion, I bet I can get her to do anything I want," Gregory drawled, his smile widening as he slid his gaze toward Chloe, who had stepped out from behind him, and was now standing at Kellan's side. "Once I get my claws around the Lycan's throat, you'll take the cross off for me. Won't you, sweetheart?"

Kellan snarled as another bitter wind swept through the clearing, shaking the leaves in the trees, catching at their clothes and hair. As the witch's tangled locks were blown back from her gaunt, hollow-eyed face, Noah, who stood a little ways off to Kellan's left, made a sharp sound of disbelief. "Sienna?" the human croaked, shaking his head. "What the hell are you doing here?"

"You know her?" Aiden grunted with a thick note of disbelief.

"Yeah." Though Noah looked as if he was staring at a ghost, the golden-haired witch gave no sign that she recognized him, simply returning his stare with those cold, expressionless eyes that gave nothing away. "At least, I used to know her," he rasped. "But she didn't look like…this."

"I imagine she might have been beautiful at one time," Gregory murmured, "before grief ravaged her features. But that would have been a lifetime ago, and Sienna has a new life now. One that ties her to me. You see, we've made a deal."

"What kind of deal?" Noah demanded, struggling even harder against the witch's power, the tendons in his dark throat straining beneath his skin. "Whatever he's promised you, Sienna, it's a lie!"

The Casus tsked under his breath, his sun-streaked hair brushing his shoulders as he shook his head. "You have it all wrong, because I didn't seek out the witch. She came to me," he explained, his ice-blue eyes shining with laughter. "I was already halfway back to Meridian, after that little human bitch shot me up in Washington, when Sienna reached in and used her power to pull me back. Took her a while to get me on my feet again, but she was determined to make it happen."

"But why?" Chloe asked the woman. "What could you possibly need him for?"

Before the witch could respond, Gregory came a few steps closer, his bright gaze landing on Chloe as he drew in a slow, deep breath. "God, you smell good," he drawled, stroking two fingers against the hard edge of his jaw, a wicked smile touching his lips. "Sweet and warm…and powerful. If I'd had any idea you were going to be this tempting, I'd have come after you a long time ago."

"Stay the fuck away from her!" Kellan roared, his

body racked with agonizing pain as he strained against the witch's power with everything that he had. But no matter how savagely he fought the hold she had over his body, he couldn't break free. And he was out of time. In the next instant, Gregory threw back his head, a deep-throated laugh rumbling up from his chest as the bastard gave himself over to the change, taking his true form. DeKreznick's clothing ripped as his body transformed into the monstrous shape of the Casus, leathery gray skin stretched over his towering frame and wolf-shaped head, his jaws gaping with jagged, deadly fangs. He let out a stark, guttural howl, then lowered his head, his nostrils flaring as he settled his bloodthirsty gaze back on Chloe.

"Get the hell out of here!" Kellan shouted at her. "Start running, now!"

"No," SHE WHISPERED, knowing she should be terrified. And yet, it wasn't thoughts of her own safety that filled her head. Instead, all she could think about was the fact that Kellan had been willing to give his life for hers. That he'd left her that night to track down Gregory on his own.

"Christ, Chloe." His deep voice was ravaged with fear, his eyes burning with preternatural fire as he stared down at her. *Please, run.*

"And leave you?" She shook her head. "I'm sorry, but I can't do that."

"You *can* do it. The Merrick's power will make you fast, honey. Just run," he pleaded in a hoarse rasp. "Do *not* let him get close to you."

"I'm staying here." It wasn't easy, but she managed to tear her gaze from Kellan's and moved to stand in front of him, while focusing her concentration inward. She could feel something building within her, and it wasn't the Merrick, the primal creature already taking up space within her body. No...this was an unknown force, and yet, it felt strangely familiar. It thrummed with promise and power, and with a deep breath, Chloe surrendered... giving herself over to it, frightened, but willing to do whatever it took to keep Kellan and the others alive.

"Holy shit," Aiden muttered, his deep voice thick with awe. "Look at her."

She heard Kellan whisper her name at her back as she lifted her hands toward the Casus. Chloe didn't understand what was happening, but her hands were suddenly...*glowing*, her skin shimmering as if a great, blinding light was burning within her.

"Do you feel that?" Gabby whispered, lifting her face to the air as a shocking wave of warmth swept through the clearing, chasing away the cold.

"What is it?" Chloe asked her, while a rush of noise filled her ears, as if she was standing beneath the jet engine of an airplane. The trees thrashed even harder, their leaves torn from the branches as that surreal wave of warmth grew stronger...the breeze more violent. Chloe knew the others were shouting, but their raised voices were drowned out by the sound of the wind, and with a sharp jolt of shock, she realized the powerful blast of air was coming from her—from her hands!

Panic swept through her, keeping company with the fear, and then, in the midst of the chaos, Gabby Reyker's voice reached out to her. "It's going to be okay. Everything you need is here."

Clenching her teeth, Chloe watched as the Casus struggled against the powerful force of the wind, fighting to reach her. "I don't know what to do!" she screamed, her skin glowing so bright that it hurt her eyes.

"You have the means inside you, but your Mallory powers are still weak," Gabby whispered within her mind. "You can find the catalyst you need inside the wolf's heart."

"Damn it, I don't understand!"

"Look inside him!" Gabby instructed her, the vampire's voice becoming strong and firm. "It's there. What you need, it's burning within him."

The witch's hair whipped around her frail body as she continued to hold the others in place, the Casus still fighting to make his way toward her, and Chloe knew she had to do something. With her arms still stretched out before her, she closed her eyes and tried to follow Gabby's instructions. She tuned everything else out, and thought of nothing but Kellan. About how much she loved him. About the stunning fact that he'd been willing to give his life for hers…and suddenly she understood what the vampire had meant. She could literally *feel* the powerful emotions burning inside him, molten and pure, and her pulse roared as she basked in their warmth, somehow soaking them into her system, until they were rushing through her veins and her thundering heart.

As Chloe lifted her lashes, she could see that she was glowing brighter, the fiery light that was shining inside her now burning in her fingertips as she narrowed her gaze on the Casus, who was clearly using everything he had to battle against the hot, hurricane-force winds rushing against him.

It's your Mallory powers, the Merrick told her, adding its strength to the blast. *They're channeling the Lycan's emotions into the fuel they need.*

Her Mallory powers? Oh, God…was the curse truly coming to an end? If so, it explained so many things—like the way she'd been able to interact so easily with Kellan's friends, without throwing the group's emotions completely out of balance. But then, it also meant Kellan's desire for her had been real, which seemed too good to be true. Could it honestly be over?

You bet your ass it is, the Merrick shouted, sounding as if it was actually enjoying itself.

Looking over her shoulder, Chloe stared up into Kellan's gorgeous face, wishing she could tell him how she felt, but she knew he couldn't hear the hoarse words spilling from her lips, the deafening sound of the wind drowning her out.

She could see that he was using every ounce of strength he possessed to fight against the witch's hold, determined to protect her. Blood trickled from the corner of his left eye like a crimson tear, more blood streaming from his nose, his veins raised beneath his skin as his muscles bulged, while his eyes burned with furious intent. "I'm not going to lose you!" he growled, his guttural words echoing through her mind, the same as Gabby's had, almost as if Chloe could hear whoever she focused her attention on, which was more than a little unusual. But considering she was glowing with light and had a windstorm coming out of her hands, it wasn't as if something "unusual" should have come as a shock.

"I'm not letting him take you from me, Chloe. Not when I've finally found you," Kellan snarled, and as she watched, his body began to change into his *were* form. His bones began to pop and crack, his body gaining inches in muscle and height, his clothes shredding as his skin darkened and auburn fur spread over his changing physique. He was breathtaking and massive, so much bigger than an actual wolf, with fur and fangs and a muzzled face, but a body that still retained shades of the man in the powerful arms and legs.

Chloe stared, more than a little amazed by the primal, predatory beauty of his beast. He looked as if he could tear mountains apart with his bare hands, his glowing green eyes burning with visceral rage…and on the other side of the clearing, Sienna cried out in pain.

Tearing her gaze from Kellan, Chloe looked toward the witch, who was screaming, "Gregory, hurry! I don't think I can hold him any longer! He's too strong!"

"You have to!" the Casus roared as he fought to take a step forward, struggling to work against the fiery wind blasting from Chloe's hands. "Don't let him go until I've got her!"

"Never!" Kellan snarled, and suddenly one claw-tipped arm was wrapping around Chloe from behind, pulling her tight against the scorching heat of his chest. As if his touch was the thing she'd needed to fully charge her Mallory powers, she shuddered with an electrifying jolt, suddenly feeling as if she could blast Gregory to hell and back. But just as she was opening her mouth to warn Kellan and the others to brace themselves, he set her aside and charged across the clearing, tackling Gregory to the ground. They skidded across the snow-covered clearing, disappearing into the edge of the trees. Their graveled snarls filled the air, and Chloe lowered her hands, fear twisting her insides as she stared into the shadowed woods. She started to head toward the trees, when Kierland, who was still locked in place by Sienna's power, roared for her to stay back. The primal, savage sounds of the battle continued, and then Gregory came crawling into the clearing, and it was clear from the Casus's bloodied form as he struggled to get to his feet that the Lycan was winning the fight. With his claws dripping red at his sides, Kellan stalked from the trees, his bright eyes burning with determination as he headed toward the Casus, and Chloe had never seen anything so mesmerizing in her entire life.

"Get up, you bastard." The snarled words were garbled within the muzzled shape of Kellan's mouth, but Chloe could still understand what he'd said. The Casus curled his lip over his jagged fangs and finally staggered to his feet, only to drop down on a knee as Kellan stalked closer. The Lycan raised one powerful arm, the moonlight glinting against his deadly claws as he prepared to deal the deathblow, when the ground began to shake with a violent, roaring tremor. Gregory's ice-blue eyes went wide with panic, and he lurched to his feet… trying to run, but his body seemed frozen in place as a thick, black smoke billowed up from the ground beneath him, encircling him as it wrapped around his legs.

"What's happening?" Chloe yelled, watching as several hideous-looking black claws materialized out of the smoke, sinking into Gregory's leathery flesh, stark cries of pain ripping from his chest as the claws sank deep into his body.

"He's dying, and the Casus shades are trying to pull him back into Meridian before the witch can save him again," Gabby shouted. "Kellan, you need to be careful! Move back!"

He growled, starting to step back, but Gregory reached forward with his long arms and grabbed one of Kellan's wrists. Chloe started screaming, terrified that the Casus would drag Kellan into the ring of smoke with him. While the Lycan ripped his claws across Gregory's arm, fighting to break free, the heat in Chloe's body intensified to a molten, pulsing fire, a breathtaking wave of power building inside her, climbing higher…and higher, until she suddenly lifted her hands again, flexing her fingers toward the Casus. And this time, instead of a powerful wind, she blasted him with white, blinding beams of light. They were like some kind of supernatural laser that scorched his leathery flesh, the power of the beams knocking him away from Kellan and deeper into the smoke, the claws now ripping into his chest.

"Sienna, help me!" the Casus screamed, reaching toward the golden-haired witch, but she shook her head, taking a step back…and then another.

"You can't help me now," she said flatly, her gaunt face devoid of emotion. "I'll have to find another." Then, in a flash of light, she vanished.

"You bitch!" Gregory roared, while the black claws pulled him deeper into the smoke, digging into his leathery skin.

"Tell your buddies in the pit we're coming for them," Kierland growled, and as he stepped forward, Chloe realized the witch's hold on the others was now gone.

"This isn't over," the Casus sneered, locking his hate-filled gaze with hers.

"You're wrong. It ends now," Chloe told him, and in the next instant her power shot out in an explosive, shocking blast of light that knocked everyone to the ground, her own body thrown back nearly twenty feet, until she slammed painfully into a tree. As she struggled to lift her head, she saw that Gregory had vanished, nothing left but a scorched, smoking ring of fire that circled the place where he'd stood. With a shuddering breath, she managed to shift her gaze toward Kellan, who was already running toward her, but her eyes slid closed…and then there was nothing but the darkness, as soothing and calm as a tropical breeze wrapping around her….

As if listening through a thick veil of fog, she could hear a raw sound tear from Kellan's throat as he clutched her body against his chest, her head lolling back over his arm. "No! This isn't… Damn it, she's not supposed to die!" His hoarse, broken words were little more than a ravaged scrape of sound. "I'm the one meant to die. Not her!"

"She isn't dying," Gabby murmured, her voice so close that Chloe realized the vampire must be kneeling on the ground beside her. Gabby's cold hand touched her cheek, and she said, "It's just going to take her body a few days to recoup from the strain. That was a helluva jolt of power she experienced. It would have shocked anyone's system."

"Where did it come from?" he croaked, sounding as if he was crying.

"It was her Mallory powers. Either the curse was ending on its own, or her determination to save you burned it out of her. Whatever the answer, you're a lucky man, Kellan Scott. To create the kind of power she just did, she must love you more than her own life. And Lycan, a love like that never dies."

Kellan shuddered, a low groan vibrating through his body as he crushed Chloe against the heavy beat of his heart, and though she wanted to comfort him…to tell him she was okay, the darkness pulled her deeper…and she drifted away…the calming waves rolling over her head, taking her under….

CHAPTER TWENTY-ONE

Harrow House, England
Monday night

IF THERE WAS ONE THING on earth that couldn't be done, it was separating a Lycan from the woman he loved. Though the others had continuously pestered him to get some sleep and let one of them sit with Chloe for a while, Kellan refused to leave her bedside. They'd arrived back at Harrow House late the previous night…and while Olivia and Saige had been ecstatic to have their men back at home, they were all sick over Jamison. After months of conflict, the war had finally taken its toll on their group, and no one could quite believe that the young archaeologist was gone. They'd known it would only be a matter of time before they suffered casualties, but it didn't make Jamison's loss any easier to accept.

And Kellan could only thank God that he hadn't lost Chloe.

After she'd lost consciousness in the clearing, Kellan had carried her back to the Sabin compound and placed her on the bed in his room. The next morning, when Kierland had come to check on how she was doing, he'd shocked the hell out of Kellan with a bone-crushing hug, his brother's deep voice hoarse with emotion as he'd said,

"I meant to give you one of those before, but I was too pissed at you for scaring the hell out of me."

A crooked grin had touched the corner of Kellan's mouth. "And now?"

"Still pissed," Kierland had replied with a gritty laugh, "but happy as hell that you're alive."

The group had set off for England later that morning, thanking Juliana Sabin for her help and promising to send her some much-needed supplies, then had parted ways with the Grangers once they'd made it out of the Wasteland. Just before they'd arrived back at Harrow House, Morgan had said, "Just to let you know, if you ever pull a stunt like this again, Kell, there's a good chance that I'll kill you myself."

Aiden and Quinn had seconded the playful threat, and Kellan had hugged Chloe closer to his chest as he said, "Don't worry. I plan on keeping myself in one piece from here on out."

Though the little witch had yet to regain consciousness for any significant amount of time, she would open her eyes every now and then, giving him a tired smile before softly drifting back to sleep, her body slowly recovering from the extreme exertion of the attack she'd waged against Gregory DeKrcznick. But for the past five hours, she'd been waking up more frequently, and Kellan was hopeful that it wouldn't be long now before she had fully recovered. And in the meantime, he was enjoying their brief conversations. Just a few hours ago, she'd opened her eyes and looked around his bedroom as she'd asked, "Where am I?"

"You're in my room at Harrow House, honey."

"Sweet," she'd murmured, her eyes already drifting closed as he'd pressed a smile into the palm of her hand.

She'd woken up a few more times since then, and each time she'd asked a question that Kellan had done his best to answer. So far, he'd explained that they were still waiting to pick up the tracking signal for Spark, which meant that the assassin was most likely still in the Wasteland. He'd also told her that they'd heard from Garrick, and the soldier had managed to get Raine's family safely to the Watchmen compound in Rome. She'd even asked about the death journal that they'd taken from Spark, and he'd told her that Kierland was trying to find someone who could decipher the passages that had been written in that strange, archaic language.

But each time they talked, Chloe would drift back to sleep, and Kellan was currently praying that she would wake up for good, because there was so much he wanted to tell her. So many things he wanted to share with her. Hell, he was even excited about taking her downstairs and showing her around, knowing she was going to love living at Harrow House as much as he did. She might have been a loner for most of her life, but he knew that was only because of the curse. The time Chloe had spent with his friends in the Wasteland had shown him that she was hungry for contact with others, and he had no doubt that she was going to make strong friendships among the Watchmen. And of course, she'd have Olivia and Jamie there with her, her sister and niece nearly as desperate as Kellan was for her to fully regain consciousness.

Sitting in a chair that he'd pulled up close to her bedside, Kellan had just taken hold of her hand, when she lifted those long lashes again, this time revealing clear, luminous eyes that no longer held that hazy veil of exhaustion. "You're still here," she whispered, her cheeks warming with a beautiful rush of color.

"I'm insulted you look so surprised," he teased with a lopsided smile. "And just so you know, I'm never leaving."

"Oh." She licked her bottom lip and blinked those long, dark lashes, her provocative scent rising with the heat of her body. "You...um, look like you want to say something."

"I'm ready to say a lot of things," he murmured, rubbing his thumb over her delicate knuckles, her small hand shaking in his. "You ready to hear them?"

Her shallow breaths were starting to come a little faster. "I...I don't know."

"Too bad." Wanting to be closer to her, Kellan sat beside her on the edge of the bed and took her precious face in his hands. "God, there's so much I want to say to you, Chloe, but I guess I'll start with this. What I wanted to tell you before, but couldn't, is that you're the *only* woman I'll ever want. The only one I'll ever need. And I don't just want you *for now*, like I told you I did. I want you forever. That's what I've wanted all along."

Tears glistened in her eyes. "Why didn't you tell me before?"

"Because I knew I was dying, and I didn't want you to care about me." He looked away, pulling a hand down his face as he blew out a rough breath. "Hell, that's not true. And I refuse to lie to you. The truth is, I *wanted* you to care about me. I wanted it more than anything. I just...I didn't want to make you think we had a future together, when I didn't believe I was going to be around much longer. I thought it was all over for me, and I didn't want you to get hurt." He cleared his throat, and another deep, ragged breath slipped past his lips as he locked his gaze back on hers, his voice shaking as he said, "The truth is...I've fallen in love with you."

He'd expected to have an argument on his hands, thinking he would have to convince her, but she simply gave him a shy smile and whispered, "I know."

His brows lifted. "You know?"

With a nod, she said, "I know it sounds crazy, but I...I saw into your heart when we were in the clearing. I saw exactly how you feel about me, Kell."

"What you saw inside of me," he rasped, his heart pounding to a deep, resonating beat as he took hold of her hand again, "it's real, Chloe. Every ounce of it. I swear it's as real as it gets, and it doesn't have a damn thing to do with that bloody curse."

"Don't worry. I know the curse has ended, so I won't keep throwing it in your face. But, are you sure this is what you want?" Using her free hand to push his hair back from his brow, she said, "You're only twenty-seven, Kell. And I've heard it can take a Lycan years to finish sowing his oats."

A wry smile touched the corner of his mouth. "Trust me, honey, I got an early start. Compared to you, I'm an old man."

She bit her lip, looking away. "I just don't want you to have any regrets."

"Chloe, look at me."

"I am," she told him, bringing her gaze back to his.

Kellan moved closer, surrounding her with his heat as he leaned over her. "No, I mean really look at me." He waited until she was staring deep into his eyes before saying, "I *love* you, Chloe Harcourt. As in till death do us part. As in my fangs in your throat, the second

you're out of this bed, so that you're marked. *As mine.* As
something that belongs to me. Something I will kill for.
Something I'm willing to die for, and I wouldn't change
anything about you. Not a single thing," he vowed in
a husky voice, his mouth suddenly kicking up with a
crooked grin. "Hell, I even love it that you can kick my
ass if I ever piss you off. You are one powerful little
badass, sweetheart."

She gave a soft, breathless laugh. "Only because of
you. *You* were my strength."

He gave her a quizzical smile, and she explained. "It
was what I found inside of you when I looked that fully
unleashed my Mallory powers. It was you, Kell. Your
love was what gave me the strength to blow that jerk
away."

"Wow," he breathed out, his throat tight with emotion.
"That's…intense."

Her mouth curled with a wobbly grin. "I know."

"And you finally believe the curse has nothing to do
with my feelings for you?" he pressed.

"What happened in that clearing was proof that it's
over, Kell. But, even without proof, I wouldn't have let
some stupid curse keep us apart. I trust you, and I believe
in you. So no matter what life throws at us, if you're sure
that you want me, I'm yours."

"I want you, Chloe. But…" He swallowed, then forced
out the bitter words, knowing they had to be said. "But
there are going to be times when you'll hear about things
that I've done in the past. And you won't be proud of
them. It could make a difference."

She shook her head, the look in her eyes damn near
stealing his breath. "Anything I hear will only make
me proud of the man you've become. No one is perfect,

Kellan, and I wouldn't want you to be. So long as you can be faithful to me, we can get through everything else."

"Trust me, sweetheart. Fidelity is never going to be a problem. When Lycans truly lose their hearts, they lose them forever."

Softly, she said, "You know, I never gave you any reason to think I didn't find you worthy."

He snorted. "Yeah, well, I had plenty of reasons on my own."

"But all that matters is the now, Kell."

"Speaking of the now," he said in a low voice, his pulse suddenly picking up speed, "isn't there something you want to tell me?"

"Is there?" she asked, giving him an innocent blink.

"The others, they…uh, they think you love me."

She smiled, but didn't say anything, and a deep groan vibrated in his chest. "Damn it, I'm not too proud to beg," he rasped, staring deep into her beautiful eyes. "I want your love, Chloe. I want it more than anything. And I know…I know I might be flawed as hell, that you deserve better, but damn it, I can't let anyone else have you, because there's no one else who's ever going to love you the way that I do."

Her smile trembled, her eyes flooding with tears. "Then it's a good thing I fell madly in love with you days ago."

Kellan's head spun in reaction, and he had to press his forehead against hers, his breathing choppy and hard as he tried to take it all in. Despite what Gabby had told him, he'd been afraid to let himself believe that Chloe might actually love him, too. It was simply too good to be true—and yet, he'd seen the truth shining in her eyes just now, when she'd given him the breathtaking words. It'd been there before, but he'd been too blind to see it. Too stubborn. But not anymore. "God, you have no idea how good it feels to hear you say that."

"Why are you surprised?" she whispered, gently placing her cool hand on the hot skin at the back of his neck. "I would have thought it was pretty obvious how I feel about you."

"You never said anything," he grunted, fighting for control, when all he wanted was to rip the sheet away from her sweet little body...and show her just how badly he wanted her, his cock already hard and aching.

"Well, I'm saying it now. I love you, Kellan Scott. I love you so much it hurts."

"God, that sounds sweet. Don't stop now," he rumbled, pulling her into his arms as he lay down beside her. "Keep it coming. I could live off this stuff. It's like manna from heaven."

"I love you," she giggled, placing a playful kiss to his nose. "And I'll keep on loving you forever," she added, trailing her lips down the side of his throat.

Thinking of a conversation he'd had with Aiden back in December, when they'd been trying to get Olivia and Jamie to England, he said, "You know what you are? You're my miracle, Chloe."

She laid her cheek against the pillow and locked her bright gaze with his. "What do you mean?"

Trailing his fingers down the sensual curve of her spine, he said, "For so long, I've been jealous of what my friends have found, certain I could never find anything like that for myself. That I wasn't worthy of it. And then you became a part of my life, and I swear it's even more amazing than I'd thought it could be." He shook his head a little, his face hot with color, his voice dropping as he said, "So I guess…I guess I must have done something right, after all. Because there's no way in hell a woman like you would ever end up with a loser. When you look at me, Chloe, I feel proud. For the first time in my life, I feel proud of the man I've become."

"You should feel proud, Kell. What you did for me, it was amazing. But I can't believe I almost lost you," she whispered, sifting her fingers through his hair.

"All I can say is thank God for that antidote."

"Will they be able to use it on Juliana's brother?"

He shook his head. "I'm afraid not. The two strains are completely different. But when we left, Juliana was trying to convince Gabby to help her make one that might work on Micah."

"I still can't believe you were willing to die for me," she told him, her eyes darkening with emotion. The possessive look on her beautiful face made him even harder, his cock practically bursting the confines of his jeans.

"I'm willing to do anything for you." Thick, husky words that held more than a little of the wolf in them, and she shivered in reaction.

"Then take me to the nearest shower and get in there with me," she said with a warm smile, reaching for the buttons on the front of his shirt. "Because what I want is your bite."

Heat rose beneath his skin, what little blood had been left in his brain quickly heading south. "Are you sure?" he demanded in a gritty voice, barely able to get the words past the knot of lust in his throat.

"Oh, I'm sure," she whispered, lifting her smoldering gaze to his. "I've never been more sure of anything in my life."

THEY DIDN'T TALK as he carried her into the bathroom, his breath coming as fast and as jagged as hers. He left her propped against the wall in his private bathroom as he reached into the shower and set the water on full heat, then turned back and stripped off the T-shirt she'd been wearing and his clothes. With a wicked smile, he carried her into the water with him, holding her tight as the jets pulsed down on them, the spray feeling wonderful on her aching muscles, while the air filled with warm, sensual steam. Though Chloe could sense how close he was to losing control, he took his time soaping her body, delighting over her in a way that made her heart pound. She no longer felt self-conscious about her figure, the heat in his eyes burning her insecurities to ash.

She knew she wasn't the most beautiful woman in the world, but in Kellan's eyes, she was…and that was all that mattered.

"What do you want, Kell? What will make you happy? After everything you've been through, you deserve that."

The corner of his mouth twitched, his deep voice thick with hunger as he said, "I want so much with you, Chloe. I want to build a life with you. Sit around and watch football. Play cheesy board games. Go on picnics. Cook breakfast." With a mischievous grin, he waggled his brows, saying, "Get you on some sunny Caribbean beach for our honeymoon in nothing but a string bikini."

"A bikini?" she groaned. "Can I at least stop by Cara's on the way and get a bigger set of boobs first?"

"Absolutely not," he argued, sliding his soapy hands possessively over her chest. "No way in hell are you messing with these beauties. They are world-class perfection, and they're *mine*."

"Jeez, you *must* love me," she drawled, snuffling a soft burst of laughter. "I thought guys always went for the hefty tatas."

"I couldn't care less about other tatas," he rumbled, her toes curling as he stroked his thumbs over her sensitive nipples. "I only care about these."

"Like I said, it must be love."

He gave her a quick, devastating kiss, then drew back, the look in his eyes making her melt. "You know what I want? I want to enjoy you, Chloe. Everything about you, for the rest of my life. Learn all the miracles that make you who you are. Be your best friend, your lover, your everything. I'll worship you, protect you and love you till the day I die. And then I'll defy whatever higher powers are out there to try and keep me away from you, because I won't even let death come between us."

"Wow," she whispered, completely dazzled.

"And you're going to marry me."

Her eyes went wide. "I am?"

"Oh, yeah," he breathed out, wrapping one arm around her waist and pulling her so close she had to tilt her head back to see his face. His eyes burned, glowing with a primal, possessive fire as he stroked a hand down the side of her throat and over her shoulder. "We'll get married as soon as possible, but first I want to mark you as mine. Bind you to me in a way that can never be undone."

She licked her lips. "I want that, too, Kell."

His voice dropped to a deep, husky rasp. "And there's something else I want," he told her, and she smiled, knowing from the breathtaking look in his eyes that it was going to be good. "I want to come inside you when I make my bite. You okay with that?"

Chloe's heart beat so hard, she was surprised it stayed inside her chest, excitement and happiness churning together into a strange, exhilarating rush that seared her veins, and she clung to his arms for support, her head spinning. "I'm more than okay with it. But...I could get pregnant. You know I'm not on the Pill."

He kissed the water droplets from her cheek, and with a tremor of emotion in his dark words, he said, "I know, honey. We could make a baby. Right here. Right now."

"And you wouldn't mind?" she whispered, her pulse roaring in her ears like a heavy rain.

He drew back his head just far enough that he could stare into her eyes, his hands stroking over her bottom. "To be honest, I can't think of anything more incredible than creating a family with you. I never would have thought that I could be so lucky, but I'm done fighting fate, Chloe. From now on, I'm going to enjoy what it gives me."

"No more guilt?" she asked, looping her arms around his powerful neck, her nipples pressed against the heavy muscles of his chest.

His eyes tightened a little, but then he shook his head as he said, "I'll always feel bad about the way I lived before you. But what's important is the man I've become. Because of you. With you by my side, I can hold my head high for the rest of my life."

"I love you," she told him, pressing a tender kiss to

his mouth…his chin…the masculine edge of his jaw. "I love you so much."

"I love you more," he groaned, lifting her off the floor as he pinned her against the wall of the shower. Chloe eagerly wrapped her legs around his waist, and he took her mouth with a raw, demanding kiss as he pushed deep inside the tight, cushiony depths of her body. She came instantly, the dark, devastating pleasure tearing through her with stunning force, and he swallowed the sound of her screams before ripping his mouth from hers.

"You feel so fucking good," he growled, shunting deeper, until it felt like he was sinking into the hot glow of bliss burning inside her. She'd never seen him look so feral in his human form as he did in that moment, with his fangs dropping beneath his upper lip, his glowing eyes heavy-lidded with lust as he cut a hungry look toward the side of her throat. The primal Merrick inside her rose up, purring with anticipation as Chloe tilted her head to the side, offering him what he wanted. He made a thick animal kind of sound in the back of his throat, before nuzzling his face against the curve of her shoulder. She felt him draw in a slow, shuddering breath, his tongue flicking against her skin, and then he sank his fangs deep, burying them into her sensitive flesh and making the primal bite.

Chloe had expected pain, and it was there. But there was so much pleasure that the sharp burn didn't matter, and she screamed again as she arched against him, telling him how much she loved him and needed him and wanted him. He shook with a violent tremor, his claws digging into the warm tiles, shattering them, and then he was coming inside her with so much force, she could feel the explosive burst of heat deep inside her. Kellan growled against her throat, then pulled his fangs free, his hips shoving against her with deep, hammering thrusts as his head fell back, a guttural roar of satisfaction tearing from his chest, and they lost themselves in that thundering, pleasure-drenched storm, battered by the blistering waves of sensation, holding on to one another as tightly as they could.

When they were finally able to move again, Kellan dried her off with a soft towel and they collapsed into bed together—the distant, sultry sound of Aiden playing blues on his piano drifting through the halls of the house. In a deep, dark rasp, Kellan told her how mouthwatering she'd tasted...how much he'd loved sinking his fangs into her...coming deep inside her, and what began as a long, lazy kiss turned into fire and passion. Needing everything he could give her, Chloe sank her fangs into his strong throat, feeding from his vein as he sent her into another long, scalding orgasm that left her melting in a warm, soothing darkness. Minutes later, when she'd finally come back to this world, she found herself lying in his arms, her face close to his as they shared a pillow, the backs of his fingers rubbing possessive circles into her stomach, as if there was already life growing inside her.

In a voice that was husky from her passionate cries, she said, "I still can't believe that I'm here with you, and that we made it through, Kell. If it weren't for the horror of what happened, losing one of your friends, everything would be...perfect."

"I'll make things perfect for you, Chloe. I promise."

"I don't need perfection. All I need is you. Because I can't be whole without you," she told him, reaching out and tucking a damp, auburn strand of hair behind his ear. When she caught his bemused expression, she asked, "What is it?"

"I was just thinking that I set out to rescue you, but you're the one who's rescued me. I thought I needed to go to the Wasteland to make a difference. To change the way my family and friends saw me. But really, what I needed was *you*."

"Kellan," she whispered.

"Yeah."

"In case you hadn't noticed, you've got me."

With a deliciously deep, husky rumble of happiness, he pulled her tighter against him, touching his mouth to the warm pulse of the bite mark he'd left at her throat, his lips tender and soft against her skin. "And I'll be keeping you, my beautiful little witch. Forever."

With a smile of pure, incandescent joy, Chloe wrapped her arms around him, holding him to her…determined to never let him go. "Lycan, I wouldn't have it any other way."

* * * * *

But the battle still isn't finished.
See how Seth succumbs to passion in
RUSH OF DARKNESS

GLOSSARY OF TERMS
for the Primal Instinct Series

The Ancient Clans: Nonhuman races whose existence has been kept secret from the majority of humans for thousands of years, their abilities differing as widely as their physiology. Some only partially alter when in their primal forms, like the Merrick. Others fully transform, able to take the shape of an animal, similar to those who compose the Watchmen.

These are but a few of the various ancient clans that remain in existence today:

The Merrick: One of the most powerful of the ancient clans, the Merrick were forced to mate with humans after years of war against the Casus had decimated their numbers. Their bloodlines eventually became dormant, dwelling within their human descendants, until the return of the Casus and the time of their awakening. In order to feed the primal parts of their nature, the newly awakened Merrick must consume blood whilst having sex. Characteristics: When in Merrick form, the males have fangs, talons, flattened noses and massive, heavily muscled physiques. The females have fangs and talons.

The Awakenings: Each time a Casus shade returns to this world, it causes the primal blood within one of the

Merrick descendants to rise within them, or awaken, so that they might battle against their ancient enemy.

The Buchanans: One of the strongest Merrick blood-lines, the Buchanans were not only the first of the Merrick to awaken, but they also each possess an unusual power or "gift." Ian has a strange sense of premonition that comes to him in dreams, Saige can "hear" things from physical objects when she touches them and Riley's telekinetic powers enable him to control physical objects with his mind.

The Casus: Meaning *violent death,* the Casus are an immortal race of preternatural monsters who were imprisoned by the Merrick and the Consortium over a thousand years ago for their mindless killing sprees. Recently, however, they have begun escaping from their holding ground, returning to this world and taking over the bodies of "human hosts" who have dormant Casus blood running through their veins. The escaped Casus now prey upon the newly awakened Merrick, feeding on their flesh for power, as well as revenge. Characteristics: When in Casus form, they have muzzled faces, wolf-shaped heads, leathery gray skin, ridged backs and long, curved claws. The males have ice-blue eyes, while the females have eyes that are pale green.

Meridian: The metaphysical holding ground where the Casus were imprisoned for their crimes against the other clans…as well as humanity. Although it was created by the original Consortium, no one knows how to find it until a journal is discovered that claims the Dark

Markers are not only the keys that will open the gate to Meridian, but that they will also form a map that leads to the prison's hidden location.

Shades: Because of their immortality, the Casus can't die in Meridian. They have simply wasted away to "shades" of the powerful creatures they once were, which is why they're forced to take human hosts when they return to this world.

The Deschanel: Also known as vampires, the Deschanel are one of the most powerful of the ancient clans, rivaling the strength of the Merrick and the shape-shifters. Although duality is a common feature among many of the clans, the trait is especially strong within the Deschanel, whose very natures are a dichotomy of opposites—of both darkness and light—which makes them complex friends…and dangerous enemies. Characteristics: Pale, pure gray eyes that glow after they've taken a blood feeding. Despite their power and strength, they move with a smooth, effortless grace that is uncommon among human males of their size. They also have incredibly long life-spans, until such time as they finally take a mate.

The Burning: The body of an unmated Deschanel male runs cold until he finds his mate. The phenomenon is referred to as being "in heat" or "burning," since his body begins warming from the moment he finds her.

The Förmyndares: As the Protectors of the Deschanel, it is the duty of these warriors to destroy any threats to the vampire clans.

Nesting Grounds: Ancient, sprawling castlelike communities where Deschanel family units, or nests, live for security, which are protected by powerful magic that keeps them hidden from the outside world. The grounds are located throughout Scandinavia and other parts of Europe.

The Witches: Although there are many witch clans still in existence, their powers vary greatly from one clan to another.

The Boudreaux: A carefree clan of witches whose specialty is beauty spells.

The Mallory: A powerful clan of witches whose diverse powers were bound by a curse. Because of the centuries-old curse, they now magnify the emotions of those in their presence to extreme levels.

The Reavess: A clan of witches who can communicate mentally with those in their families. They access their considerable power through the use of spells, and will bond their true loves to them through sex. They are also able to assume the traits possessed by their mates during "joining."

The Saville: A snobbish clan of witches who have little power.

The Regan: An aggressive clan responsible for hunting several rival clans to near extinction. Characteristics: long noses, pointed ears and deeply cleft chins.

The Kenly: A mountain-dwelling clan nearly hunted to extinction by the Regan. Characteristics: short statures and large, doelike eyes.

The Feardacha: One of several ancient clans that reside in Ireland. They are extremely superstitious, believing that the dead should never go unchecked. As a precaution, they tattoo pagan symbols on their hands and arms, believing the symbols will draw to them any evil souls that manage to escape from hell, so that they might kill them once again. Characteristics: tattoos, mocha-colored skin and pale green eyes.

The Vassayre: One of the more reclusive clans, they seldom come out of the underground caves where they dwell. Characteristics: dark markings around their sunken eyes.

The Deuchar: One of the most violent of the ancient clans, they are the mortal enemy of the Shaevan.

The Shaevan: One of several ancient clans that reside in France.

The Shape-shifters: A richly diverse, powerful collection of clans whose members can take either the complete or partial shape of a beast.

The Prime Predators: Consisting of the most dangerous, predatory animal species, they are the most aggressive breeds of shape-shifters, well-known for their legendary sex drives and their unquestionable devotion to their mates. In order to claim a mate, a Prime must bite the one who holds their heart, marking them with their fangs while taking their blood into their bodies. They are also known for their incomparable skill as warriors and their strong healing abilities. Examples: the tigers, jaguars and lycanthropes.

The Lycanthropes: Also known as werewolves, they are formidable warriors who can actually change humans to their species with the power of their bite if they are in wolf form. However, in order to mark their mates, they must make a bite with their fangs whilst still in human form.

The Raptors: One of the rarest breeds of shifters, the Raptors are known for being ruthless warriors and possessive, utterly devoted lovers. Although they do not completely shift form, they are able to release powerful wings from their backs that enable them to fly, as well as sharp talons from their fingertips for fighting.

The Charteris: Dragon shape-shifters who possess the ability to control fire, and whose bodies burn with a dangerous heat when making love to a woman who holds their heart. It is believed that no pure-blooded Charteris are still in existence.

The Archives: The records that belonged to the original Consortium which are believed to hold vital information about the ancient clans. Though the new Consortium has spent years searching for them, the archives have fallen into the hands of the Collective Army.

The Collective Army: A militant organization of human mercenaries devoted to purging the world of all preternatural life. In an ironic twist, the Collective Army now finds itself partnered with the Kraven and the Casus, in exchange for information that they believe will enable them to exterminate the remaining nonhuman species.

The Consortium: A body of officials comprised of representatives from each of the remaining ancient clans, the Consortium is a sort of preternatural United Nations. Their purpose is to settle disputes and keep peace among the differing species, while working to hide the existence of the remaining clans from the human world. Over a thousand years ago, the original Consortium helped the Merrick imprison the Casus, after the Casus's relentless killing of humans threatened to expose the existence of the nonhuman races. The council fashioned the Dark Markers in order to destroy the immortal killers, only to be murdered by the newly created Collective Army before they could complete the task. Years later, the Consortium re-formed, but by then its original archives had been lost…all traces of the Dark Markers supposedly destroyed during the Collective's merciless raids, which nearly led to the destruction of the clans.

The Dark Markers: Metal crosses of enormous power that were mysteriously created by the original Consortium, they are the only known weapons capable of killing a Casus, sending its soul directly to hell. They also work as a talisman for those who wear them, offering protection from the Casus. Although it is unknown how many Dark Markers are in existence, there is a set of encrypted maps that lead to their locations. The Watchmen and the Buchanans are using these maps to help them find the Markers before they fall into enemy hands.

"Arm of Fire": Weapon mode for a Dark Marker. When held against the palm, a Dark Marker holds the power to change one's arm into an "Arm of Fire." When the cross is placed against the back of a Casus's neck, the flame-covered arm will sink into the monster's body, burning it from the inside out.

The Encrypted Maps: When Saige Buchanan discovered the first Dark Marker in Italy, she found a set of encrypted maps buried alongside the cross. The maps, which lead to the hidden locations of the Dark Markers, had been wrapped in oilcloth and preserved by some kind of spell.

The Death-Walkers: The demented souls of clansmen and -women who were sent to hell for their sadistic crimes, and who are now managing to return to our world. It is unknown how to kill them, but they can be burned by a combination of holy water and salt. Driven mad by their time in hell, they are a formidable force of evil, seeking to create chaos and war among the remaining clans simply because they want to watch the world bleed. Characteristics: Although they retain certain traits from their original species, each of the Death-Walkers has cadaverously white skin and small horns that protrude from their temples, as well as deadly fangs and claws.

"The Eve Effect": A phenomenon that affects various

breeds of shape-shifters, causing them to be drawn to certain females who touch the primal hungers of both the man and the beast. If a male falls in love with one of these females and bites her, she will be bonded to him as his mate for the rest of their lives.

The Infettato: Humans who have been infected by the bite of a Death-Walker. Once turned, they become the "walking dead" and it is impossible for them to regain their humanity. They live only to consume flesh, tracking their prey by scent and blindly obeying the orders of those who made them. As they feed, they become stronger, and they can only be killed when their hearts are removed from their chests and burned. Characteristics: Mottled, yellowish skin, gaunt faces and sunken eyes. Black skin that looks as if it has been burned surrounds their eyes and mouths.

The Kraven: The offspring of female Deschanel vampires who were raped by Casus males prior to their imprisonment. Treated little better than slaves and considered an embarrassing symbol of weakness, the Kraven have been such a closely guarded secret within the Deschanel clan that the Watchmen have only recently become aware of their existence. Although their motivation is still unclear, the Kraven are working to facilitate the return of the Casus. Characteristics: They are believed to have long life-spans, and their fangs can be released only at night, causing their eyes to glow a deep, blood-red crimson. They can also easily pass for human, but can only be killed when a wooden stake is driven through their heart.

The Wasteland: A cold, desolate, dangerous region that

was created by powerful magic, where exiled Deschanel "nests" or family units are forced to live once the Consortium has passed judgment against them. Protected by spells that make it invisible to humans, this vast region "shares" physical space with the Scandinavian forests surrounding it.

The Watchmen: An organization of shape-shifters whose job it is to watch over the remaining ancient clans, they are considered the "eyes and ears" of the Consortium. They monitor the various nonhuman species, as well as the bloodlines of those clans that have become dormant. Prior to the recent Merrick awakenings, the most powerful Merrick bloodlines had been under Watchmen supervision. There are Watchmen compounds situated around the world, with each unit consisting of four to six warriors. Characteristics: Physical traits vary according to the specific breed of shape-shifter.

ACKNOWLEDGMENTS

As always, endless thanks to my family for being so wonderful, and for always cheering me on!!

Big hugs to Madi, Debs and Joy! You guys ROCK!

And a very special thank-you to Mary-Theresa Hussey for her incredible insight, hard work and enthusiasm. It's been such a pleasure to work with you!

REQUEST YOUR FREE BOOKS!

2 FREE NOVELS
FROM THE SUSPENSE COLLECTION
PLUS 2 FREE GIFTS!

YES! Please send me 2 FREE novels from the Suspense Collection and my 2 FREE gifts (gifts are worth about $10). After receiving them, if I don't wish to receive any more books, I can return the shipping statement marked "cancel." If I don't cancel, I will receive 3 brand-new novels every month and be billed just $5.74 per book in the U.S. or $6.24 per book in Canada. That's a saving of at least 28% off the cover price. It's quite a bargain! Shipping and handling is just 50¢ per book.* I understand that accepting the 2 free books and gifts places me under no obligation to buy anything. I can always return a shipment and cancel at any time. Even if I never buy another book, the two free books and gifts are mine to keep forever.

192/392 MDN E7PD

Name	(PLEASE PRINT)
Address	Apt. #
City	State/Prov.	Zip/Postal Code

Signature (if under 18, a parent or guardian must sign)

Mail to The Reader Service:
IN U.S.A.: P.O. Box 1867, Buffalo, NY 14240-1867
IN CANADA: P.O. Box 609, Fort Erie, Ontario L2A 5X3

Not valid for current subscribers to the Suspense Collection
or the Romance/Suspense Collection.

Want to try two free books from another line?
Call 1-800-873-8635 or visit www.morefreebooks.com.

* Terms and prices subject to change without notice. Prices do not include applicable taxes. N.Y. residents add applicable sales tax. Canadian residents will be charged applicable provincial taxes and GST. Offer not valid in Quebec. This offer is limited to one order per household. All orders subject to approval. Credit or debit balances in a customer's account(s) may be offset by any other outstanding balance owed by or to the customer. Please allow 4 to 6 weeks for delivery. Offer available while quantities last.

Your Privacy: Harlequin Books is committed to protecting your privacy. Our Privacy Policy is available online at www.eHarlequin.com or upon request from the Reader Service. From time to time we make our lists of customers available to reputable third parties who may have a product or service of interest to you. If you would prefer we not share your name and address, please check here. ☐

Help us get it right—We strive for accurate, respectful and relevant communications. To clarify or modify your communication preferences, visit us at www.ReaderService.com/consumerschoice.

MSUS10R

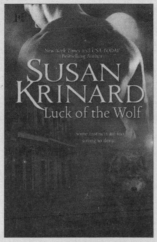

RHYANNON BYRD

77464	TOUCH OF SURRENDER	___ $7.99 U.S.	___ $9.99 CAN.
77448	TOUCH OF SEDUCTION	___ $7.99 U.S.	___ $9.99 CAN.
77423	EDGE OF DESIRE	___ $7.99 U.S.	___ $8.99 CAN.
77399	EDGE OF DANGER	___ $7.99 U.S.	___ $8.99 CAN.
77367	EDGE OF HUNGER	___ $6.99 U.S.	___ $6.99 CAN.

(limited quantities available)

TOTAL AMOUNT	$ _____
POSTAGE & HANDLING	$ _____
($1.00 FOR 1 BOOK, 50¢ for each additional)	
APPLICABLE TAXES*	$ _____
TOTAL PAYABLE	$ _____

(check or money order—please do not send cash)

To order, complete this form and send it, along with a check or money order for the total above, payable to HQN Books, to: **In the U.S.:** 3010 Walden Avenue, P.O. Box 9077, Buffalo, NY 14269-9077; **In Canada:** P.O. Box 636, Fort Erie, Ontario, L2A 5X3.

Name: _____
Address: _____ City: _____
State/Prov.: _____ Zip/Postal Code: _____
Account Number (if applicable): _____

075 CSAS

*New York residents remit applicable sales taxes.
*Canadian residents remit applicable GST and provincial taxes.

HQN™

We *are* romance™

www.HQNBooks.com

PHRB1110BL